W9-CFQ-980

Kaho Miyasaka's Profile

Kaho Miyasaka was born on October 17 under the astrological sign of Libra, in the Japanese prefecture of Chiba. Her blood type is A.

Because she hasn't been able to go shopping these past few years, she fears that she's turning into a twentysomething mail-order nerd...

Miyasaka's debut work was "Jungle Boy," which was first printed in Shôjo Comic on November 15, 1992. Currently she is a very popular author at Shôjo Comic.

Kare First Love
Vol. 1
Shôjo Edition
Story and Art by KAHO MIYASAKA

English Adaptation/Kelly Sue DeConnick
Translation/Akira Watanabe
Touch-Up Art & Lettering/Steve Dutro
Cover and Interior Design/Hidemi Sahara
Editor/Michelle Pangilinan

Managing Editor/Annette Roman
Editor-in-Chief/Alvin Lu
Production Manager/Noboru Watanabe
Sr. Director of Licensing & Acquisitions/Rika Inouye
VP of Sales/Joe Morici
VP of Marketing/Liza Coppola
Executive VP/Hyoe Narita
Publisher/Seiji Horibuchi

KARE FIRST LOVE is rated "T" for Teens. This book is recommended for ages 13 and up.
It contains mild language and suggestive situations.

© 2002 Kaho Miyasaka/Shogakukan, Inc.
First published by Shogakukan, Inc. as "Kare First Love".

The KARE FIRST LOVE logo is a trademark of VIZ, LLC. ©2004, VIZ, LLC. All rights reserved.
No portion of this book may be reproduced or transmitted by any form or by any means
without written permission from the copyright holders.

New and adapted artwork and text
©2004 VIZ, LLC

The stories, characters and incidents mentioned in this publication are entirely fictional. All rights reserved.

Printed in the U.S.A.

Published by VIZ, LLC
P.O. Box 77010
San Francisco, CA 94107

Action Edition
10 9 8 7 6 5 4 3 2 1
First printing, August 2004

www.viz.com

store.viz.com

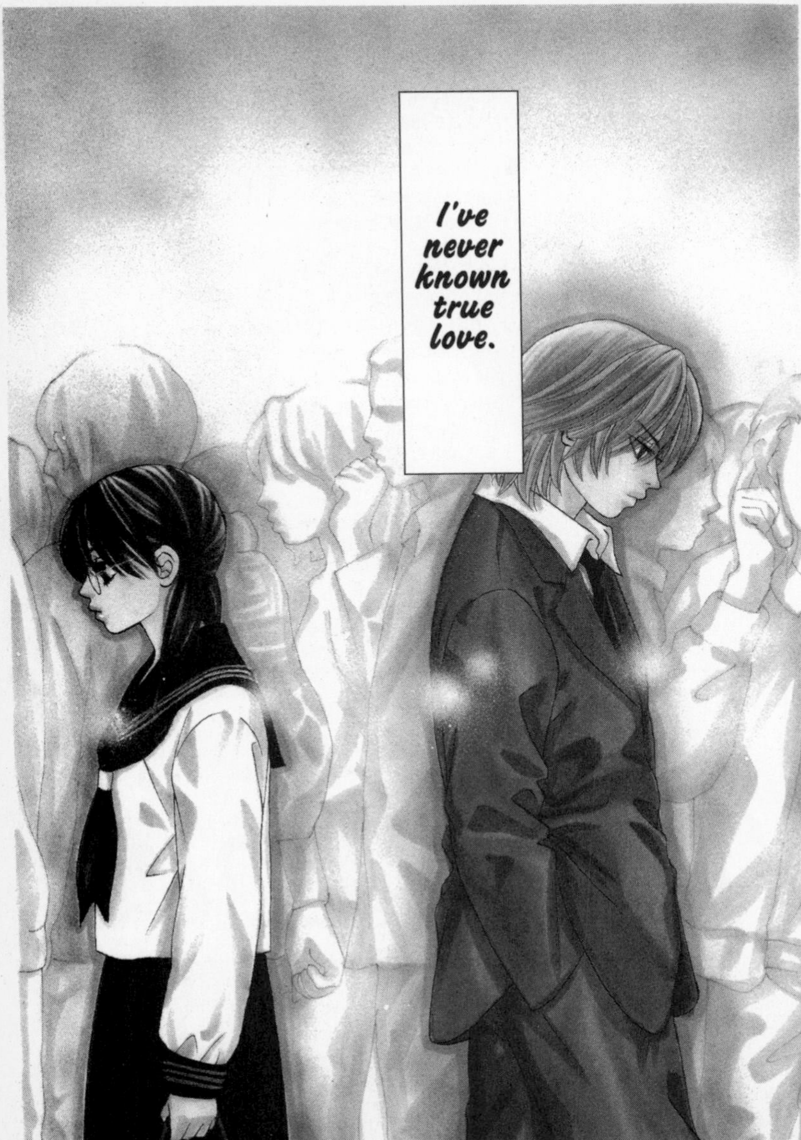
I've never known true love.

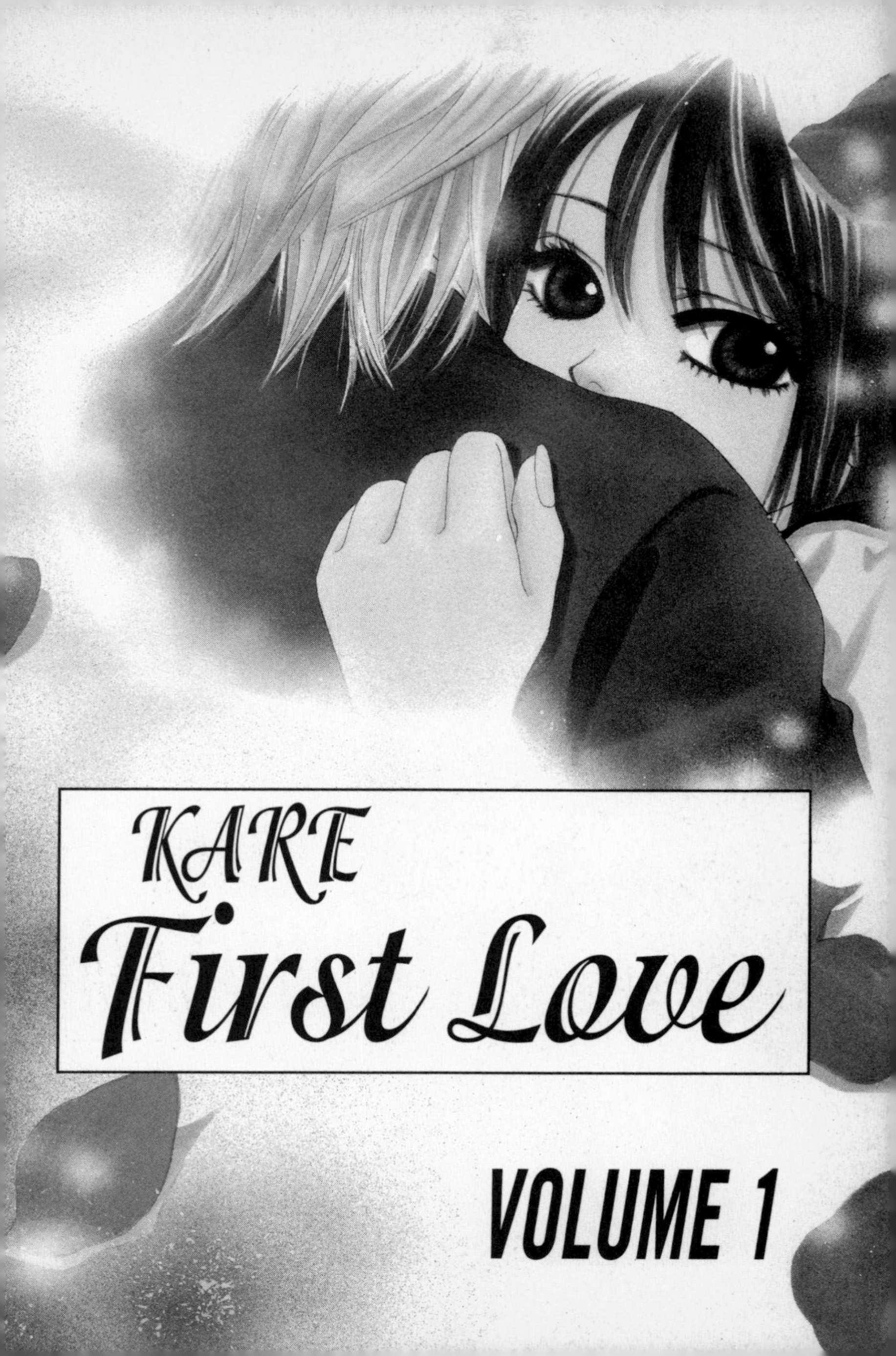
KARE
First Love
VOLUME 1

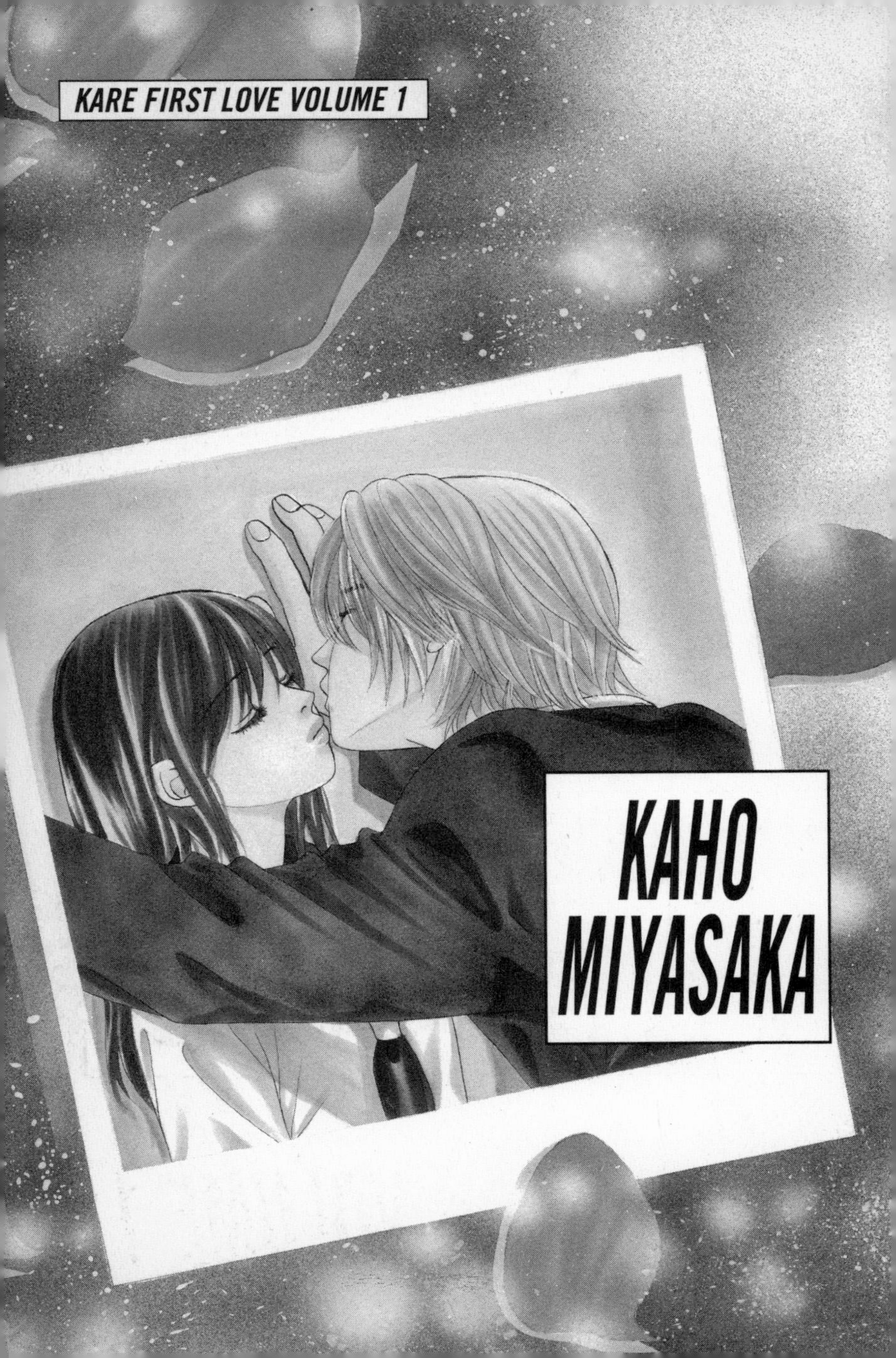
KARE FIRST LOVE VOLUME 1
KAHO MIYASAKA

KARE
First Love

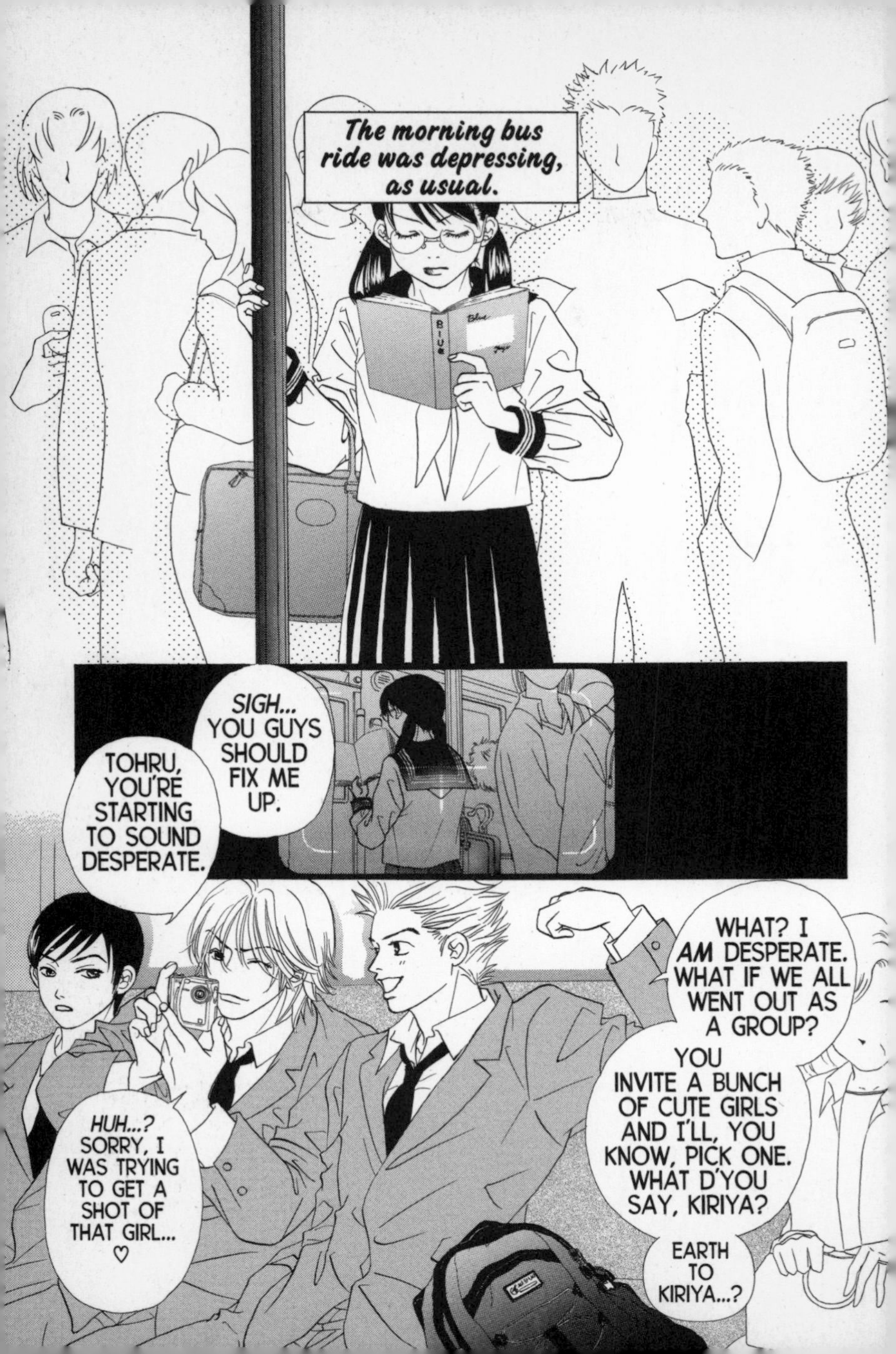
The morning bus ride was depressing, as usual.
SIGH... YOU GUYS SHOULD FIX ME UP.
TOHRU, YOU'RE STARTING TO SOUND DESPERATE.
WHAT? I *AM* DESPERATE. WHAT IF WE ALL WENT OUT AS A GROUP?
YOU INVITE A BUNCH OF CUTE GIRLS AND I'LL, YOU KNOW, PICK ONE. WHAT D'YOU SAY, KIRIYA?
EARTH TO KIRIYA...?
HUH...? SORRY, I WAS TRYING TO GET A SHOT OF THAT GIRL... ♡

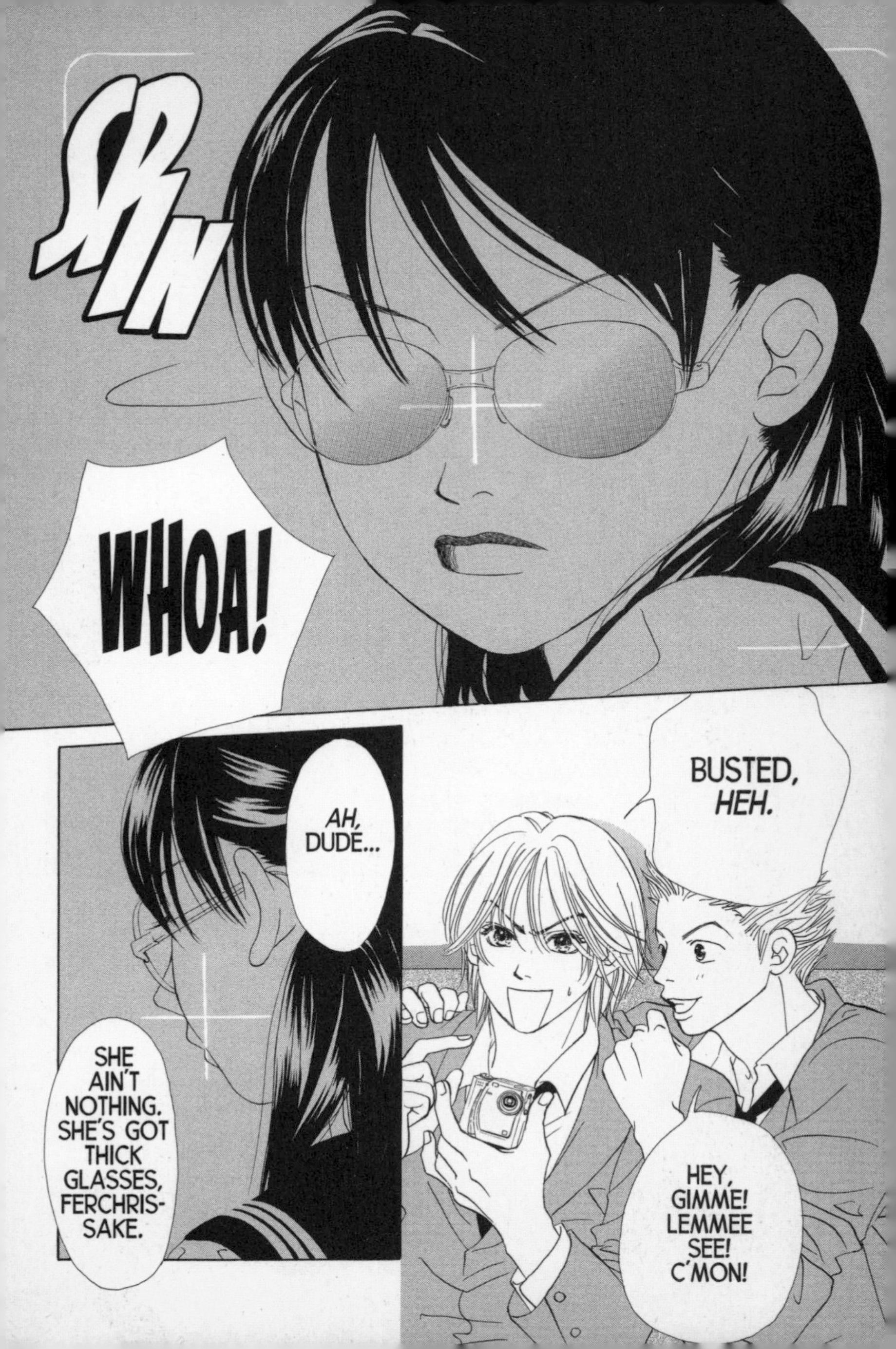
WHOA!
BUSTED, *HEH.*
HEY, GIMME! LEMMEE SEE! C'MON!
AH, DUDE...
SHE AIN'T NOTHING. SHE'S GOT THICK GLASSES, FERCHRIS-SAKE.

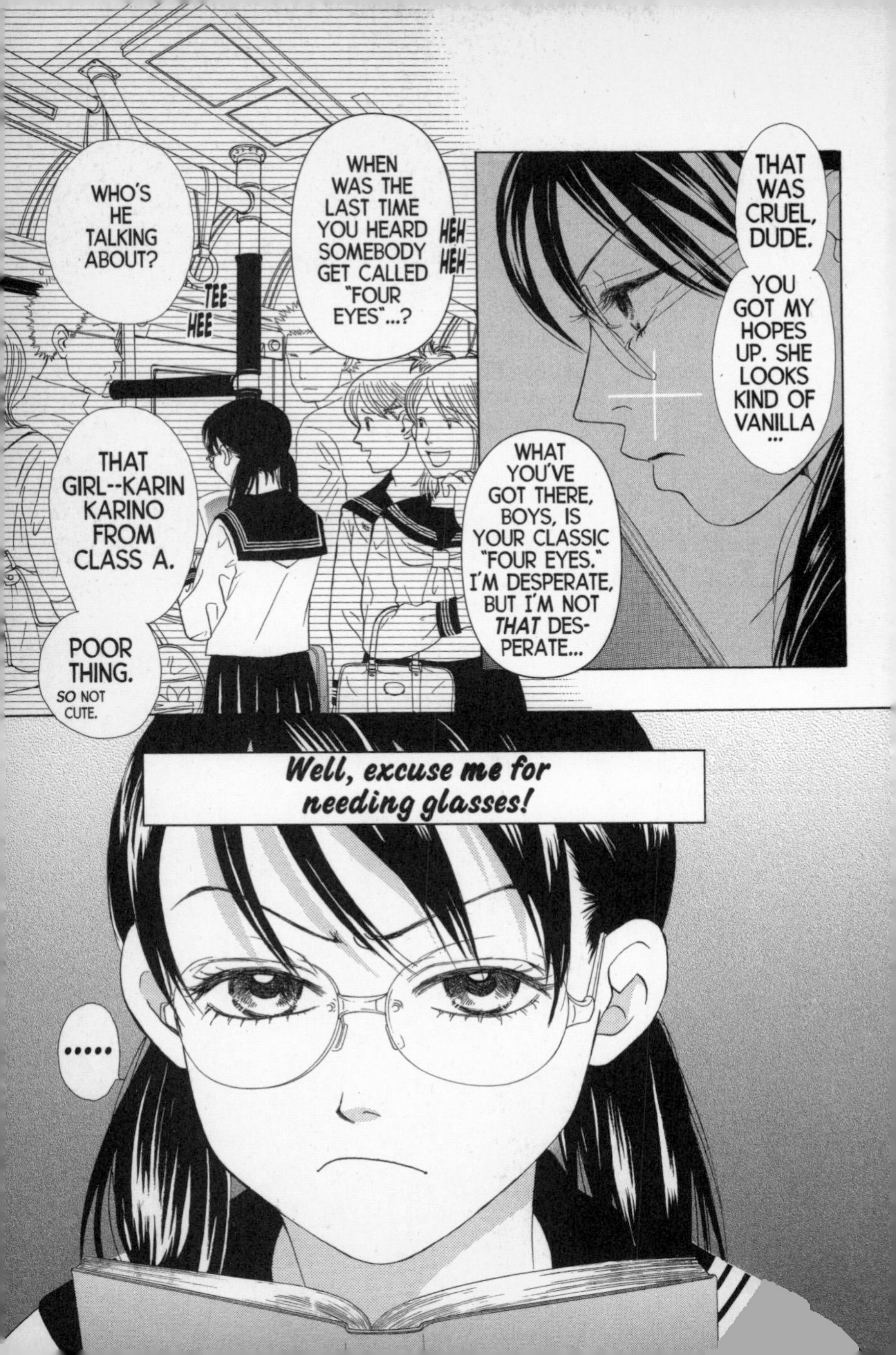
THAT WAS CRUEL, DUDE.
YOU GOT MY HOPES UP. SHE LOOKS KIND OF VANILLA...
WHAT YOU'VE GOT THERE, BOYS, IS YOUR CLASSIC "FOUR EYES." I'M DESPERATE, BUT I'M NOT *THAT* DESPERATE...
WHEN WAS THE LAST TIME YOU HEARD SOMEBODY GET CALLED "FOUR EYES"...?
HEH HEH
WHO'S HE TALKING ABOUT?
TEE HEE
THAT GIRL--KARIN KARINO FROM CLASS A.
POOR THING.
SO NOT CUTE.
Well, excuse me for needing glasses!
......

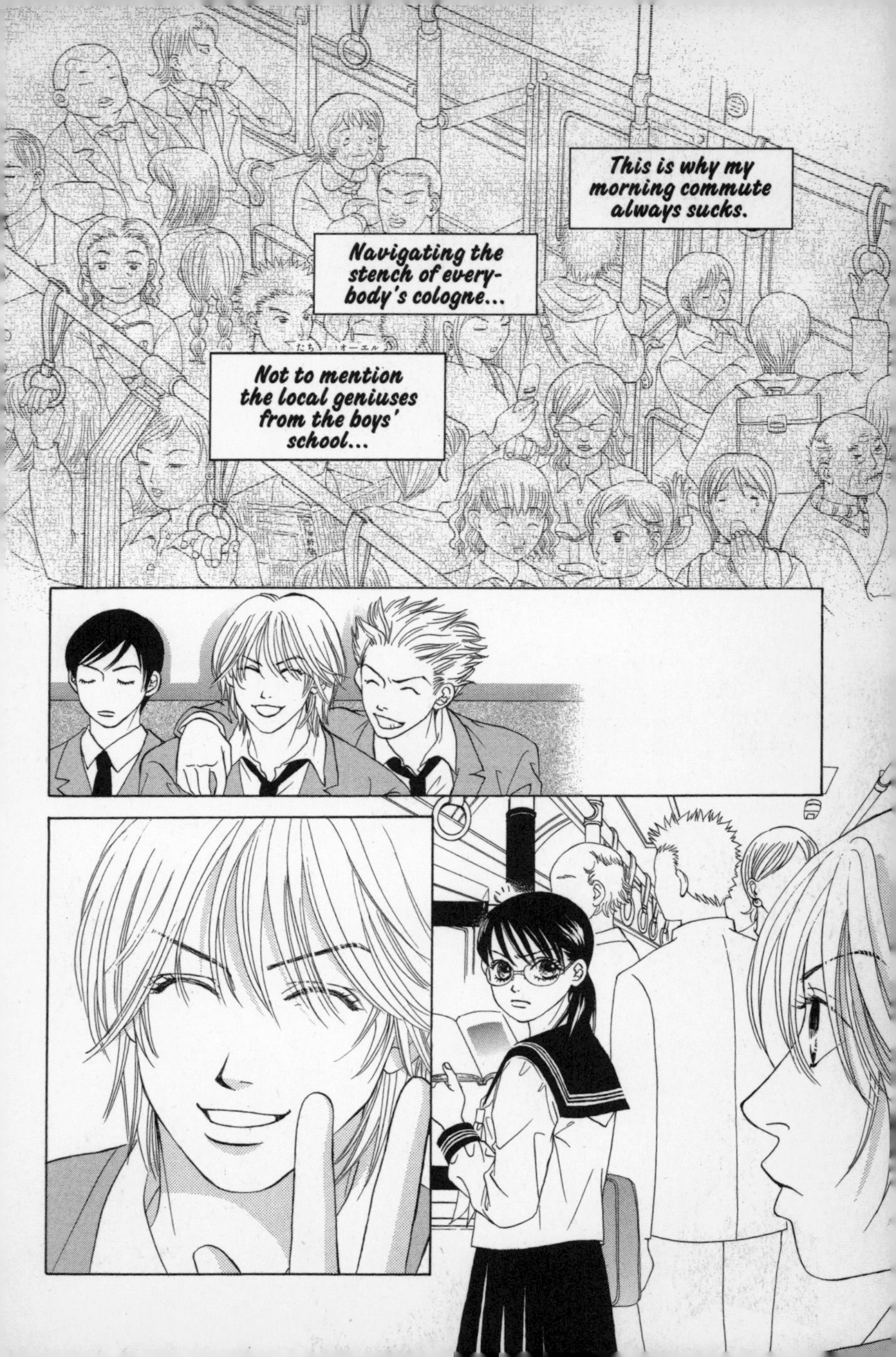
This is why my morning commute always sucks.
Navigating the stench of every-body's cologne...
Not to mention the local geniuses from the boys' school...

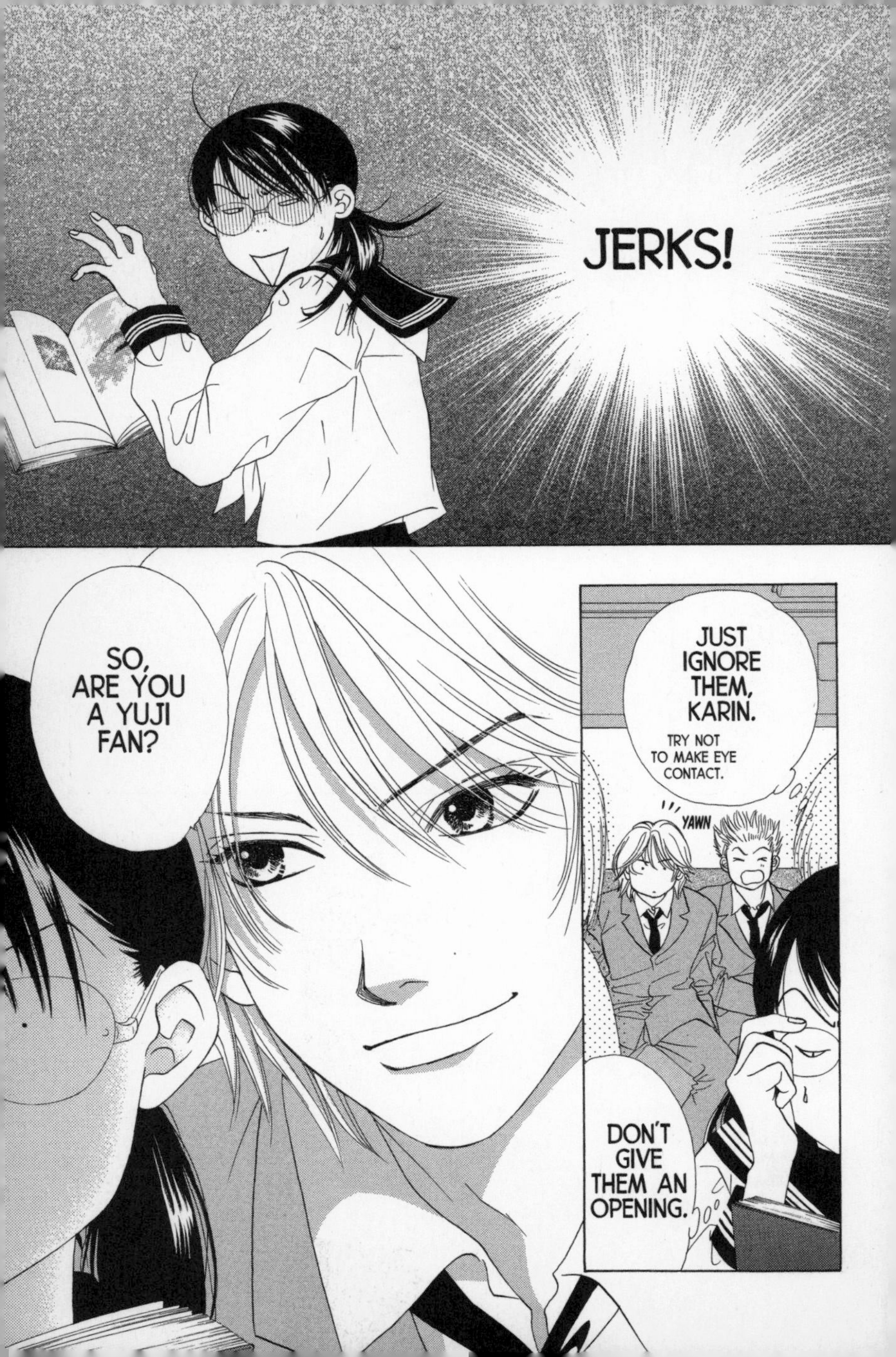
JERKS!
JUST IGNORE THEM, KARIN.
TRY NOT TO MAKE EYE CONTACT.
YAWN
DON'T GIVE THEM AN OPENING.
SO, ARE YOU A YUJI FAN?

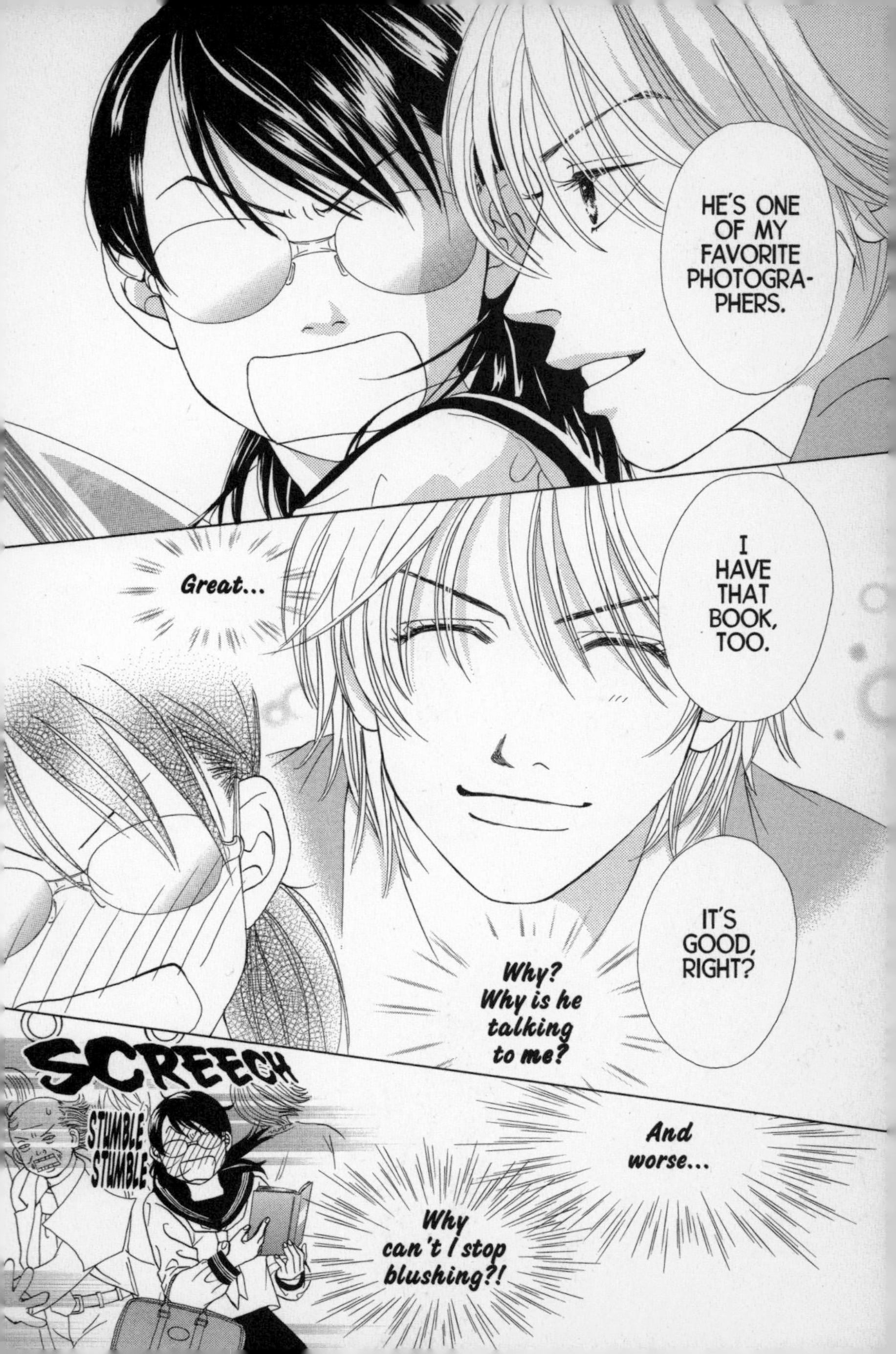
HE'S ONE OF MY FAVORITE PHOTOGRA-PHERS.
I HAVE THAT BOOK, TOO.
Great...
IT'S GOOD, RIGHT?
Why? Why is he talking to me?
And worse...
SCREECH
STUMBLE STUMBLE
Why can't I stop blushing?!

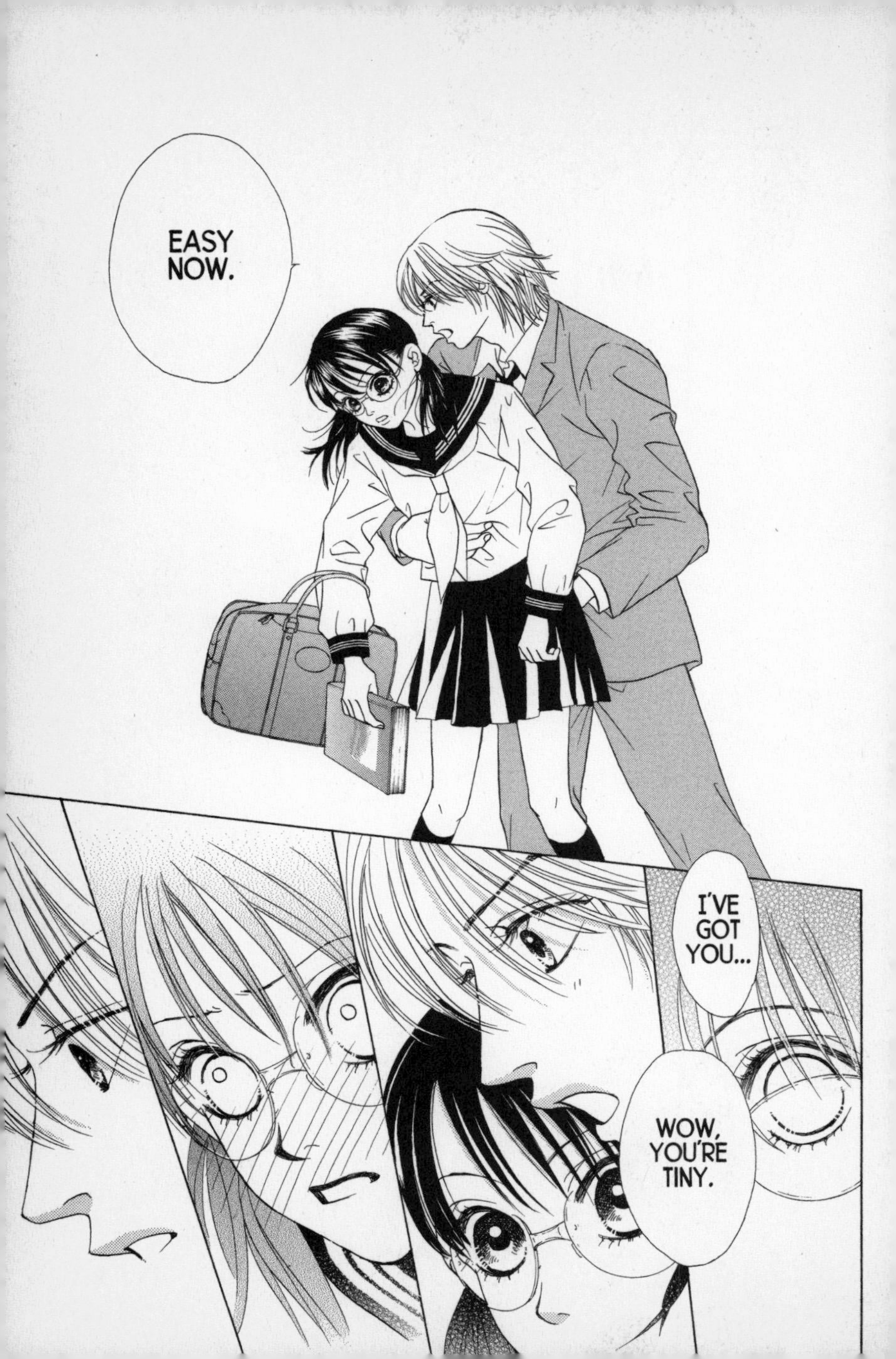
EASY NOW.
I'VE GOT YOU...
WOW, YOU'RE TINY.

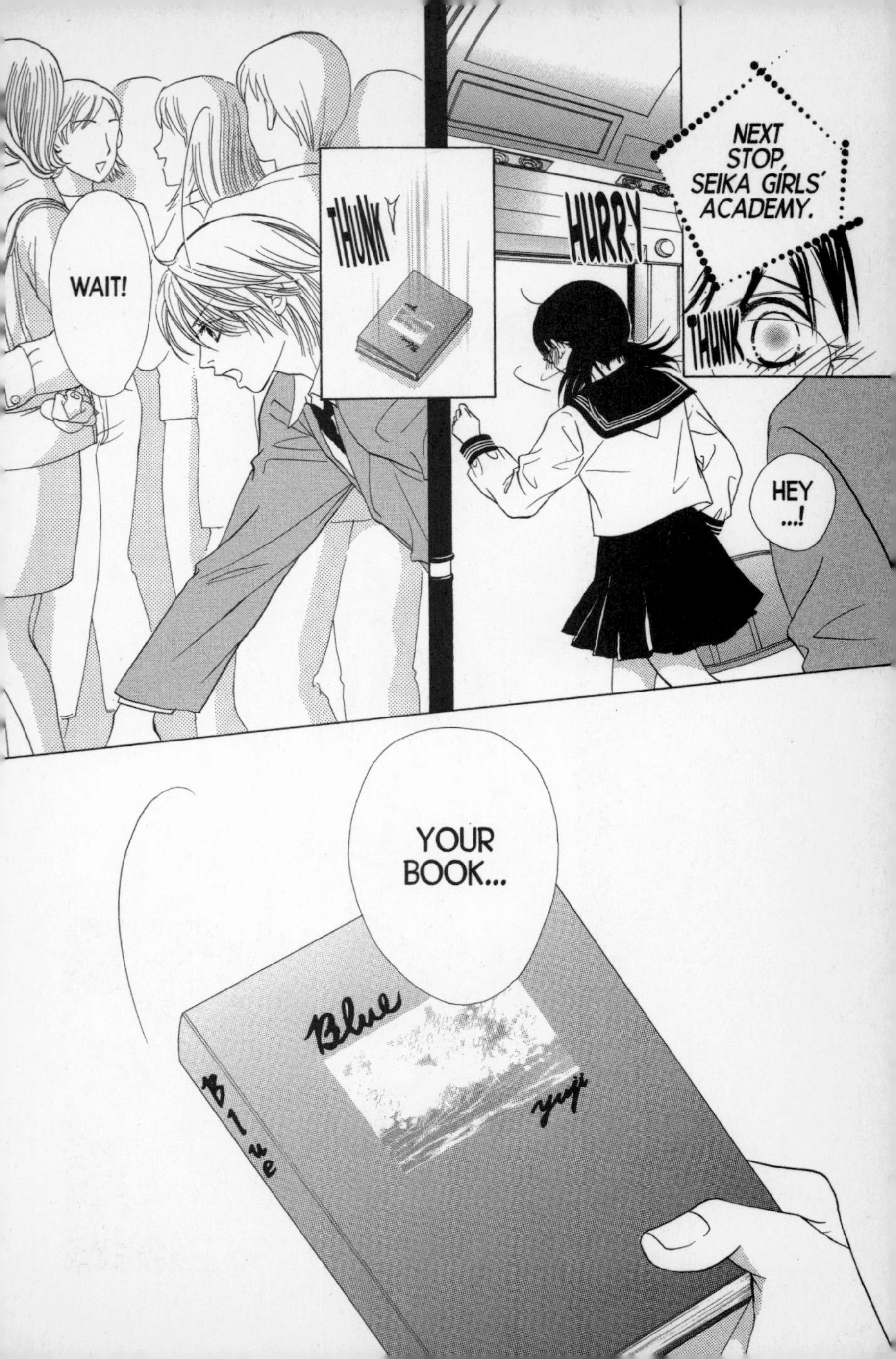
NEXT STOP, SEIKA GIRLS' ACADEMY.
THUNK
HURRY
HEY ...!
THUNK
WAIT!
YOUR BOOK...
Blue
yuji
Blue

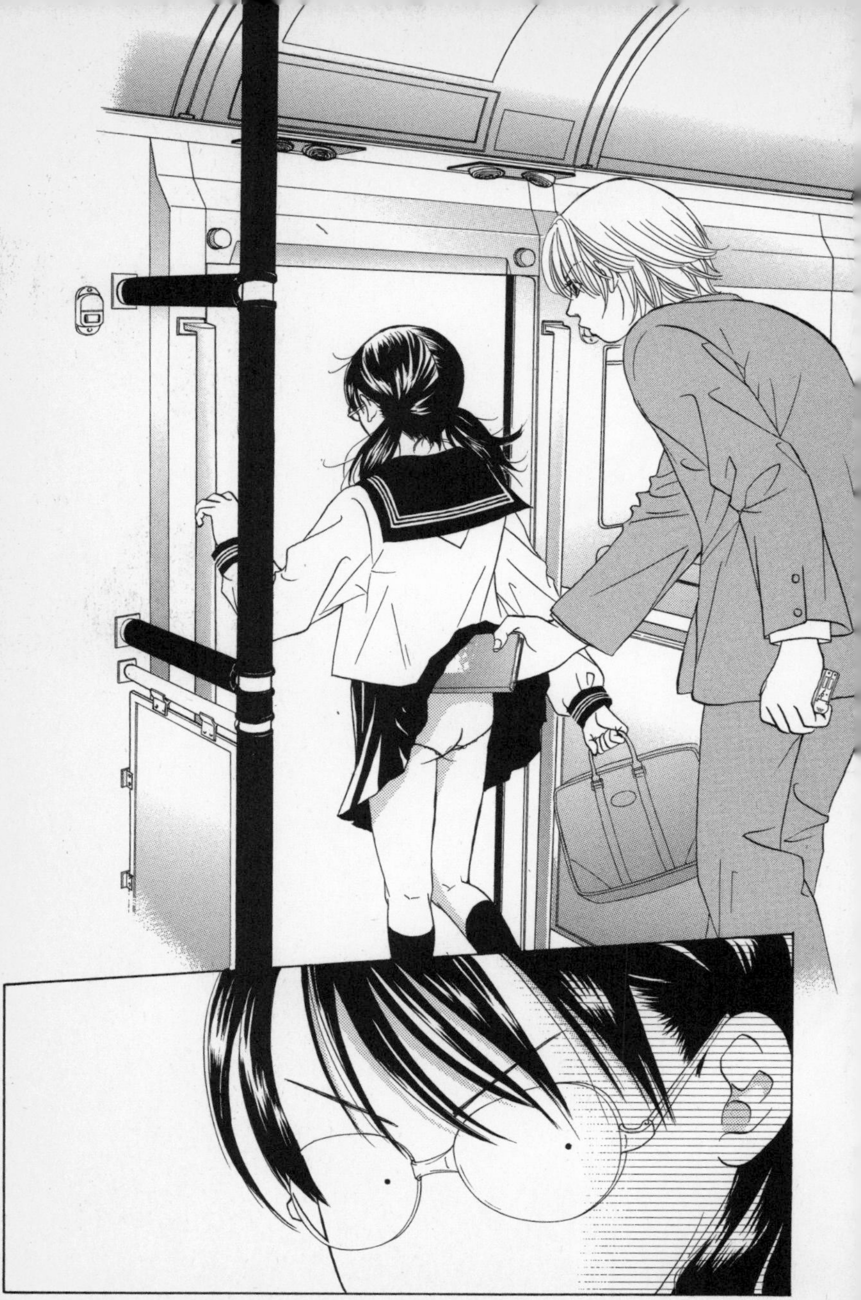

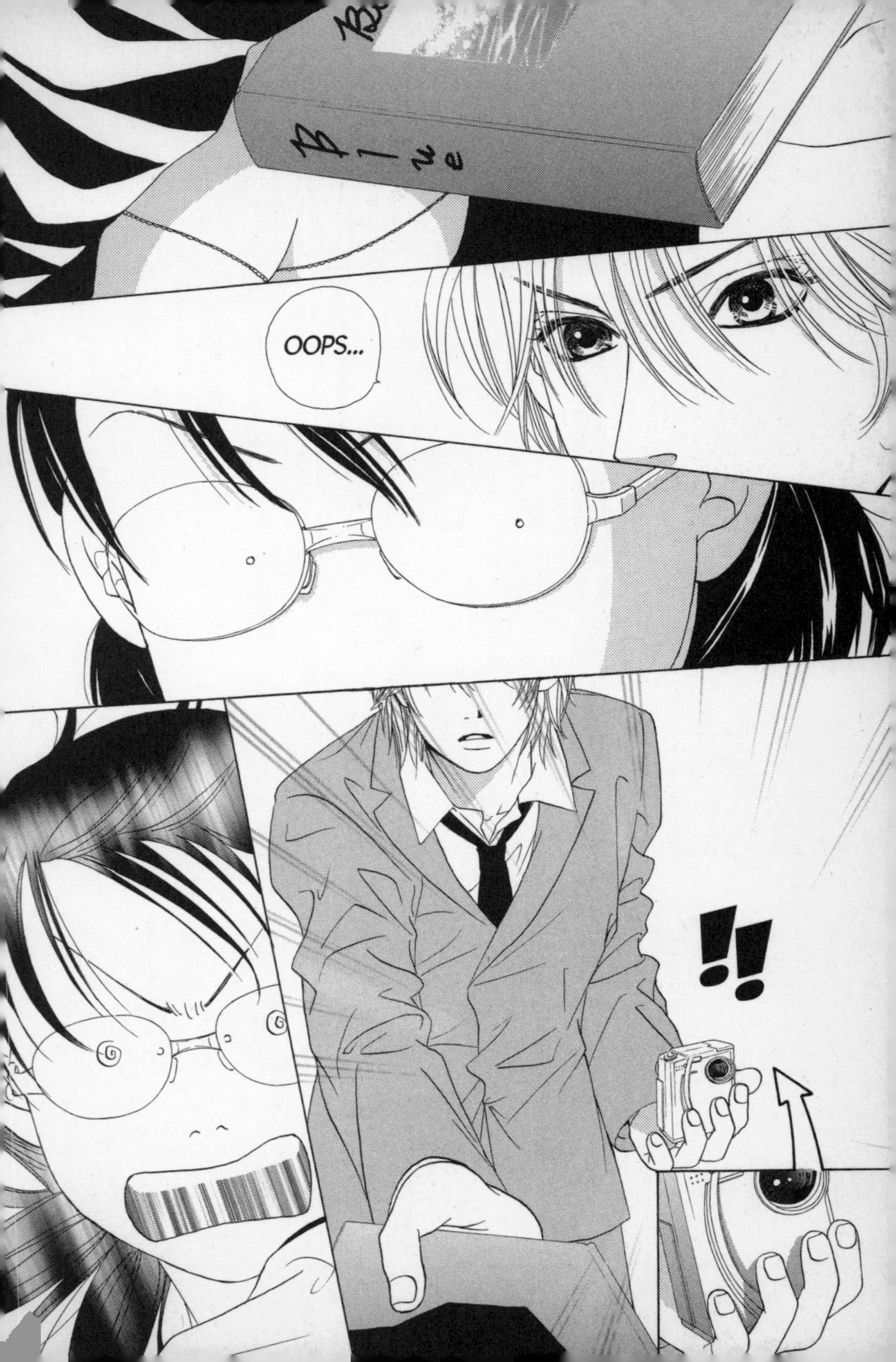
Blue
OOPS...
!!

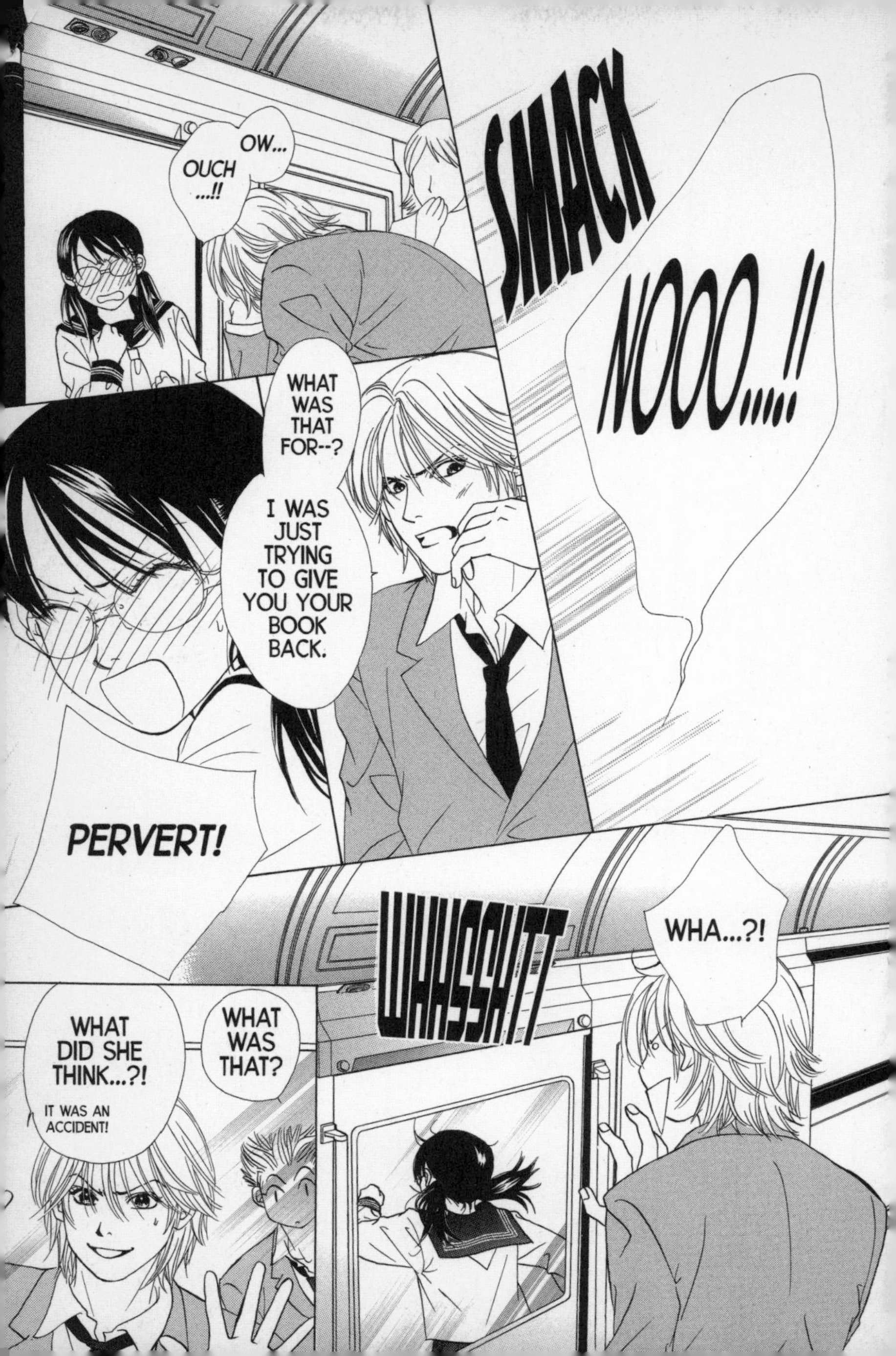
SMACK
NOOO...!!
OW...
OUCH
...!!
WHAT WAS THAT FOR--?
I WAS JUST TRYING TO GIVE YOU YOUR BOOK BACK.
PERVERT!
WHA...?!
WHHSSHTT
WHAT WAS THAT?
WHAT DID SHE THINK...?!
IT WAS AN ACCIDENT!

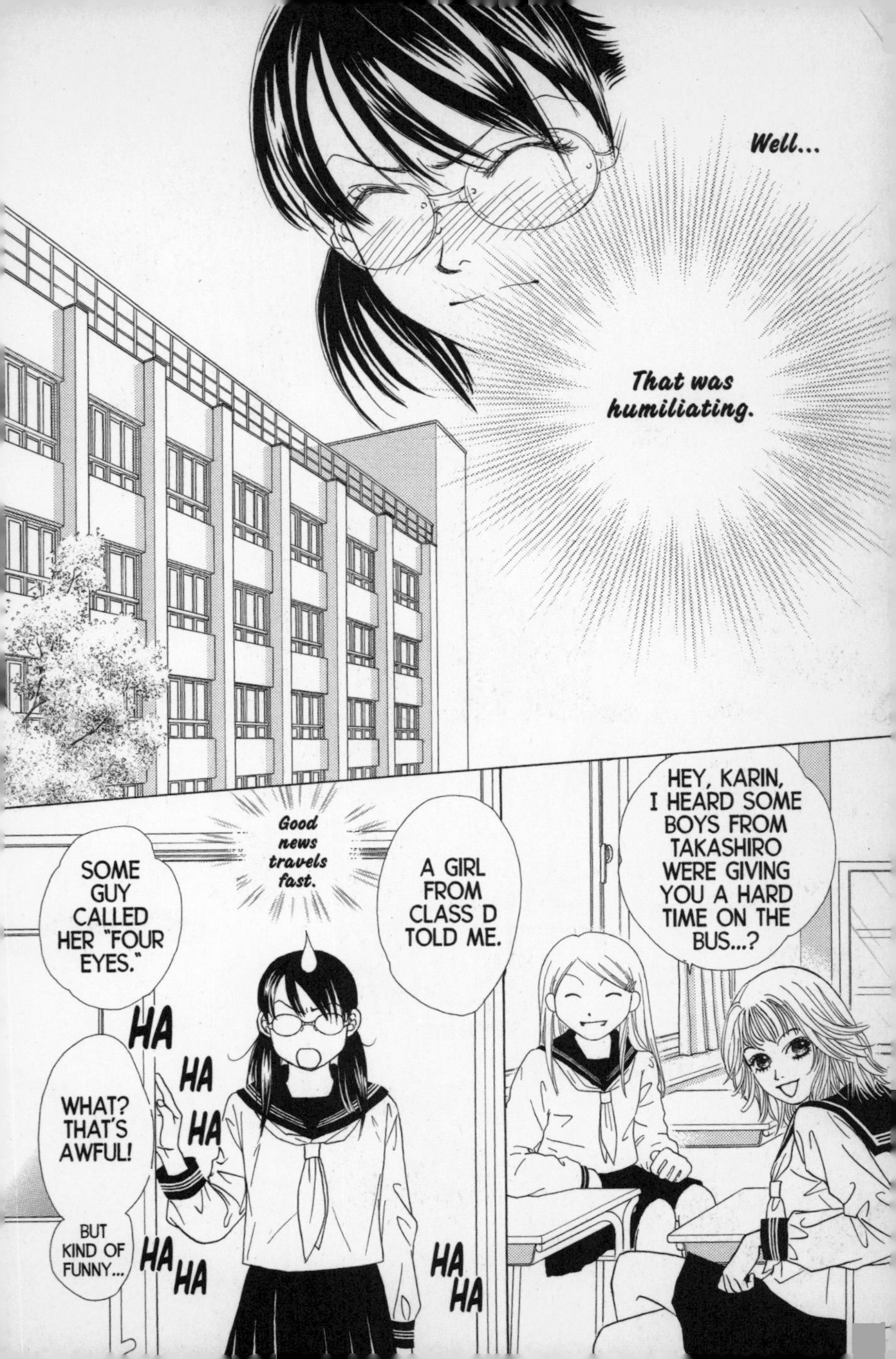
Well...
That was humiliating.
HEY, KARIN, I HEARD SOME BOYS FROM TAKASHIRO WERE GIVING YOU A HARD TIME ON THE BUS...?
A GIRL FROM CLASS D TOLD ME.
Good news travels fast.
SOME GUY CALLED HER "FOUR EYES."
HA HA HA
WHAT? THAT'S AWFUL!
BUT KIND OF FUNNY...
HA HA
HA HA

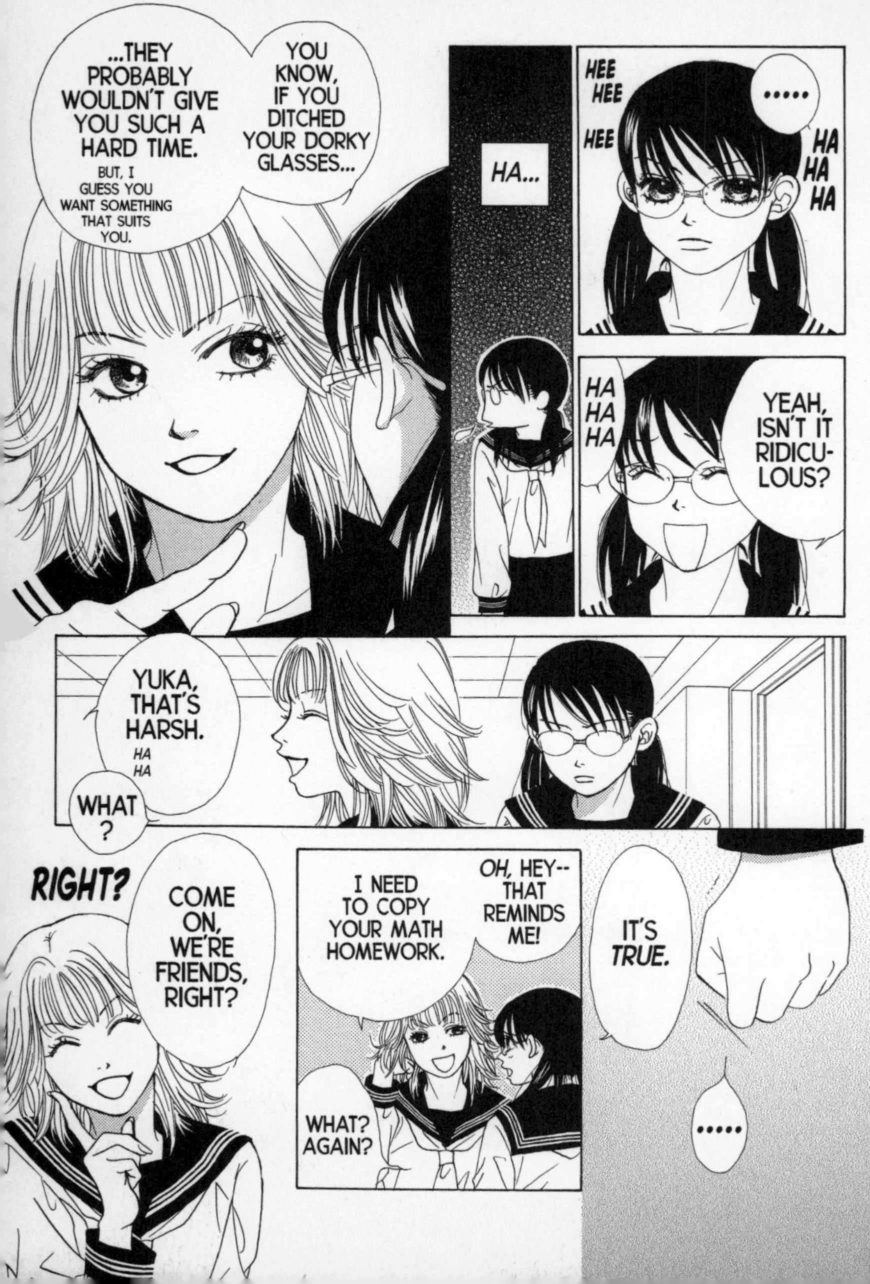
HEE HEE HEE
.....
HA HA HA
HA HA HA
YEAH, ISN'T IT RIDICULOUS?
HA...
YOU KNOW, IF YOU DITCHED YOUR DORKY GLASSES...
...THEY PROBABLY WOULDN'T GIVE YOU SUCH A HARD TIME.
BUT, I GUESS YOU WANT SOMETHING THAT SUITS YOU.
YUKA, THAT'S HARSH.
HA HA
WHAT?
IT'S TRUE.
.....
OH, HEY-- THAT REMINDS ME!
I NEED TO COPY YOUR MATH HOMEWORK.
WHAT? AGAIN?
RIGHT?
COME ON, WE'RE FRIENDS, RIGHT?

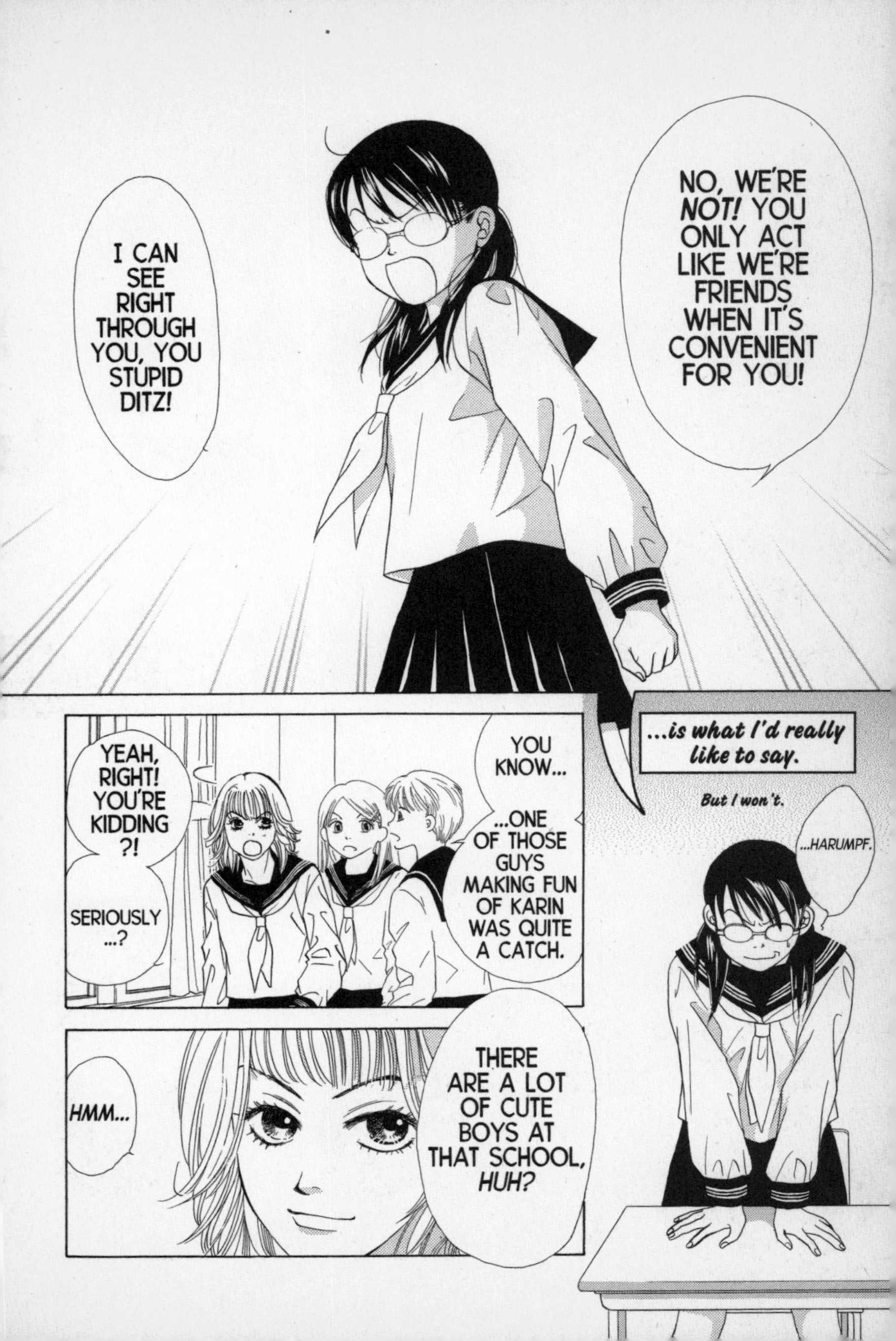
NO, WE'RE *NOT!* YOU ONLY ACT LIKE WE'RE FRIENDS WHEN IT'S CONVENIENT FOR YOU!
I CAN SEE RIGHT THROUGH YOU, YOU STUPID DITZ!
...is what I'd really like to say.
But I won't.
...HARUMPF.
YOU KNOW...
...ONE OF THOSE GUYS MAKING FUN OF KARIN WAS QUITE A CATCH.
YEAH, RIGHT! YOU'RE KIDDING ?!
SERIOUSLY ...?
THERE ARE A LOT OF CUTE BOYS AT THAT SCHOOL, *HUH?*
HMM...

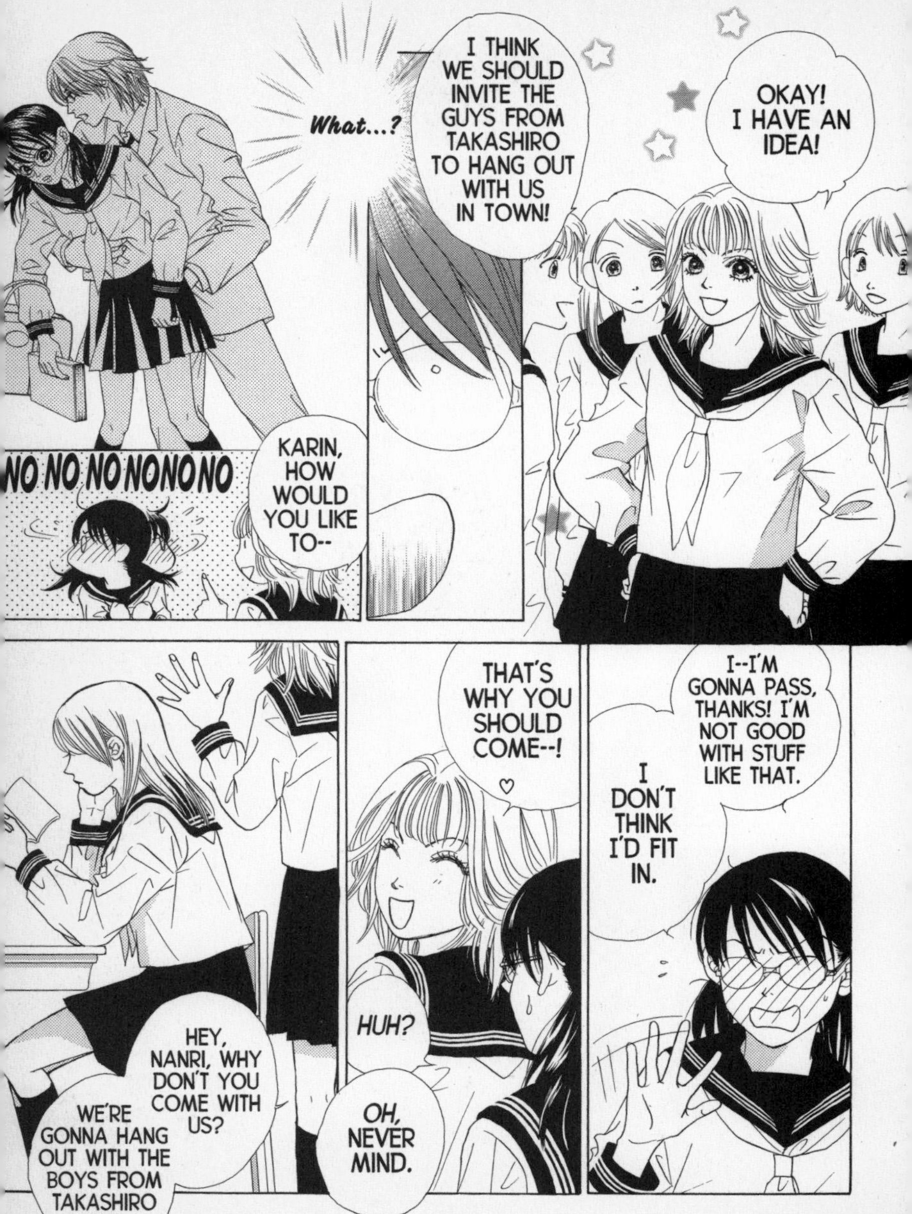
OKAY! I HAVE AN IDEA!
I THINK WE SHOULD INVITE THE GUYS FROM TAKASHIRO TO HANG OUT WITH US IN TOWN!
What...?
KARIN, HOW WOULD YOU LIKE TO--
NO NO NO NONONO
I--I'M GONNA PASS, THANKS! I'M NOT GOOD WITH STUFF LIKE THAT.
I DON'T THINK I'D FIT IN.
THAT'S WHY YOU SHOULD COME--! ♡
HUH?
OH, NEVER MIND.
HEY, NANRI, WHY DON'T YOU COME WITH US?
WE'RE GONNA HANG OUT WITH THE BOYS FROM TAKASHIRO HIGH.

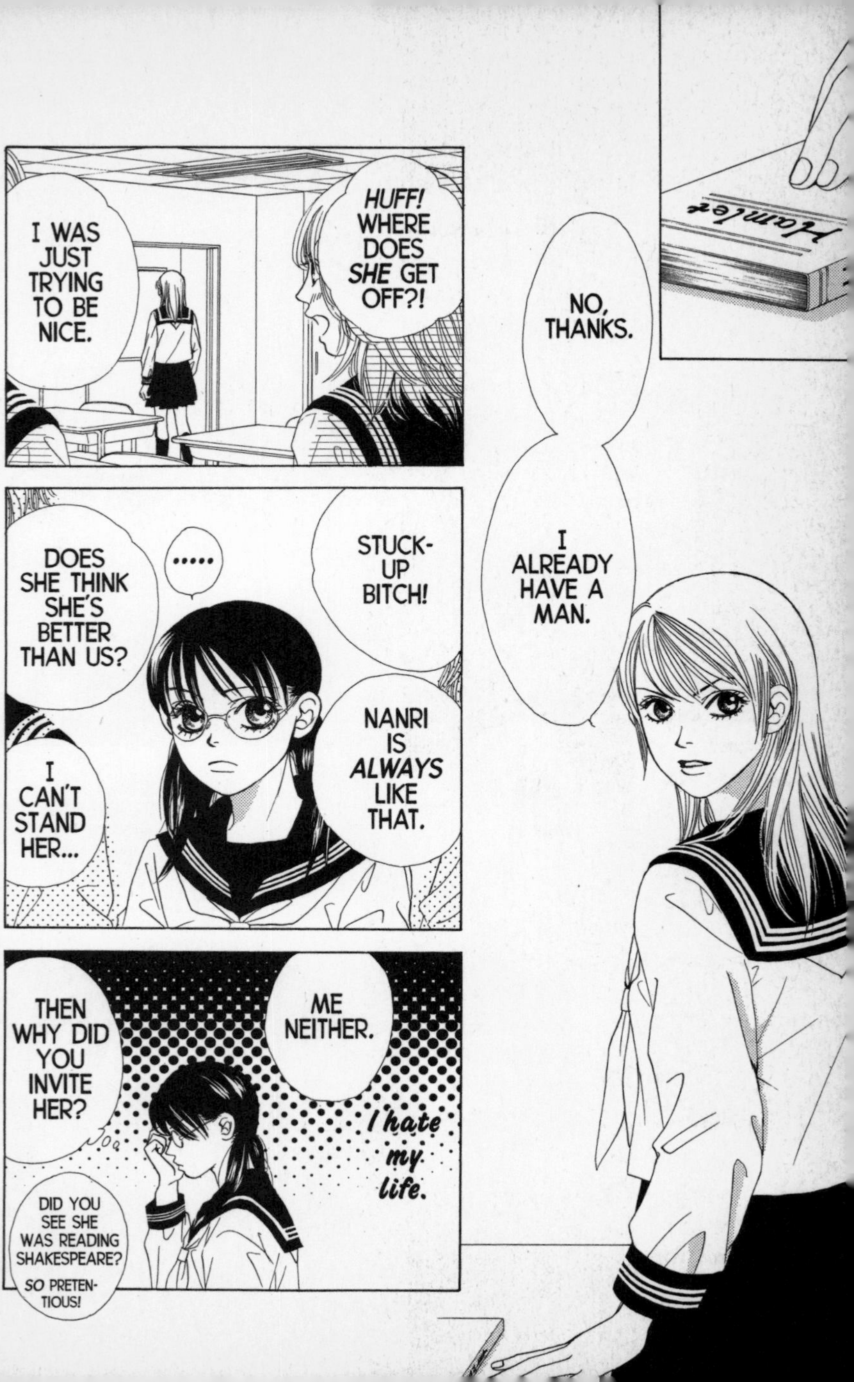
Hamlet
NO, THANKS.
I ALREADY HAVE A MAN.
HUFF! WHERE DOES *SHE* GET OFF?!
I WAS JUST TRYING TO BE NICE.
STUCK-UP BITCH!
.....
DOES SHE THINK SHE'S BETTER THAN US?
NANRI IS *ALWAYS* LIKE THAT.
I CAN'T STAND HER...
ME NEITHER.
THEN WHY DID YOU INVITE HER?
I hate my life.
DID YOU SEE SHE WAS READING SHAKESPEARE?
SO PRETEN-TIOUS!

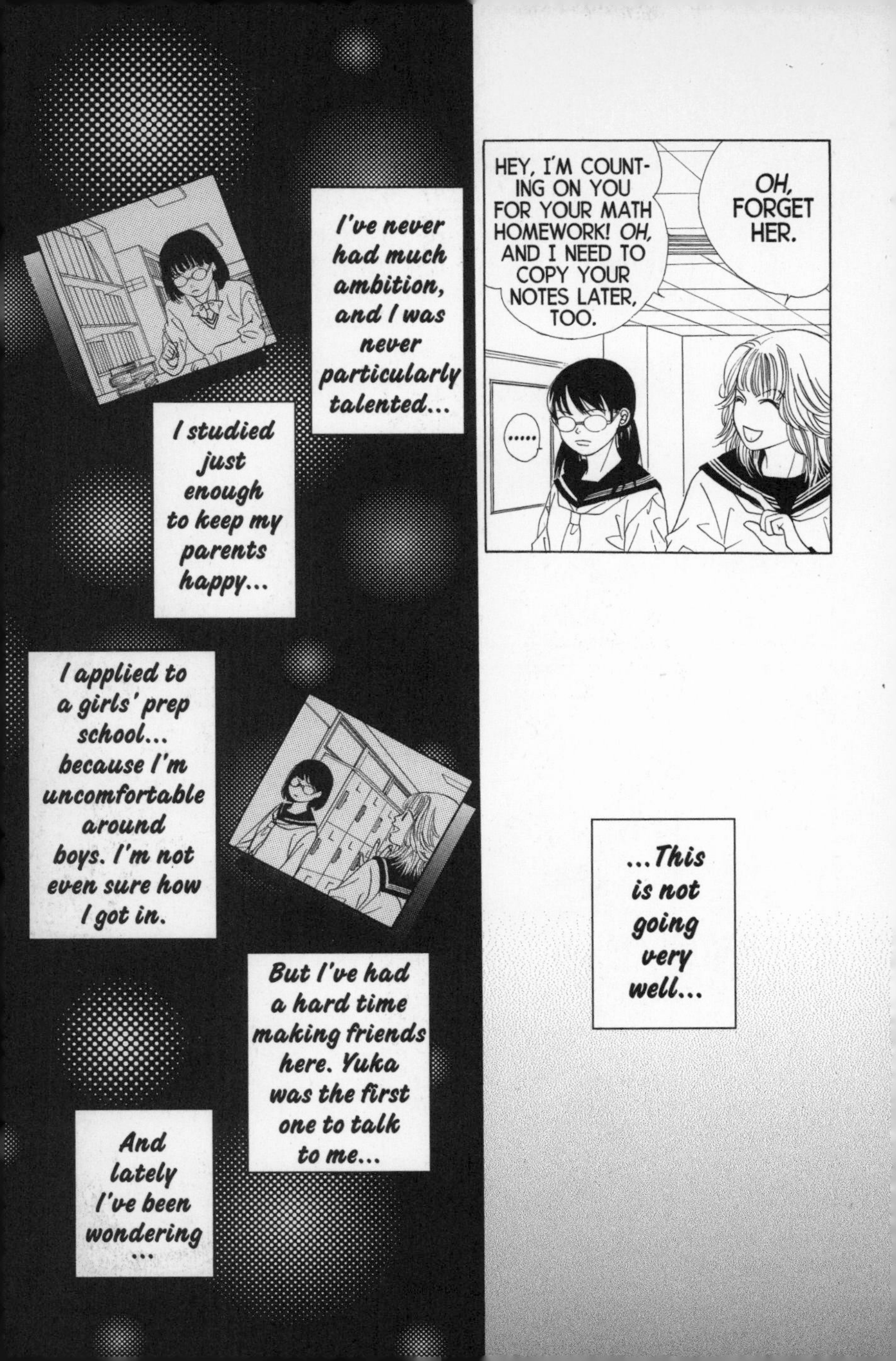
OH, FORGET HER.
HEY, I'M COUNTING ON YOU FOR YOUR MATH HOMEWORK! OH, AND I NEED TO COPY YOUR NOTES LATER, TOO.
.....
...This is not going very well...
I've never had much ambition, and I was never particularly talented...
I studied just enough to keep my parents happy...
I applied to a girls' prep school... because I'm uncomfortable around boys. I'm not even sure how I got in.
But I've had a hard time making friends here. Yuka was the first one to talk to me...
And lately I've been wondering ...

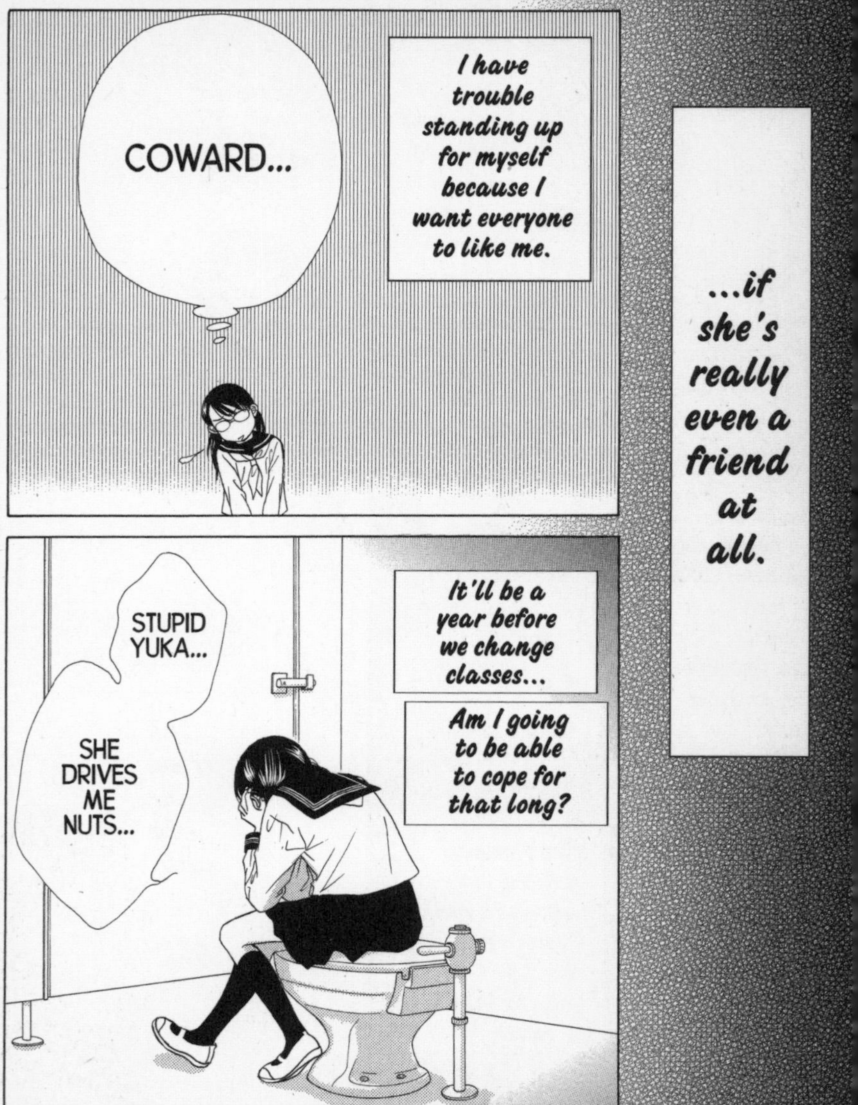
...if she's really even a friend at all.
I have trouble standing up for myself because I want everyone to like me.
COWARD...
It'll be a year before we change classes...
Am I going to be able to cope for that long?
STUPID YUKA...
SHE DRIVES ME NUTS...

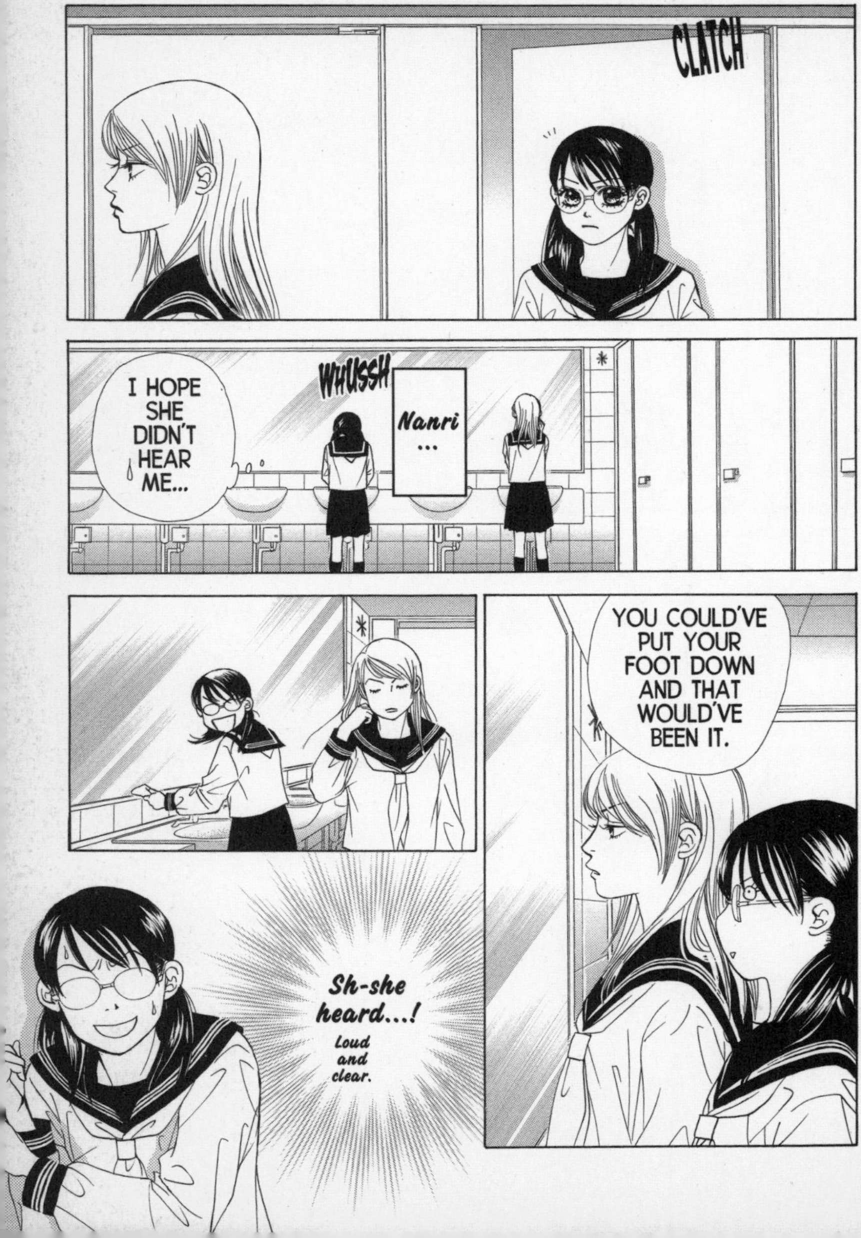
CLATCH
Nanri ...
WHUSSH
I HOPE SHE DIDN'T HEAR ME...
YOU COULD'VE PUT YOUR FOOT DOWN AND THAT WOULD'VE BEEN IT.
Sh-she heard...!
Loud and clear.

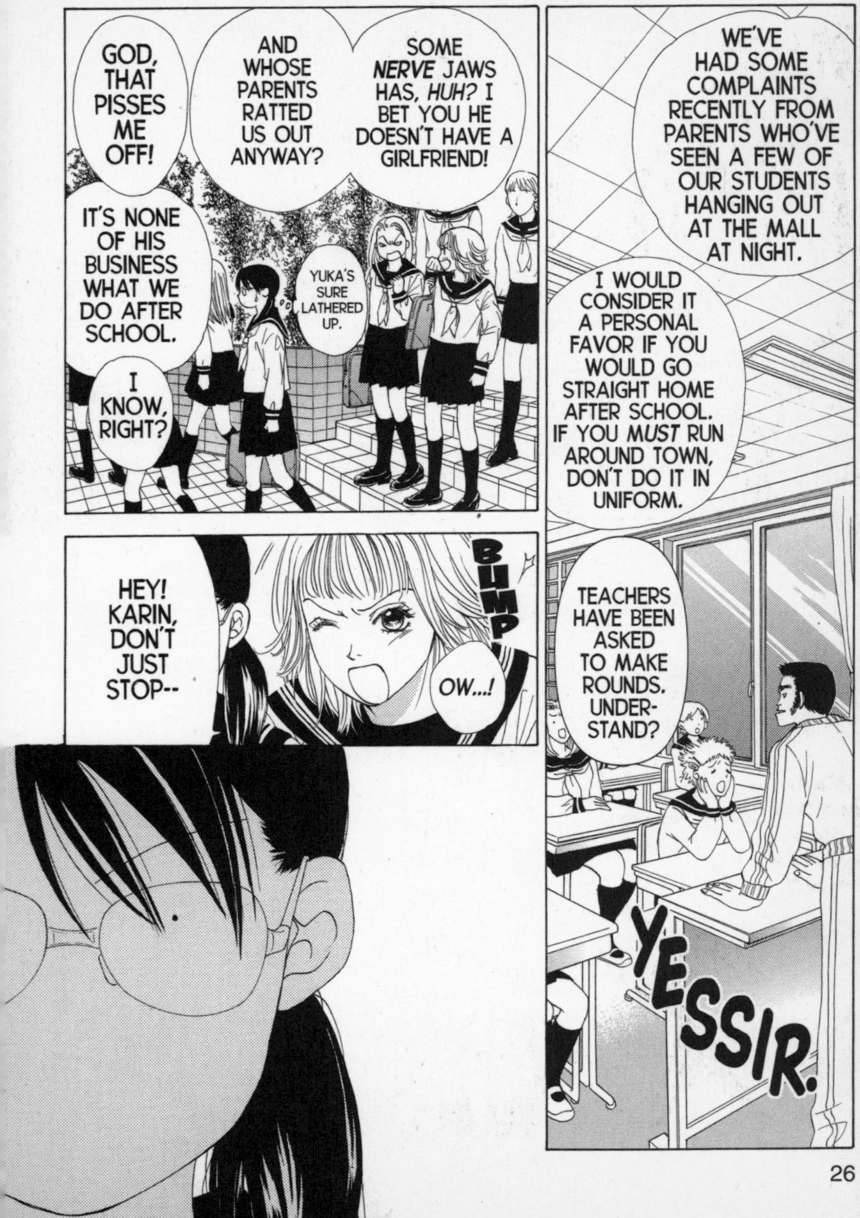

WE'VE HAD SOME COMPLAINTS RECENTLY FROM PARENTS WHO'VE SEEN A FEW OF OUR STUDENTS HANGING OUT AT THE MALL AT NIGHT.
I WOULD CONSIDER IT A PERSONAL FAVOR IF YOU WOULD GO STRAIGHT HOME AFTER SCHOOL. IF YOU *MUST* RUN AROUND TOWN, DON'T DO IT IN UNIFORM.
TEACHERS HAVE BEEN ASKED TO MAKE ROUNDS. UNDER-STAND?
YESSIR.
SOME *NERVE* JAWS HAS, *HUH?* I BET YOU HE DOESN'T HAVE A GIRLFRIEND!
AND WHOSE PARENTS RATTED US OUT ANYWAY?
GOD, THAT PISSES ME OFF!
YUKA'S SURE LATHERED UP.
IT'S NONE OF HIS BUSINESS WHAT WE DO AFTER SCHOOL.
I KNOW, RIGHT?
BUMP
OW...!
HEY! KARIN, DON'T JUST STOP--

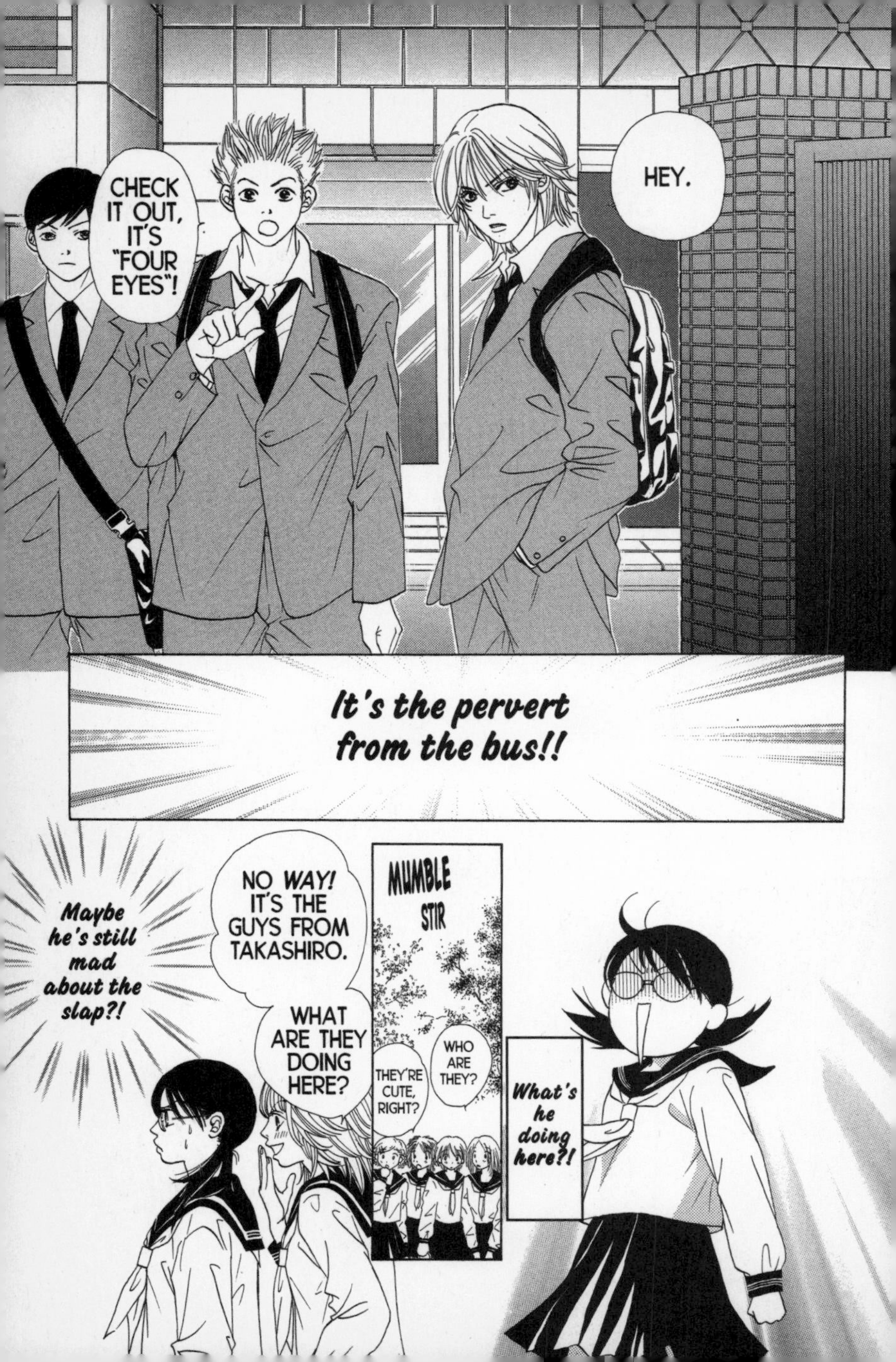
HEY.
CHECK IT OUT, IT'S "FOUR EYES"!
It's the pervert from the bus!!
What's he doing here?!
MUMBLE
STIR
WHO ARE THEY?
THEY'RE CUTE, RIGHT?
NO WAY! IT'S THE GUYS FROM TAKASHIRO.
WHAT ARE THEY DOING HERE?
Maybe he's still mad about the slap?!

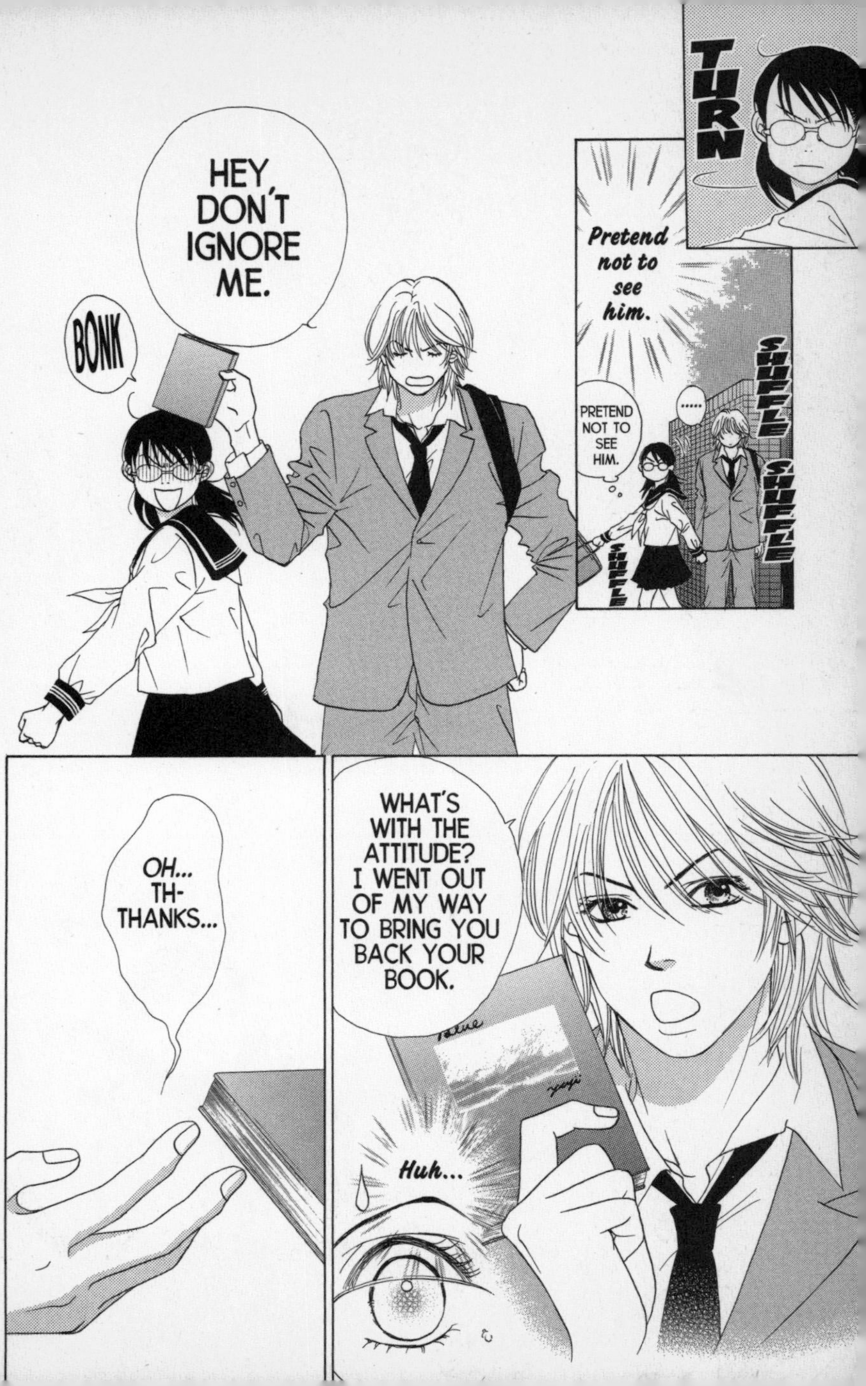
TURN
Pretend not to see him.
SHUFFLE
SHUFFLE
......
PRETEND NOT TO SEE HIM.
SHUFFLE
HEY DON'T IGNORE ME.
BONK
WHAT'S WITH THE ATTITUDE? I WENT OUT OF MY WAY TO BRING YOU BACK YOUR BOOK.
Huh...
OH... TH- THANKS...

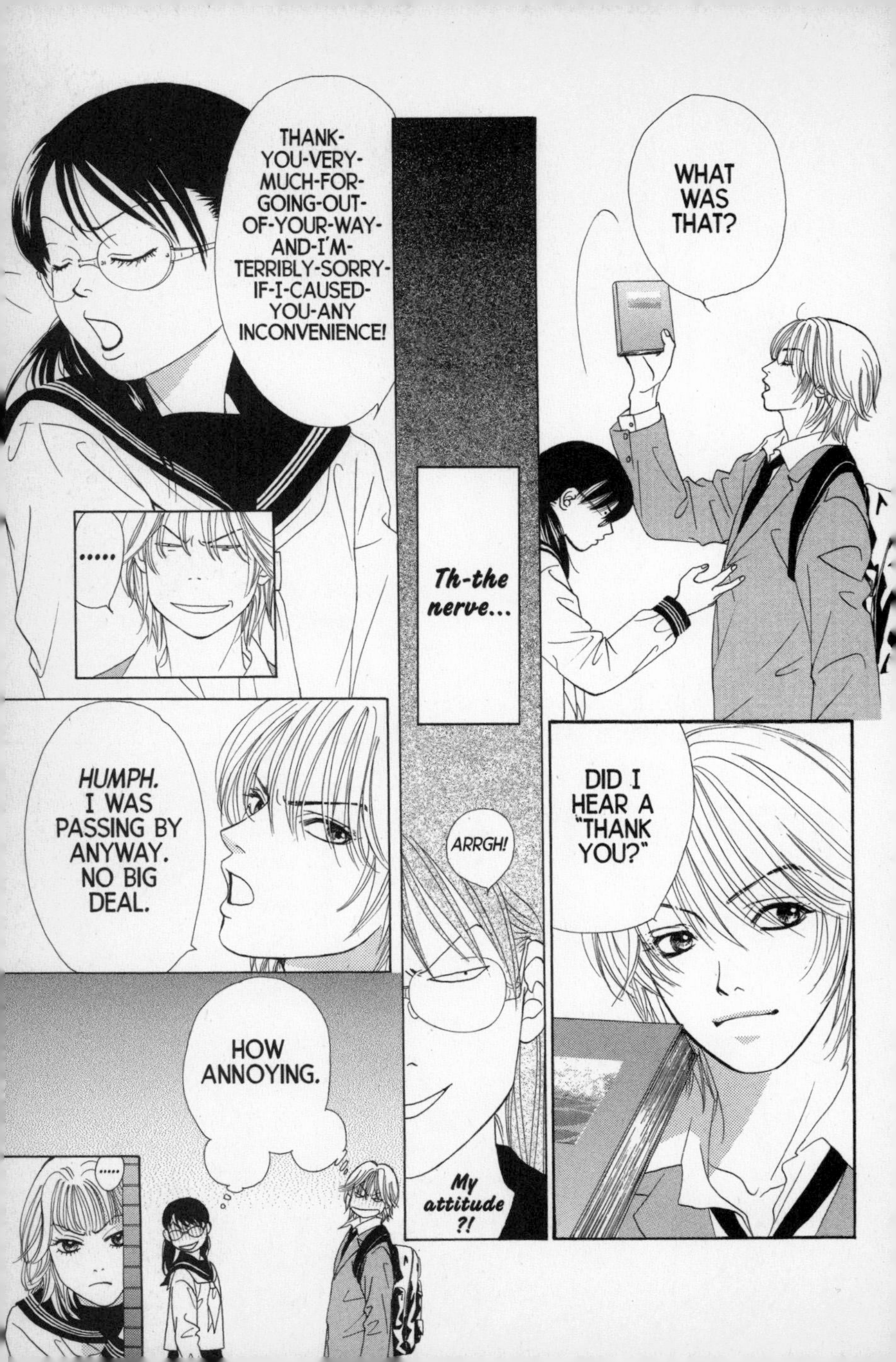

WHAT WAS THAT?
Th-the nerve...
THANK-YOU-VERY-MUCH-FOR-GOING-OUT-OF-YOUR-WAY-AND-I'M-TERRIBLY-SORRY-IF-I-CAUSED-YOU-ANY INCONVENIENCE!
.....
HUMPH. I WAS PASSING BY ANYWAY. NO BIG DEAL.
DID I HEAR A "THANK YOU?"
ARRGH!
My attitude?!
HOW ANNOYING.
.....

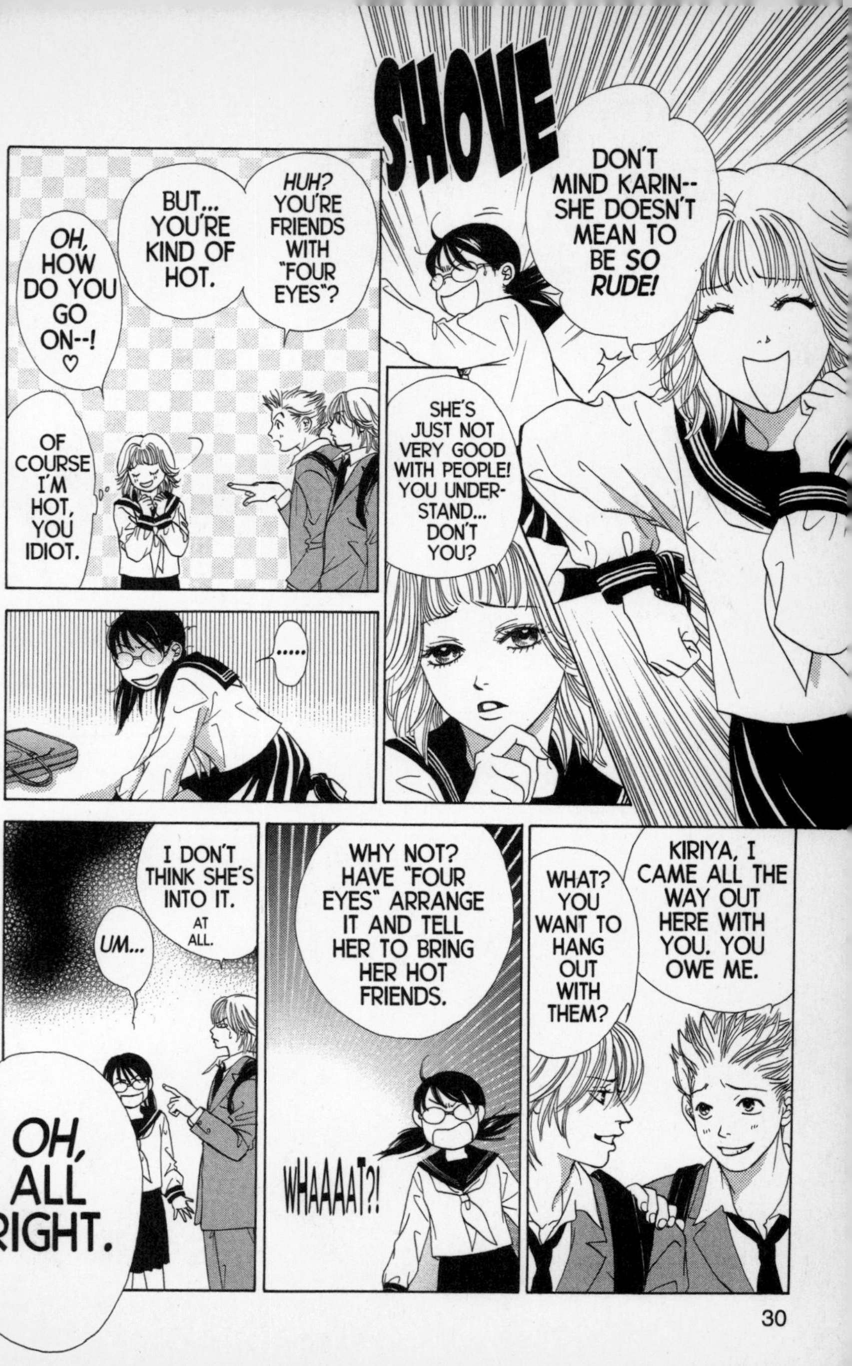
HUH? YOU'RE FRIENDS WITH "FOUR EYES"?
BUT... YOU'RE KIND OF HOT.
OH, HOW DO YOU GO ON--! ♡
OF COURSE I'M HOT, YOU IDIOT.
......
SHOVE
DON'T MIND KARIN-- SHE DOESN'T MEAN TO BE SO RUDE!
SHE'S JUST NOT VERY GOOD WITH PEOPLE! YOU UNDER-STAND... DON'T YOU?
KIRIYA, I CAME ALL THE WAY OUT HERE WITH YOU. YOU OWE ME.
WHAT? YOU WANT TO HANG OUT WITH THEM?
WHY NOT? HAVE "FOUR EYES" ARRANGE IT AND TELL HER TO BRING HER HOT FRIENDS.
WHAAAAT?!
I DON'T THINK SHE'S INTO IT. AT ALL.
UM...
OH, ALL RIGHT.

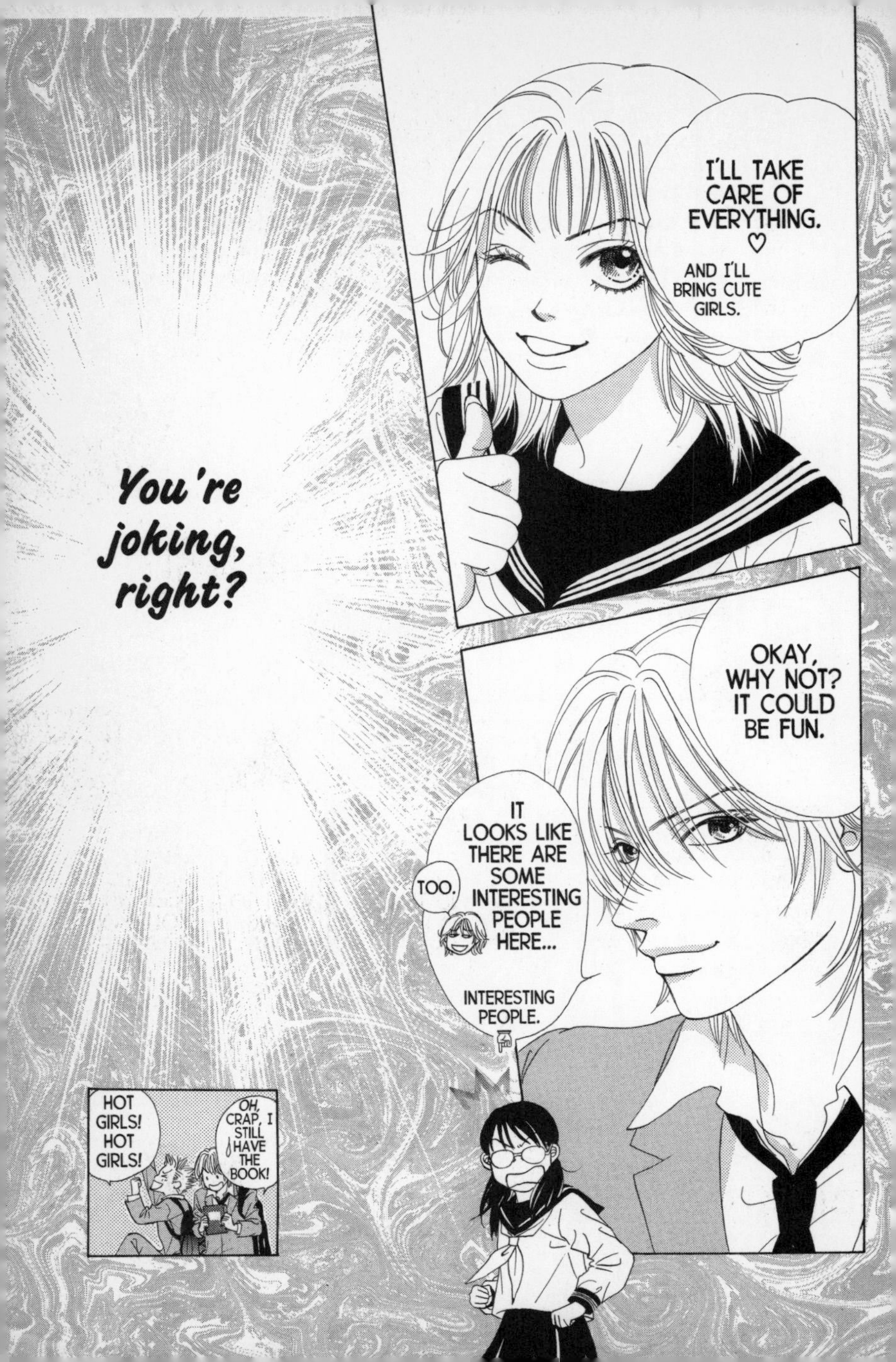
I'LL TAKE CARE OF EVERYTHING. ♡
AND I'LL BRING CUTE GIRLS.
OKAY, WHY NOT? IT COULD BE FUN.
IT LOOKS LIKE THERE ARE SOME INTERESTING PEOPLE HERE...
TOO.
INTERESTING PEOPLE.
You're joking, right?
OH, CRAP, I STILL HAVE THE BOOK!
HOT GIRLS! HOT GIRLS!

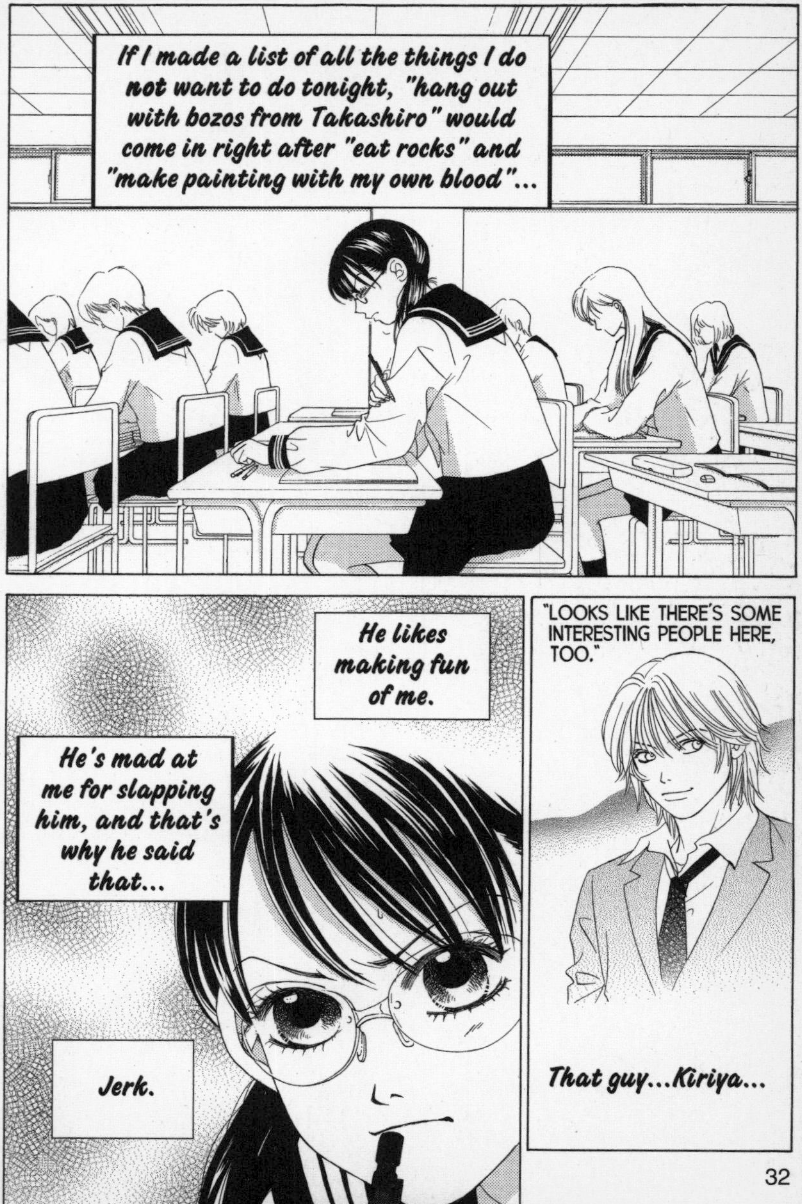
If I made a list of all the things I do not want to do tonight, "hang out with bozos from Takashiro" would come in right after "eat rocks" and "make painting with my own blood"...
"LOOKS LIKE THERE'S SOME INTERESTING PEOPLE HERE, TOO."
That guy...Kiriya...
He likes making fun of me.
He's mad at me for slapping him, and that's why he said that...
Jerk.

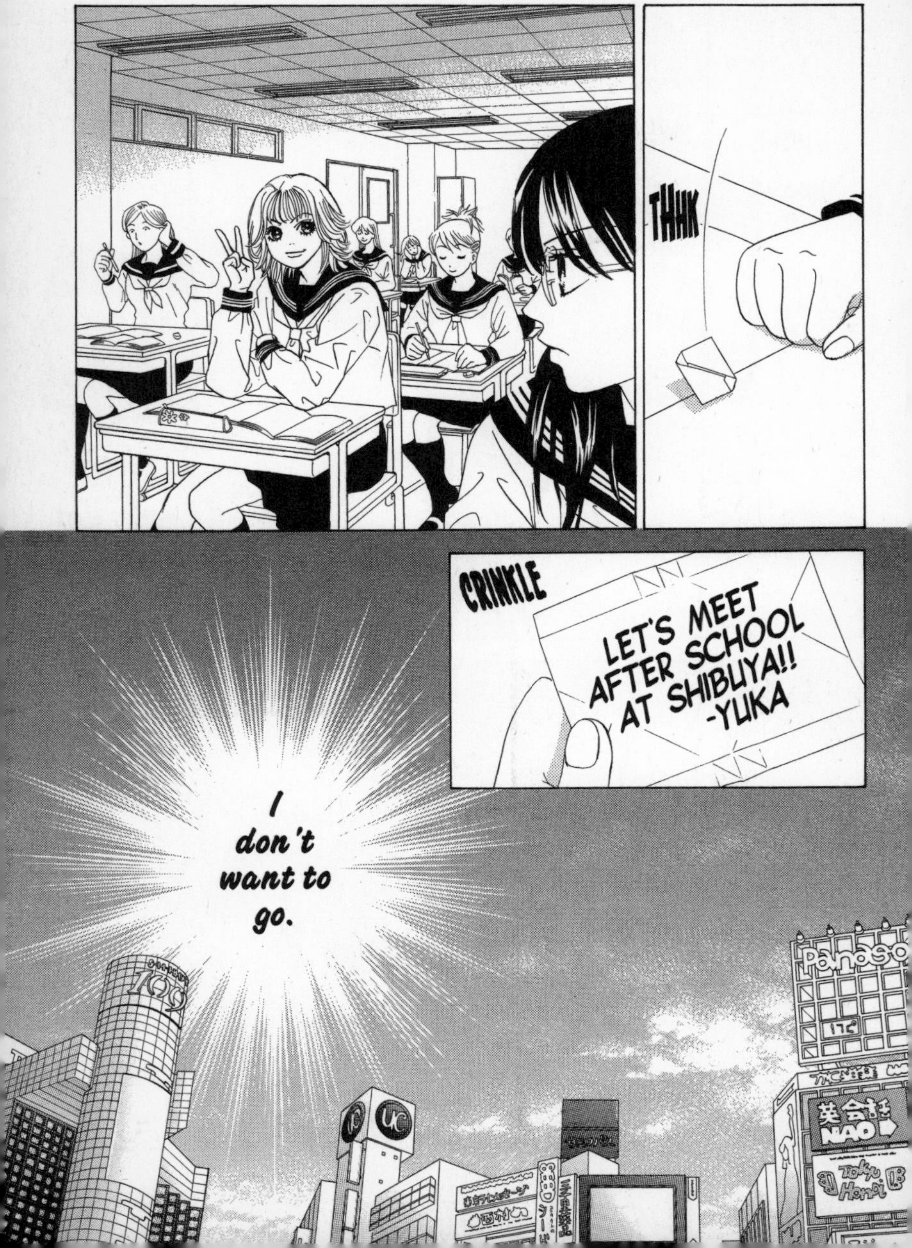
THHK
CRINKLE
LET'S MEET AFTER SCHOOL AT SHIBUYA!! -YUKA
I don't want to go.
Panaso
NAO

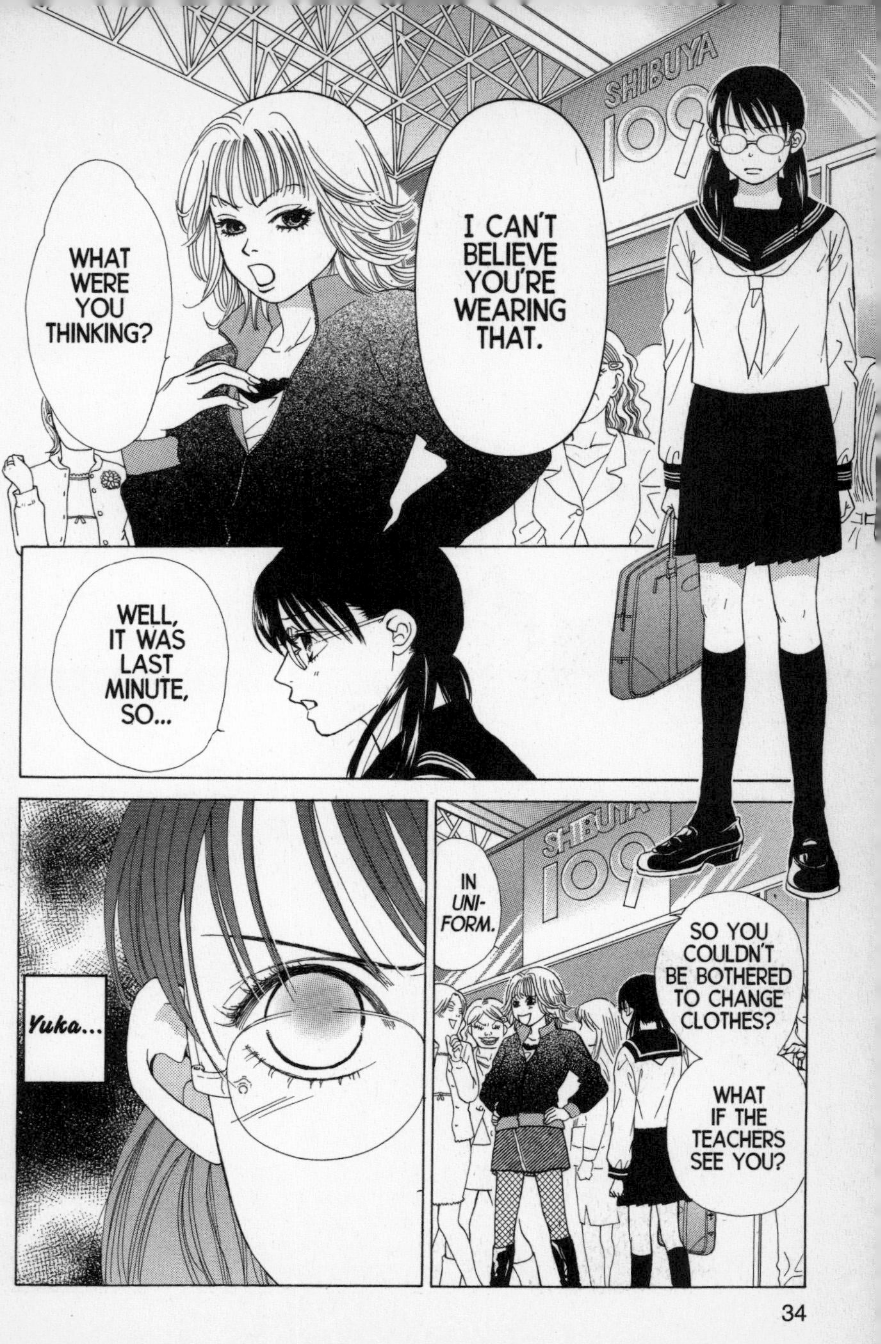
SHIBUYA
I CAN'T BELIEVE YOU'RE WEARING THAT.
WHAT WERE YOU THINKING?
WELL, IT WAS LAST MINUTE, SO...
SHIBUYA
SO YOU COULDN'T BE BOTHERED TO CHANGE CLOTHES?
WHAT IF THE TEACHERS SEE YOU?
IN *UNI-FORM.*
Yuka...

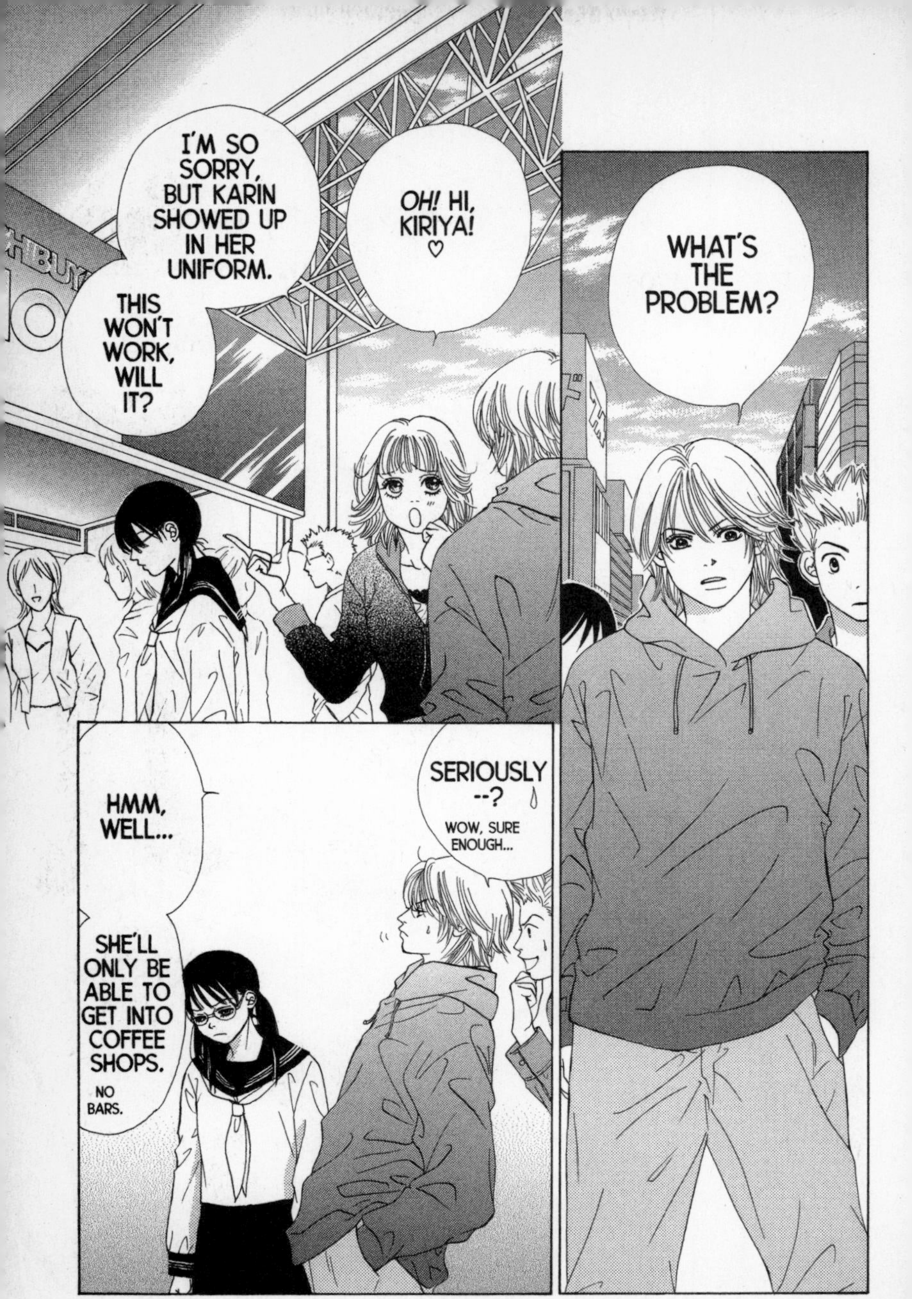
OH! HI, KIRIYA! ♡
I'M SO SORRY, BUT KARIN SHOWED UP IN HER UNIFORM.
THIS WON'T WORK, WILL IT?
WHAT'S THE PROBLEM?
SERIOUSLY --?
WOW, SURE ENOUGH...
HMM, WELL...
SHE'LL ONLY BE ABLE TO GET INTO COFFEE SHOPS.
NO BARS.

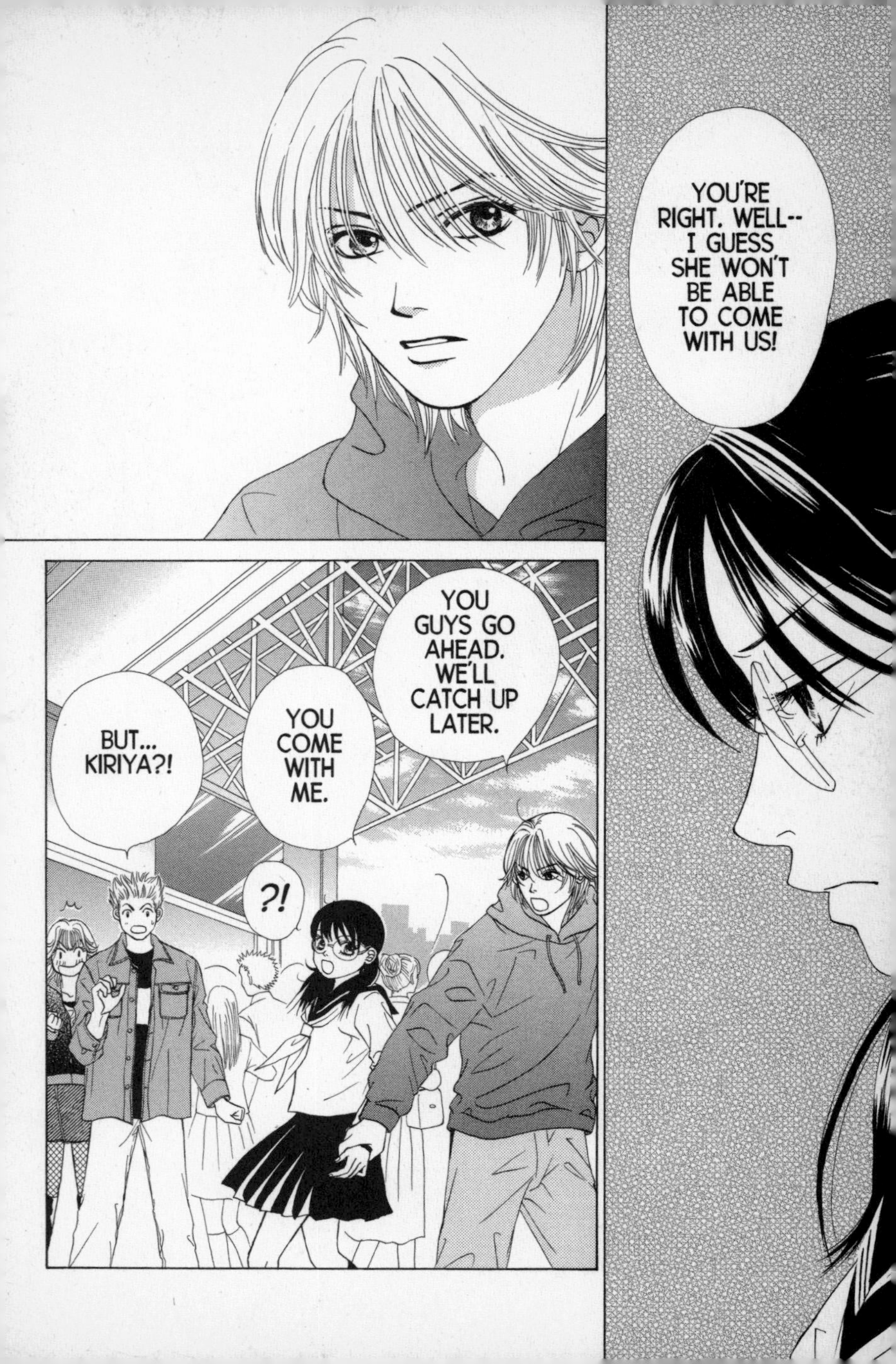
YOU'RE RIGHT. WELL-- I GUESS SHE WON'T BE ABLE TO COME WITH US!
YOU GUYS GO AHEAD. WE'LL CATCH UP LATER.
YOU COME WITH ME.
BUT... KIRIYA?!
?!

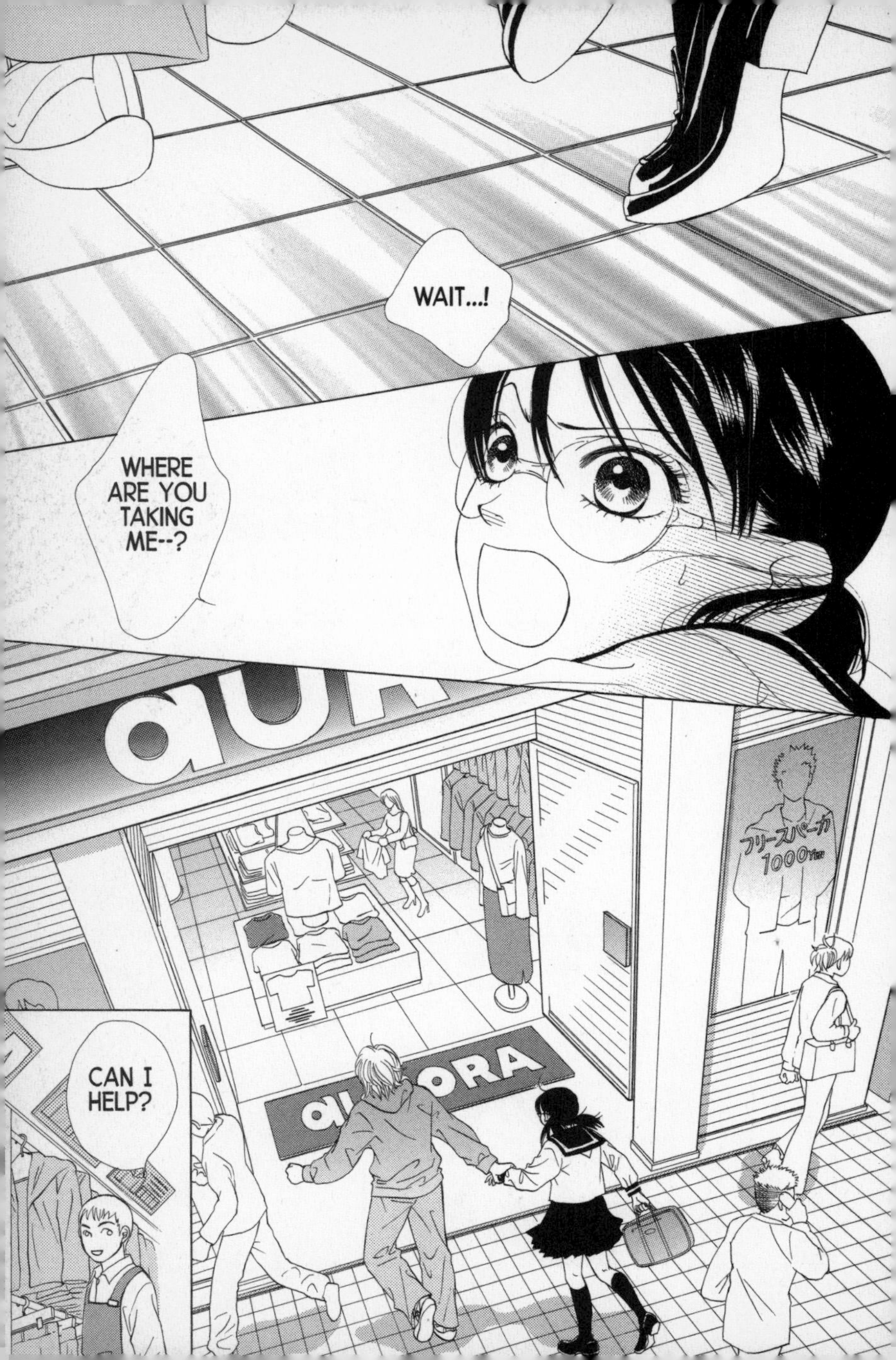
WAIT...!
WHERE ARE YOU TAKING ME--?
フリースパーカ
1000Yen
CAN I HELP?

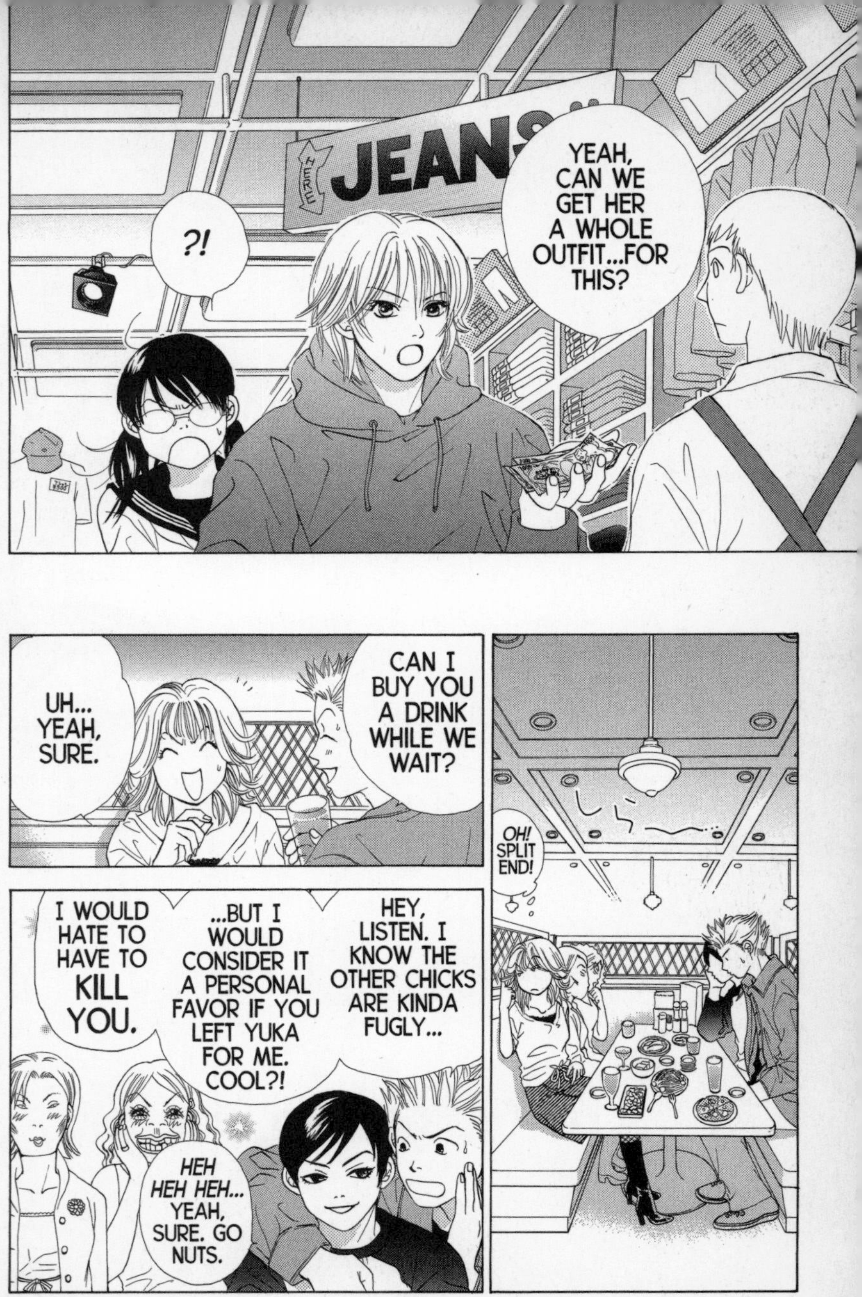
JEANS
HERE
YEAH, CAN WE GET HER A WHOLE OUTFIT...FOR THIS?
?!
OH! SPLIT END!
CAN I BUY YOU A DRINK WHILE WE WAIT?
UH... YEAH, SURE.
HEY, LISTEN. I KNOW THE OTHER CHICKS ARE KINDA FUGLY...
...BUT I WOULD CONSIDER IT A PERSONAL FAVOR IF YOU LEFT YUKA FOR ME. COOL?!
I WOULD HATE TO HAVE TO KILL YOU.
HEH HEH HEH... YEAH, SURE. GO NUTS.

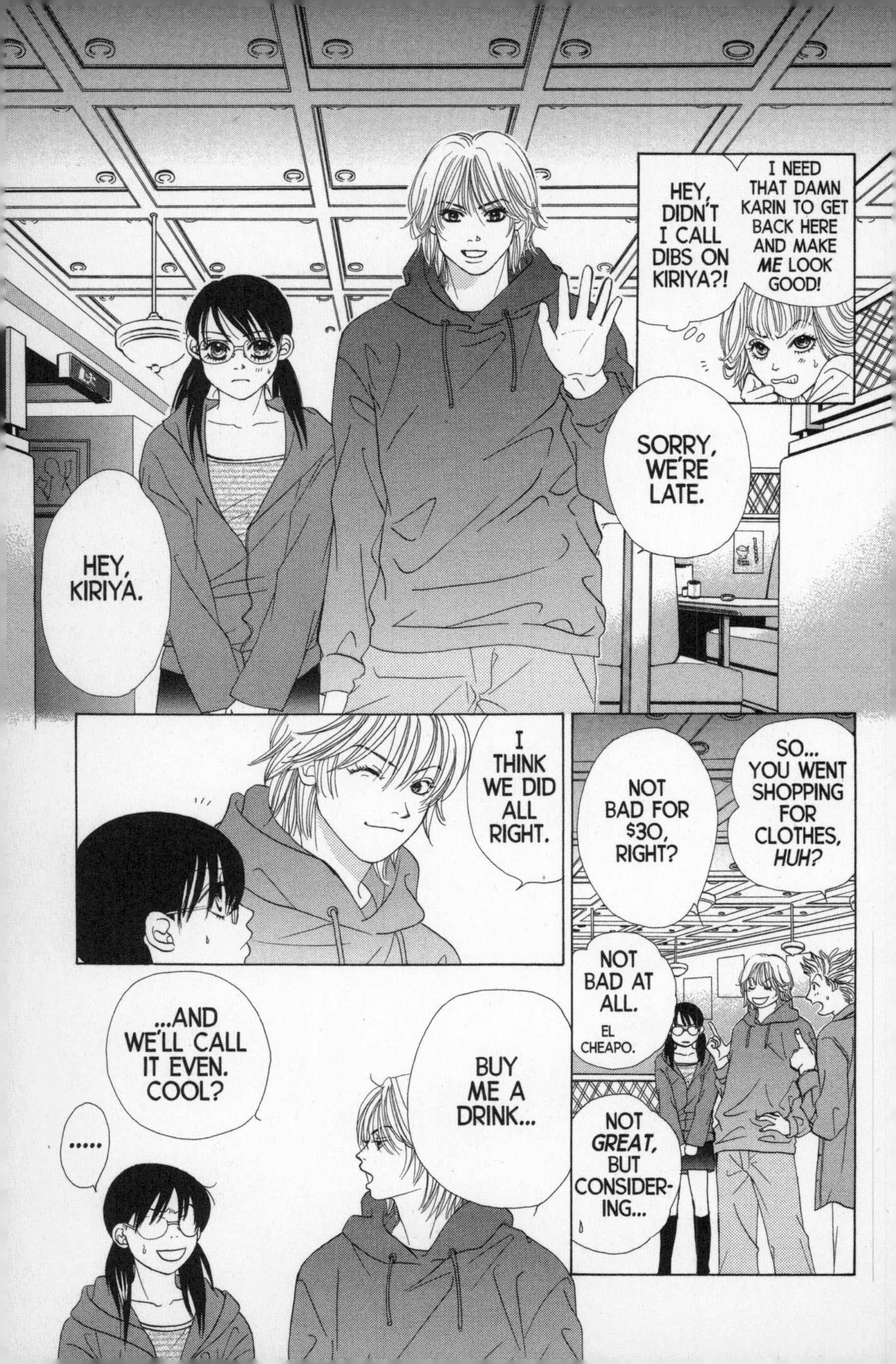
I NEED THAT DAMN KARIN TO GET BACK HERE AND MAKE *ME* LOOK GOOD!
HEY, DIDN'T I CALL DIBS ON KIRIYA?!
SORRY, WE'RE LATE.
HEY, KIRIYA.
SO... YOU WENT SHOPPING FOR CLOTHES, *HUH?*
NOT BAD FOR $30, RIGHT?
NOT BAD AT ALL.
EL CHEAPO.
NOT *GREAT,* BUT CONSIDER-ING...
I THINK WE DID ALL RIGHT.
BUY ME A DRINK...
...AND WE'LL CALL IT EVEN. COOL?
.....

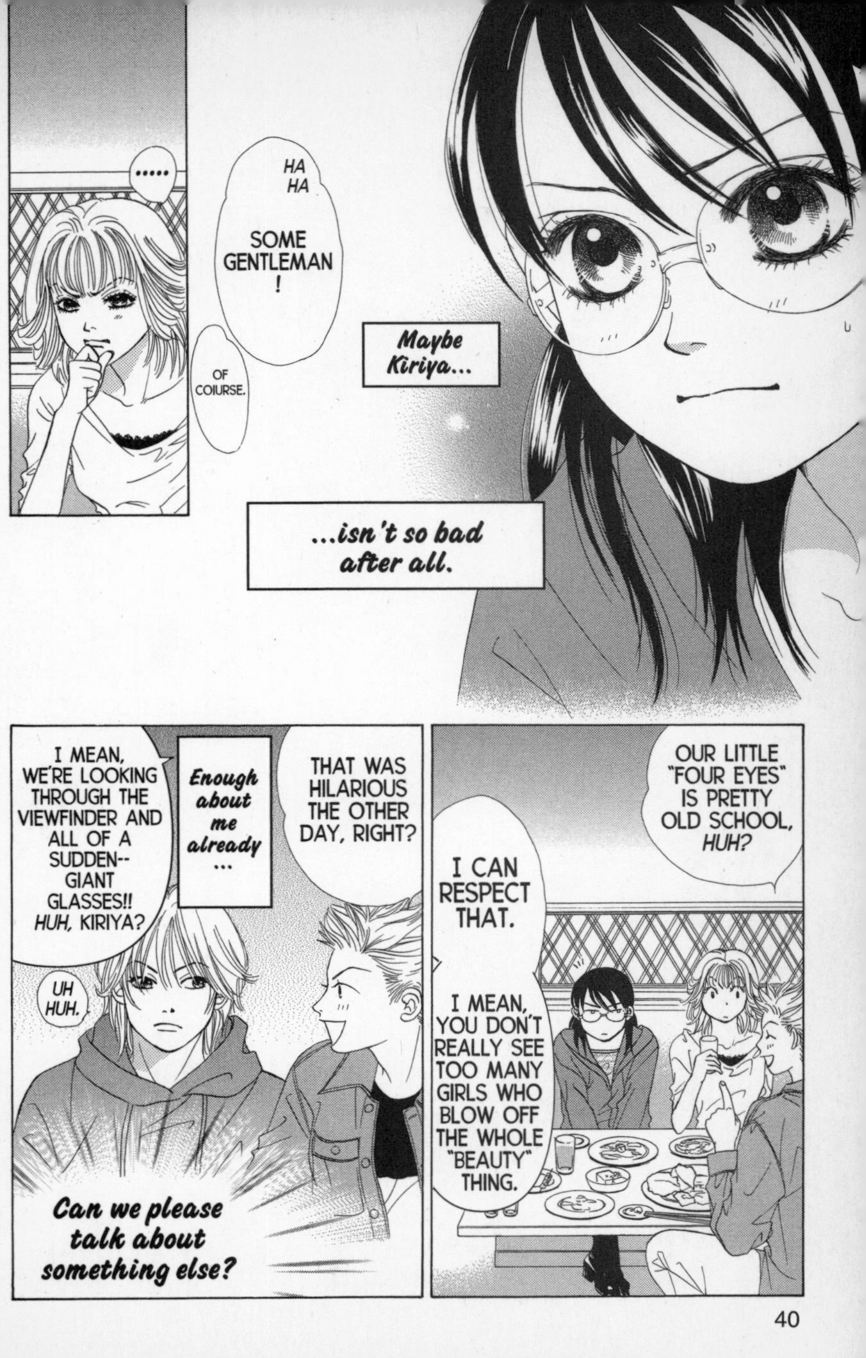

Maybe Kiriya...
...isn't so bad after all.
HA HA
SOME GENTLEMAN!
......
OF COIURSE.
OUR LITTLE "FOUR EYES" IS PRETTY OLD SCHOOL, HUH?
I CAN RESPECT THAT.
I MEAN, YOU DON'T REALLY SEE TOO MANY GIRLS WHO BLOW OFF THE WHOLE "BEAUTY" THING.
THAT WAS HILARIOUS THE OTHER DAY, RIGHT?
Enough about me already...
I MEAN, WE'RE LOOKING THROUGH THE VIEWFINDER AND ALL OF A SUDDEN-- GIANT GLASSES!! HUH, KIRIYA?
UH HUH.
Can we please talk about something else?

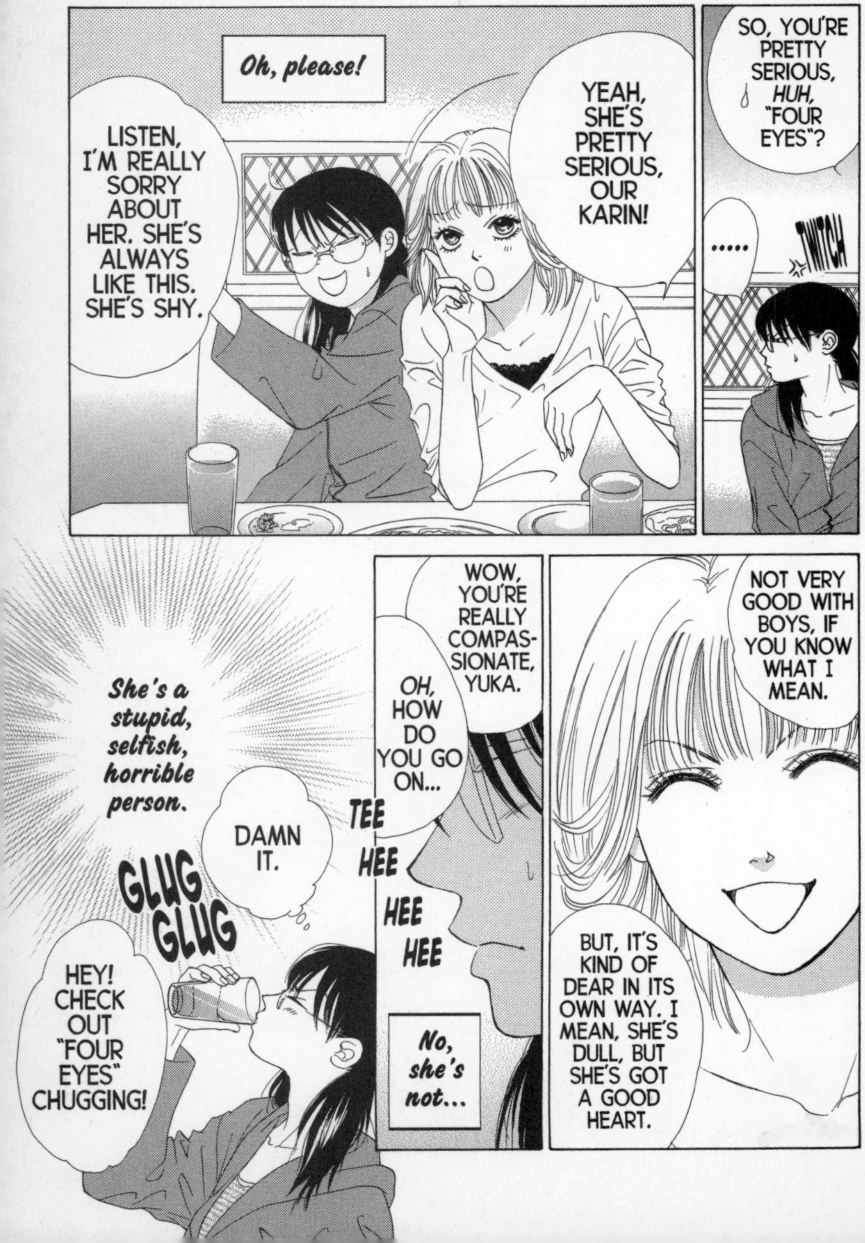

SO, YOU'RE PRETTY SERIOUS, *HUH*, "FOUR EYES"?
.....
TWITCH
YEAH, SHE'S PRETTY SERIOUS, OUR KARIN!
Oh, please!
LISTEN, I'M REALLY SORRY ABOUT HER. SHE'S ALWAYS LIKE THIS. SHE'S SHY.
NOT VERY GOOD WITH BOYS, IF YOU KNOW WHAT I MEAN.
BUT, IT'S KIND OF DEAR IN ITS OWN WAY. I MEAN, SHE'S DULL, BUT SHE'S GOT A GOOD HEART.
WOW, YOU'RE REALLY COMPAS-SIONATE, YUKA.
OH, HOW DO YOU GO ON...
TEE HEE HEE HEE
No, she's not...
She's a stupid, selfish, horrible person.
DAMN IT.
GLUG GLUG
HEY! CHECK OUT "FOUR EYES" CHUGGING!

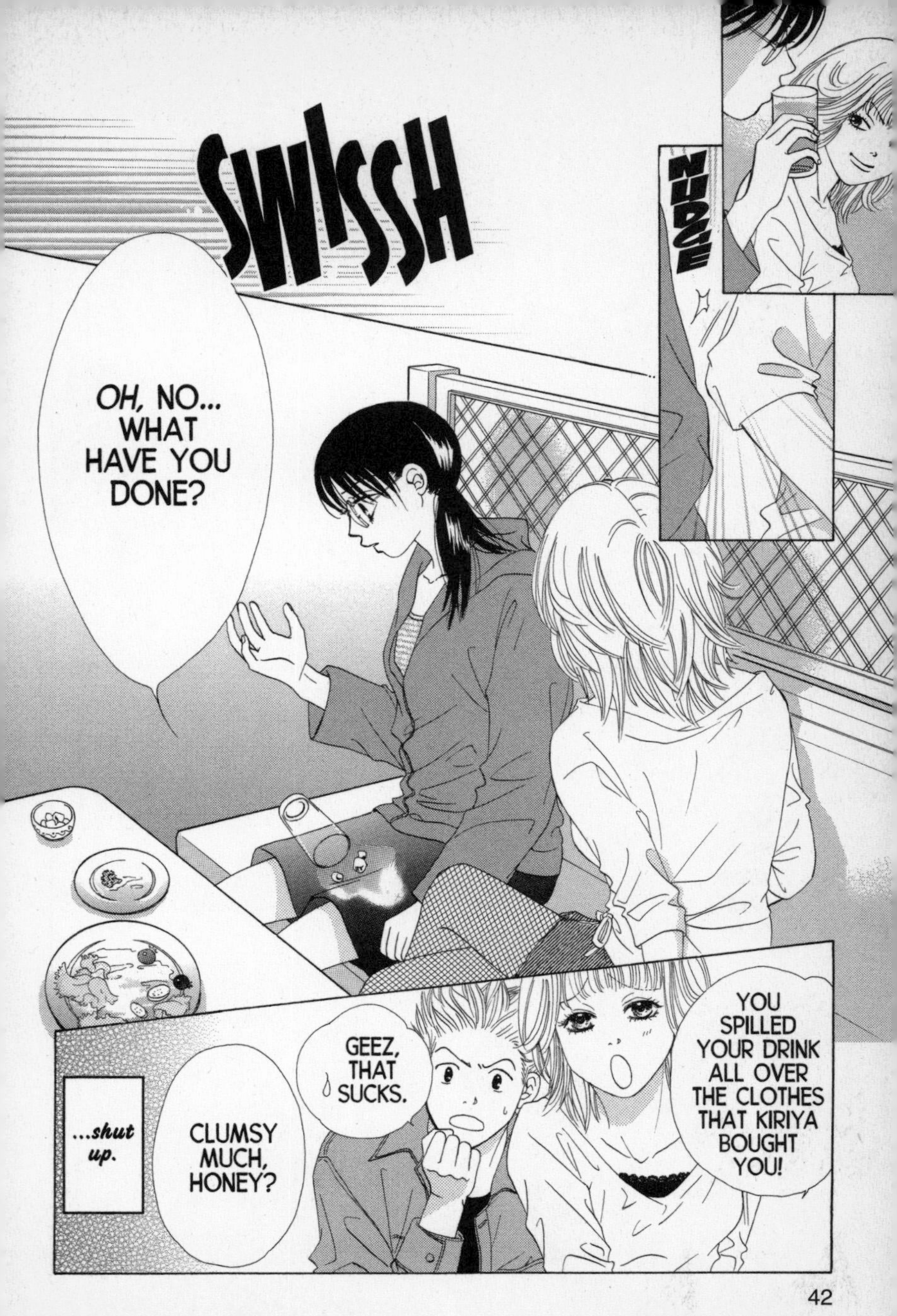
NUDGE
SWISSH
OH, NO... WHAT HAVE YOU DONE?
YOU SPILLED YOUR DRINK ALL OVER THE CLOTHES THAT KIRIYA BOUGHT YOU!
GEEZ, THAT SUCKS.
CLUMSY MUCH, HONEY?
...shut up.

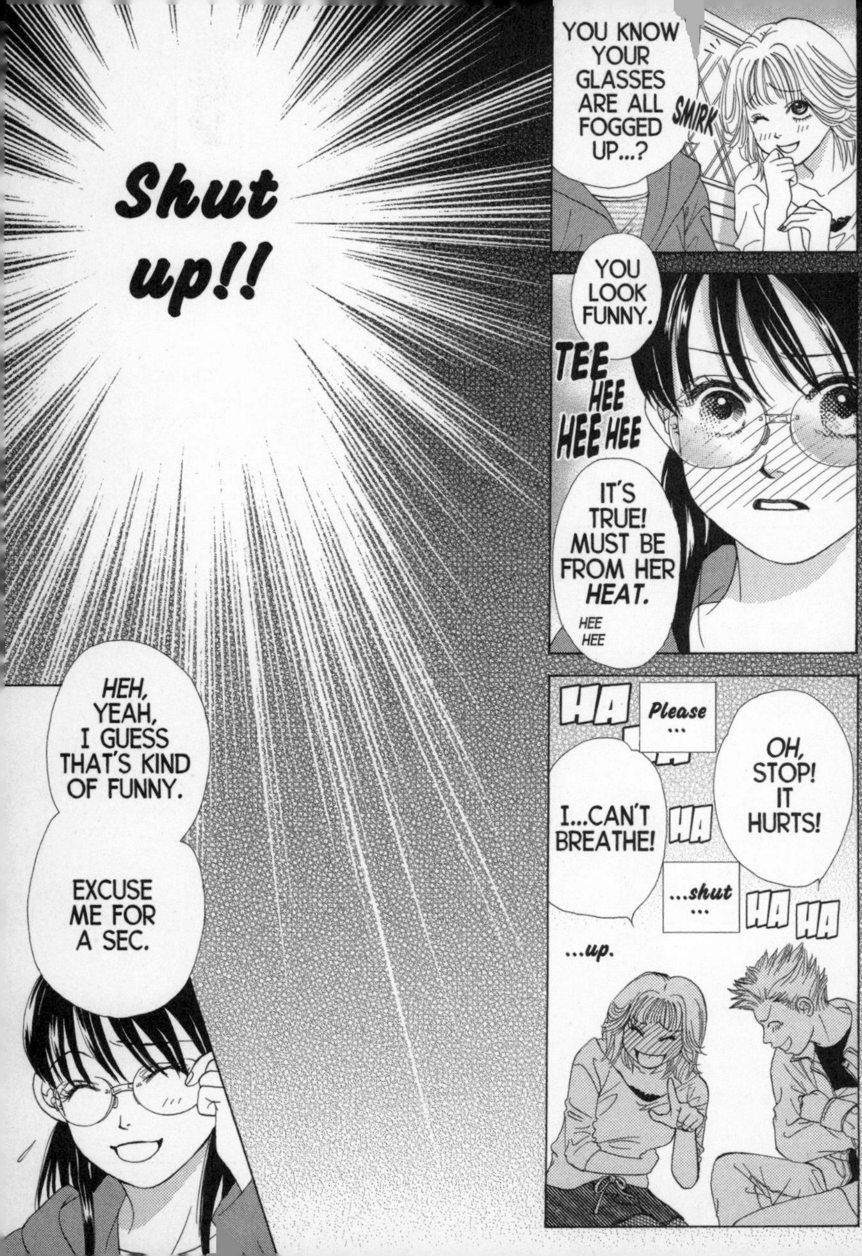

YOU KNOW YOUR GLASSES ARE ALL FOGGED UP...?
SMIRK
YOU LOOK FUNNY.
TEE HEE HEE HEE
IT'S TRUE! MUST BE FROM HER *HEAT*.
HEE HEE
HA
OH, STOP! IT HURTS!
Please ...
I...CAN'T BREATHE!
HA
...shut ...
HA HA
...up.
Shut up!!
HEH, YEAH, I GUESS THAT'S KIND OF FUNNY.
EXCUSE ME FOR A SEC.

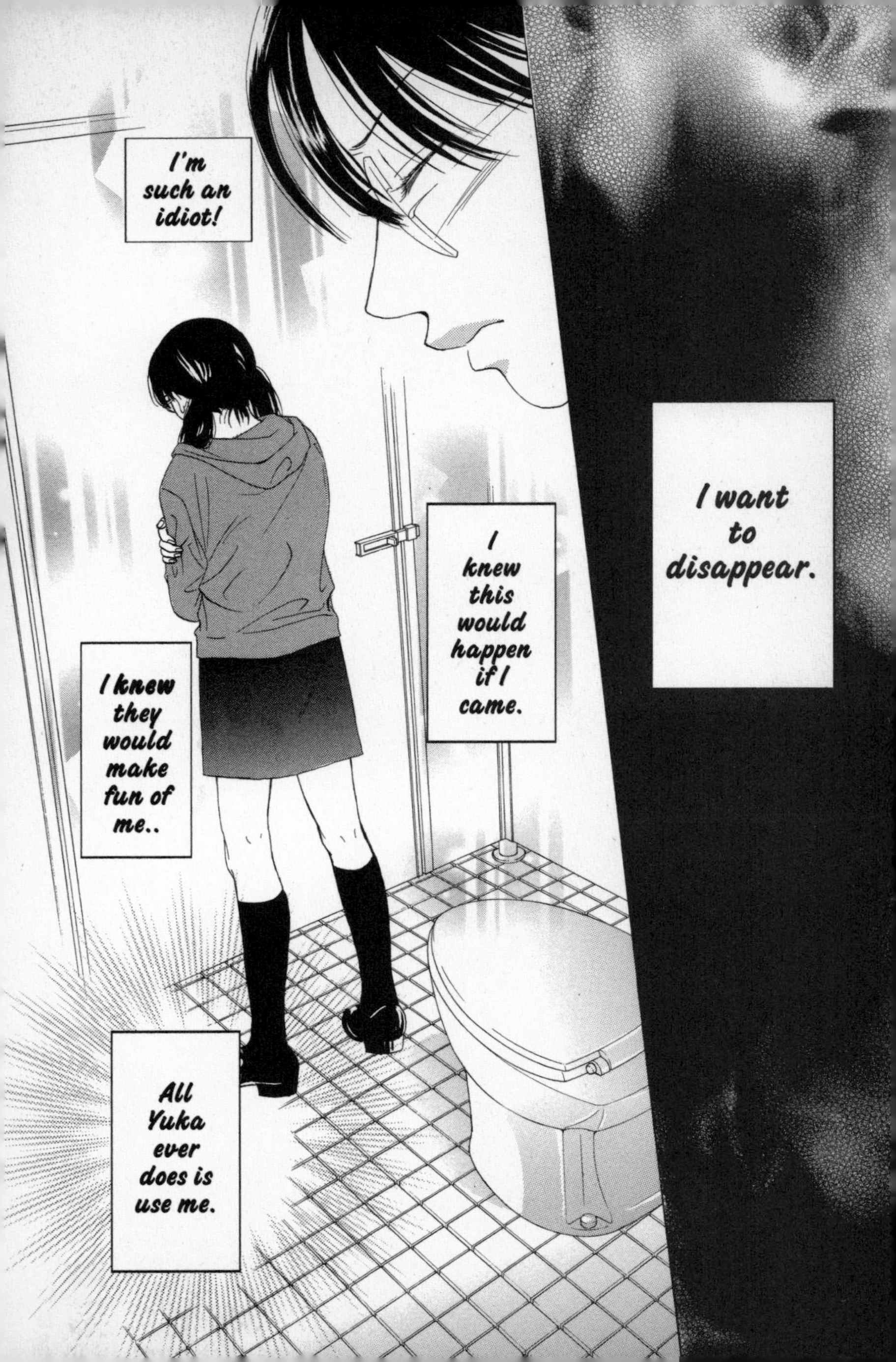
I want to disappear.
I'm such an idiot!
I knew this would happen if I came.
I knew they would make fun of me..
All Yuka ever does is use me.

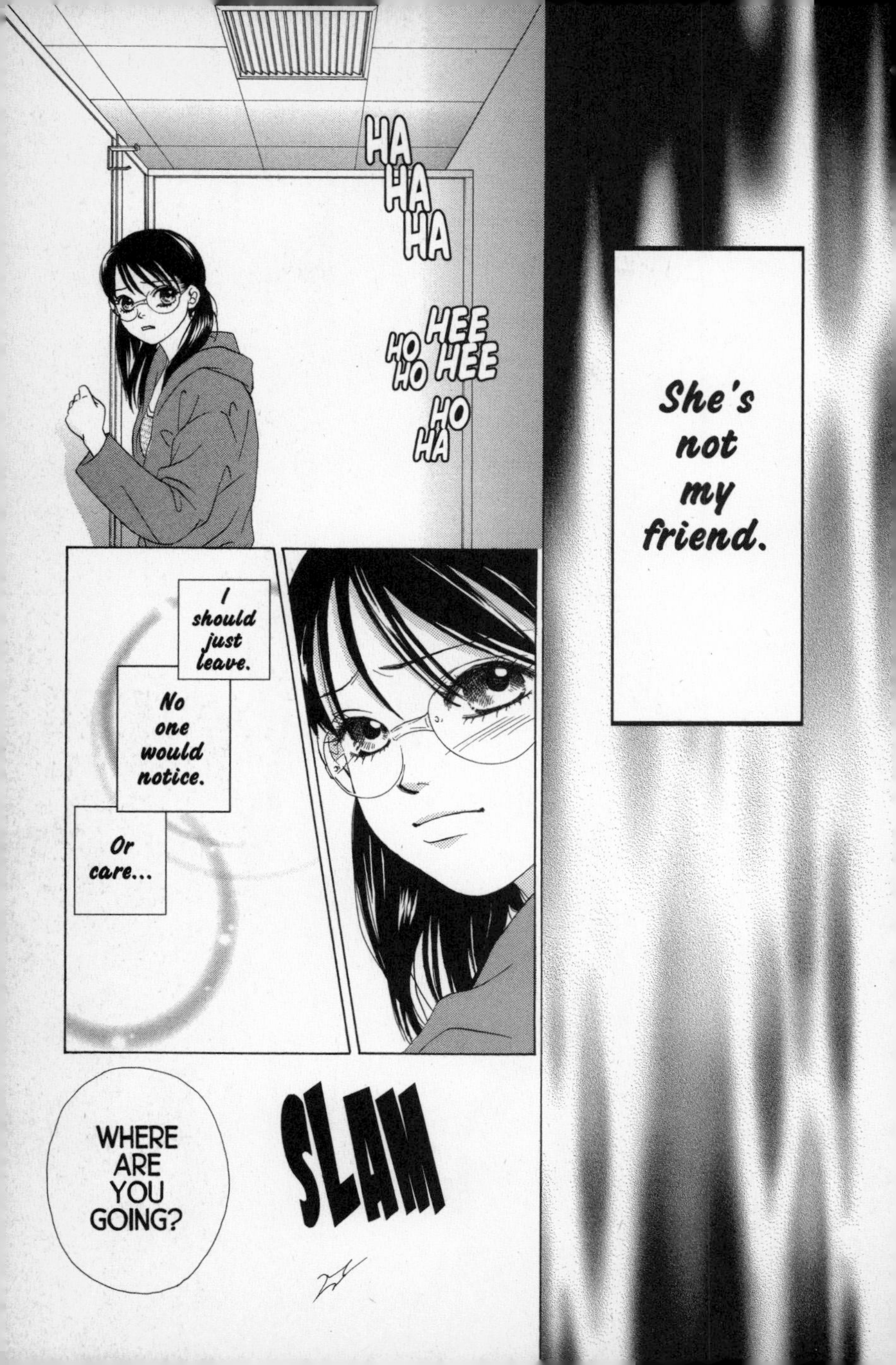
She's not my friend.
HA HA HA
HEE HEE
HO HO
HO HA
I should just leave.
No one would notice.
Or care...
SLAM
WHERE ARE YOU GOING?

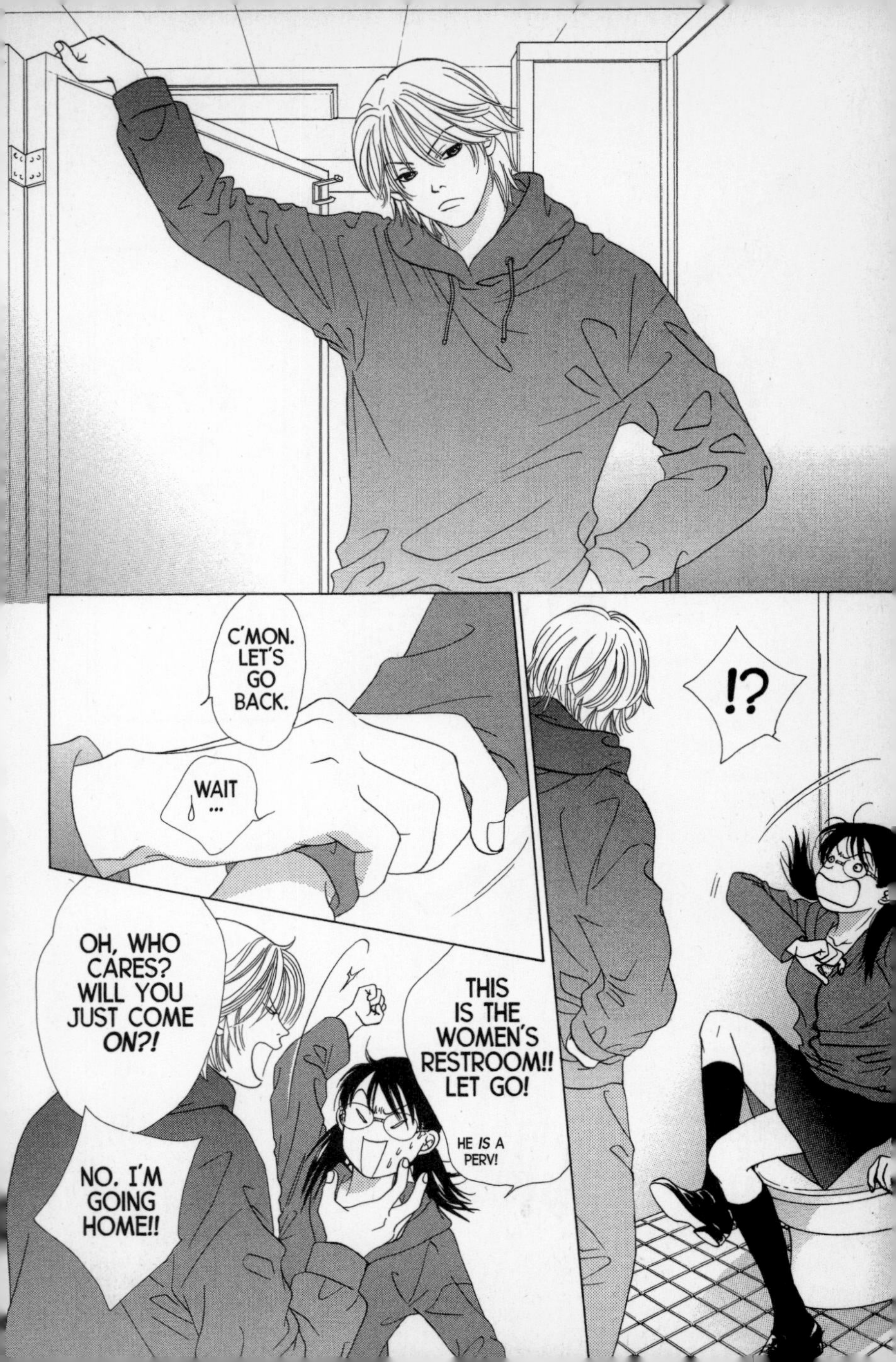

!?
C'MON. LET'S GO BACK.
WAIT ...
THIS IS THE WOMEN'S RESTROOM!! LET GO!
OH, WHO CARES? WILL YOU JUST COME *ON?!*
HE *IS* A PERV!
NO. I'M GOING HOME!!

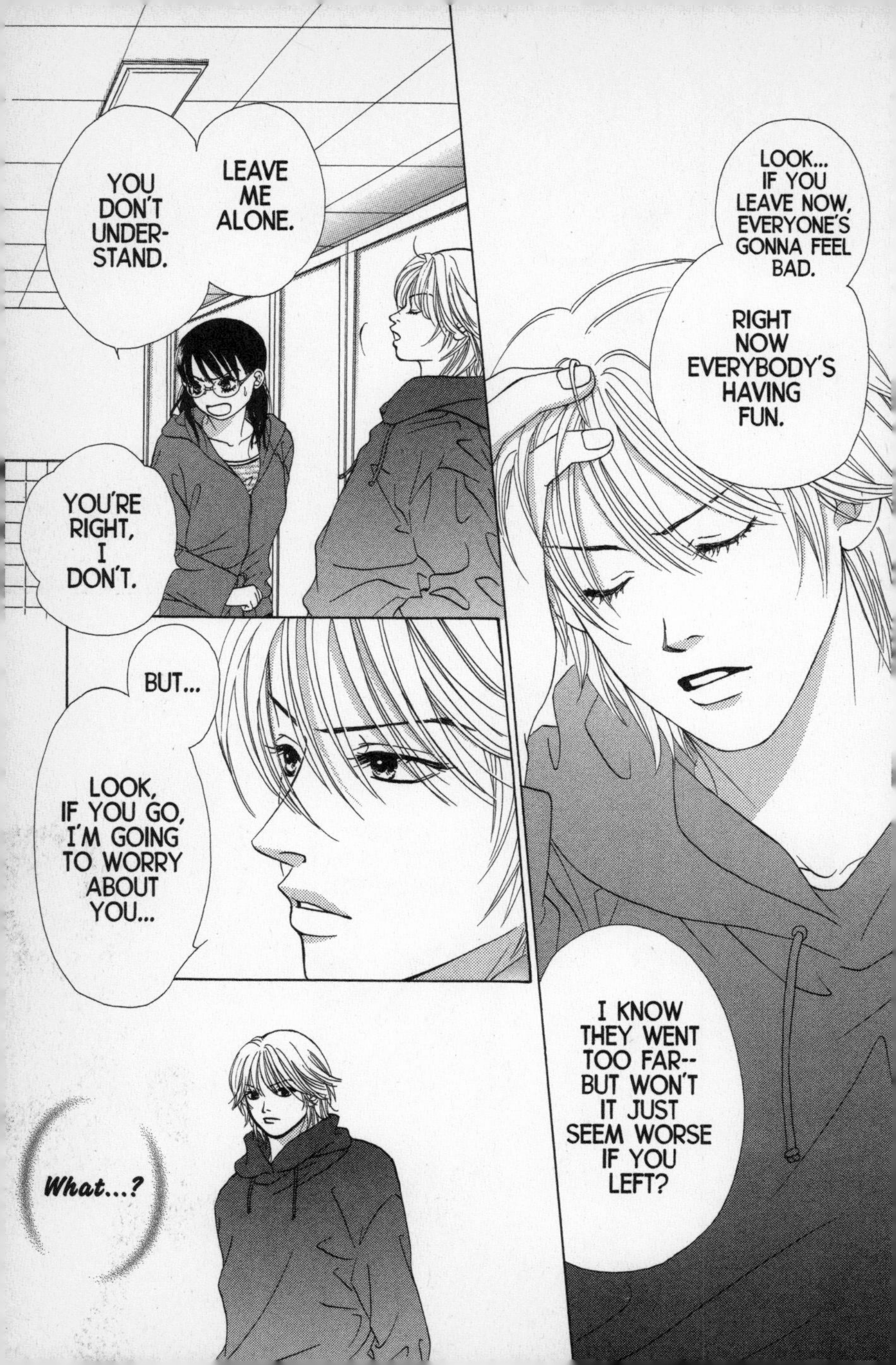
LOOK... IF YOU LEAVE NOW, EVERYONE'S GONNA FEEL BAD.
RIGHT NOW EVERYBODY'S HAVING FUN.
I KNOW THEY WENT TOO FAR-- BUT WON'T IT JUST SEEM WORSE IF YOU LEFT?
LEAVE ME ALONE.
YOU DON'T UNDER-STAND.
YOU'RE RIGHT, I DON'T.
BUT...
LOOK, IF YOU GO, I'M GOING TO WORRY ABOUT YOU...
What...?

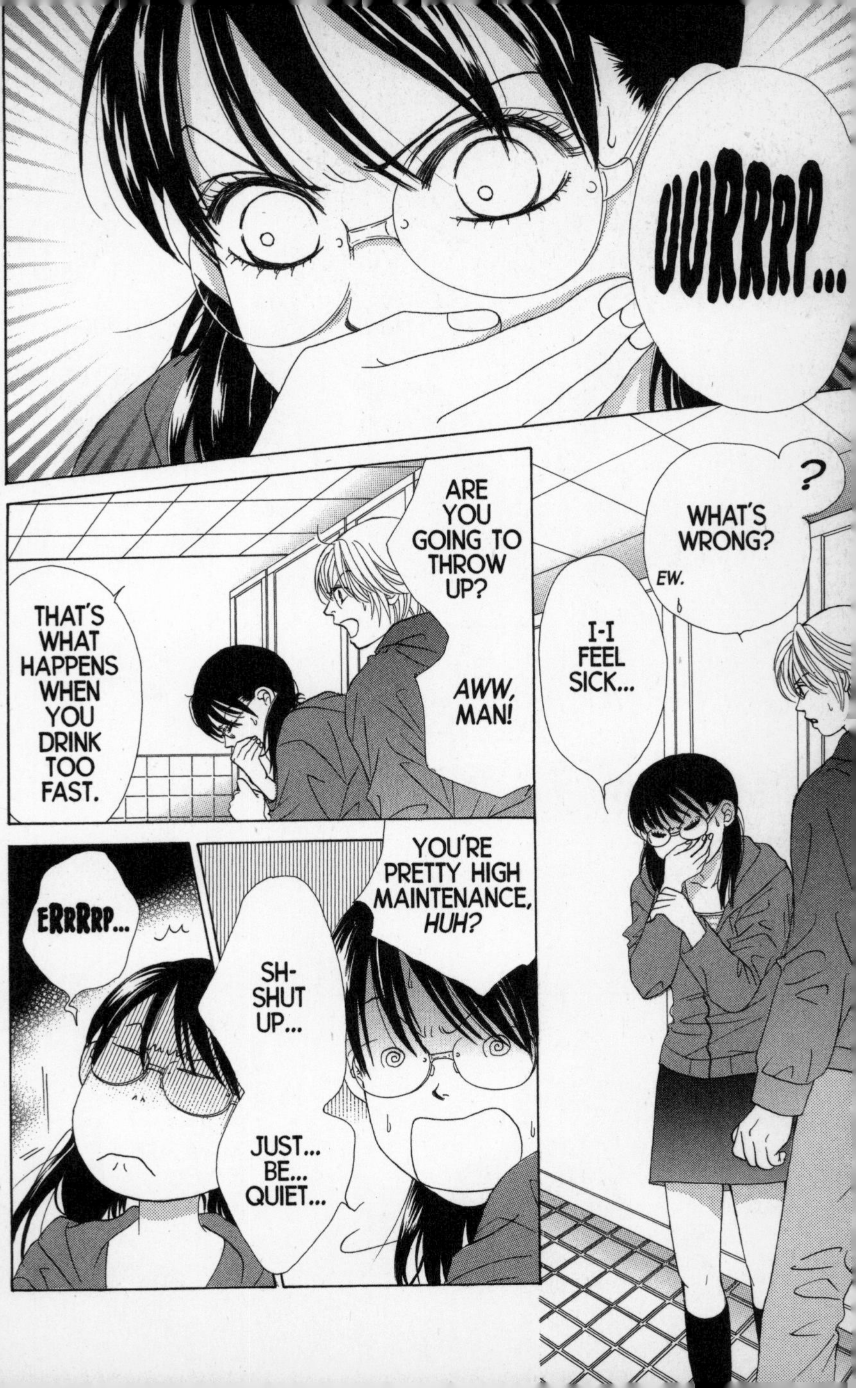
UURRRP...
?
WHAT'S WRONG?
EW.
I-I FEEL SICK...
ARE YOU GOING TO THROW UP?
AWW, MAN!
THAT'S WHAT HAPPENS WHEN YOU DRINK TOO FAST.
YOU'RE PRETTY HIGH MAINTENANCE, HUH?
SH-SHUT UP...
JUST... BE... QUIET...
ERRRRP...

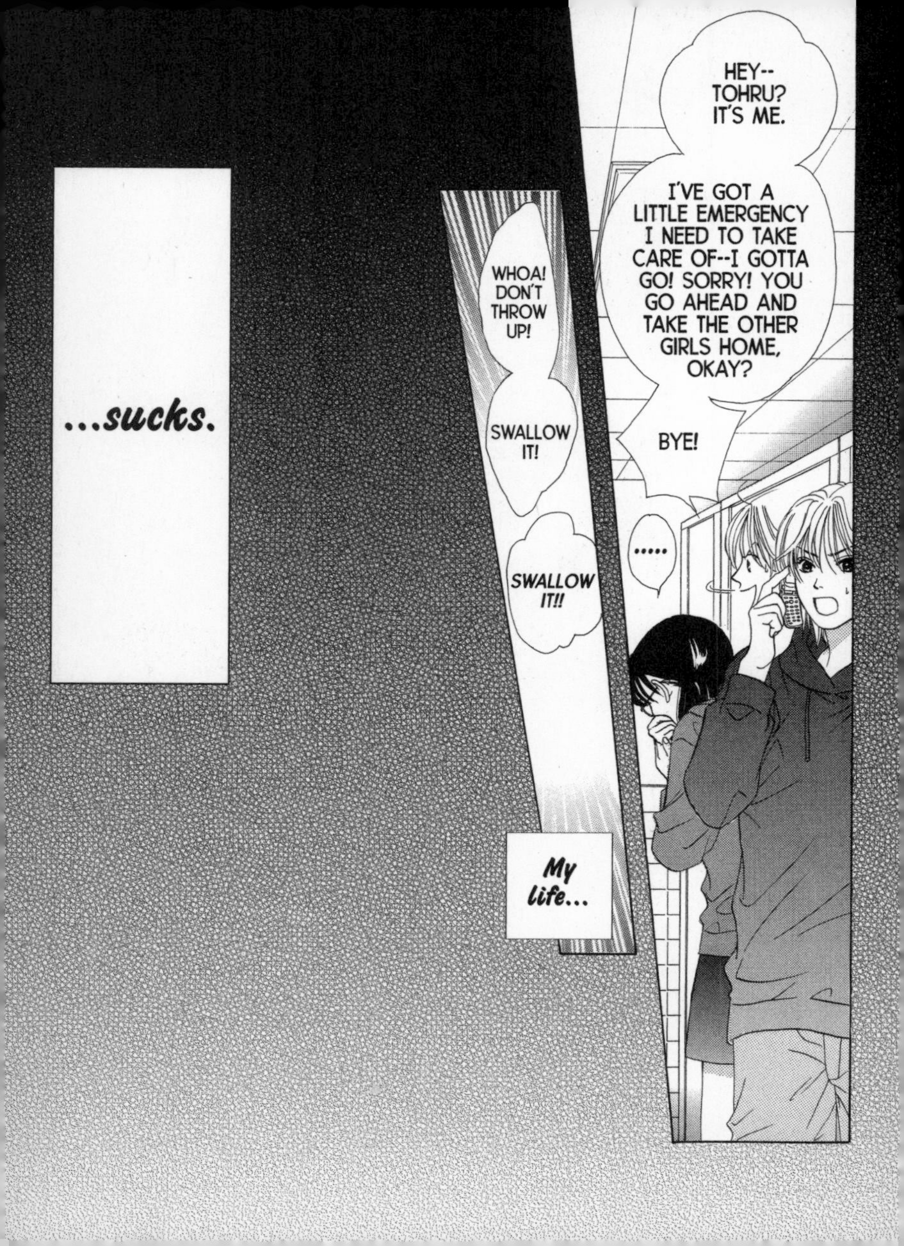
HEY-- TOHRU? IT'S ME.
I'VE GOT A LITTLE EMERGENCY I NEED TO TAKE CARE OF--I GOTTA GO! SORRY! YOU GO AHEAD AND TAKE THE OTHER GIRLS HOME, OKAY?
BYE!
......
WHOA! DON'T THROW UP!
SWALLOW IT!
SWALLOW IT!!
My life...
...sucks.

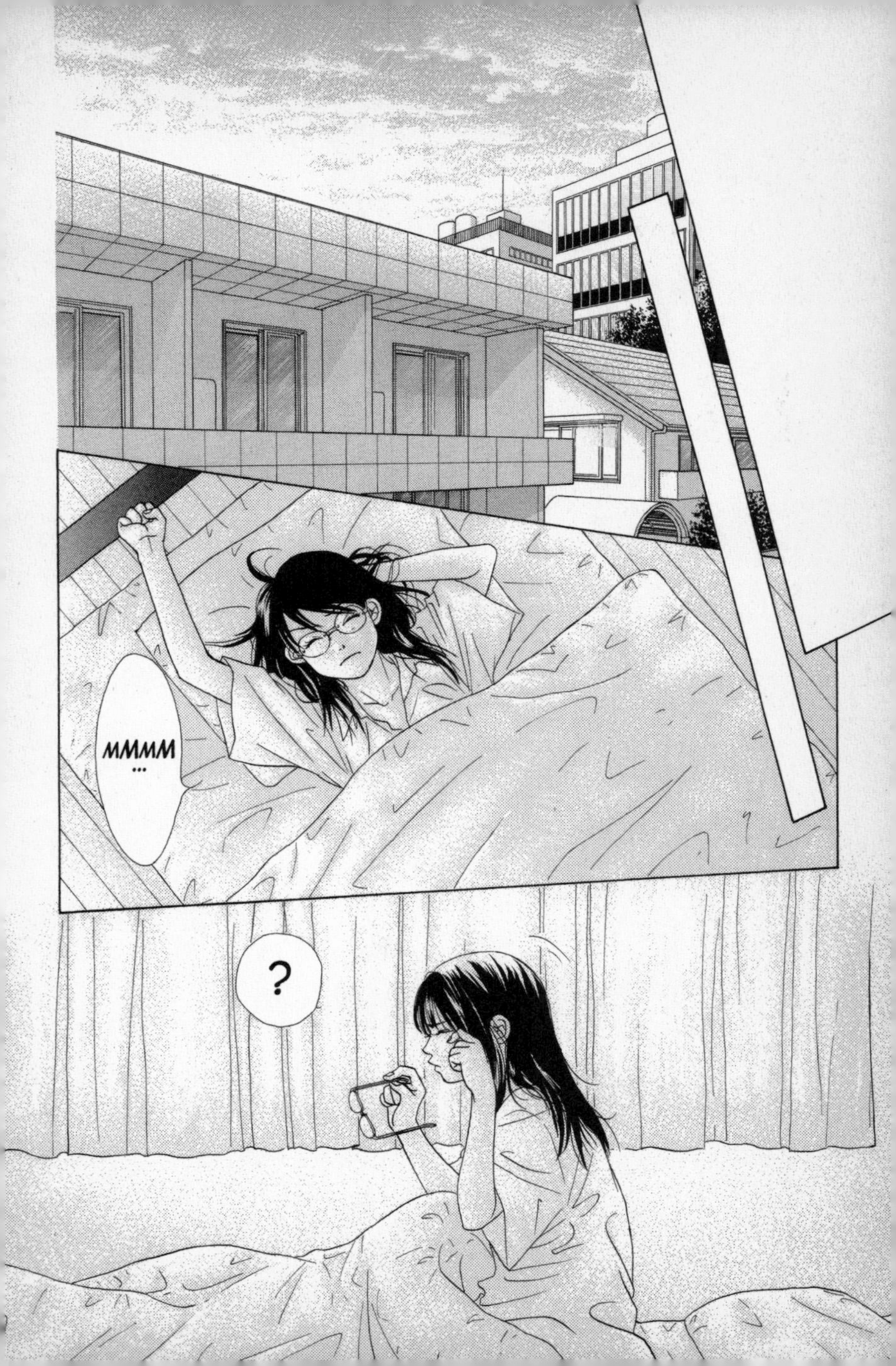
MMMM
...
?

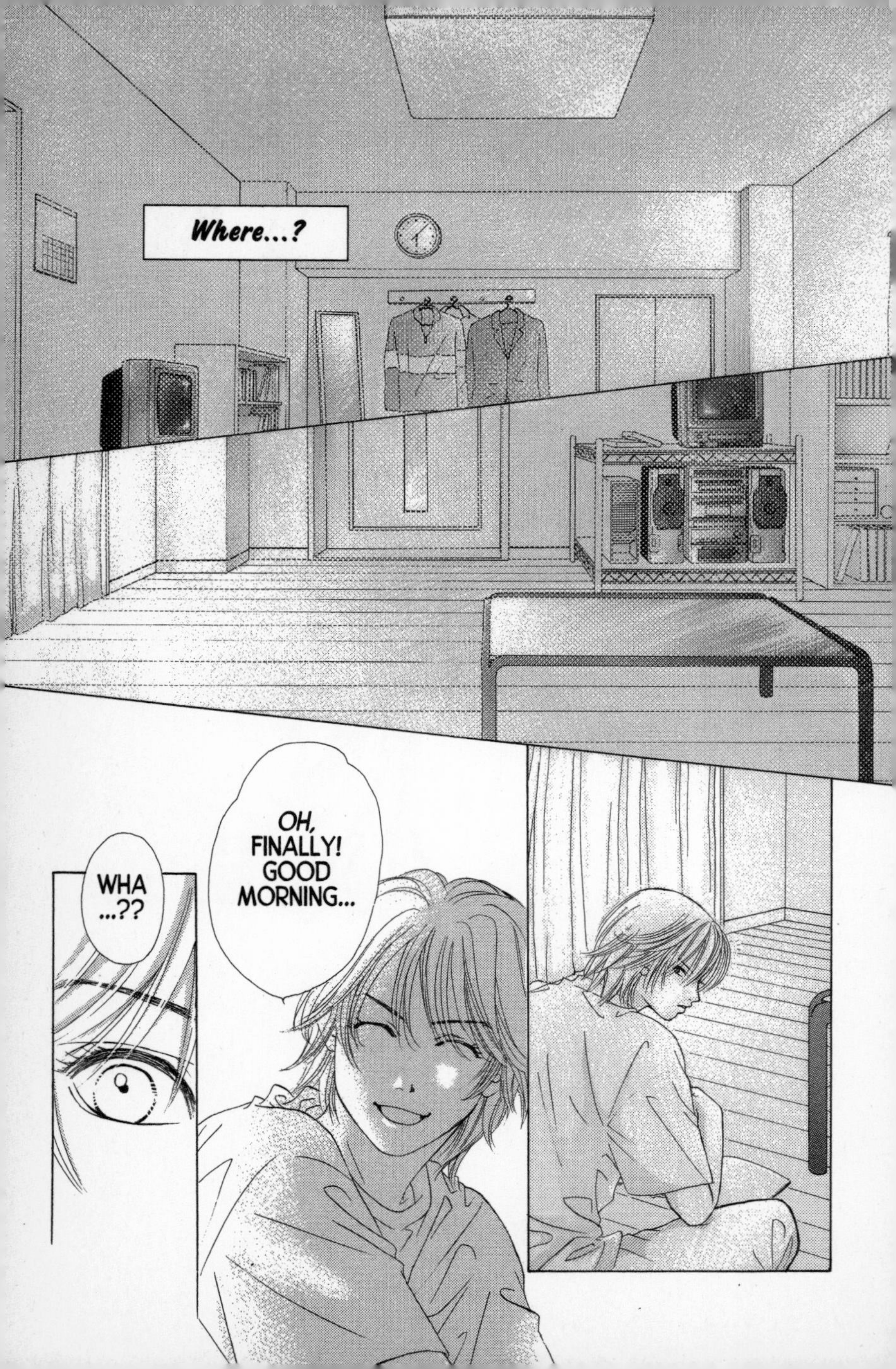
Where...?
OH, FINALLY! GOOD MORNING...
WHA ...??

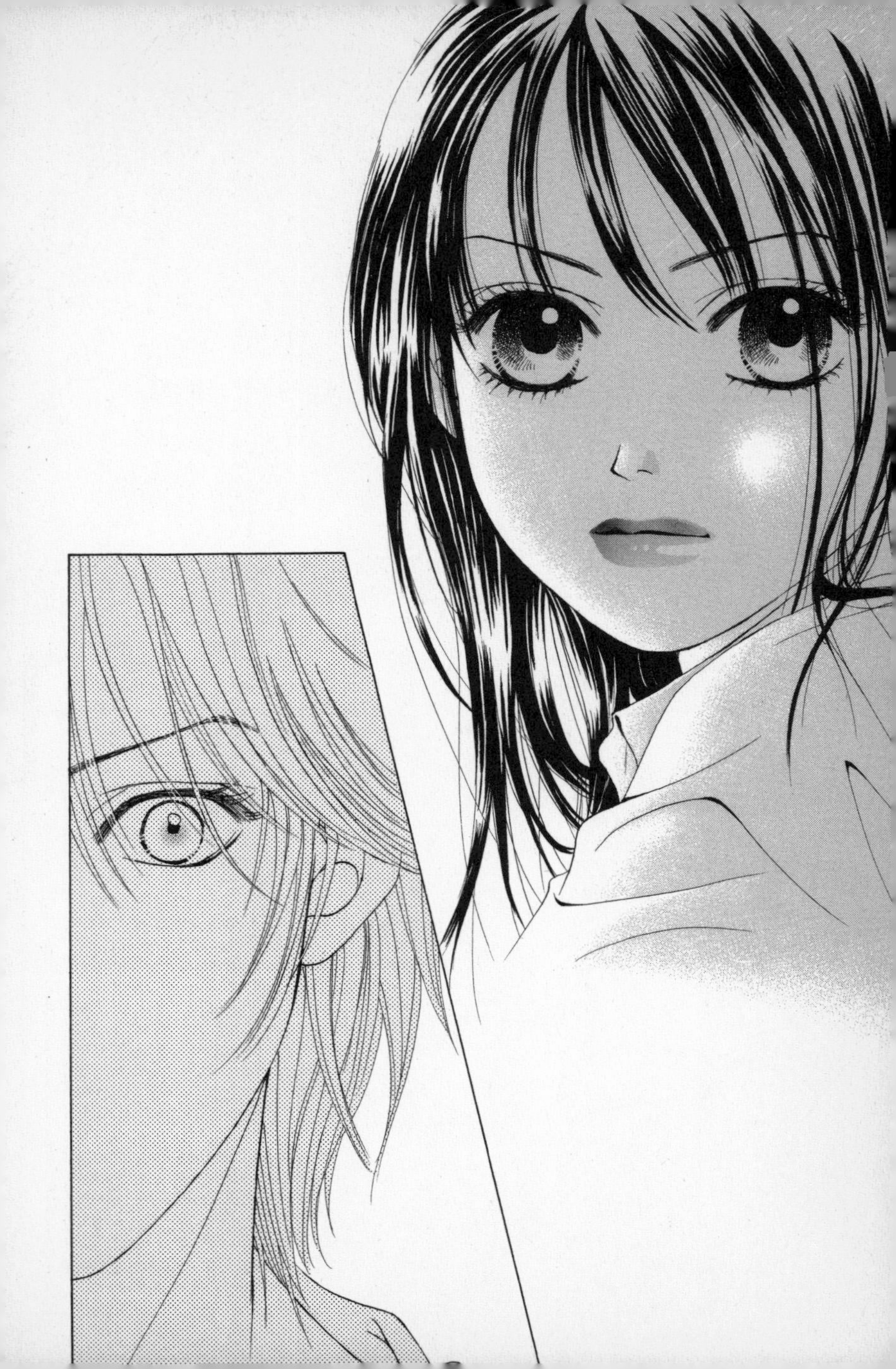

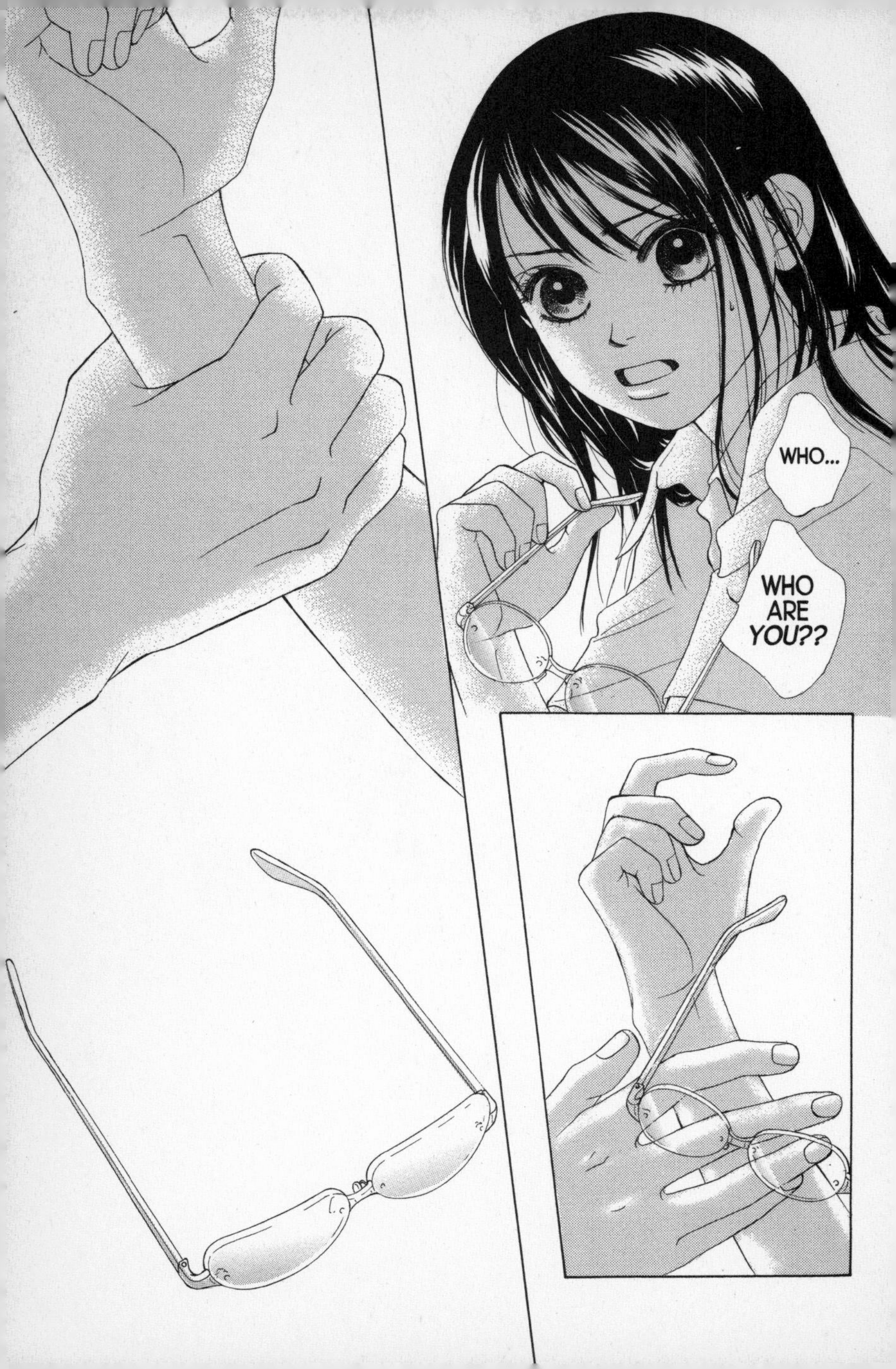
WHO...
WHO ARE *YOU*??

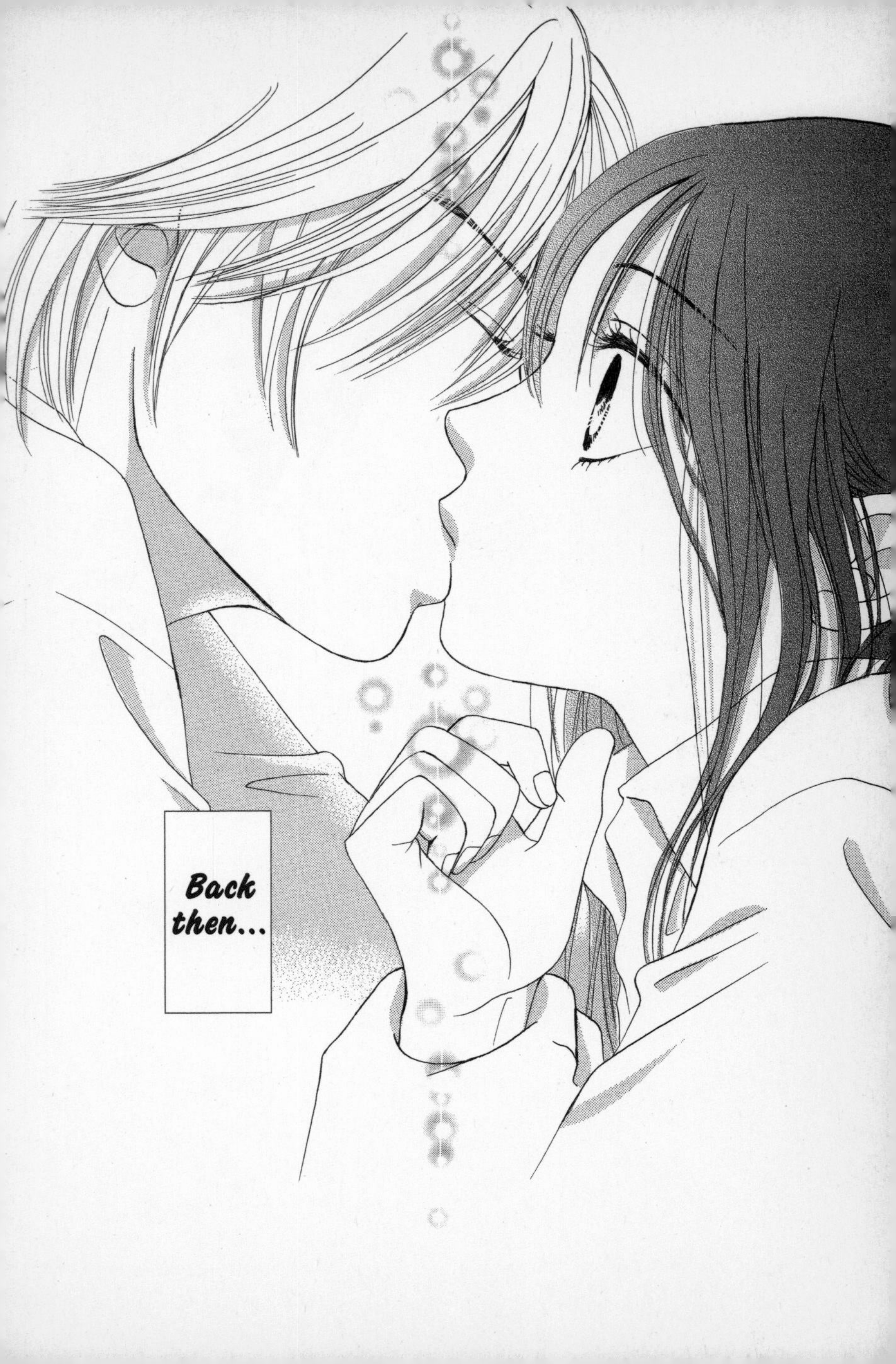
Back then...

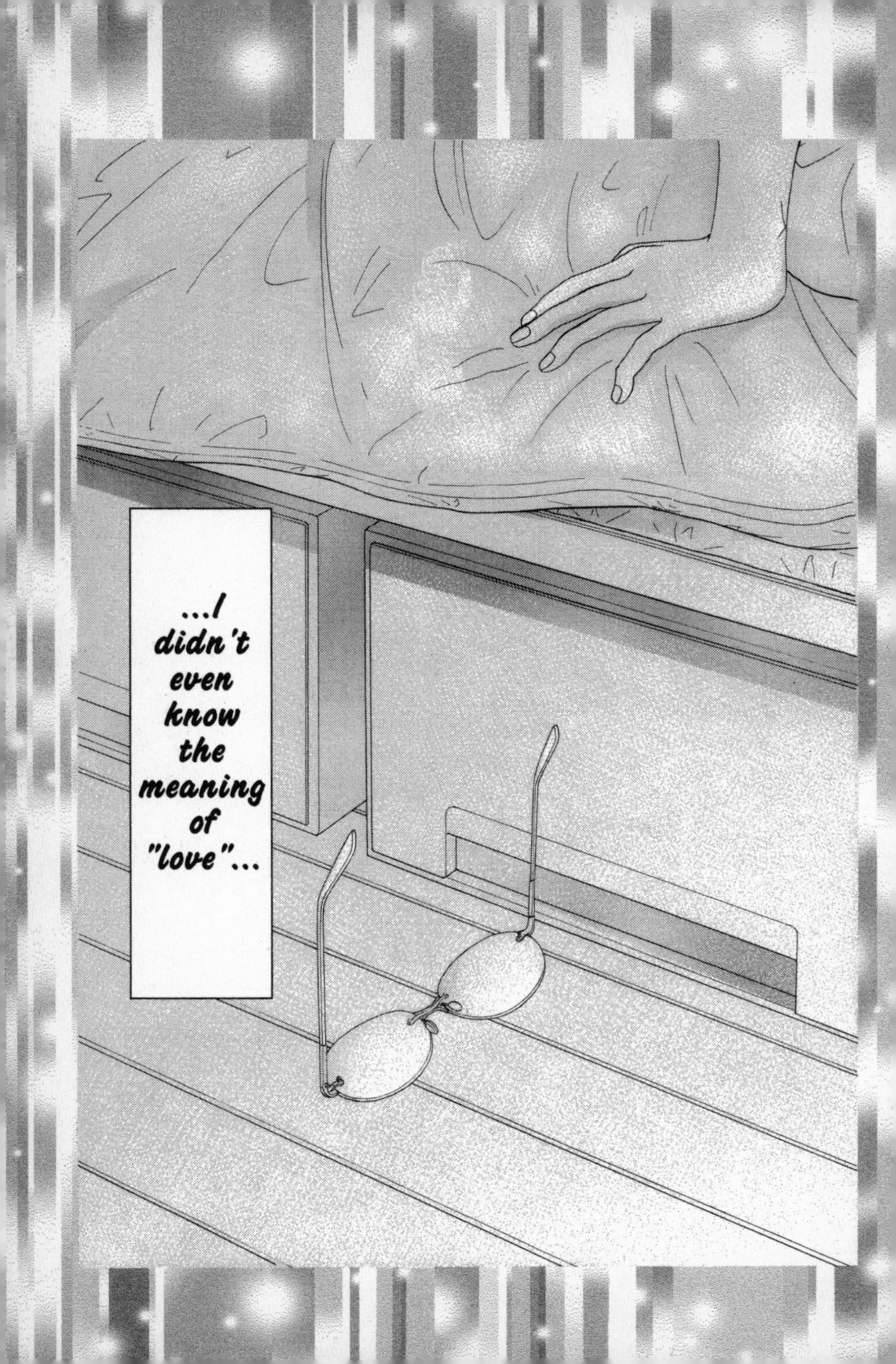
...I didn't even know the meaning of "love"...

KARE
First Love

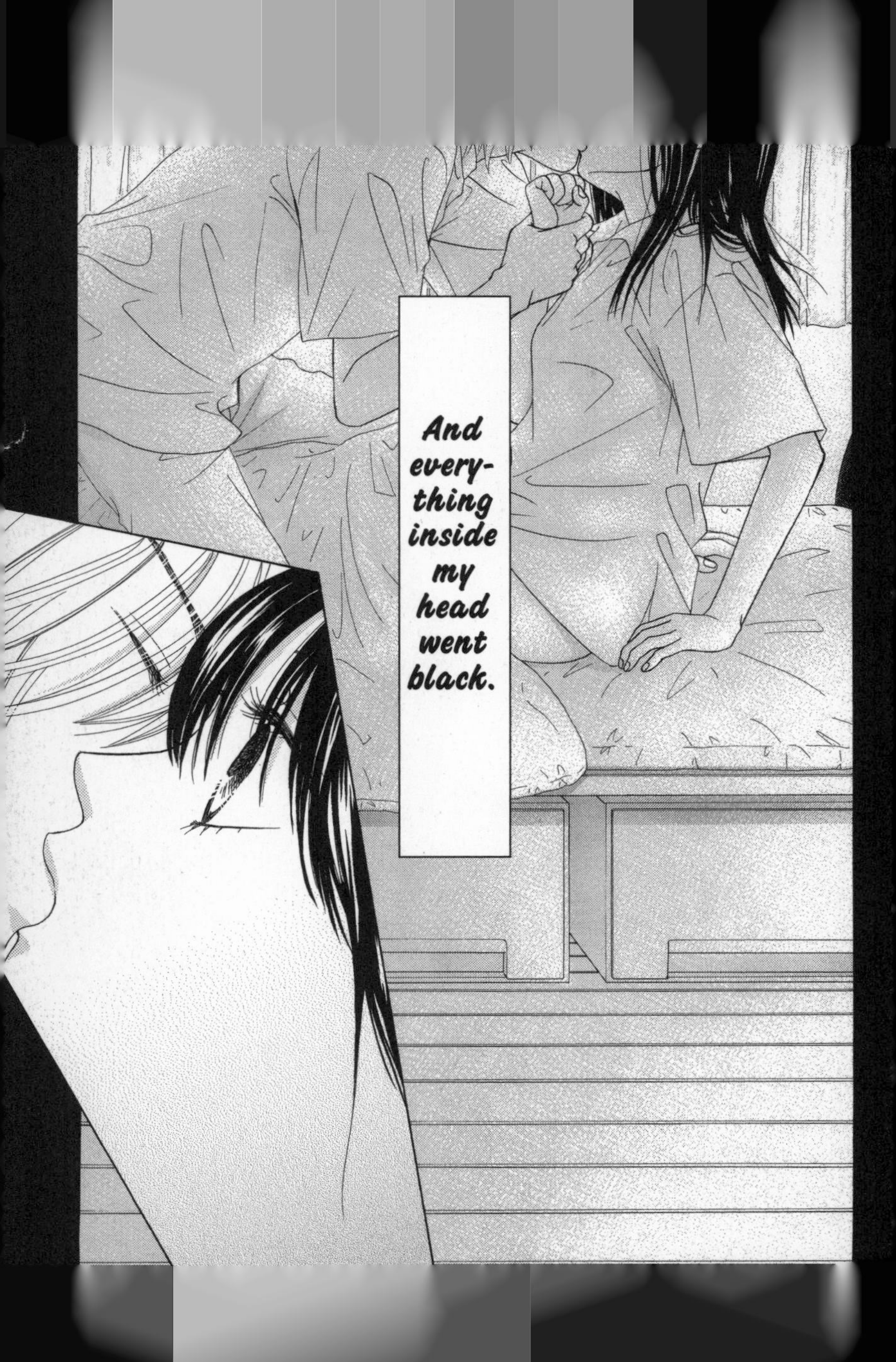
And everything inside my head went black.

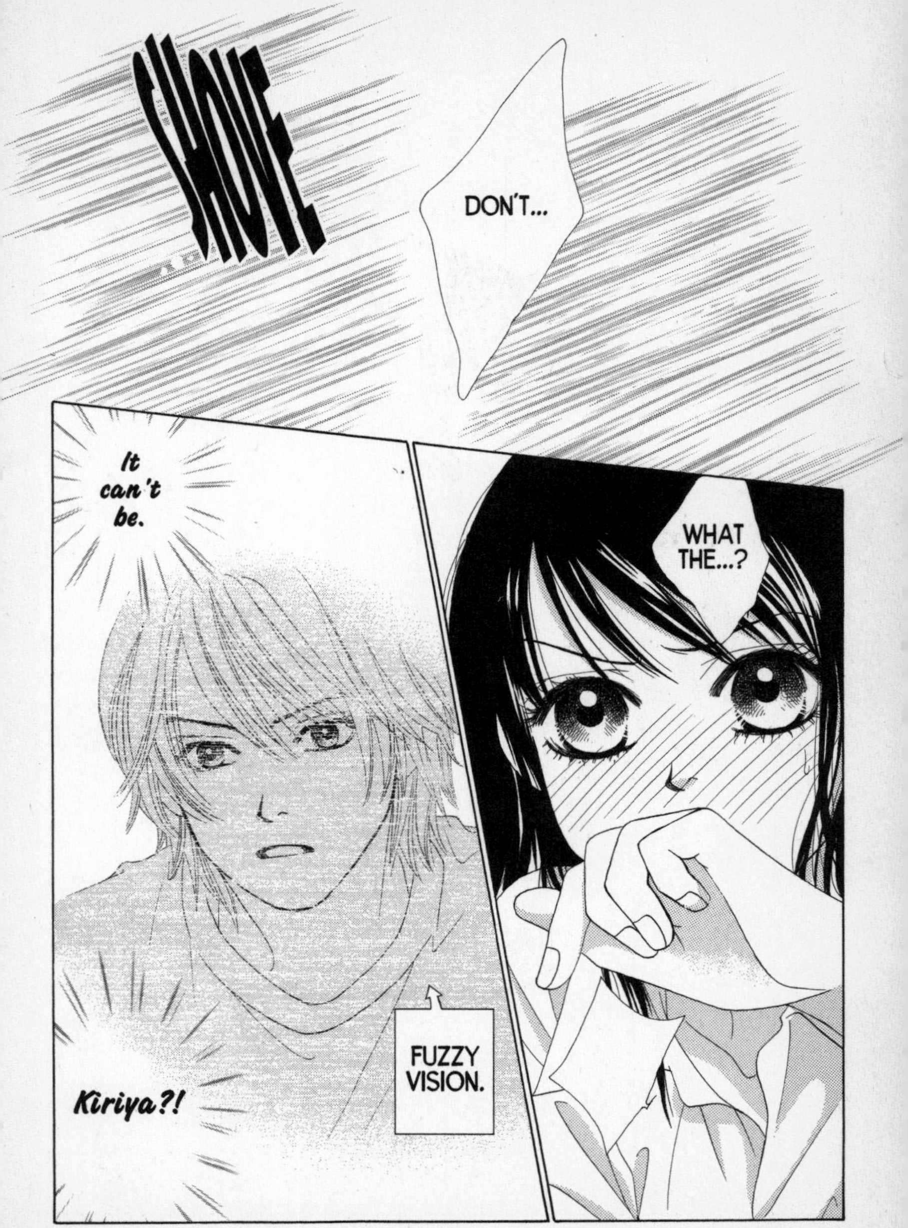
DON'T...
SHOVE
WHAT THE...?
It can't be.
FUZZY VISION.
Kiriya?!

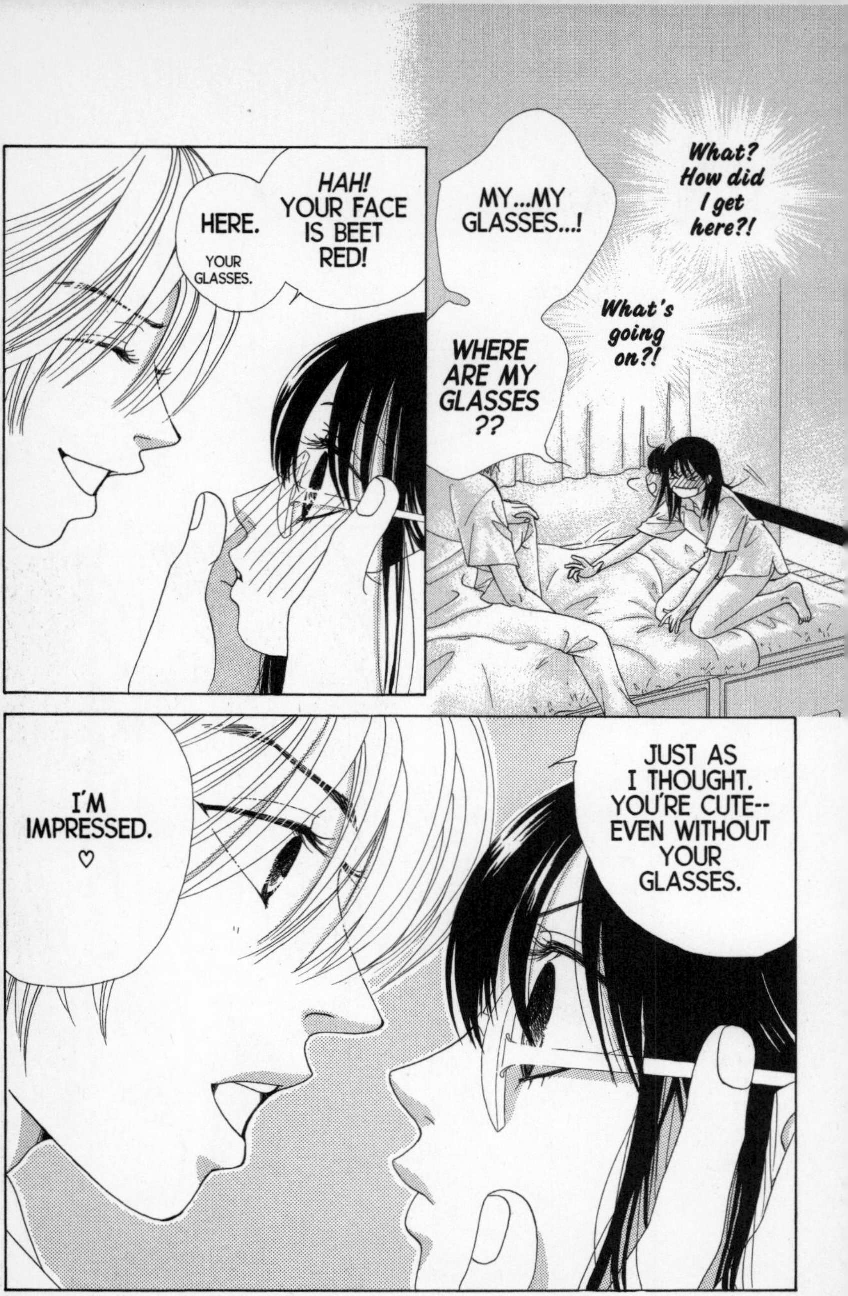
What? How did I get here?!
MY...MY GLASSES...!
What's going on?!
WHERE ARE MY GLASSES ??
HAH! YOUR FACE IS BEET RED!
HERE.
YOUR GLASSES.
JUST AS I THOUGHT. YOU'RE CUTE-- EVEN WITHOUT YOUR GLASSES.
I'M IMPRESSED. ♡

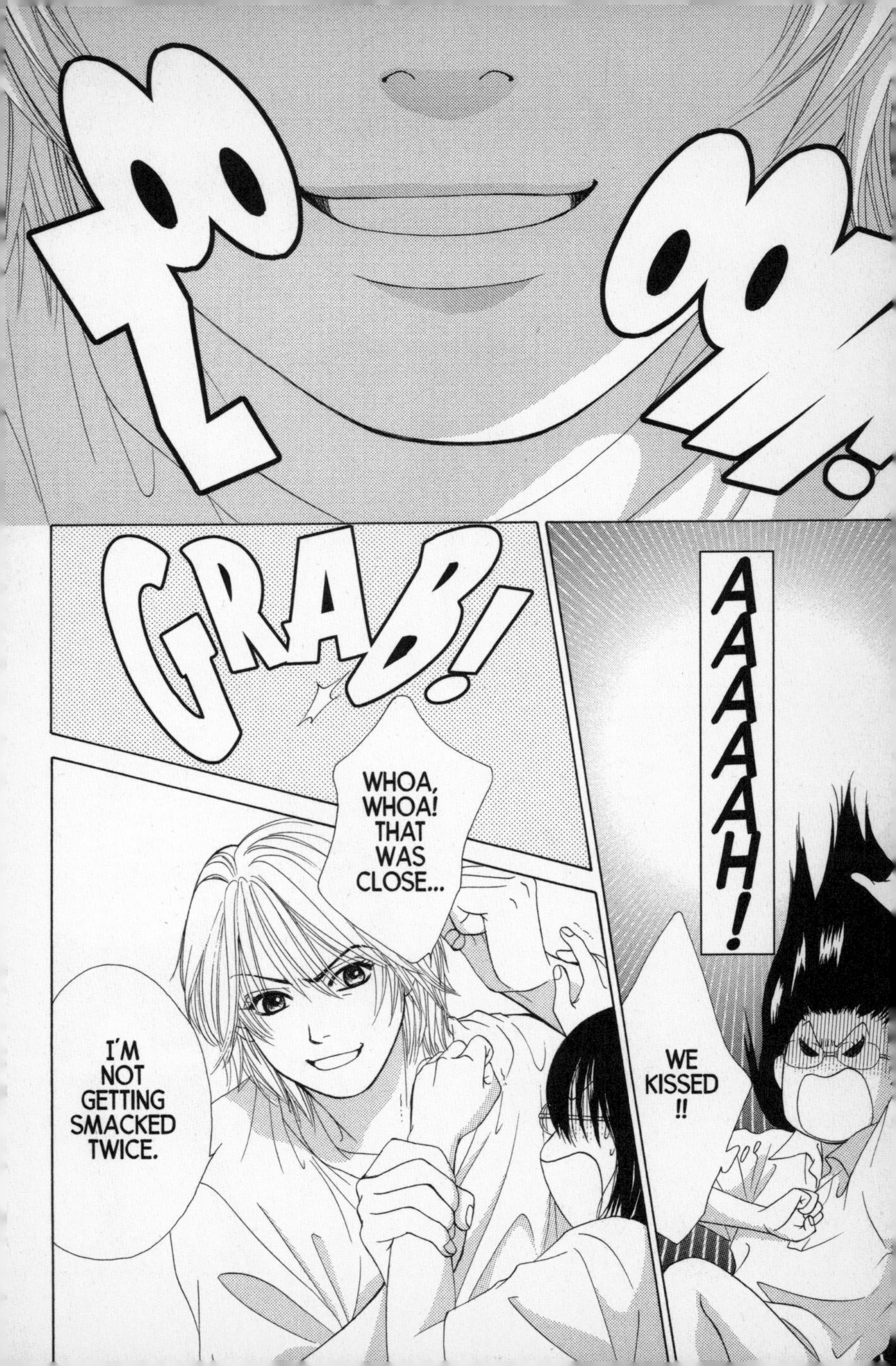
AAAAAAH!
WE KISSED !!
GRAB!
WHOA, WHOA! THAT WAS CLOSE...
I'M NOT GETTING SMACKED TWICE.

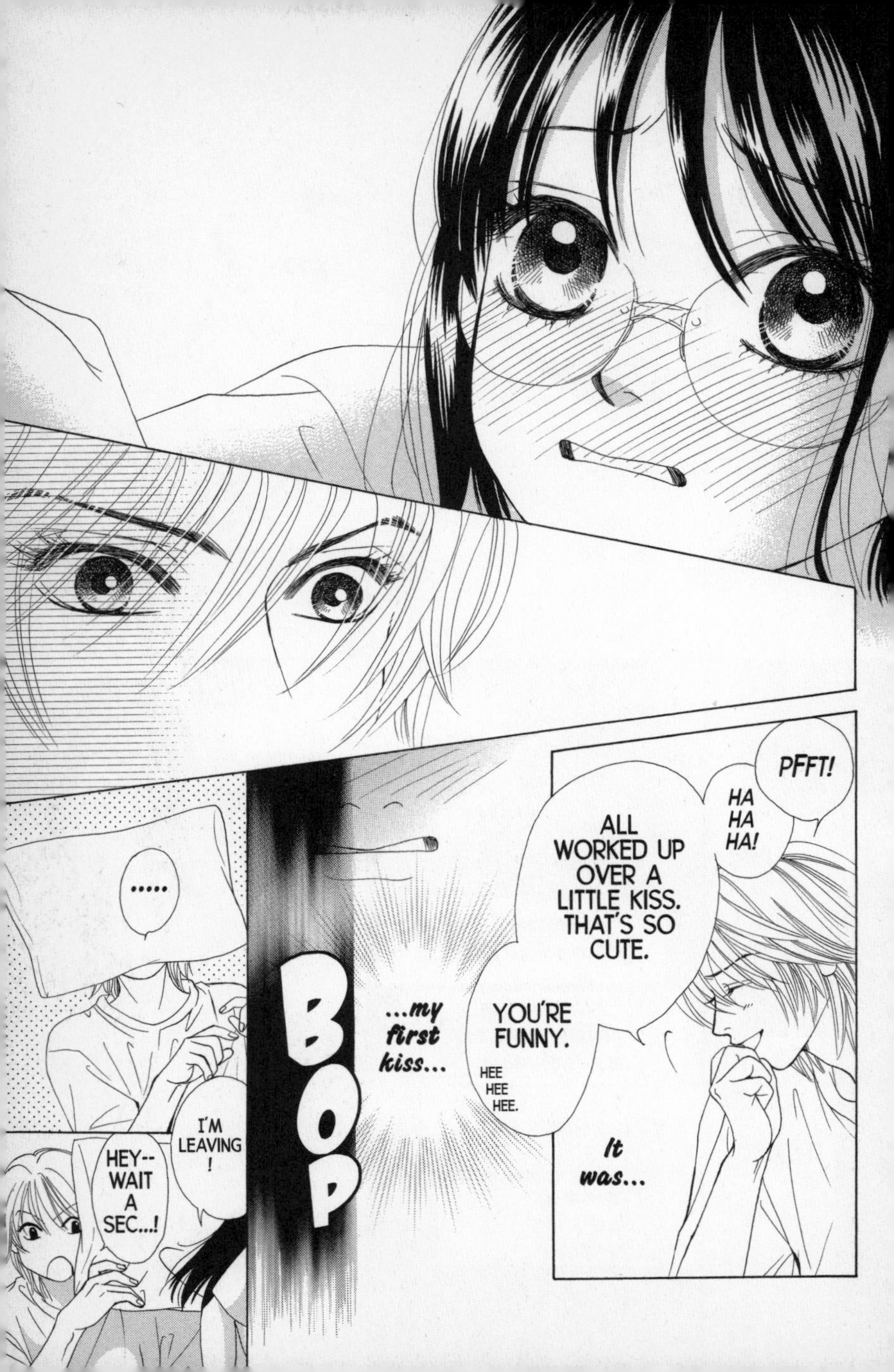
PFFT!
HA HA HA!
ALL WORKED UP OVER A LITTLE KISS. THAT'S SO CUTE.
YOU'RE FUNNY.
HEE HEE HEE.
It was...
...my first kiss...
BOP
......
I'M LEAVING!
HEY-- WAIT A SEC...!

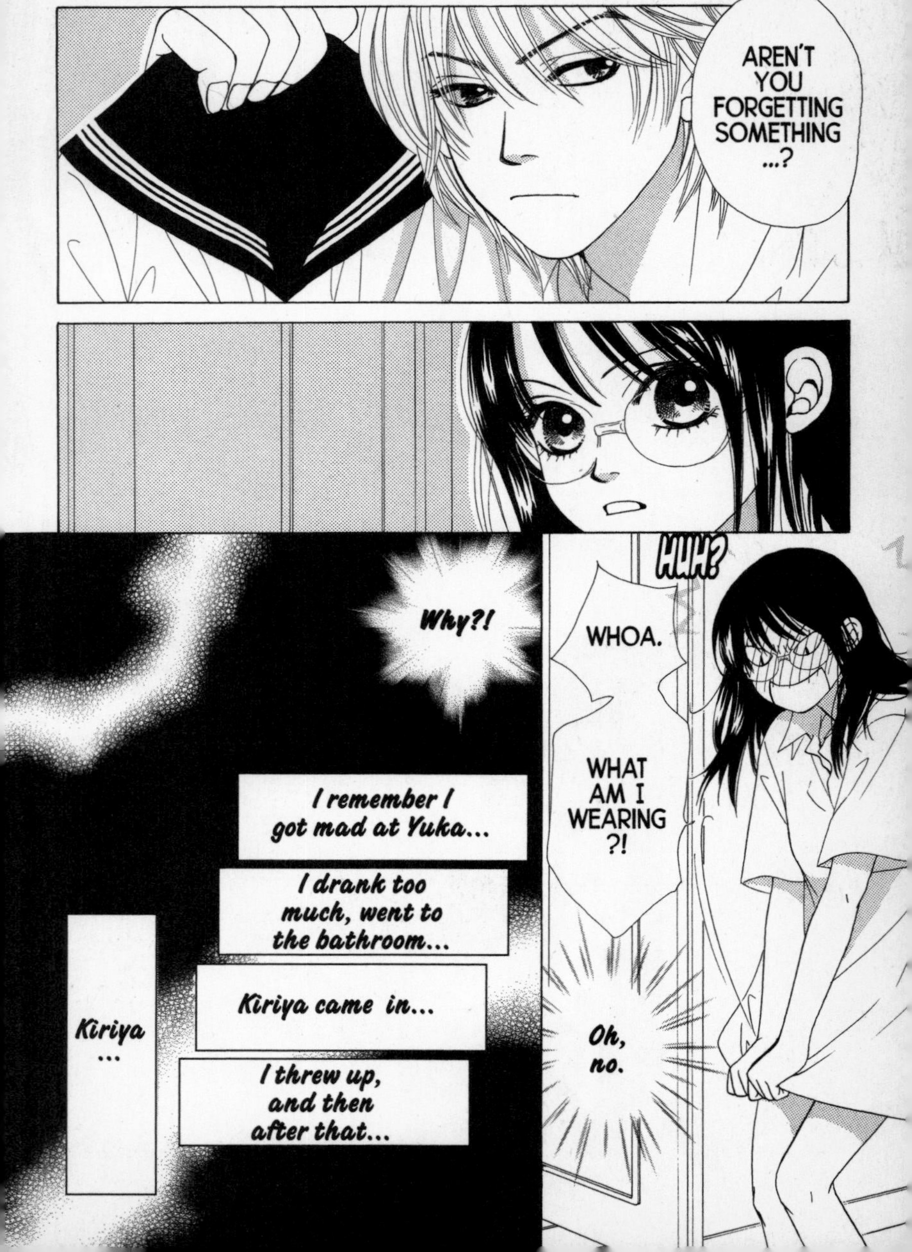
AREN'T YOU FORGETTING SOMETHING ...?
HUH?
WHOA.
WHAT AM I WEARING ?!
Oh, no.
Why?!
I remember I got mad at Yuka...
I drank too much, went to the bathroom...
Kiriya came in...
I threw up, and then after that...
Kiriya ...

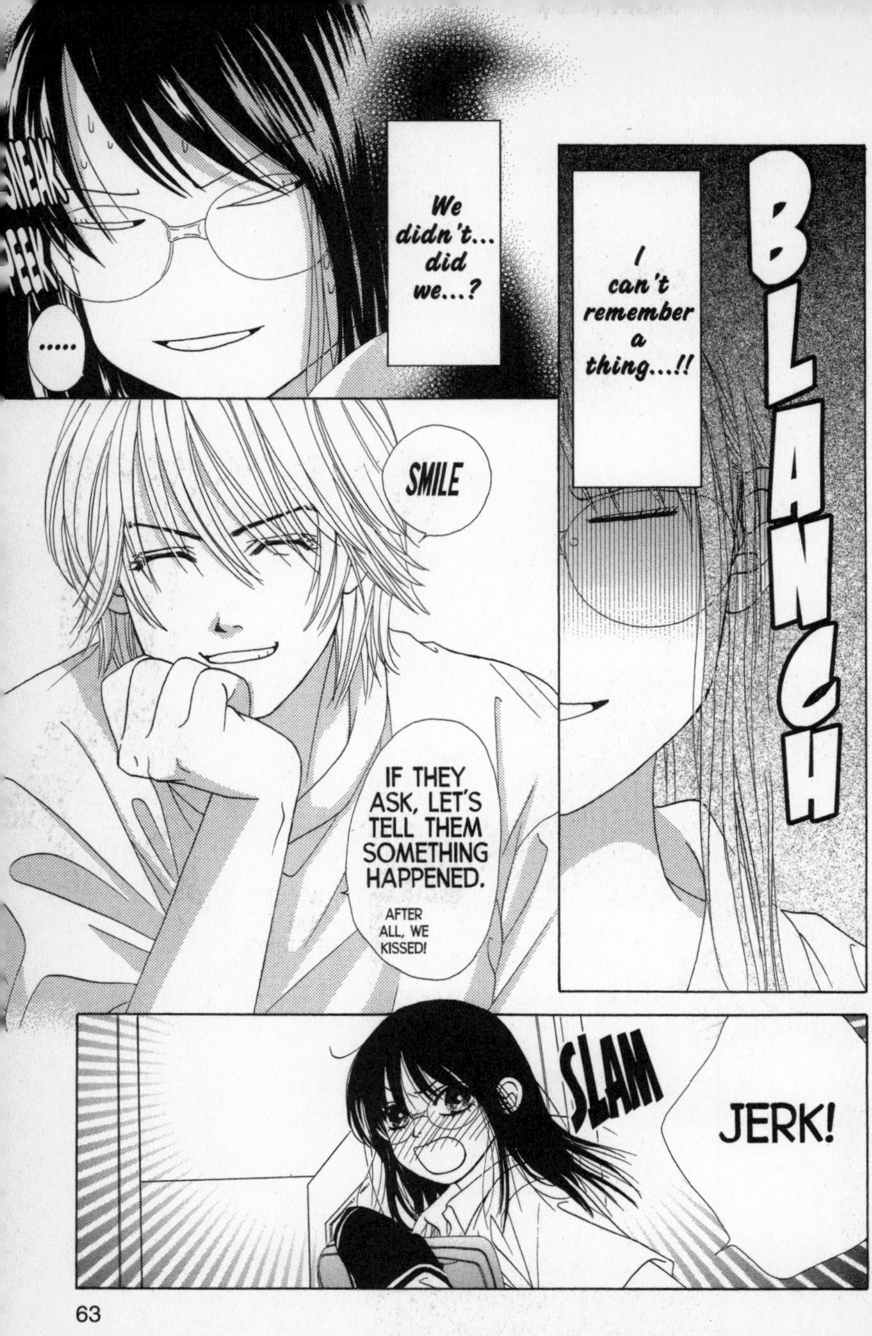
We didn't... did we...?
SNEAK PEEK
.....
I can't remember a thing...!!
BLANCH
SMILE
IF THEY ASK, LET'S TELL THEM SOMETHING HAPPENED.
AFTER ALL, WE KISSED!
JERK!
SLAM

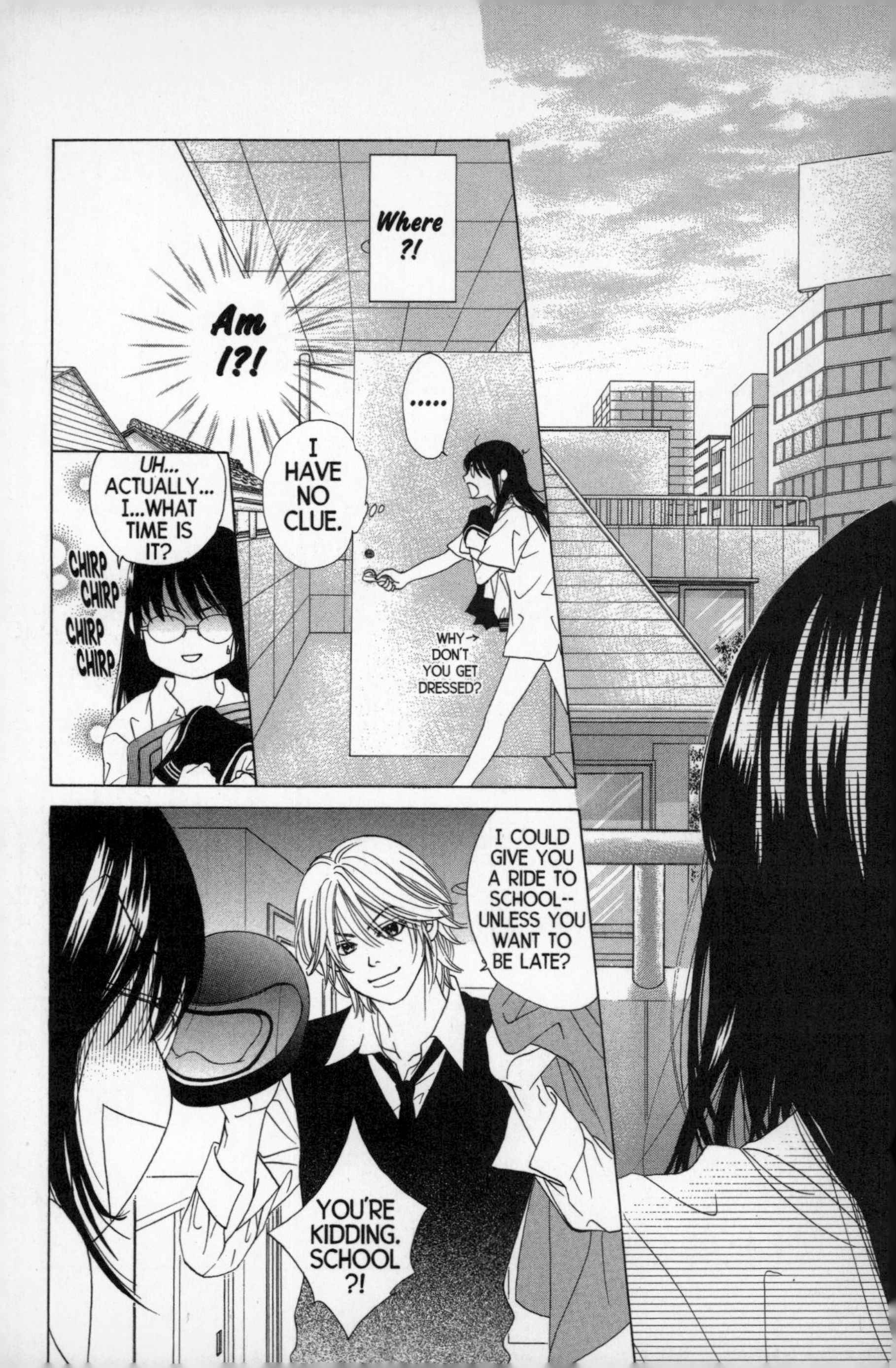
Where ?!
Am I?!
......
I HAVE NO CLUE.
WHY→ DON'T YOU GET DRESSED?
UH... ACTUALLY... I...WHAT TIME IS IT?
CHIRP CHIRP CHIRP CHIRP
I COULD GIVE YOU A RIDE TO SCHOOL-- UNLESS YOU WANT TO BE LATE?
YOU'RE KIDDING. SCHOOL ?!

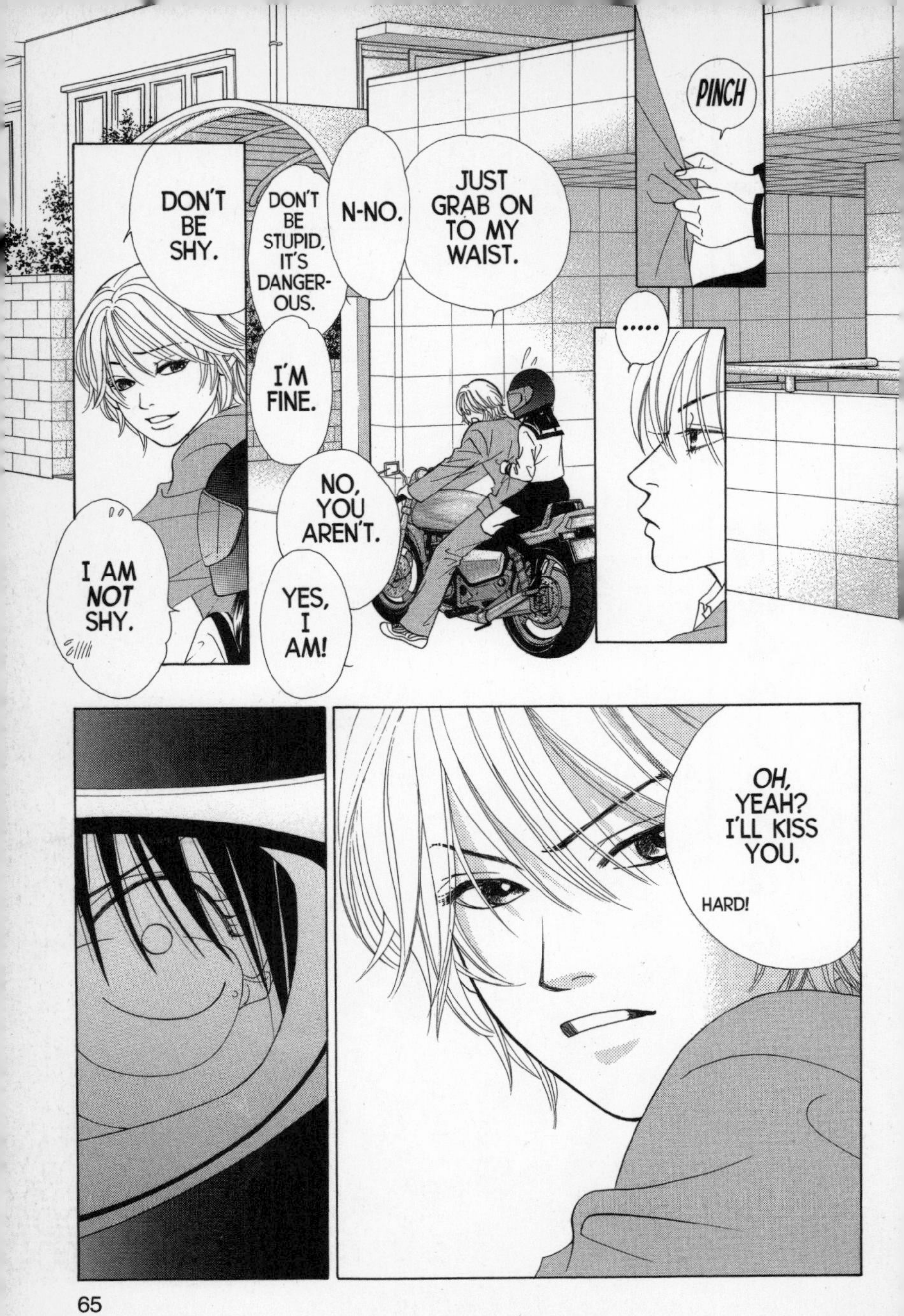
PINCH
.....
JUST GRAB ON TO MY WAIST.
N-NO.
DON'T BE STUPID, IT'S DANGER-OUS.
I'M FINE.
NO, YOU AREN'T.
YES, I AM!
DON'T BE SHY.
I AM *NOT* SHY.
OH, YEAH? I'LL KISS YOU.
HARD!

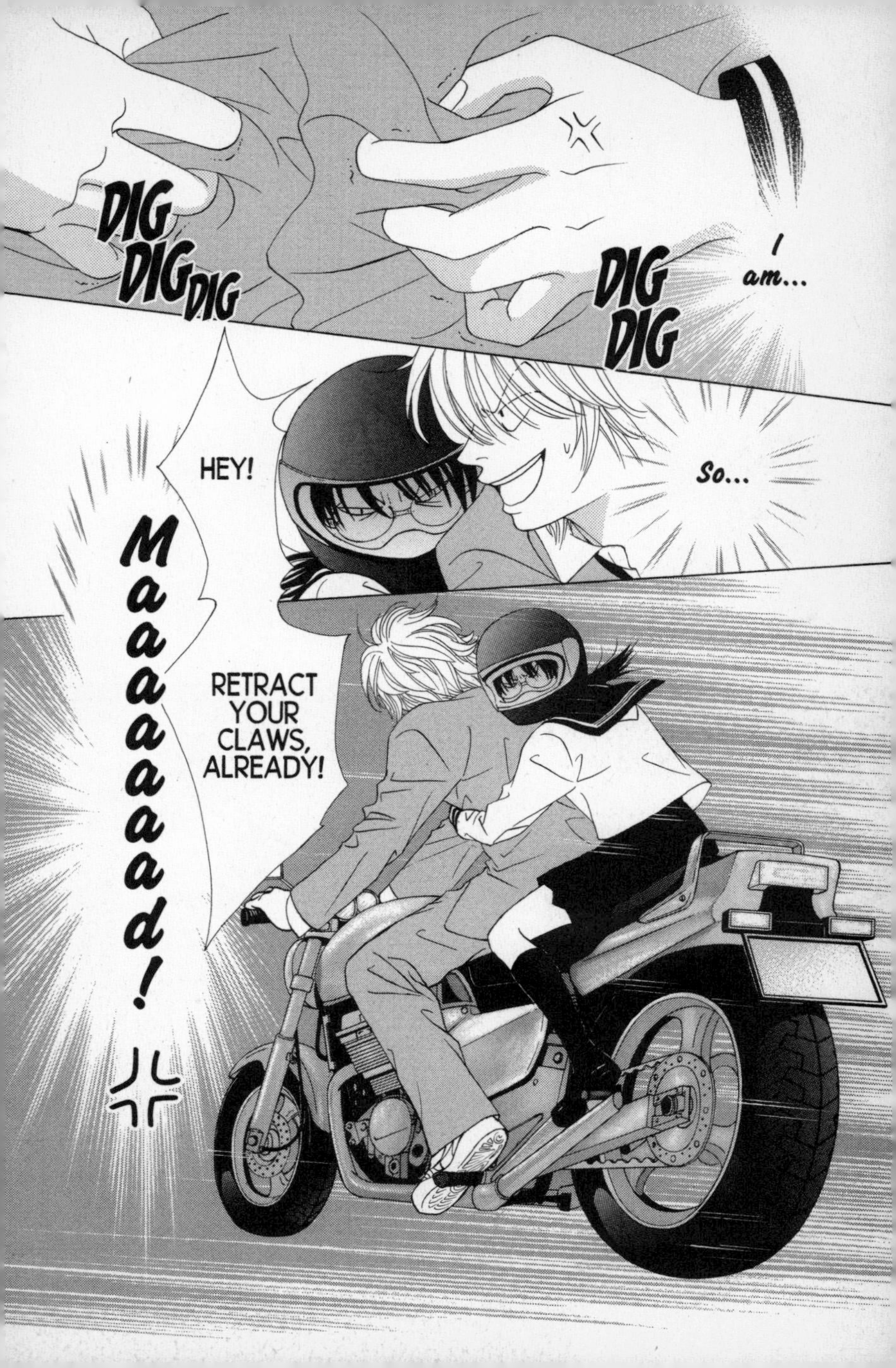
I am...
DIG DIG
DIG DIG DIG
So...
HEY!
RETRACT YOUR CLAWS, ALREADY!
Maaaaaaaad!

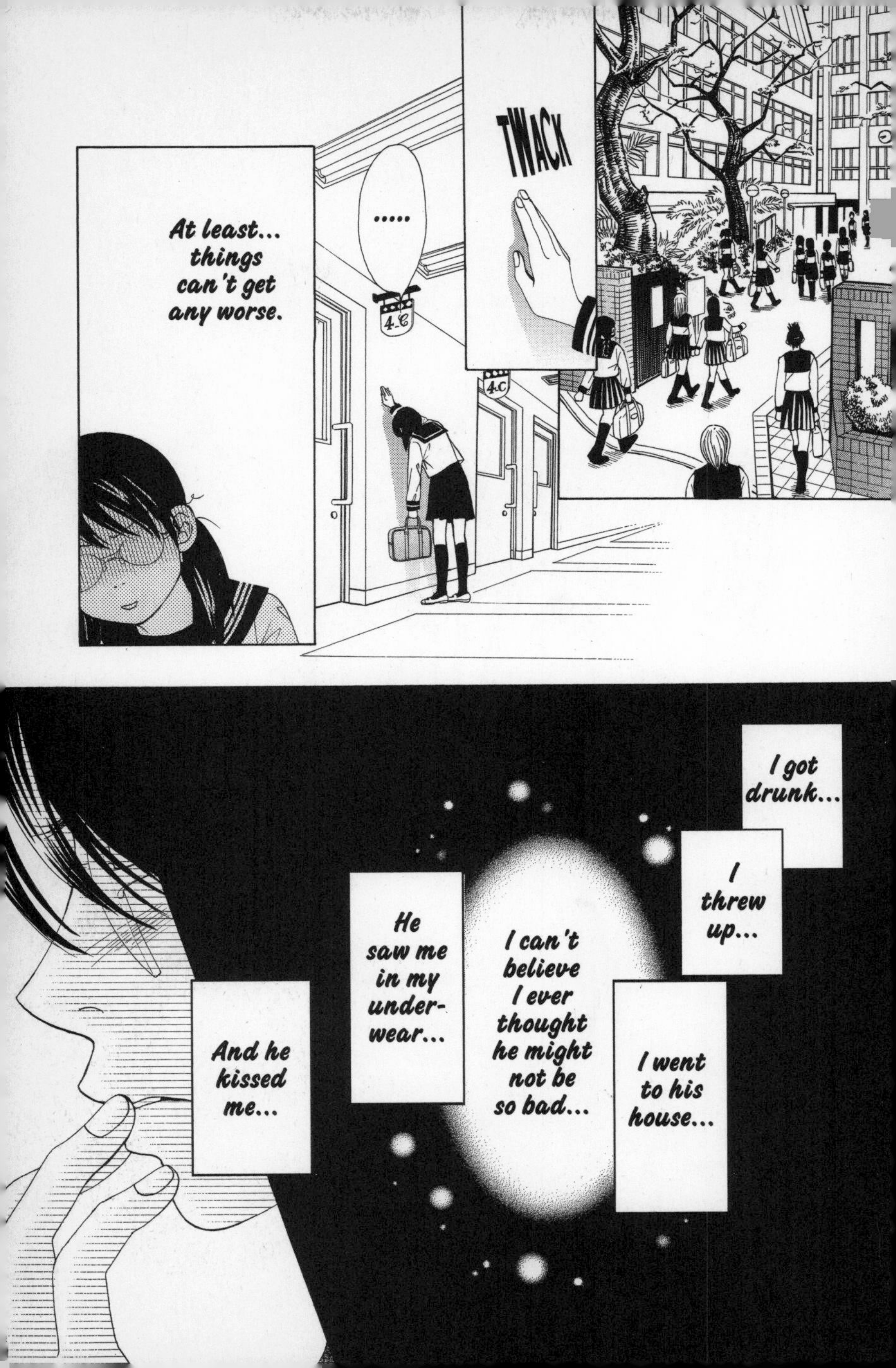
TWACK
.....
4-C
At least... things can't get any worse.
I got drunk...
I threw up...
I went to his house...
I can't believe I ever thought he might not be so bad...
He saw me in my under-wear...
And he kissed me...

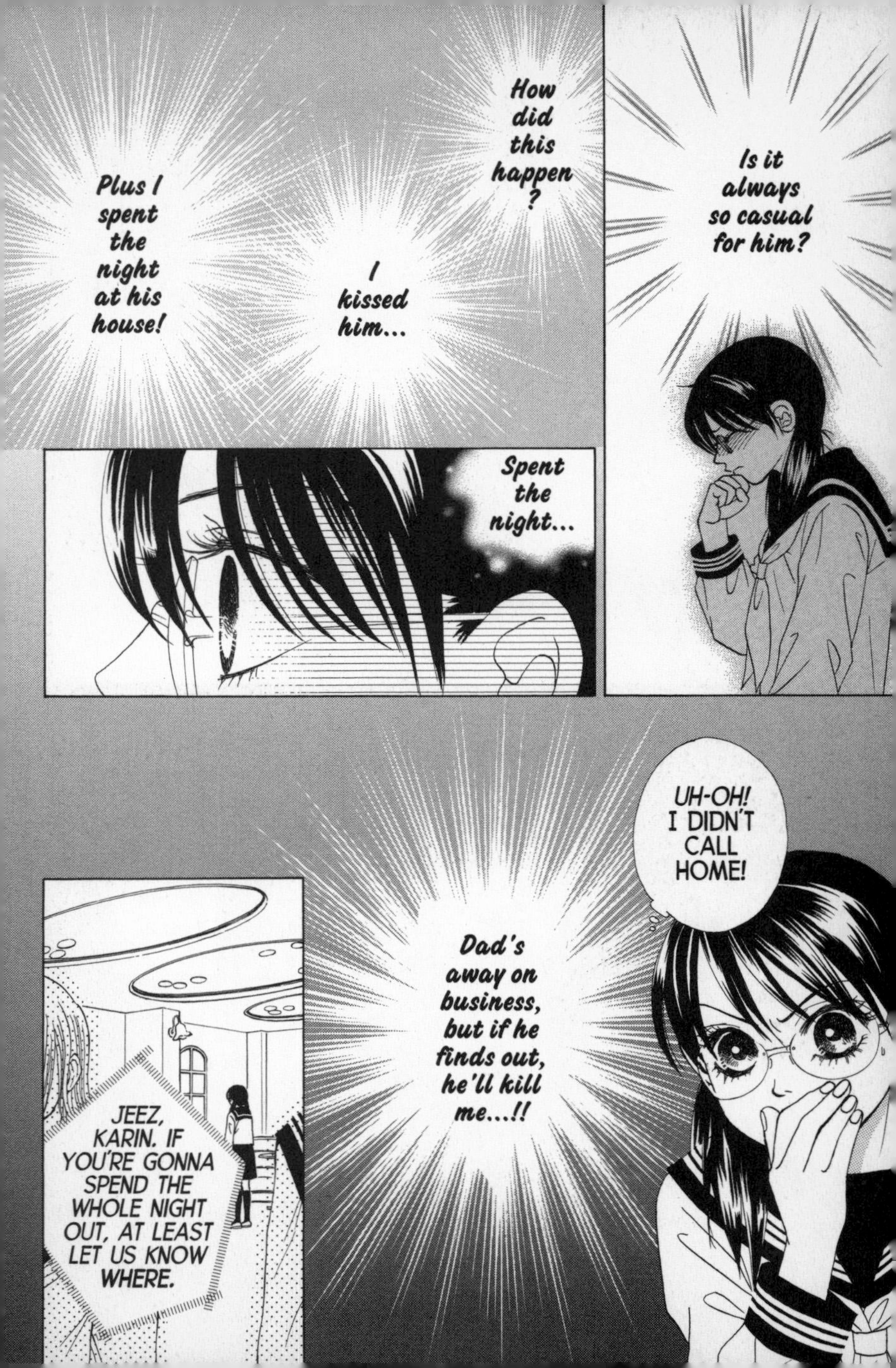
Is it always so casual for him?
How did this happen?
I kissed him...
Plus I spent the night at his house!
Spent the night...
UH-OH! I DIDN'T CALL HOME!
Dad's away on business, but if he finds out, he'll kill me...!!
JEEZ, KARIN. IF YOU'RE GONNA SPEND THE WHOLE NIGHT OUT, AT LEAST LET US KNOW WHERE.

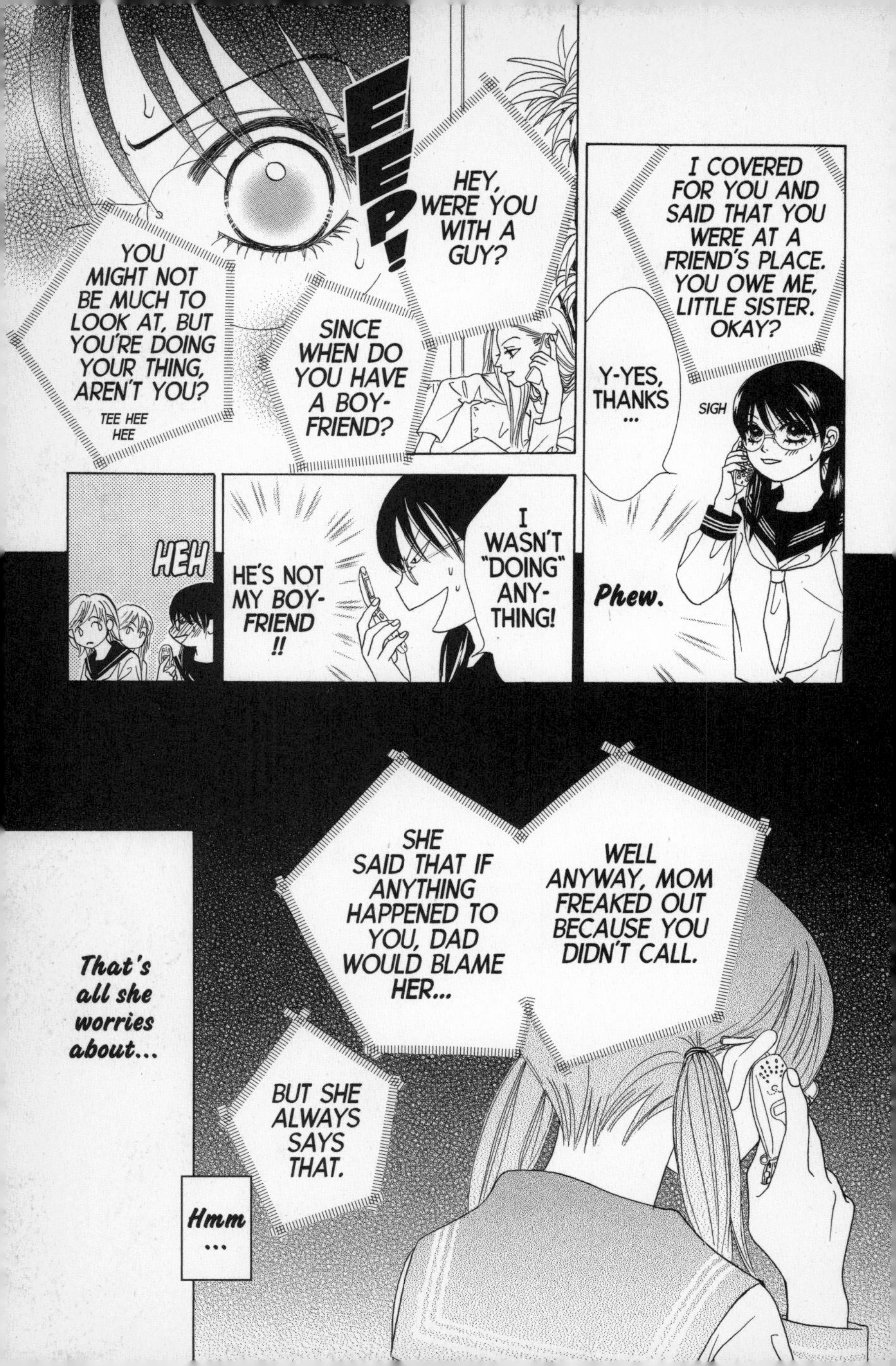
I COVERED FOR YOU AND SAID THAT YOU WERE AT A FRIEND'S PLACE. YOU OWE ME, LITTLE SISTER. OKAY?
Y-YES, THANKS ...
SIGH
Phew.
HEY, WERE YOU WITH A GUY?
EEP!
SINCE WHEN DO YOU HAVE A BOY-FRIEND?
YOU MIGHT NOT BE MUCH TO LOOK AT, BUT YOU'RE DOING YOUR THING, AREN'T YOU?
TEE HEE HEE
I WASN'T "DOING" ANY-THING!
HE'S NOT MY BOY-FRIEND !!
HEH
WELL ANYWAY, MOM FREAKED OUT BECAUSE YOU DIDN'T CALL.
SHE SAID THAT IF ANYTHING HAPPENED TO YOU, DAD WOULD BLAME HER...
BUT SHE ALWAYS SAYS THAT.
That's all she worries about...
Hmm ...

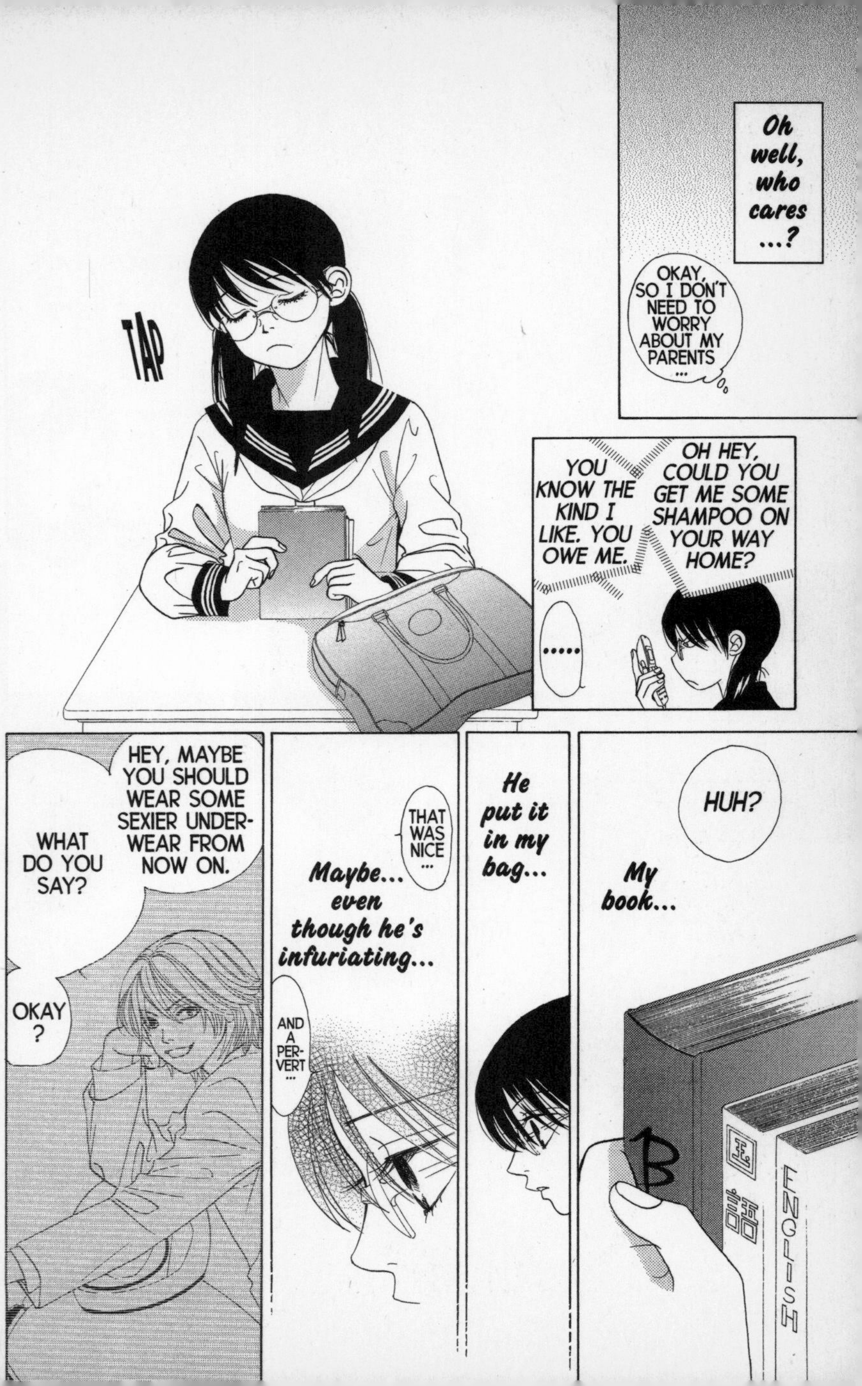
Oh well, who cares...?
OKAY, SO I DON'T NEED TO WORRY ABOUT MY PARENTS...
OH HEY, COULD YOU GET ME SOME SHAMPOO ON YOUR WAY HOME?
YOU KNOW THE KIND I LIKE. YOU OWE ME.
......
TAP
HUH?
My book...
ENGLISH
He put it in my bag...
THAT WAS NICE...
Maybe... even though he's infuriating...
AND A PERVERT...
HEY, MAYBE YOU SHOULD WEAR SOME SEXIER UNDERWEAR FROM NOW ON.
WHAT DO YOU SAY?
OKAY?

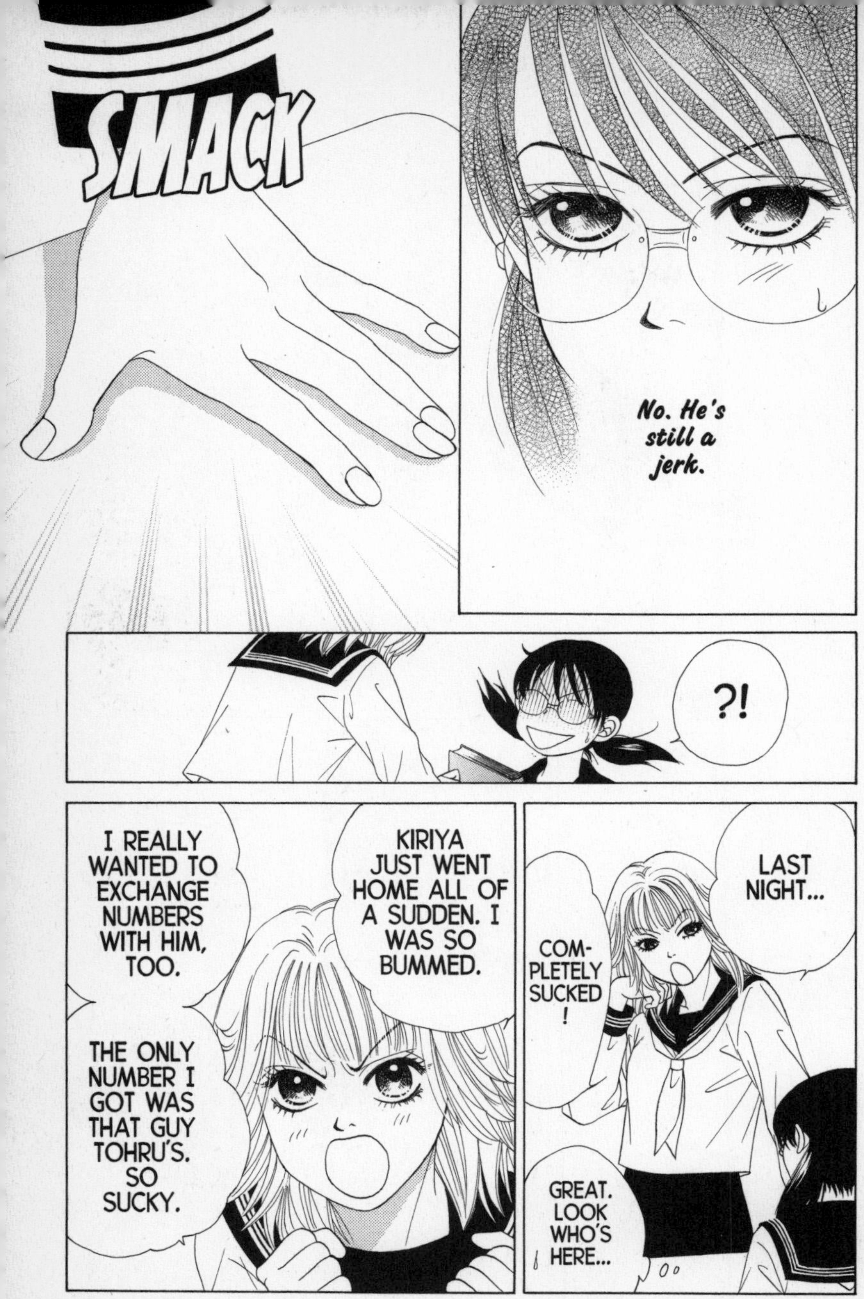

No. He's still a jerk.
SMACK
?!
LAST NIGHT...
COMPLETELY SUCKED!
GREAT. LOOK WHO'S HERE...
KIRIYA JUST WENT HOME ALL OF A SUDDEN. I WAS SO BUMMED.
I REALLY WANTED TO EXCHANGE NUMBERS WITH HIM, TOO.
THE ONLY NUMBER I GOT WAS THAT GUY TOHRU'S. SO SUCKY.

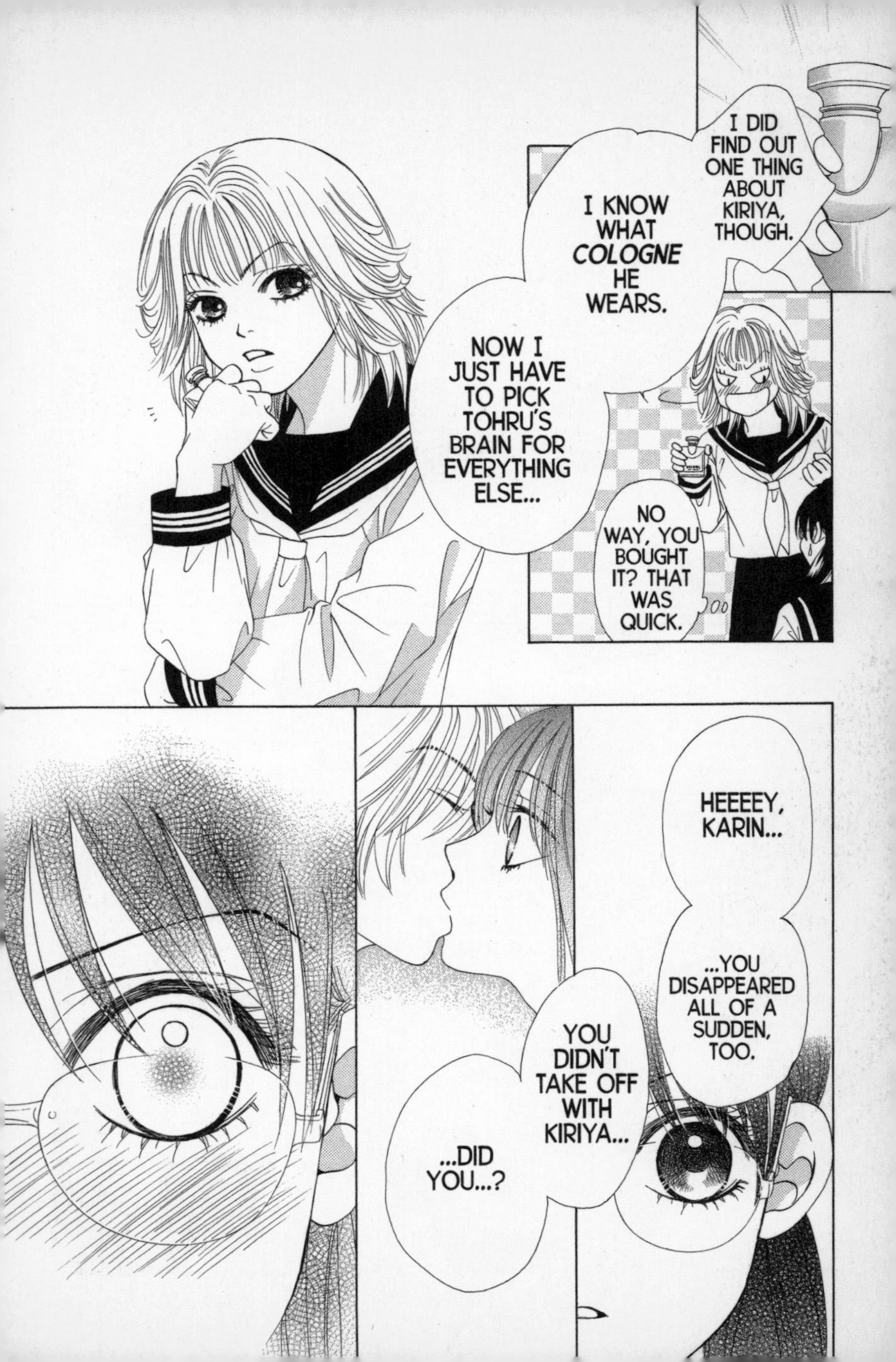
I DID FIND OUT ONE THING ABOUT KIRIYA, THOUGH.
I KNOW WHAT *COLOGNE* HE WEARS.
NO WAY, YOU BOUGHT IT? THAT WAS QUICK.
NOW I JUST HAVE TO PICK TOHRU'S BRAIN FOR EVERYTHING ELSE...
HEEEEY, KARIN...
...YOU DISAPPEARED ALL OF A SUDDEN, TOO.
YOU DIDN'T TAKE OFF WITH KIRIYA...
...DID YOU...?

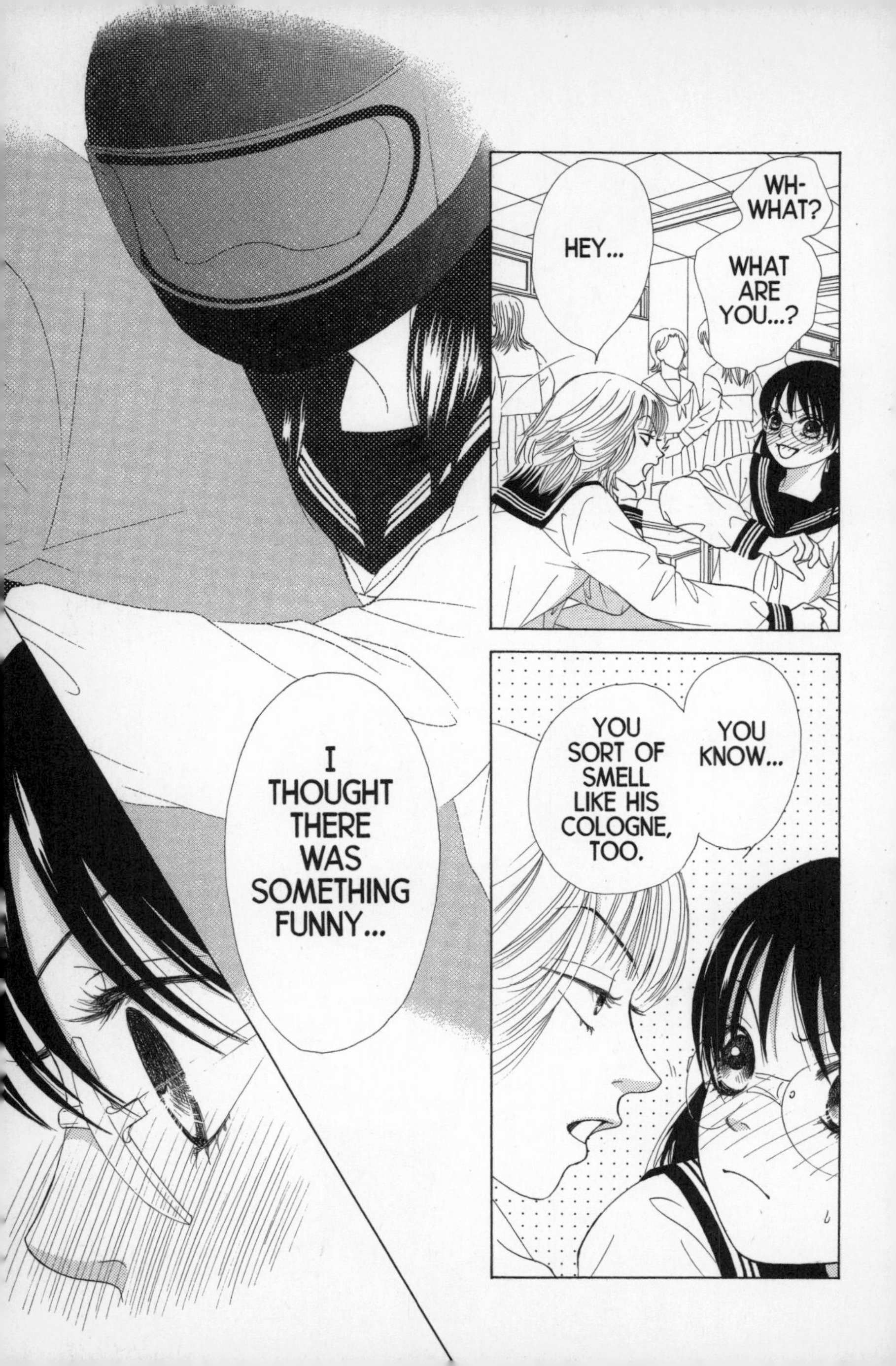
WH- WHAT?
WHAT ARE YOU...?
HEY...
YOU KNOW...
YOU SORT OF SMELL LIKE HIS COLOGNE, TOO.
I THOUGHT THERE WAS SOMETHING FUNNY...

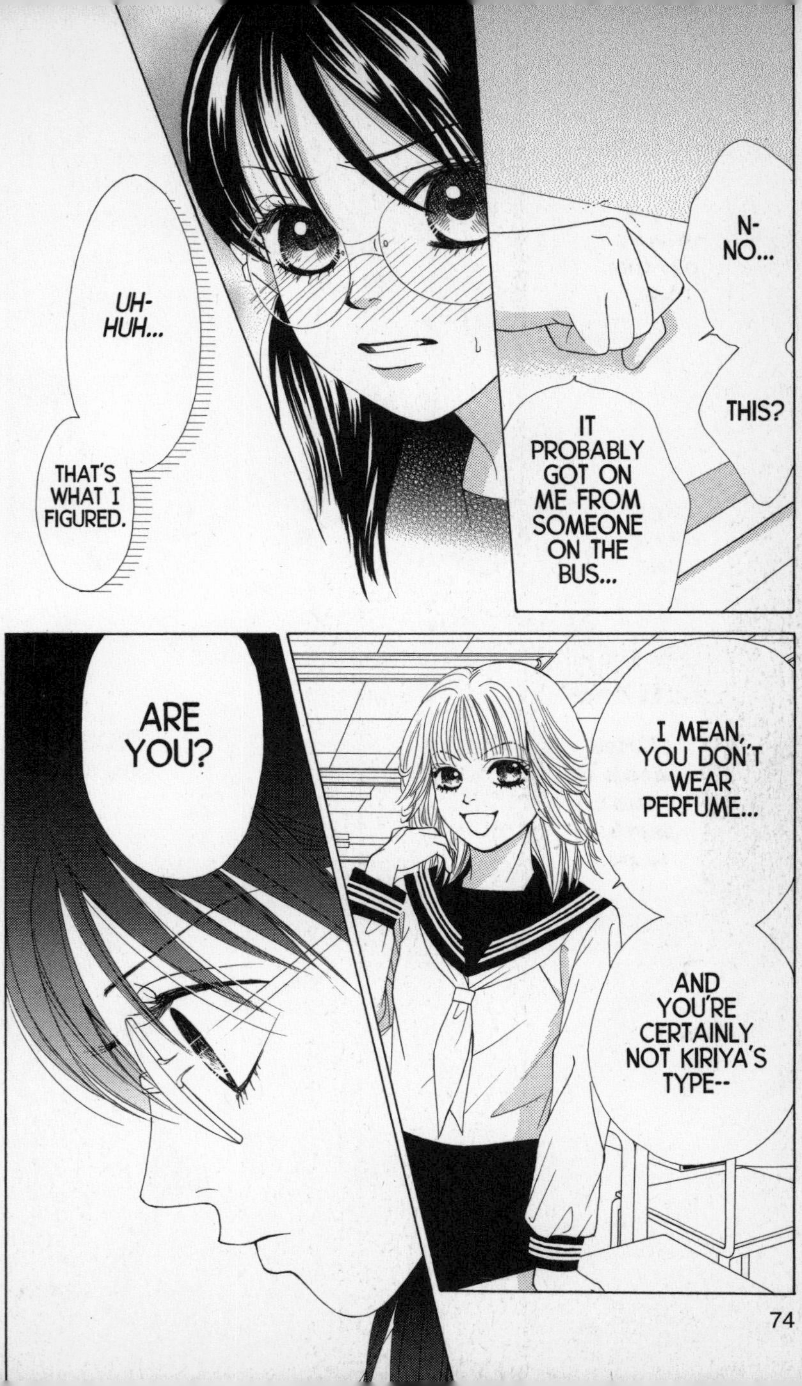
N-NO...
THIS?
IT PROBABLY GOT ON ME FROM SOMEONE ON THE BUS...
UH-HUH...
THAT'S WHAT I FIGURED.
I MEAN, YOU DON'T WEAR PERFUME...
AND YOU'RE CERTAINLY NOT KIRIYA'S TYPE--
ARE YOU?

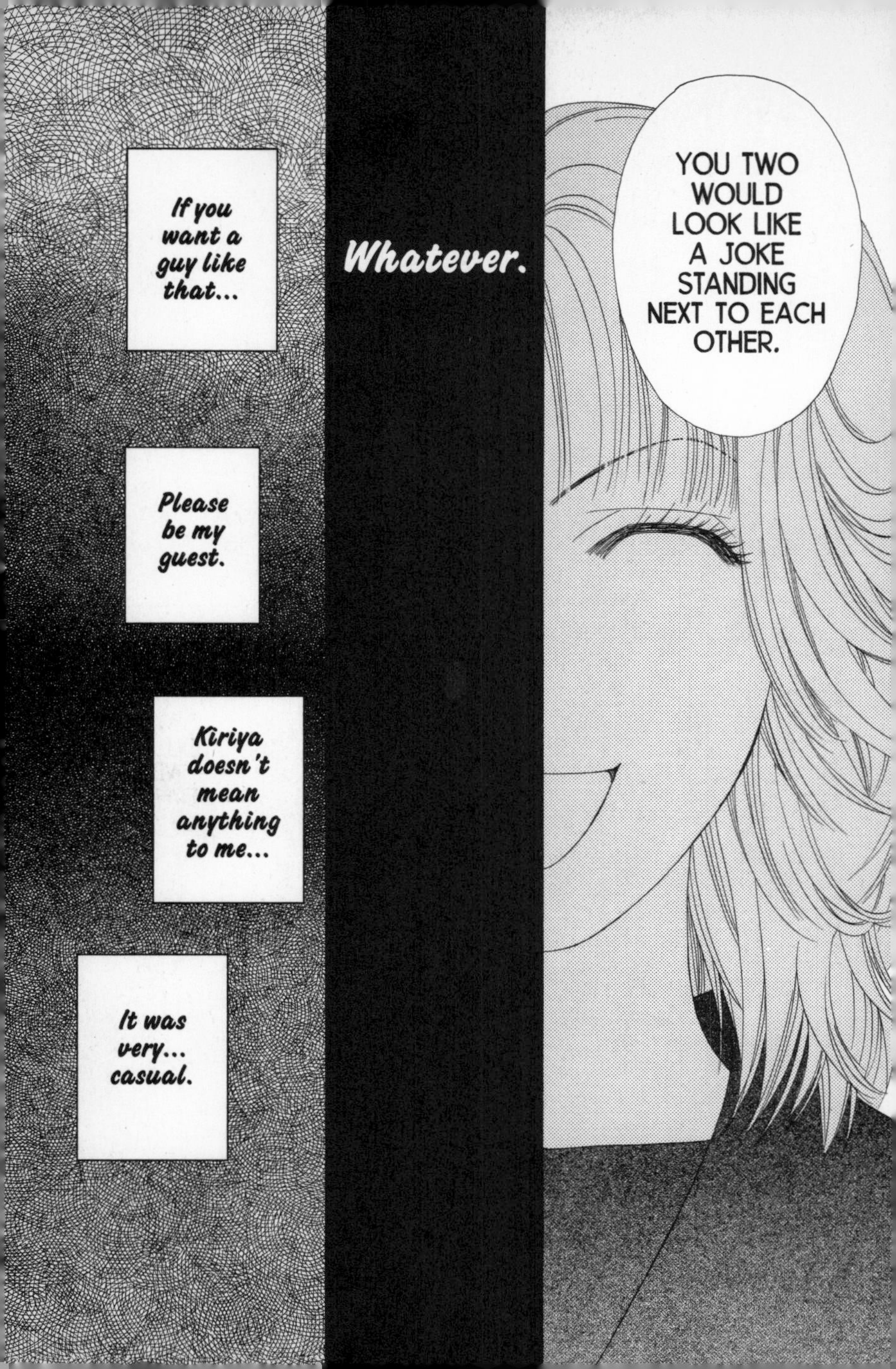
YOU TWO WOULD LOOK LIKE A JOKE STANDING NEXT TO EACH OTHER.
Whatever.
If you want a guy like that...
Please be my guest.
Kiriya doesn't mean anything to me...
It was very... casual.

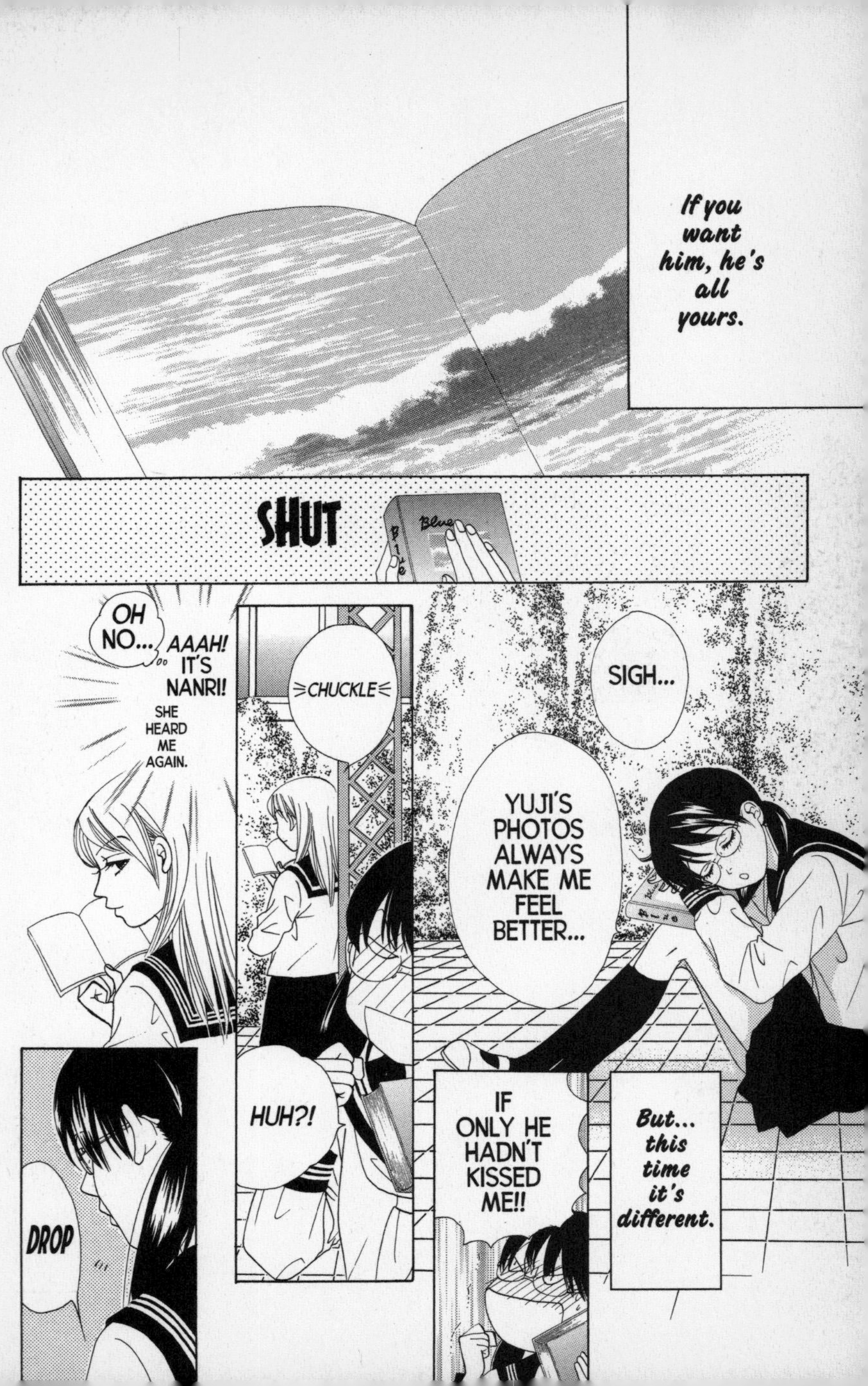
If you want him, he's all yours.
SHUT
SIGH...
YUJI'S PHOTOS ALWAYS MAKE ME FEEL BETTER...
CHUCKLE
OH NO...
AAAH! IT'S NANRI!
SHE HEARD ME AGAIN.
But... this time it's different.
IF ONLY HE HADN'T KISSED ME!!
HUH?!
DROP

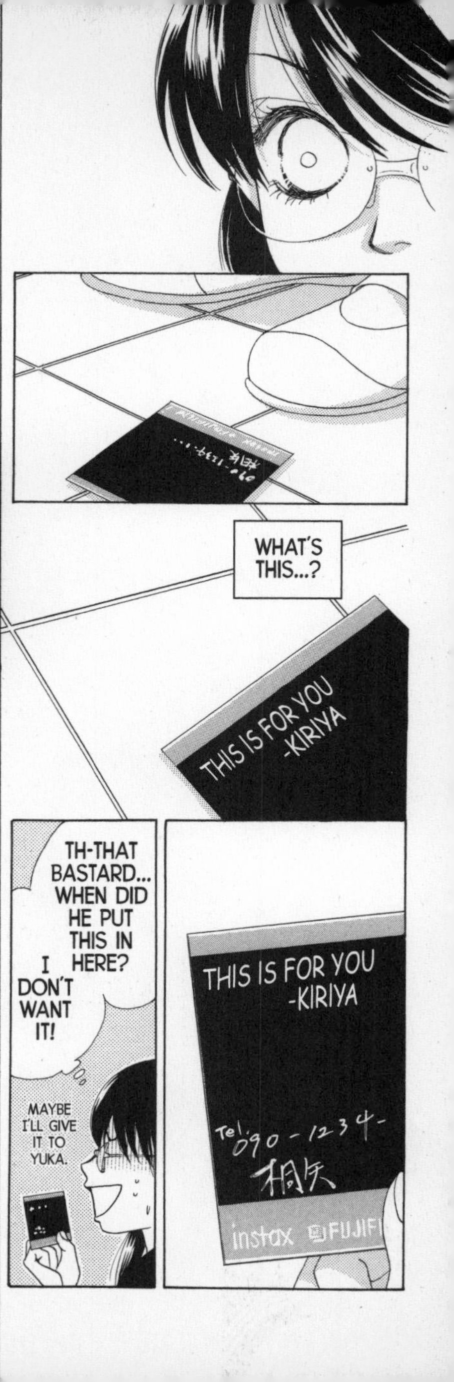
WHAT'S THIS...?
THIS IS FOR YOU -KIRIYA
THIS IS FOR YOU -KIRIYA
Tel: 090-1234-
桐矢
instax FUJIFI
TH-THAT BASTARD... WHEN DID HE PUT THIS IN HERE?
I DON'T WANT IT!
MAYBE I'LL GIVE IT TO YUKA.
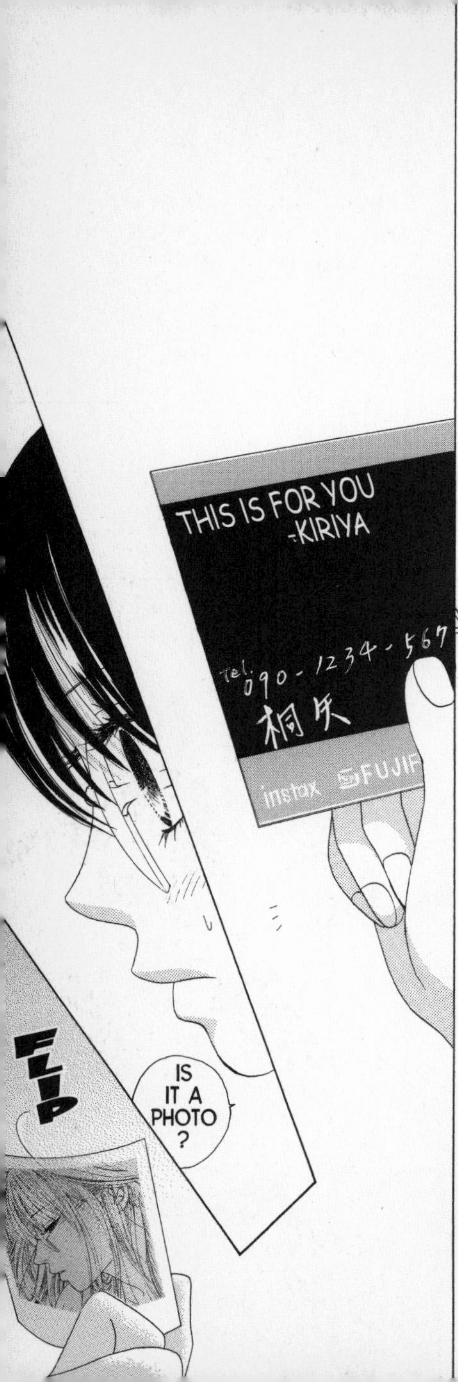
THIS IS FOR YOU -KIRIYA
Tel: 090-1234-567
桐矢
instax FUJIF
FLIP
IS IT A PHOTO?

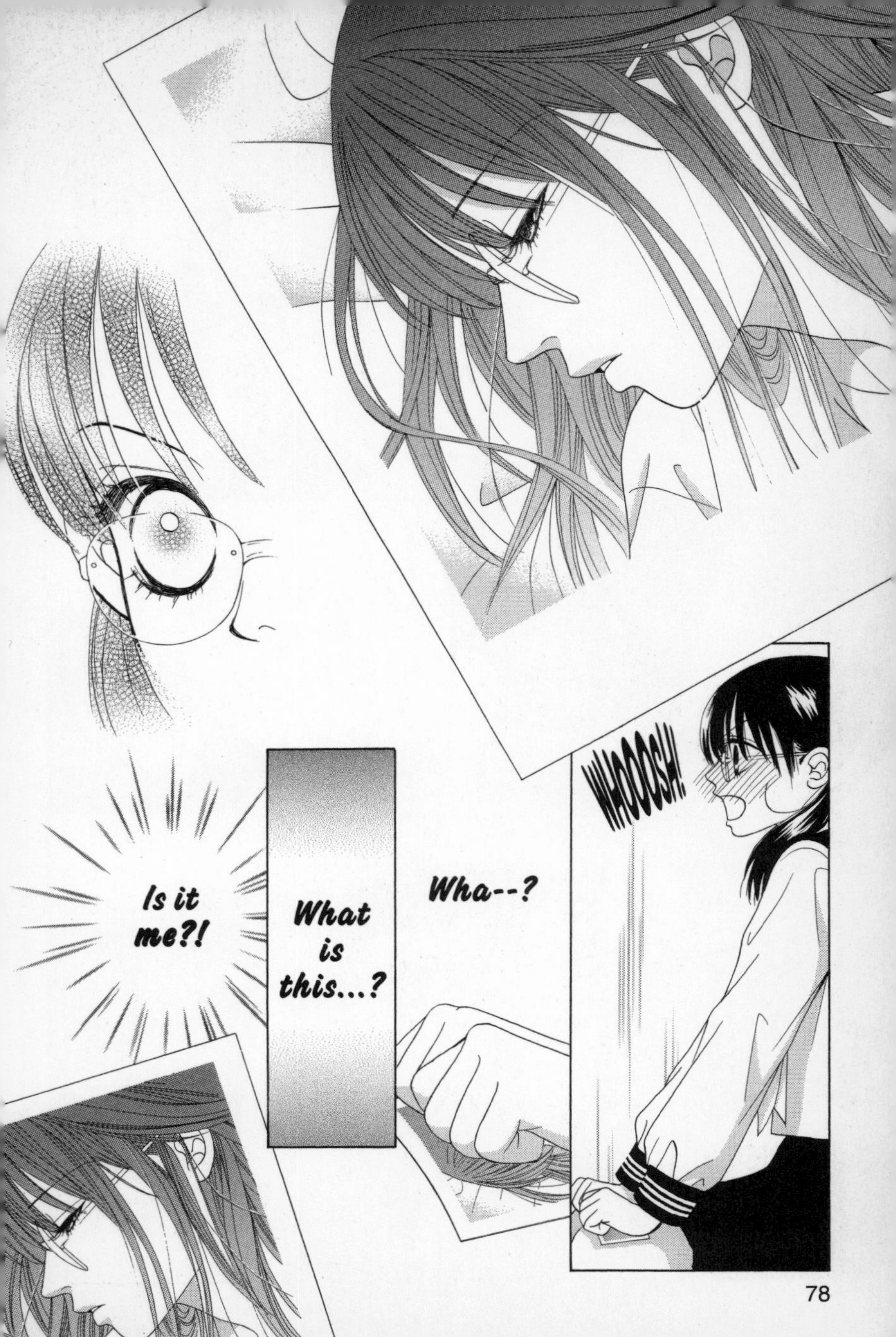
WHOOOSH!
Wha--?
What is this...?
Is it me?!

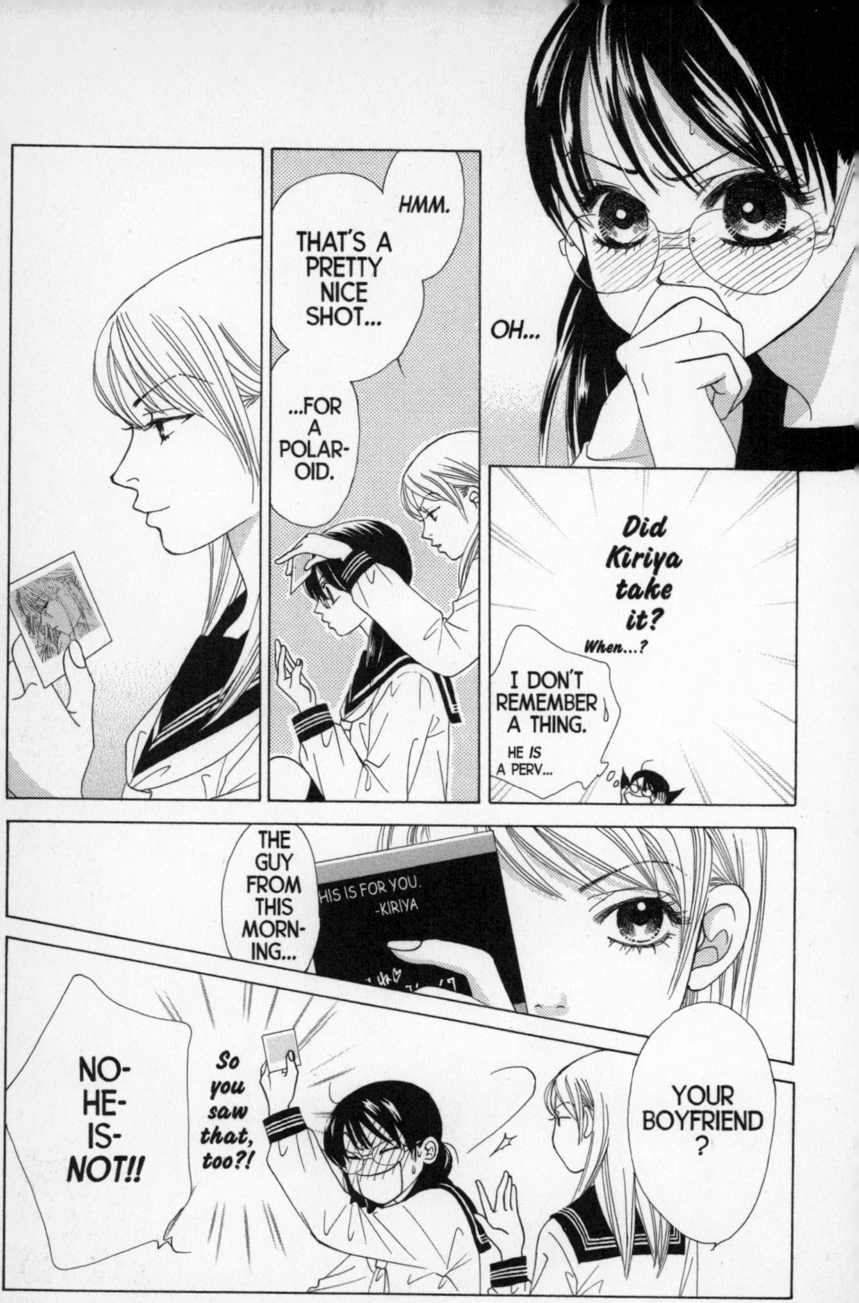
OH...
Did Kiriya take it?
When...?
I DON'T REMEMBER A THING.
HE IS A PERV...
HMM.
THAT'S A PRETTY NICE SHOT...
...FOR A POLAROID.
HIS IS FOR YOU. -KIRIYA
THE GUY FROM THIS MORNING...
YOUR BOYFRIEND?
So you saw that, too?!
NO-HE-IS-NOT!!

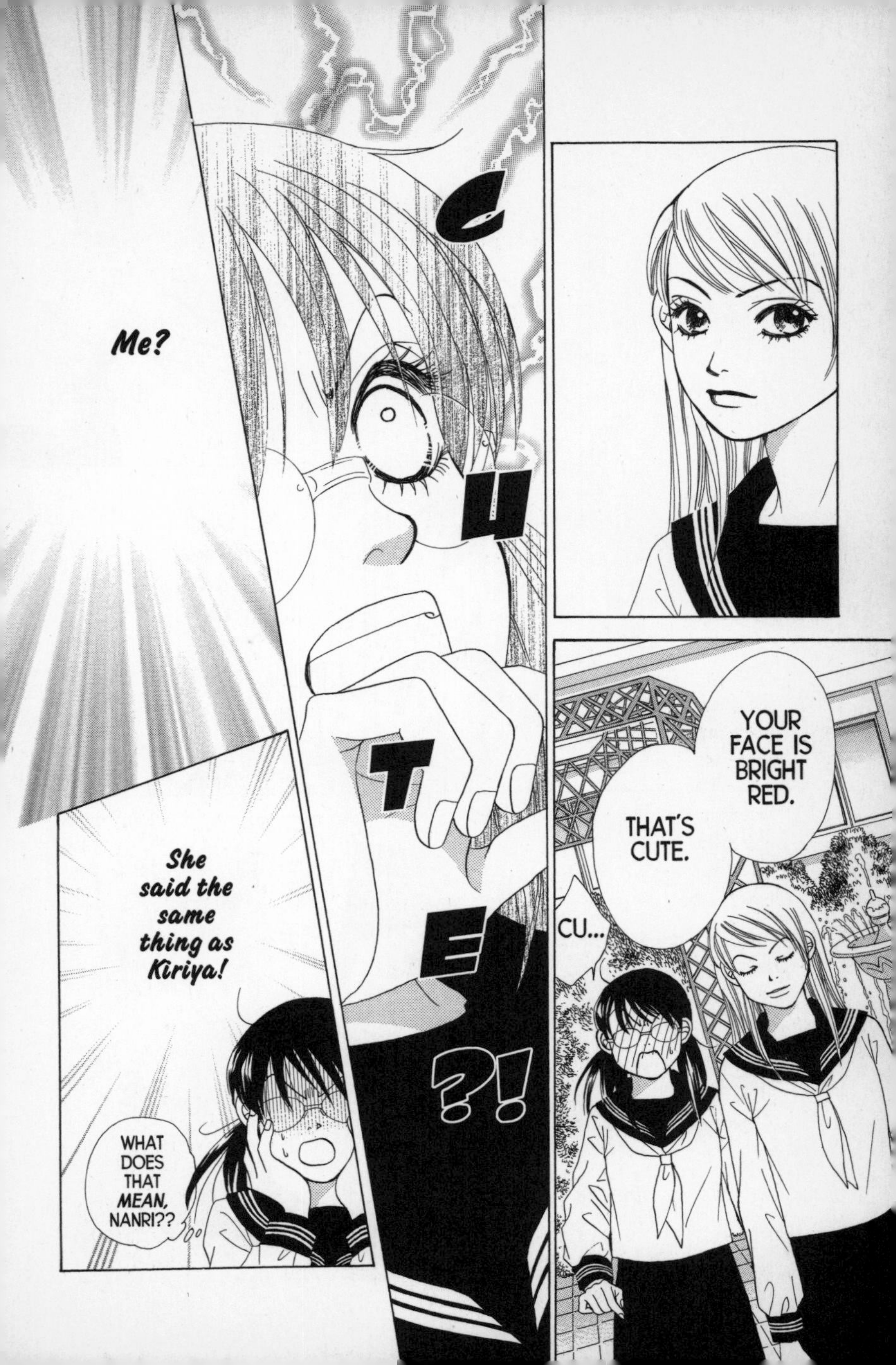
YOUR FACE IS BRIGHT RED.
THAT'S CUTE.
CU...
C U T E ?!
Me?
She said the same thing as Kiriya!
WHAT DOES THAT *MEAN*, NANRI??

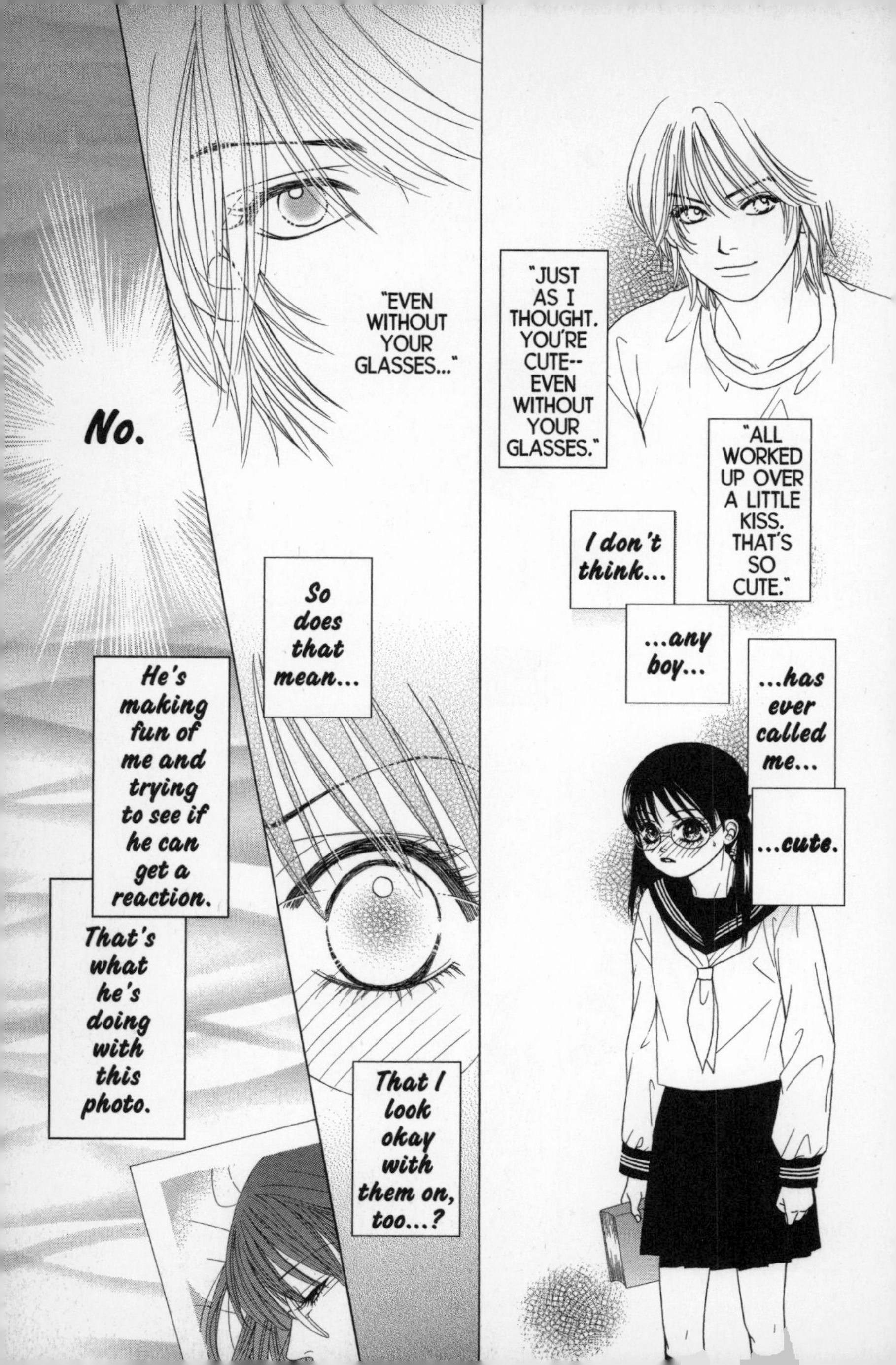
"JUST AS I THOUGHT. YOU'RE CUTE-- EVEN WITHOUT YOUR GLASSES."
"ALL WORKED UP OVER A LITTLE KISS. THAT'S SO CUTE."
I don't think...
...any boy...
...has ever called me...
...cute.
"EVEN WITHOUT YOUR GLASSES..."
So does that mean...
That I look okay with them on, too...?
No.
He's making fun of me and trying to see if he can get a reaction.
That's what he's doing with this photo.

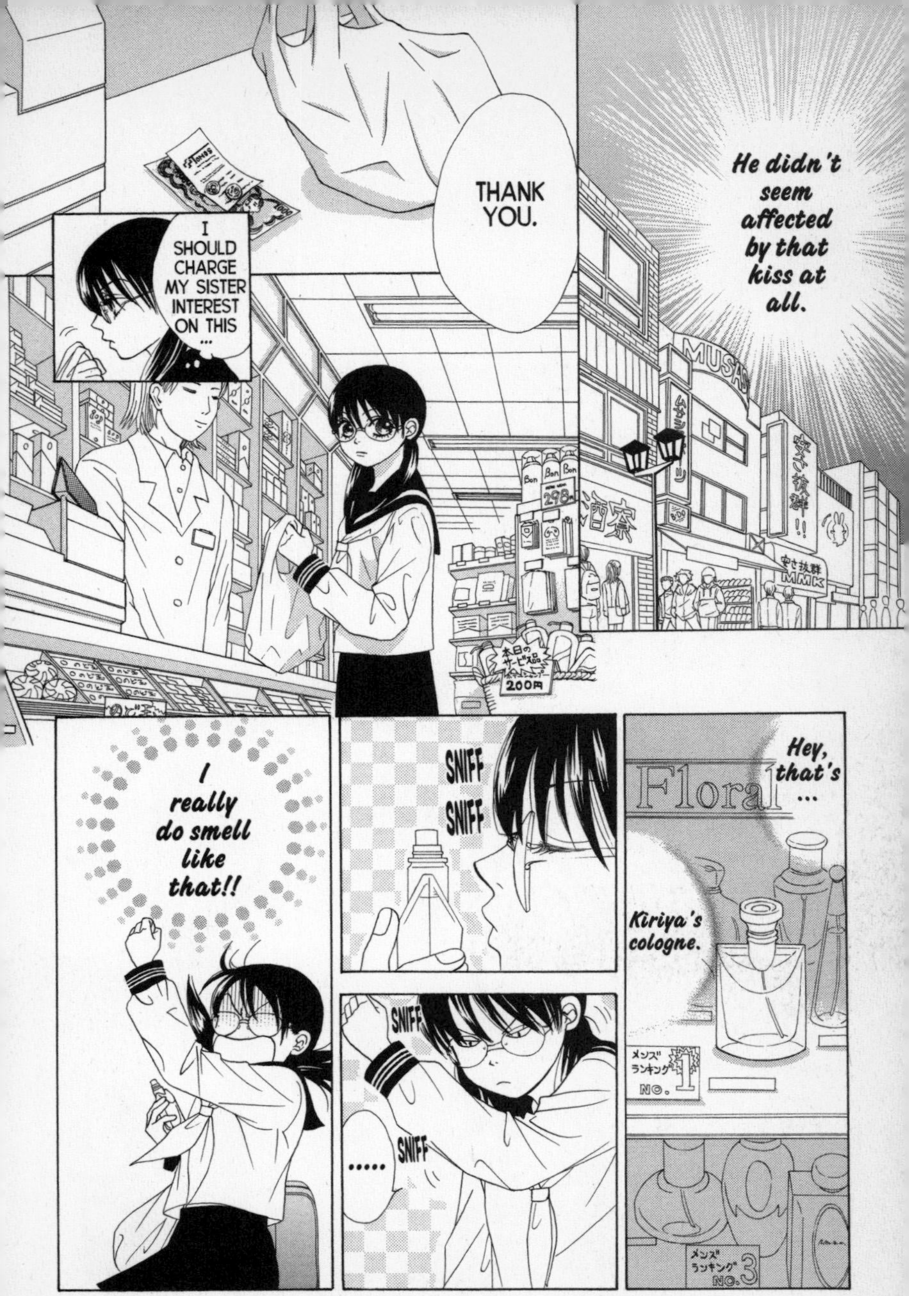
He didn't seem affected by that kiss at all.
MMK
THANK YOU.
I SHOULD CHARGE MY SISTER INTEREST ON THIS ...
Hey, that's ...
Floral
Kiriya's cologne.
メンズランキング NO. 1
メンズランキング NO. 3
SNIFF SNIFF
SNIFF
SNIFF
.....
I really do smell like that!!

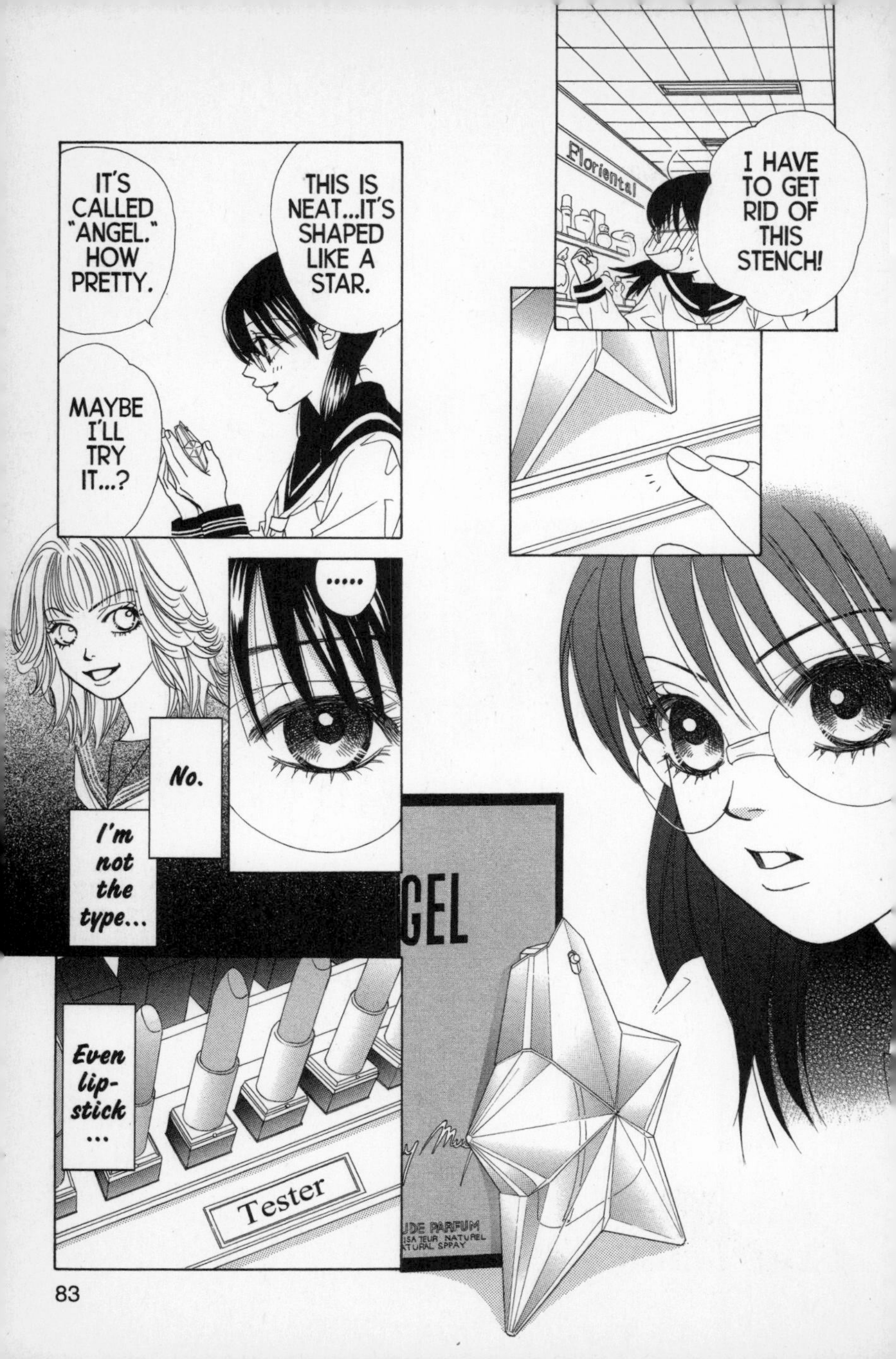

Floriental
I HAVE TO GET RID OF THIS STENCH!
THIS IS NEAT...IT'S SHAPED LIKE A STAR.
IT'S CALLED "ANGEL." HOW PRETTY.
MAYBE I'LL TRY IT...?
.....
No.
I'm not the type...
GEL
UDE PARFUM
Even lipstick...
Tester

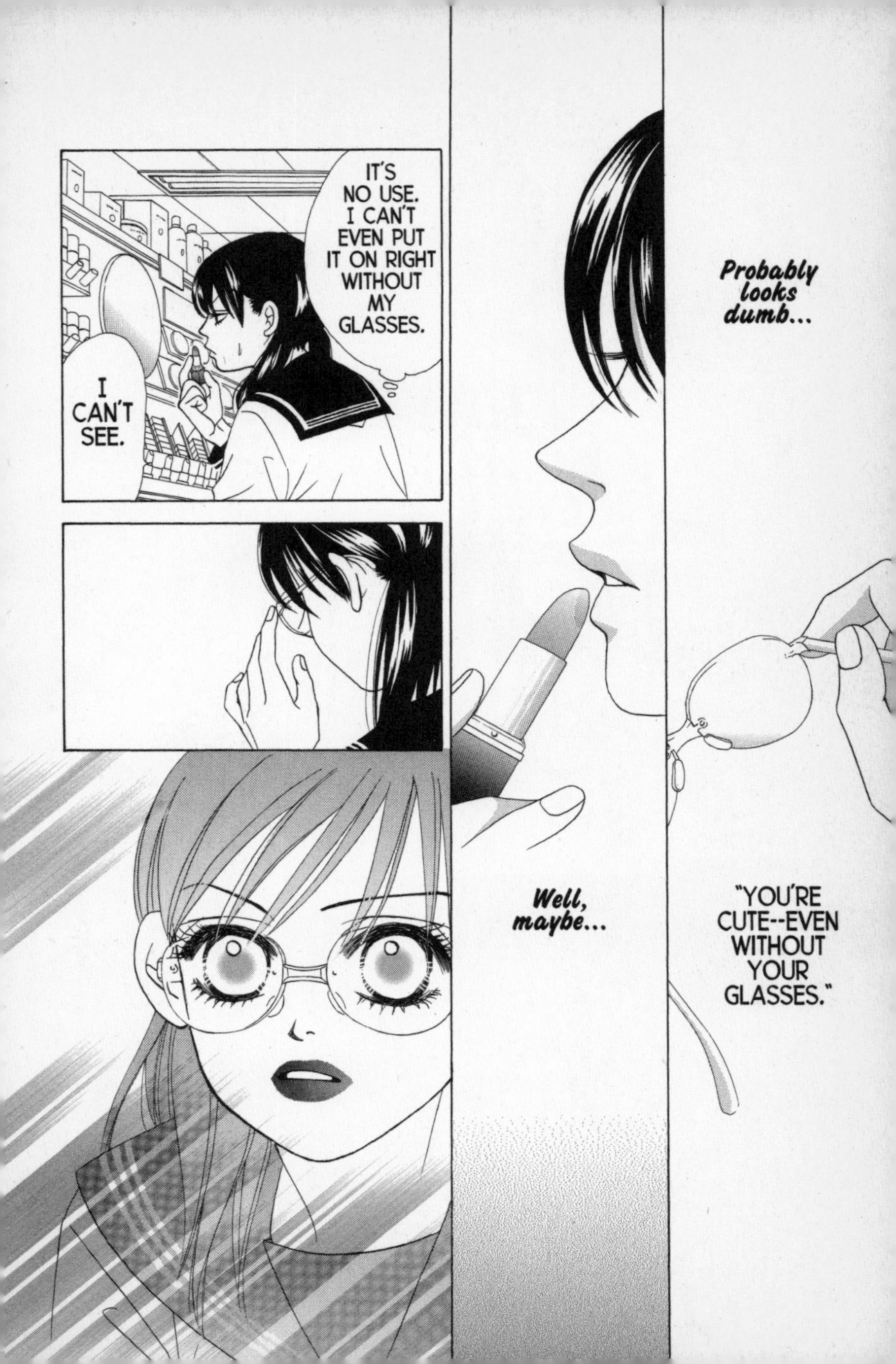
Probably looks dumb...
"YOU'RE CUTE--EVEN WITHOUT YOUR GLASSES."
Well, maybe...
IT'S NO USE. I CAN'T EVEN PUT IT ON RIGHT WITHOUT MY GLASSES.
I CAN'T SEE.

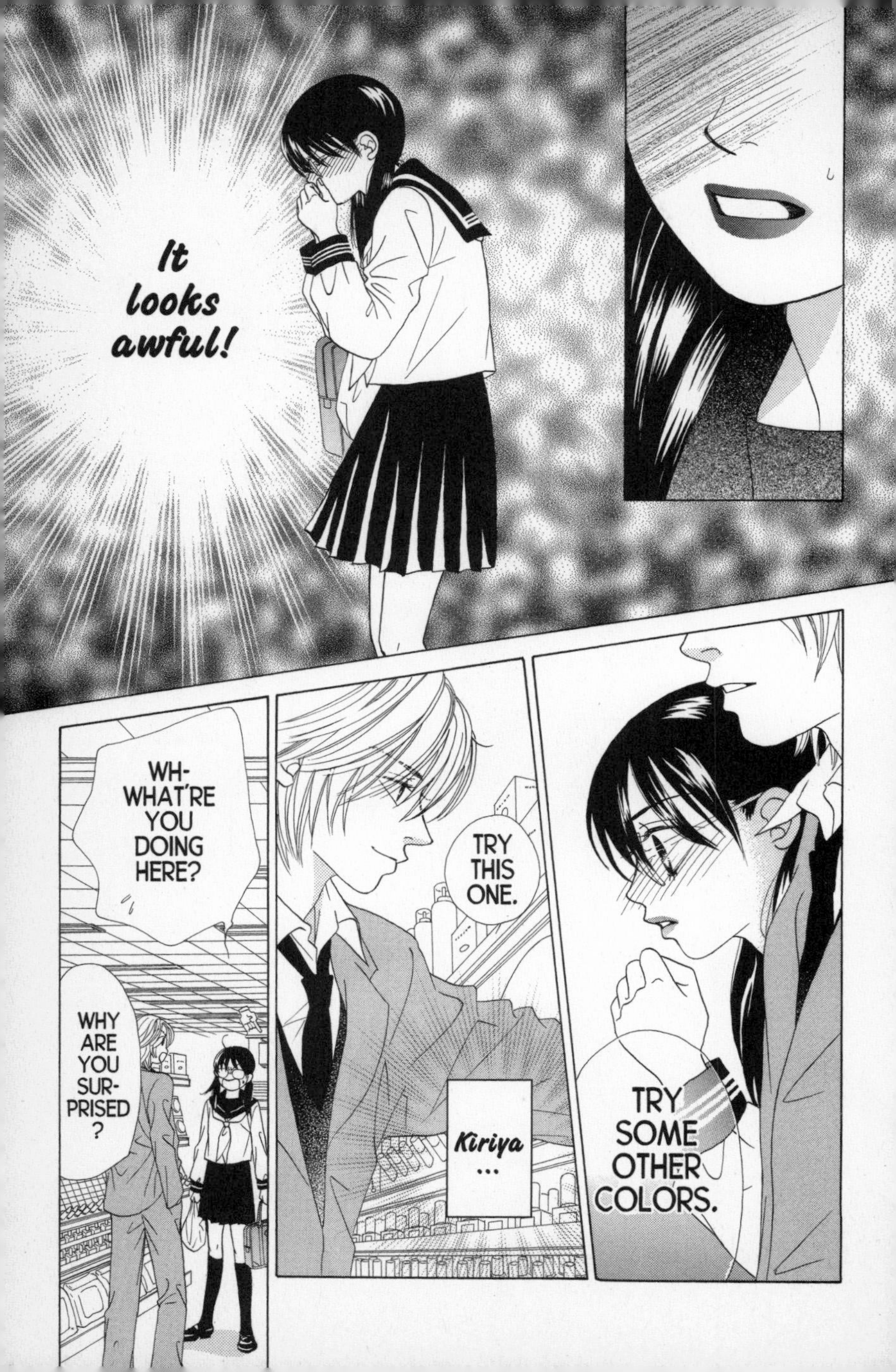
It looks awful!
TRY SOME OTHER COLORS.
TRY THIS ONE.
Kiriya ...
WH-WHAT'RE YOU DOING HERE?
WHY ARE YOU SUR-PRISED?

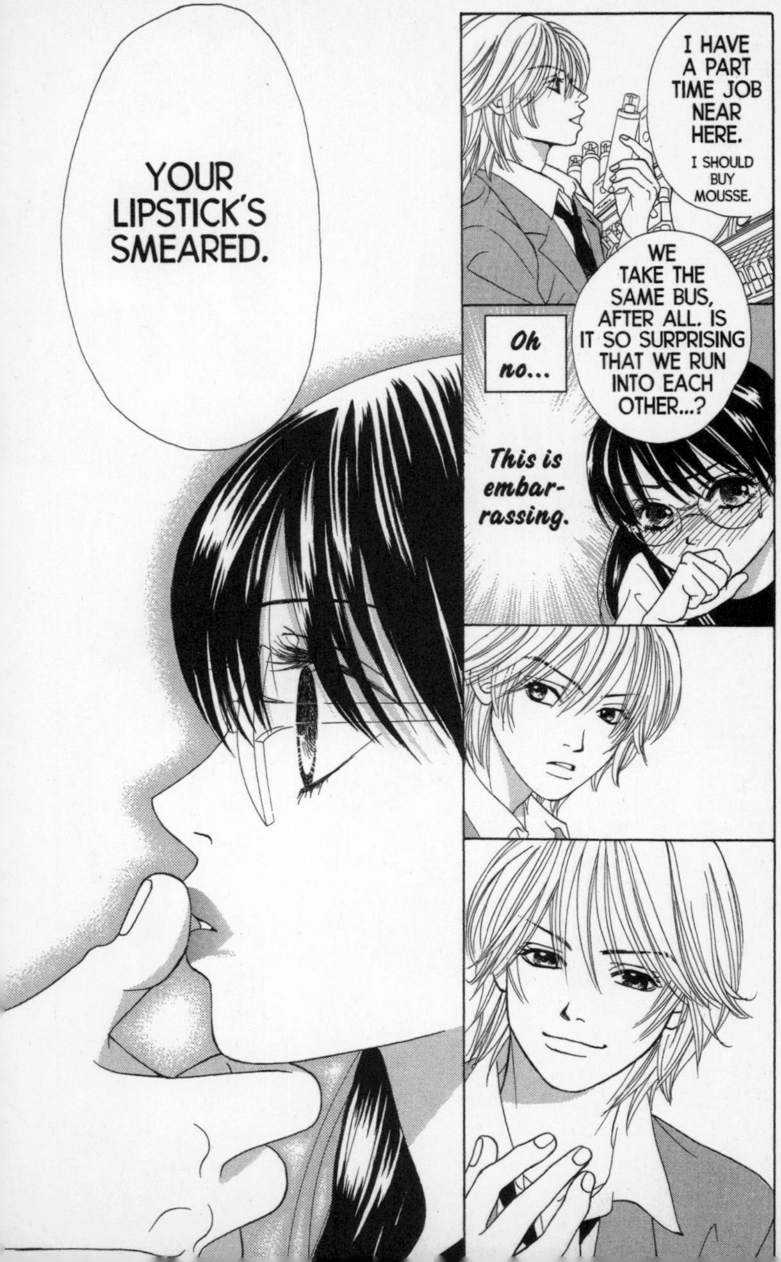
I HAVE A PART TIME JOB NEAR HERE.
I SHOULD BUY MOUSSE.
WE TAKE THE SAME BUS, AFTER ALL. IS IT SO SURPRISING THAT WE RUN INTO EACH OTHER...?
Oh no...
This is embar-rassing.
YOUR LIPSTICK'S SMEARED.

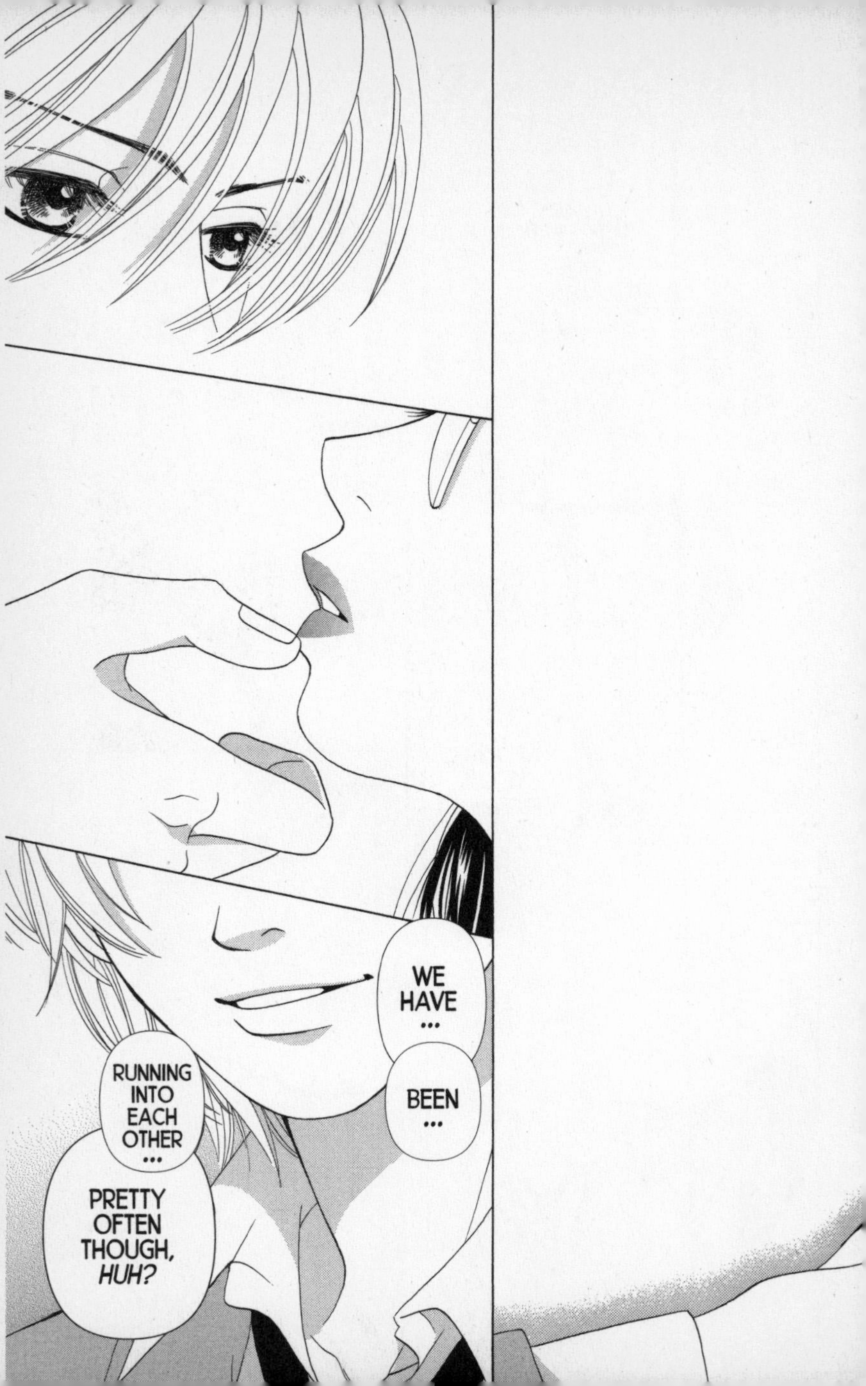
WE HAVE ...
BEEN ...
RUNNING INTO EACH OTHER ...
PRETTY OFTEN THOUGH, *HUH?*

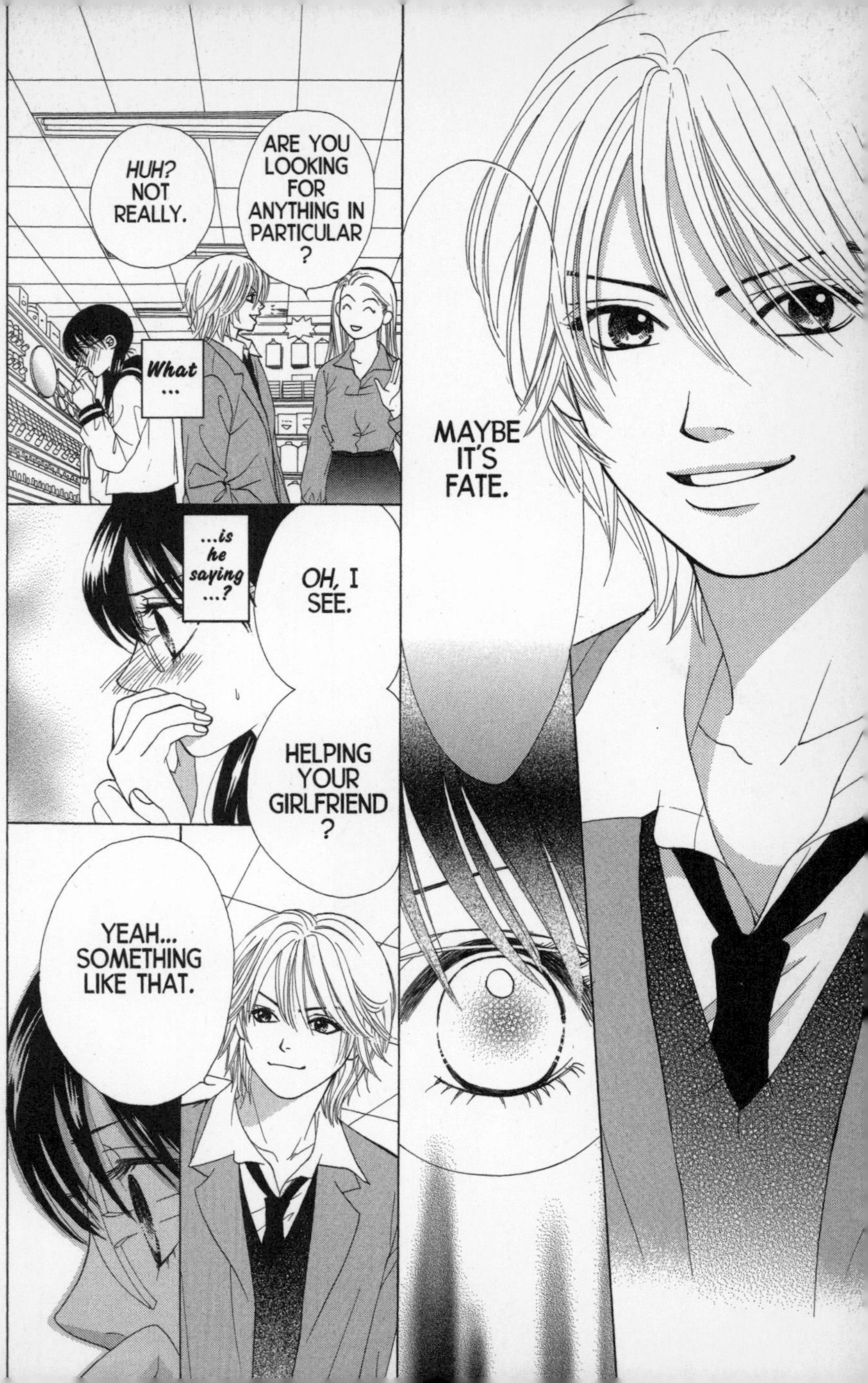
MAYBE IT'S FATE.
ARE YOU LOOKING FOR ANYTHING IN PARTICULAR?
HUH? NOT REALLY.
What...
OH, I SEE.
...is he saying...?
HELPING YOUR GIRLFRIEND?
YEAH... SOMETHING LIKE THAT.

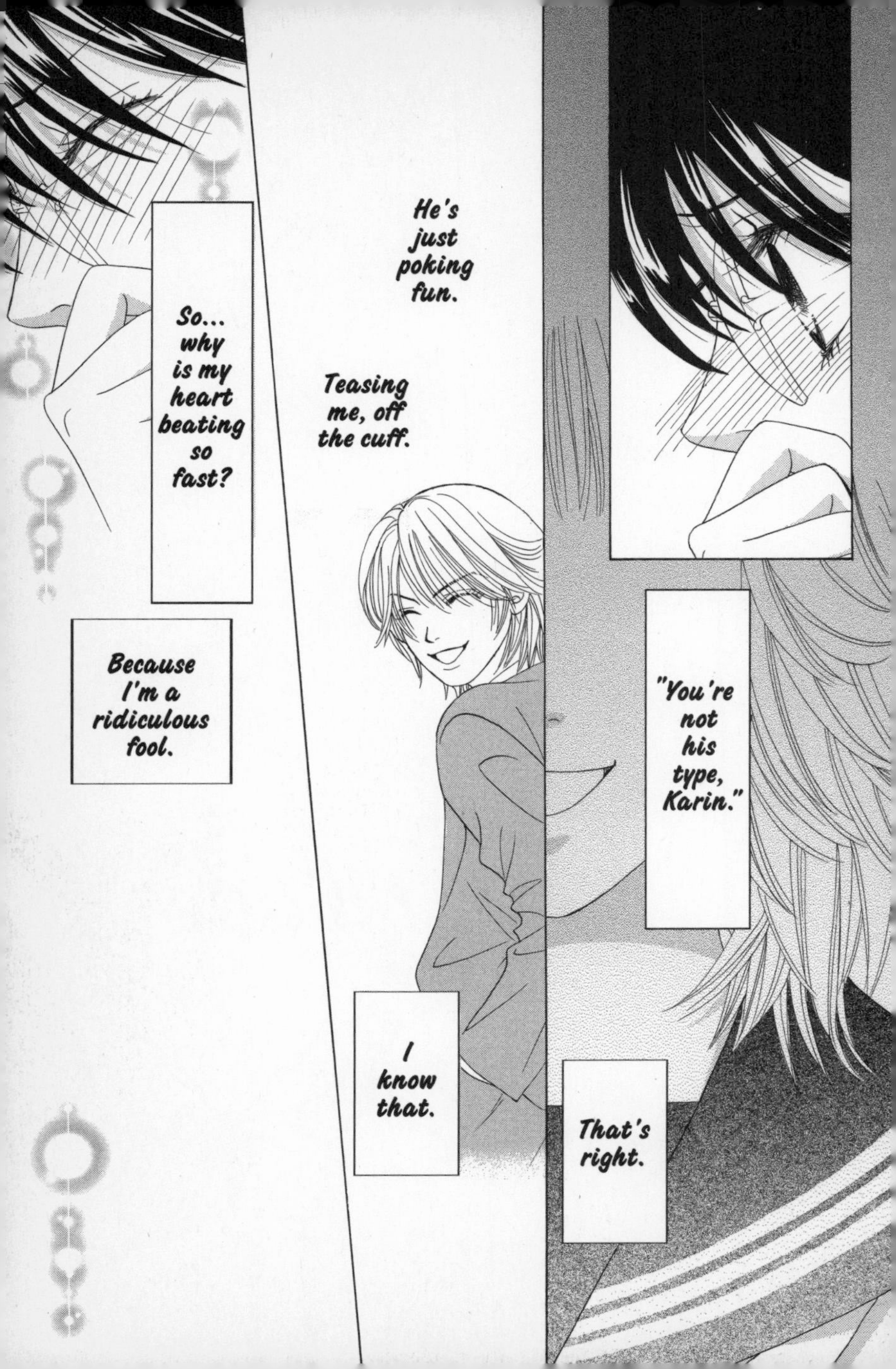
"You're not his type, Karin."
That's right.
He's just poking fun.
Teasing me, off the cuff.
I know that.
So... why is my heart beating so fast?
Because I'm a ridiculous fool.

KARE
First Love

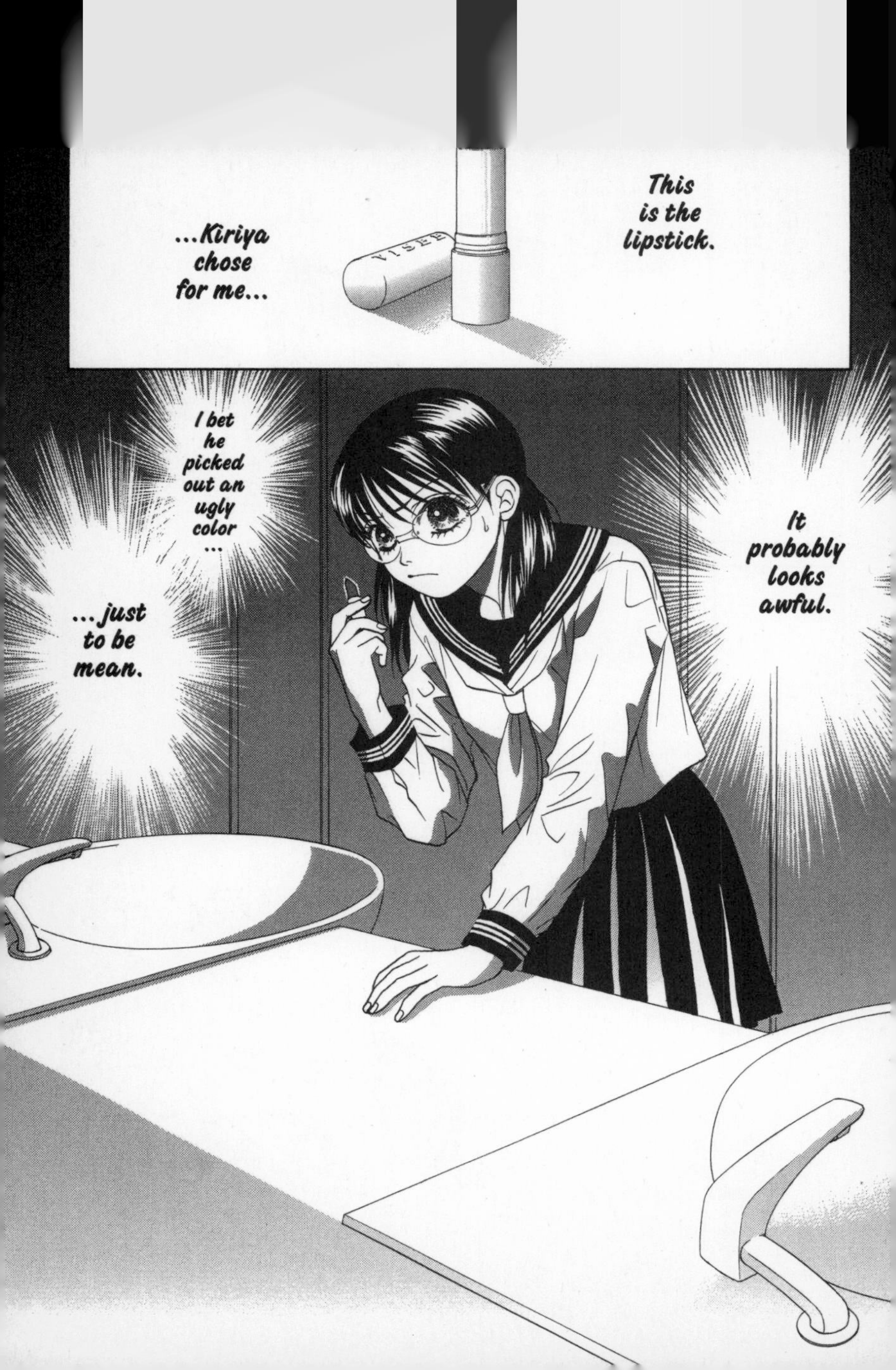
This is the lipstick.
VISEE
...Kiriya chose for me...
It probably looks awful.
I bet he picked out an ugly color...
...just to be mean.

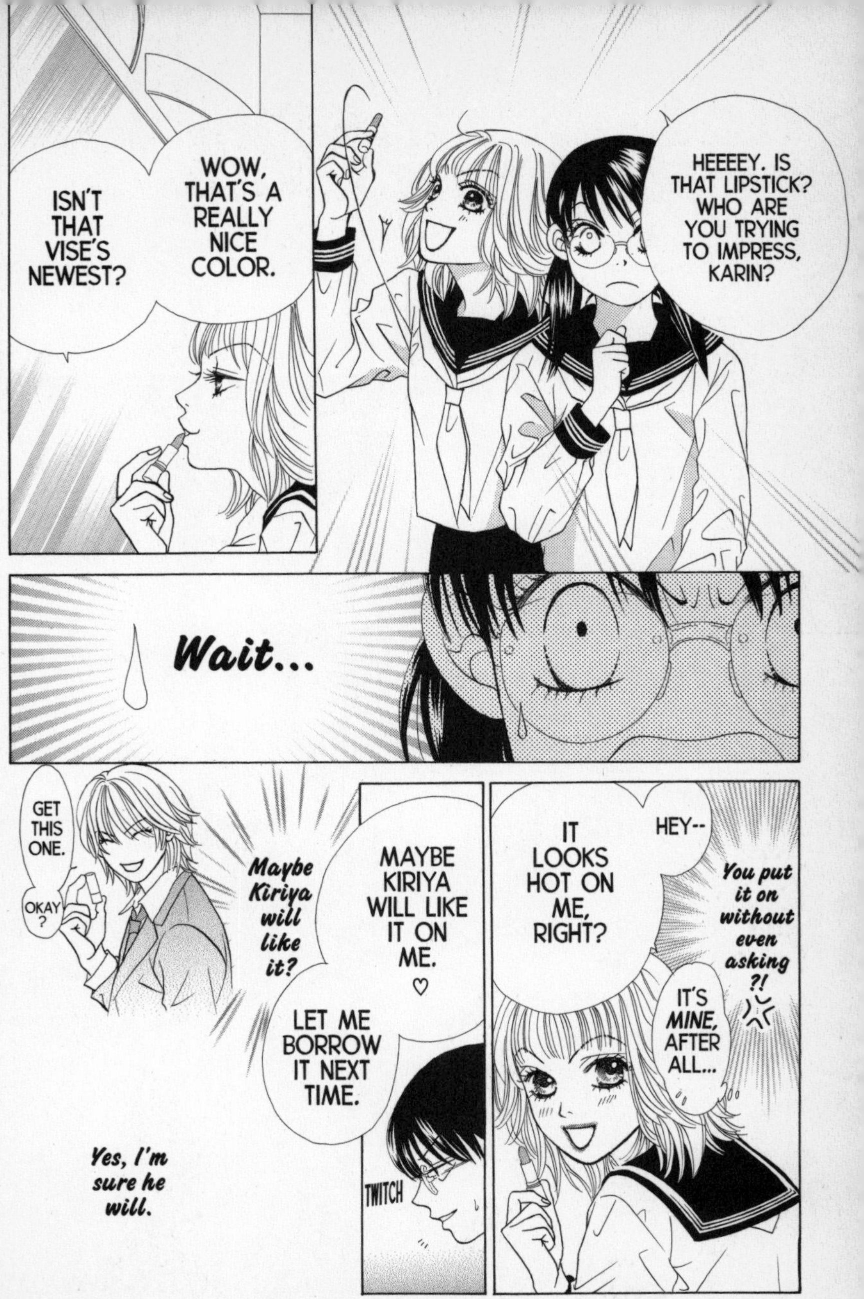

HEEEEY. IS THAT LIPSTICK? WHO ARE YOU TRYING TO IMPRESS, KARIN?
WOW, THAT'S A REALLY NICE COLOR.
ISN'T THAT VISE'S NEWEST?
Wait...
HEY--
IT LOOKS HOT ON ME, RIGHT?
You put it on without even asking?!
IT'S MINE, AFTER ALL...
MAYBE KIRIYA WILL LIKE IT ON ME. ♡
LET ME BORROW IT NEXT TIME.
TWITCH
Maybe Kiriya will like it?
GET THIS ONE.
OKAY?
Yes, I'm sure he will.

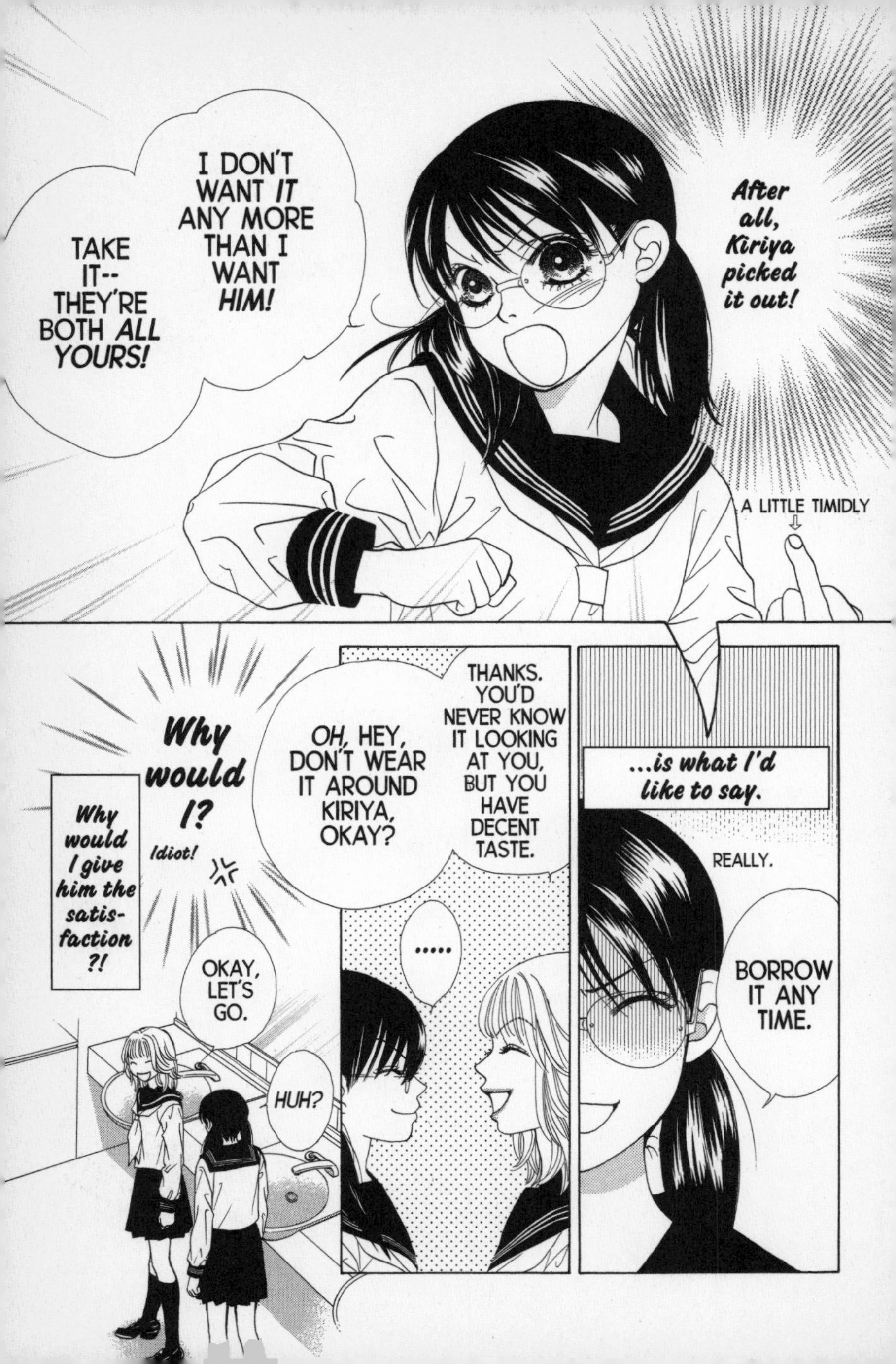
After all, Kiriya picked it out!
A LITTLE TIMIDLY
I DON'T WANT IT ANY MORE THAN I WANT HIM!
TAKE IT-- THEY'RE BOTH ALL YOURS!
...is what I'd like to say.
REALLY.
BORROW IT ANY TIME.
THANKS. YOU'D NEVER KNOW IT LOOKING AT YOU, BUT YOU HAVE DECENT TASTE.
OH, HEY, DON'T WEAR IT AROUND KIRIYA, OKAY?
......
Why would I?
Idiot!
Why would I give him the satis-faction?!
OKAY, LET'S GO.
HUH?

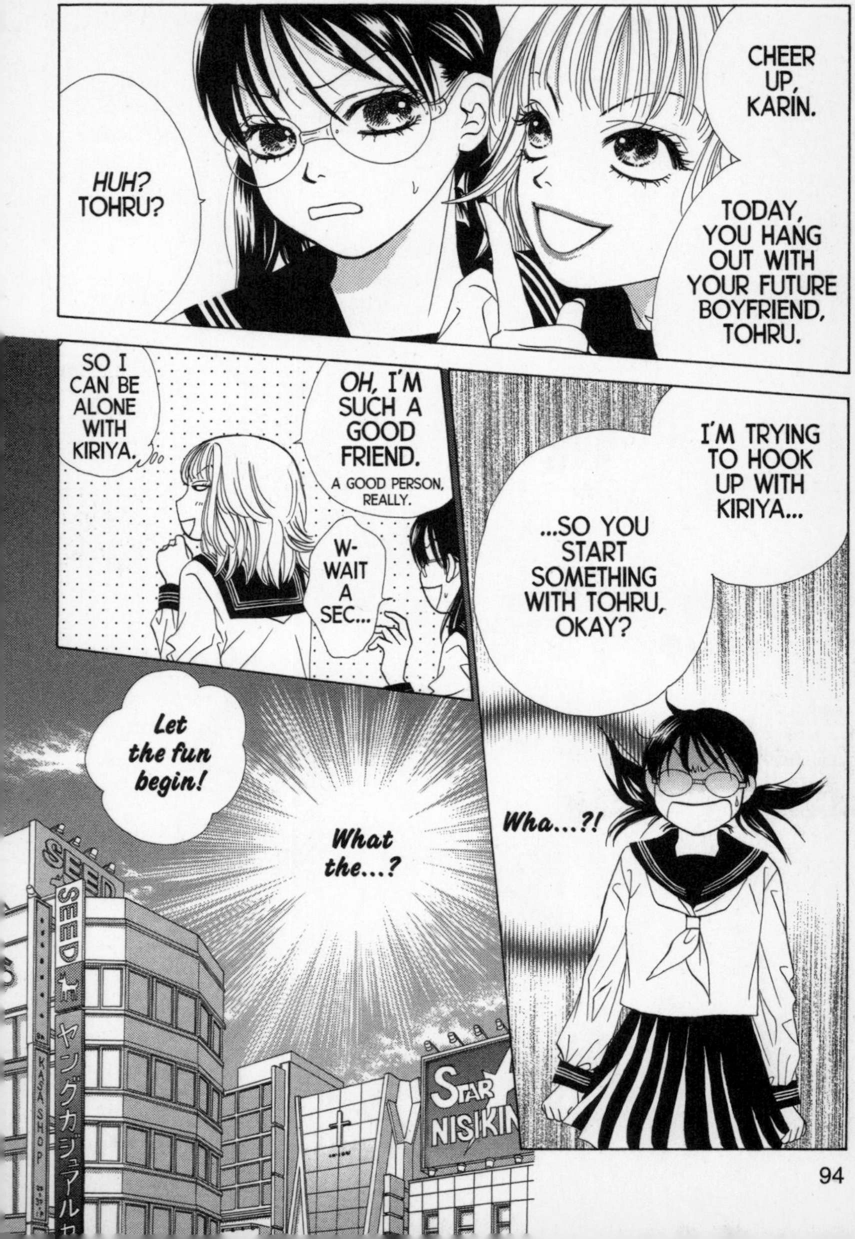
CHEER UP, KARIN.
TODAY, YOU HANG OUT WITH YOUR FUTURE BOYFRIEND, TOHRU.
HUH? TOHRU?
I'M TRYING TO HOOK UP WITH KIRIYA...
...SO YOU START SOMETHING WITH TOHRU, OKAY?
Wha...?!
OH, I'M SUCH A GOOD FRIEND.
A GOOD PERSON, REALLY.
SO I CAN BE ALONE WITH KIRIYA.
W-WAIT A SEC...
Let the fun begin!
What the...?
SEED
ヤングカジュアル
KASA SHOP
STAR
NISIKIN

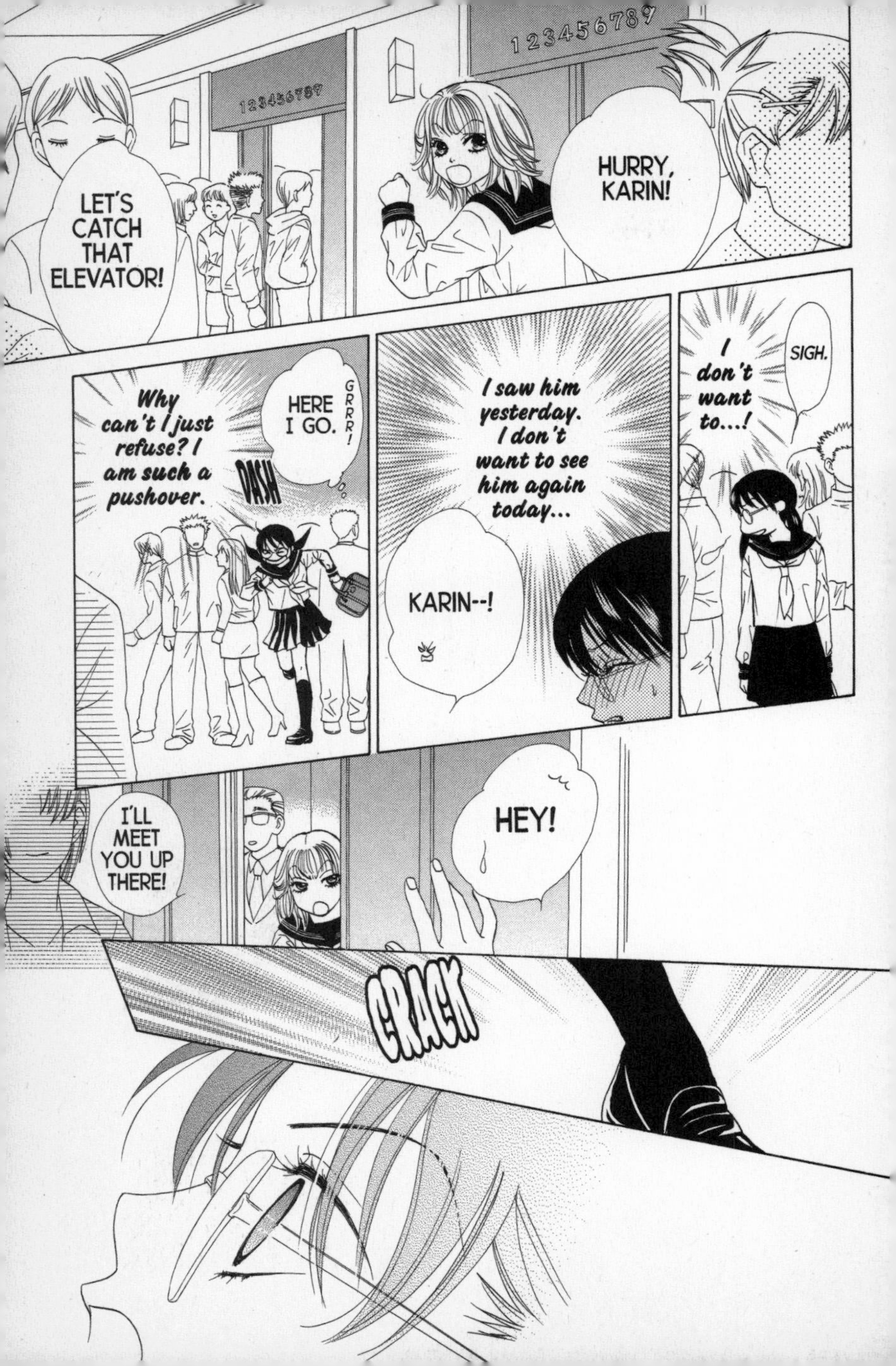

HURRY, KARIN!
LET'S CATCH THAT ELEVATOR!
SIGH.
I don't want to...!
I saw him yesterday. I don't want to see him again today...
KARIN--!
GRRR!
HERE I GO.
Why can't I just refuse? I am such a pushover.
DASH
HEY!
I'LL MEET YOU UP THERE!
CRACK

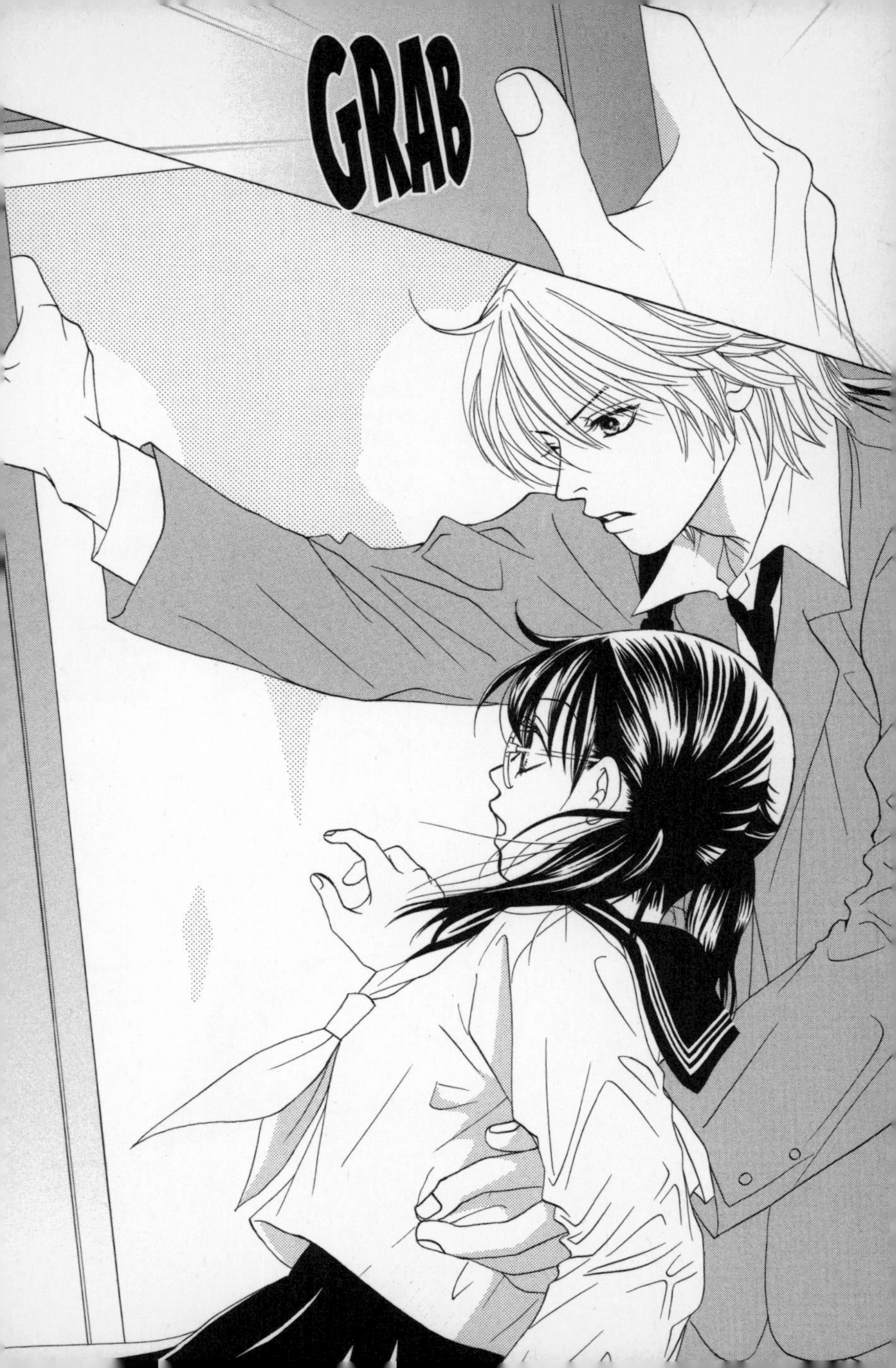
GRAB

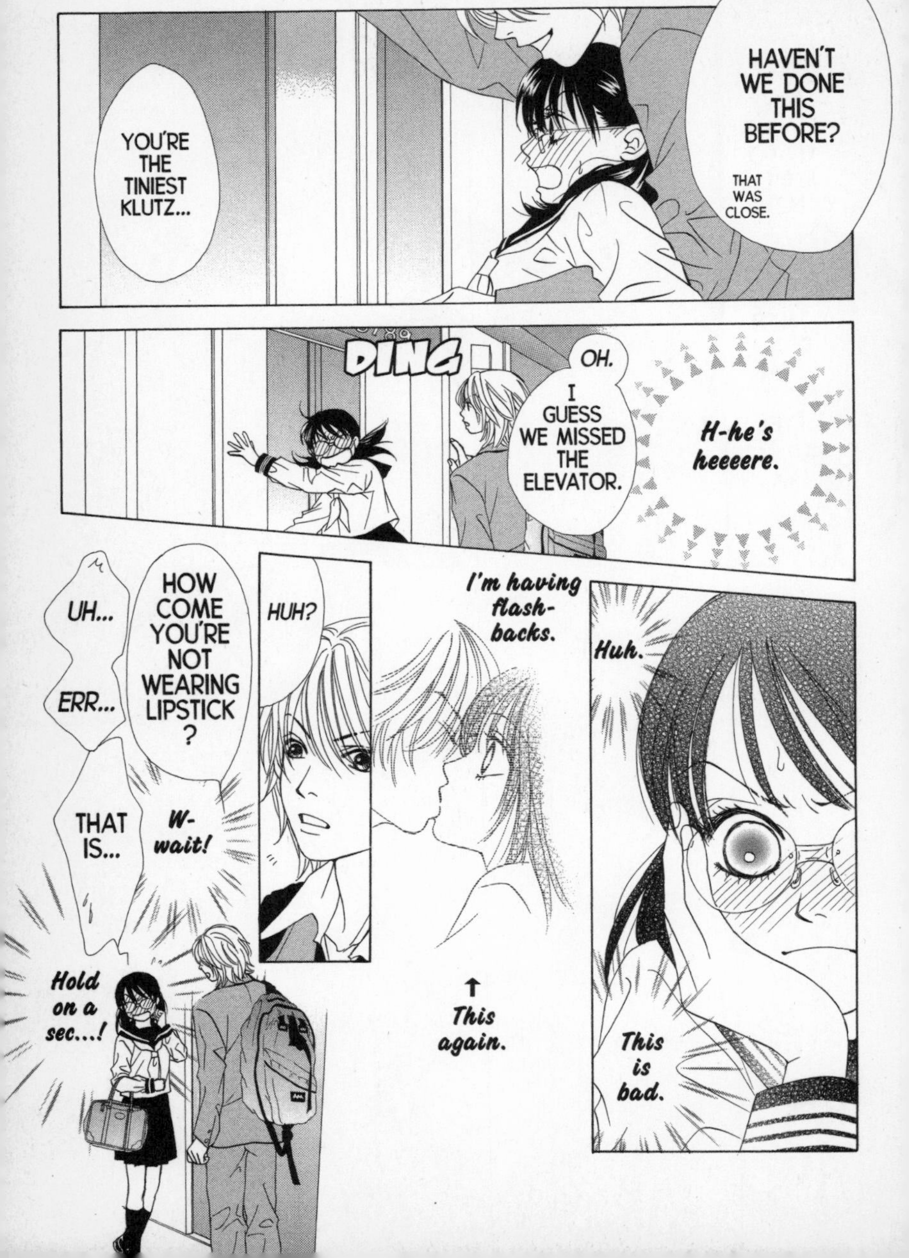
HAVEN'T WE DONE THIS BEFORE?
THAT WAS CLOSE.
YOU'RE THE TINIEST KLUTZ...
H-he's heeeere.
OH.
I GUESS WE MISSED THE ELEVATOR.
DING
Huh.
This is bad.
I'm having flash-backs.
↑ This again.
HUH?
HOW COME YOU'RE NOT WEARING LIPSTICK?
UH...
ERR...
THAT IS...
W-wait!
Hold on a sec...!

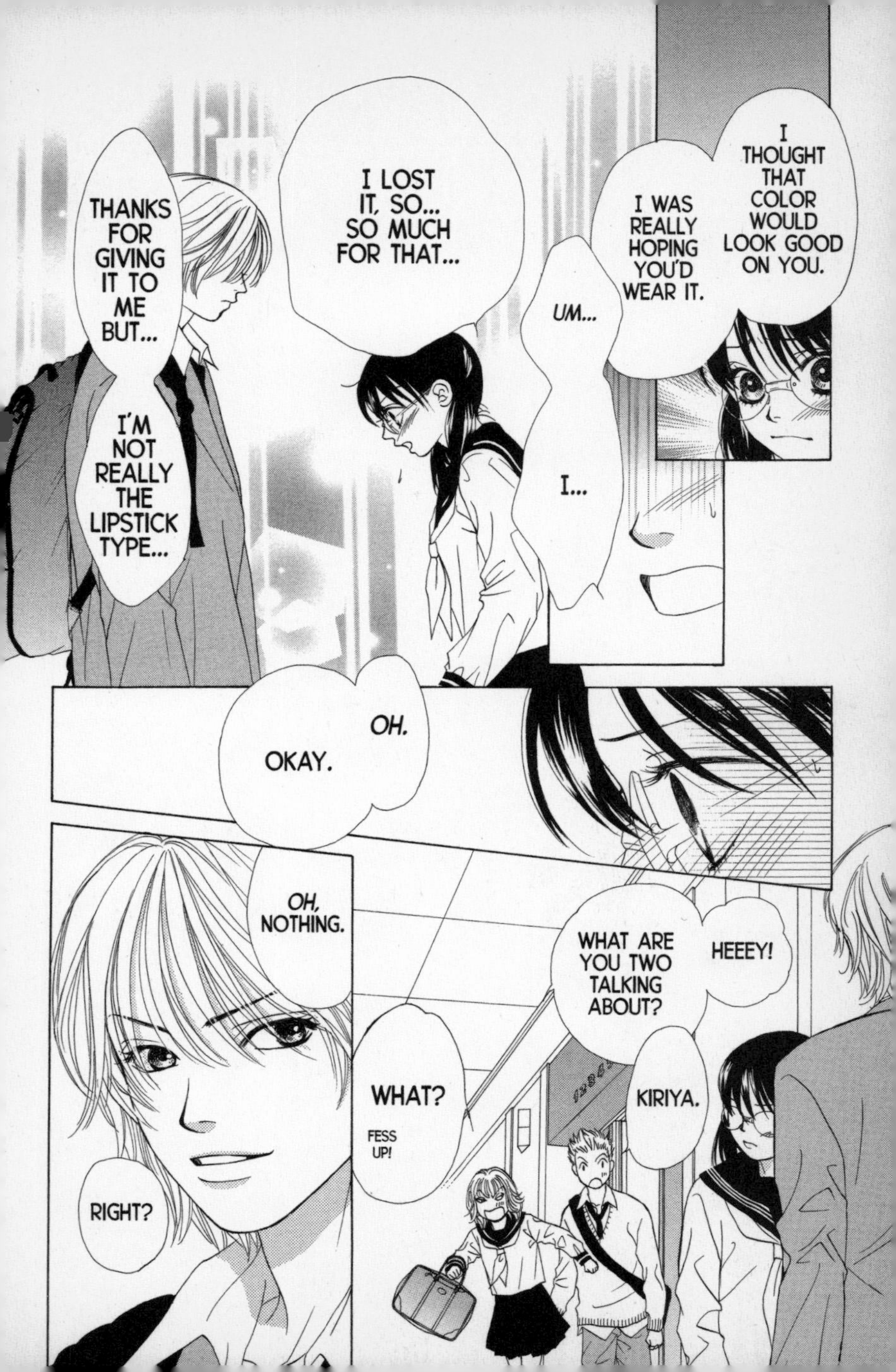
I THOUGHT THAT COLOR WOULD LOOK GOOD ON YOU.
I WAS REALLY HOPING YOU'D WEAR IT.
UM...
I...
I LOST IT, SO... SO MUCH FOR THAT...
THANKS FOR GIVING IT TO ME BUT...
I'M NOT REALLY THE LIPSTICK TYPE...
OH.
OKAY.
HEEEY!
WHAT ARE YOU TWO TALKING ABOUT?
KIRIYA.
OH, NOTHING.
WHAT?
FESS UP!
RIGHT?

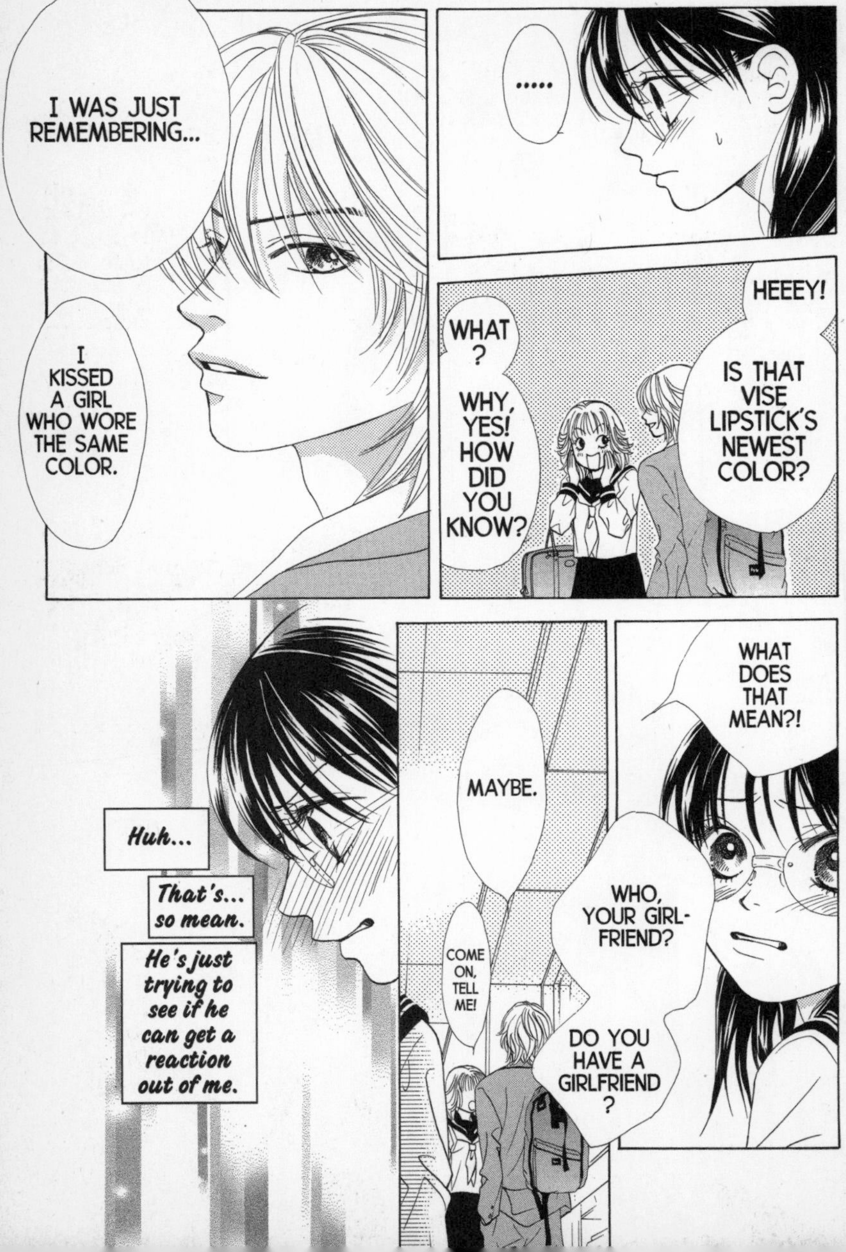
......
HEEEY!
IS THAT VISE LIPSTICK'S NEWEST COLOR?
WHAT? WHY, YES! HOW DID YOU KNOW?
I WAS JUST REMEMBERING...
I KISSED A GIRL WHO WORE THE SAME COLOR.
WHAT DOES THAT MEAN?!
WHO, YOUR GIRL-FRIEND?
DO YOU HAVE A GIRLFRIEND?
MAYBE.
COME ON, TELL ME!
Huh...
That's... so mean.
He's just trying to see if he can get a reaction out of me.

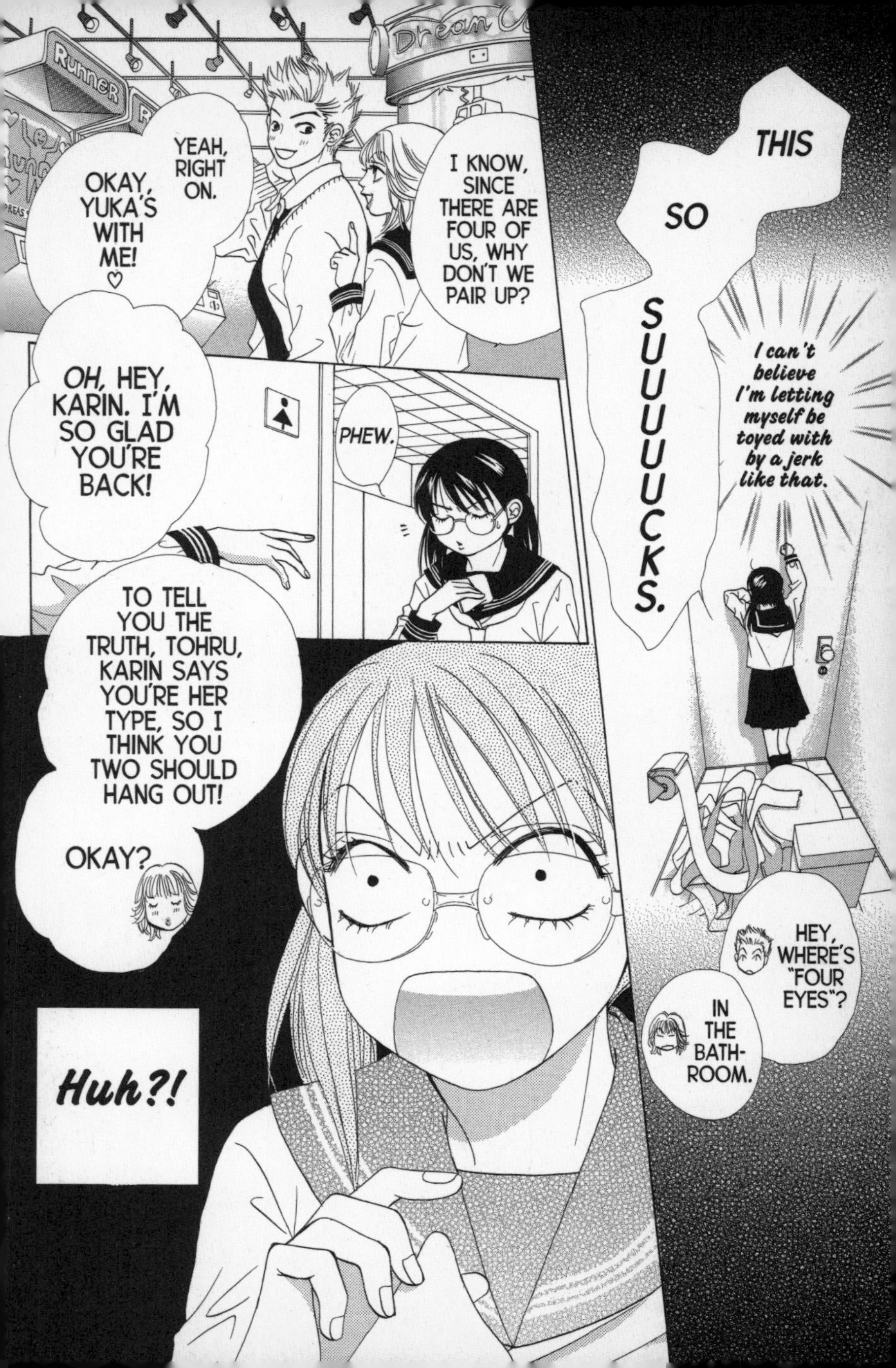

THIS SO SUUUUUCKS.
I can't believe I'm letting myself be toyed with by a jerk like that.
HEY, WHERE'S "FOUR EYES"?
IN THE BATHROOM.
I KNOW, SINCE THERE ARE FOUR OF US, WHY DON'T WE PAIR UP?
YEAH, RIGHT ON.
OKAY, YUKA'S WITH ME! ♡
PHEW.
OH, HEY, KARIN. I'M SO GLAD YOU'RE BACK!
TO TELL YOU THE TRUTH, TOHRU, KARIN SAYS YOU'RE HER TYPE, SO I THINK YOU TWO SHOULD HANG OUT!
OKAY?
Huh?!

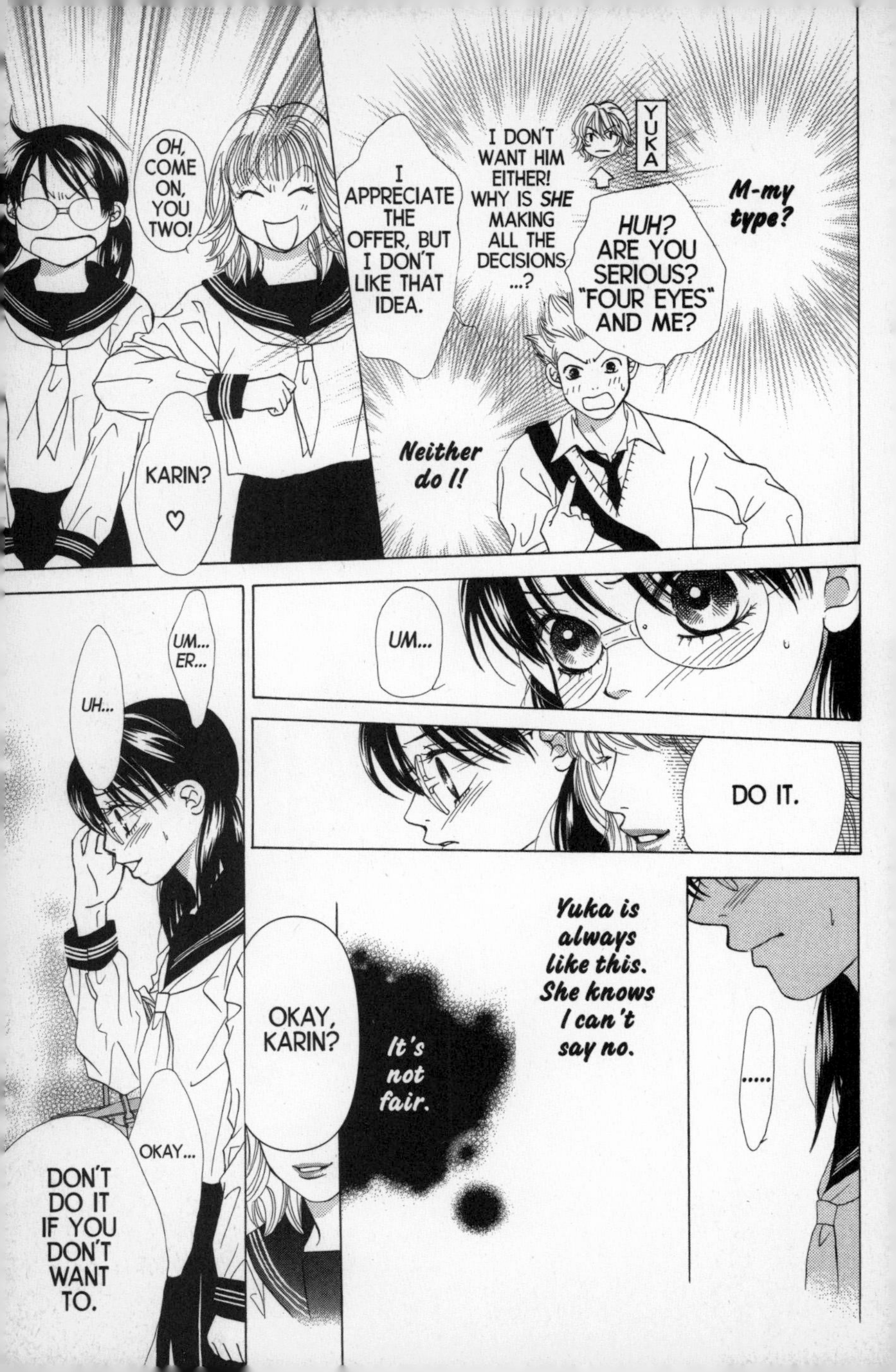
M-my type?
HUH? ARE YOU SERIOUS? "FOUR EYES" AND ME?
YUKA
I DON'T WANT HIM EITHER! WHY IS SHE MAKING ALL THE DECISIONS ...?
I APPRECIATE THE OFFER, BUT I DON'T LIKE THAT IDEA.
Neither do I!
OH, COME ON, YOU TWO!
KARIN? ♡
UM...
DO IT.
Yuka is always like this. She knows I can't say no.
.....
OKAY, KARIN?
It's not fair.
UM... ER...
UH...
OKAY...
DON'T DO IT IF YOU DON'T WANT TO.

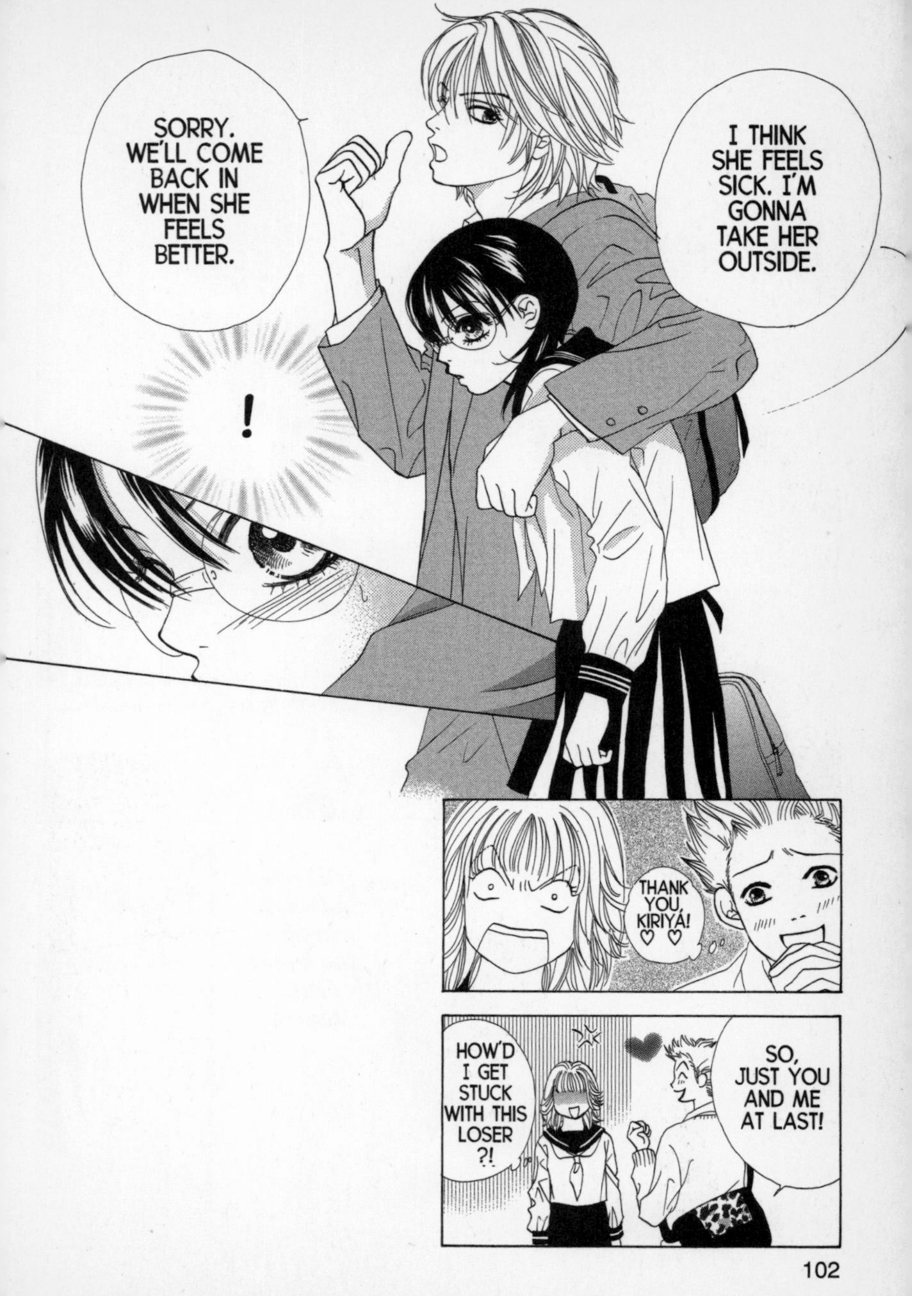
I THINK SHE FEELS SICK. I'M GONNA TAKE HER OUTSIDE.
SORRY. WE'LL COME BACK IN WHEN SHE FEELS BETTER.
!
THANK YOU, KIRIYA! ♡ ♡
SO, JUST YOU AND ME AT LAST!
HOW'D I GET STUCK WITH THIS LOSER ?!

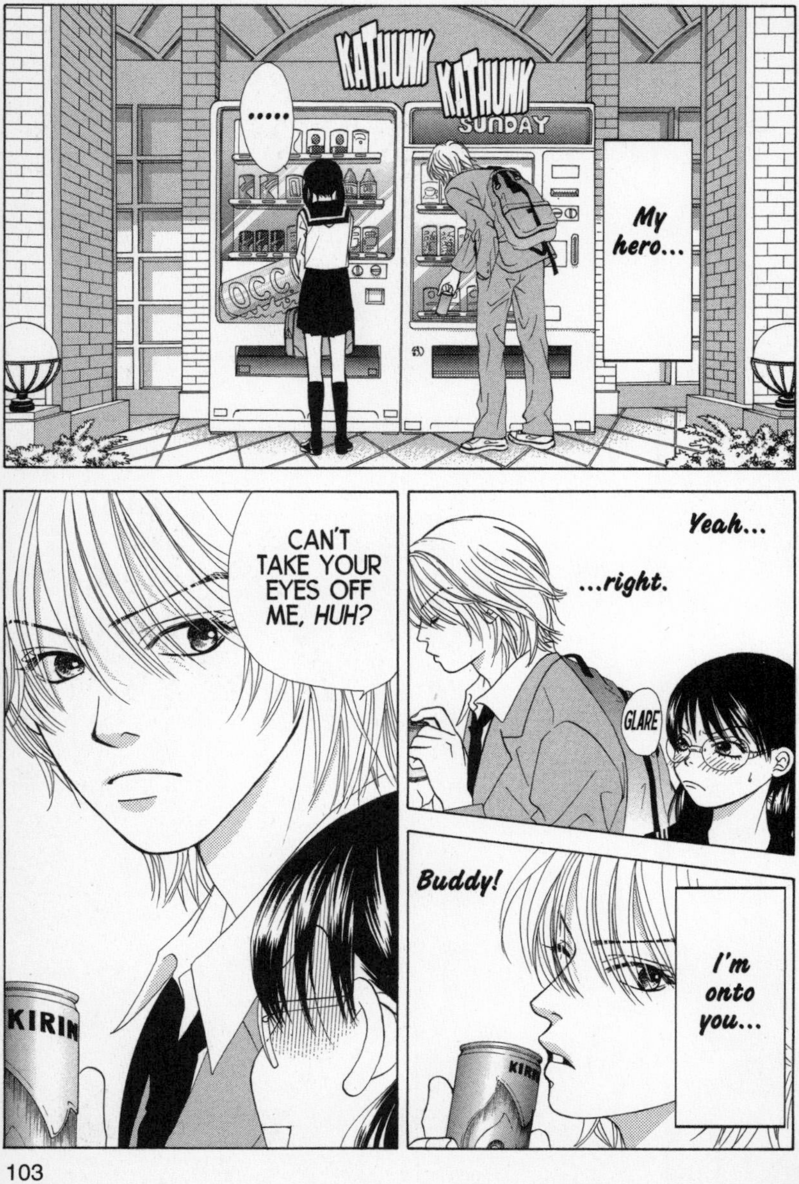
KATHUNK
KATHUNK
SUNDAY
.....
My hero...
Yeah...
...right.
GLARE
Buddy!
I'm onto you...
KIRIN
CAN'T TAKE YOUR EYES OFF ME, HUH?
KIRIN

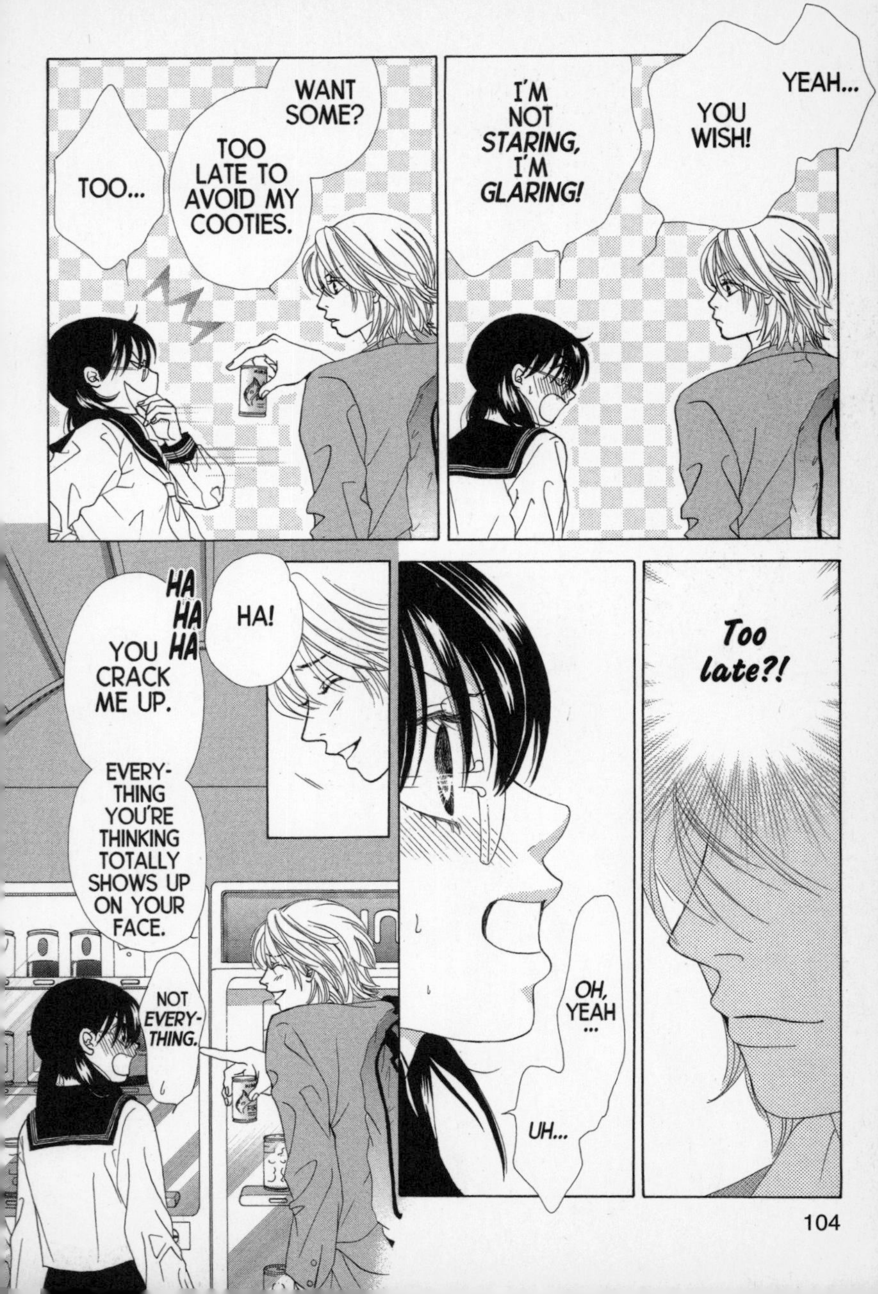
YEAH...
YOU WISH!
I'M NOT *STARING,* I'M *GLARING!*
WANT SOME?
TOO LATE TO AVOID MY COOTIES.
TOO...
Too late?!
OH, YEAH ...
UH...
HA!
HA HA HA
YOU CRACK ME UP.
EVERY-THING YOU'RE THINKING TOTALLY SHOWS UP ON YOUR FACE.
NOT *EVERY-THING.*

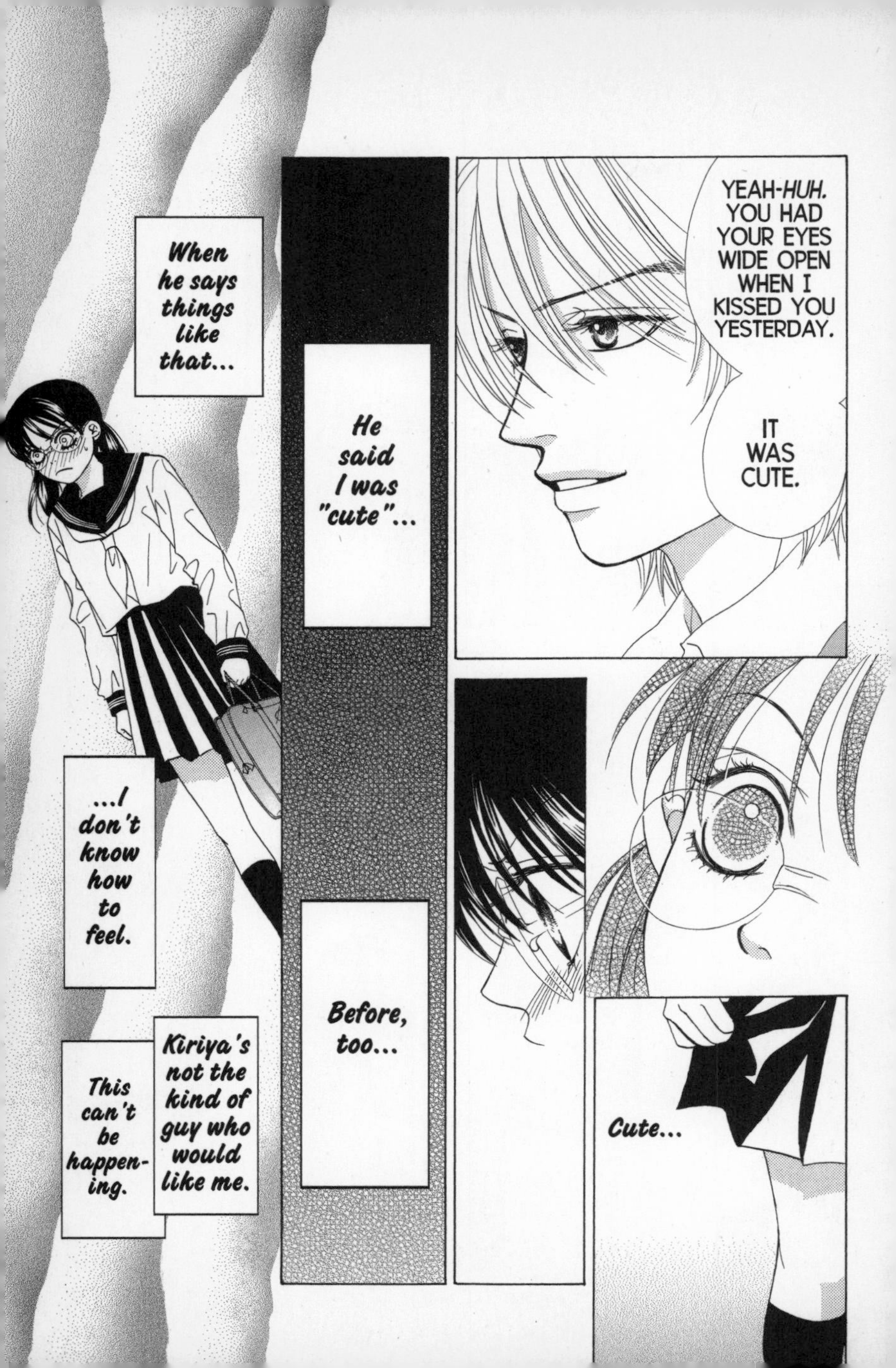
YEAH-*HUH*. YOU HAD YOUR EYES WIDE OPEN WHEN I KISSED YOU YESTERDAY.
IT WAS CUTE.
Cute...
He said I was "cute"...
Before, too...
When he says things like that...
...I don't know how to feel.
Kiriya's not the kind of guy who would like me.
This can't be happen-ing.

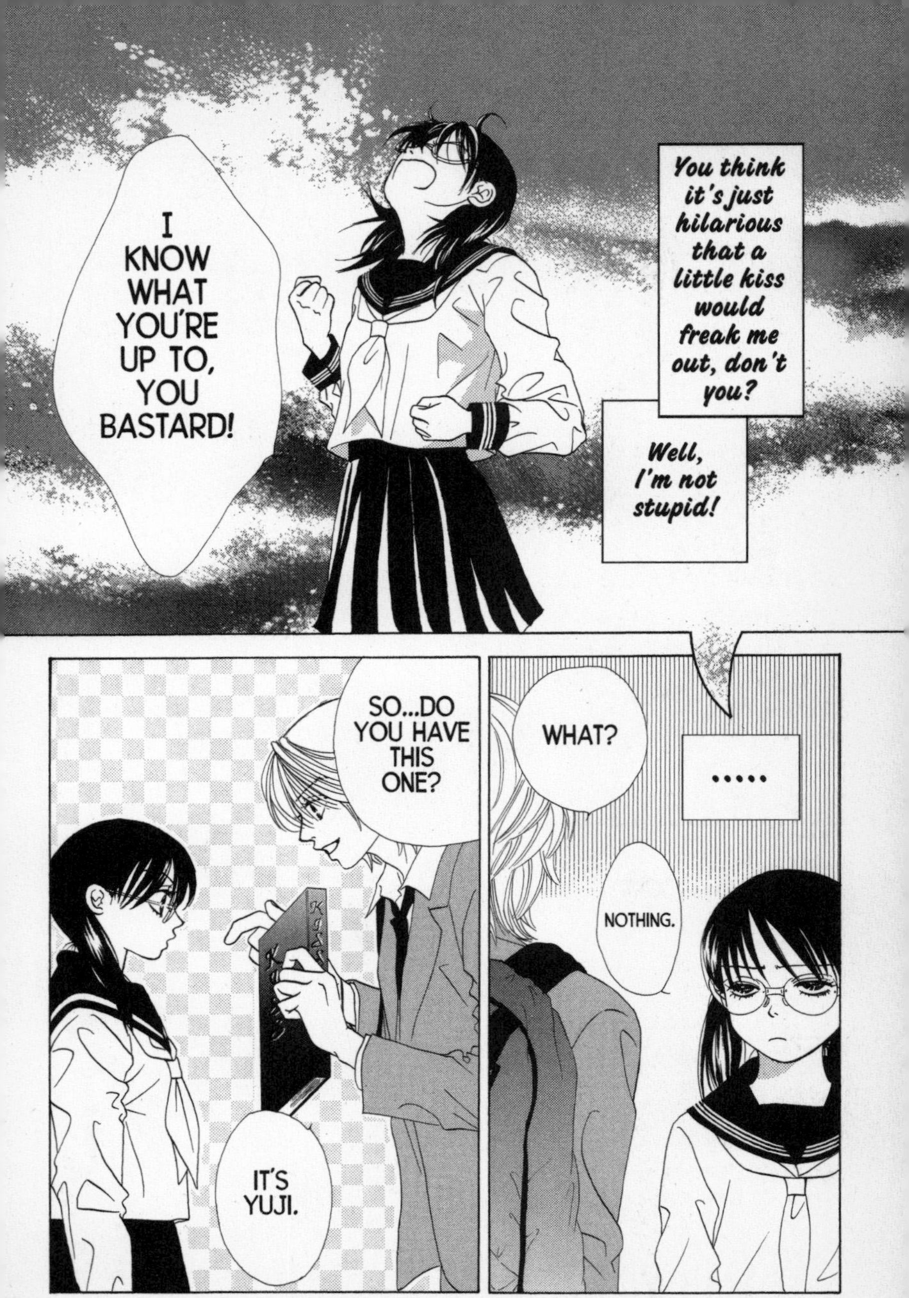
You think it's just hilarious that a little kiss would freak me out, don't you?
Well, I'm not stupid!
I KNOW WHAT YOU'RE UP TO, YOU BASTARD!
WHAT?
.....
NOTHING.
SO...DO YOU HAVE THIS ONE?
IT'S YUJI.

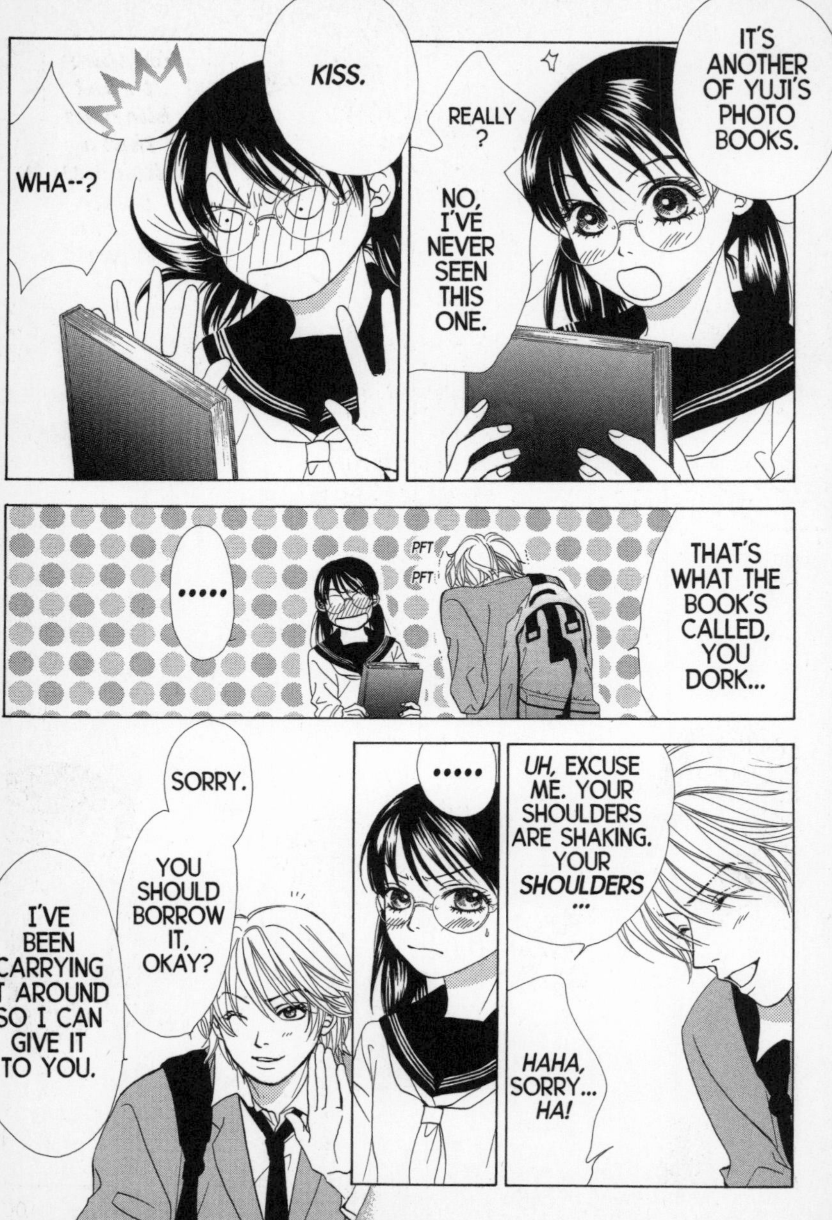
IT'S ANOTHER OF YUJI'S PHOTO BOOKS.
REALLY?
NO, I'VE NEVER SEEN THIS ONE.
KISS.
WHA--?
THAT'S WHAT THE BOOK'S CALLED, YOU DORK...
PFT
PFT
.....
UH, EXCUSE ME. YOUR SHOULDERS ARE SHAKING. YOUR *SHOULDERS*...
HAHA, SORRY... HA!
.....
SORRY.
YOU SHOULD BORROW IT, OKAY?
I'VE BEEN CARRYING IT AROUND SO I CAN GIVE IT TO YOU.

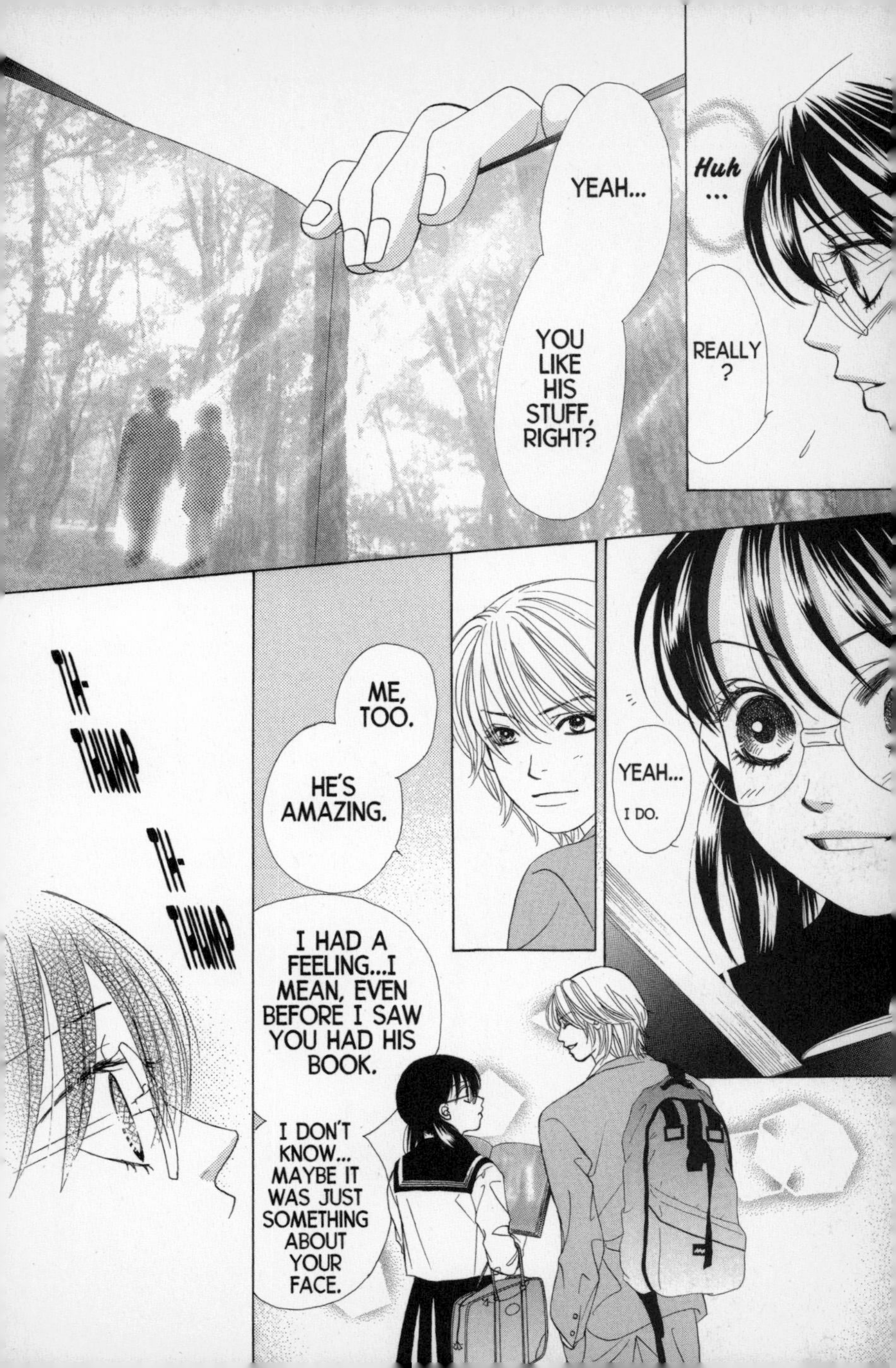

Huh...
REALLY?
YEAH...
YOU LIKE HIS STUFF, RIGHT?
YEAH...
I DO.
ME, TOO.
HE'S AMAZING.
I HAD A FEELING...I MEAN, EVEN BEFORE I SAW YOU HAD HIS BOOK.
I DON'T KNOW... MAYBE IT WAS JUST SOMETHING ABOUT YOUR FACE.
TH-THUMP
TH-THUMP

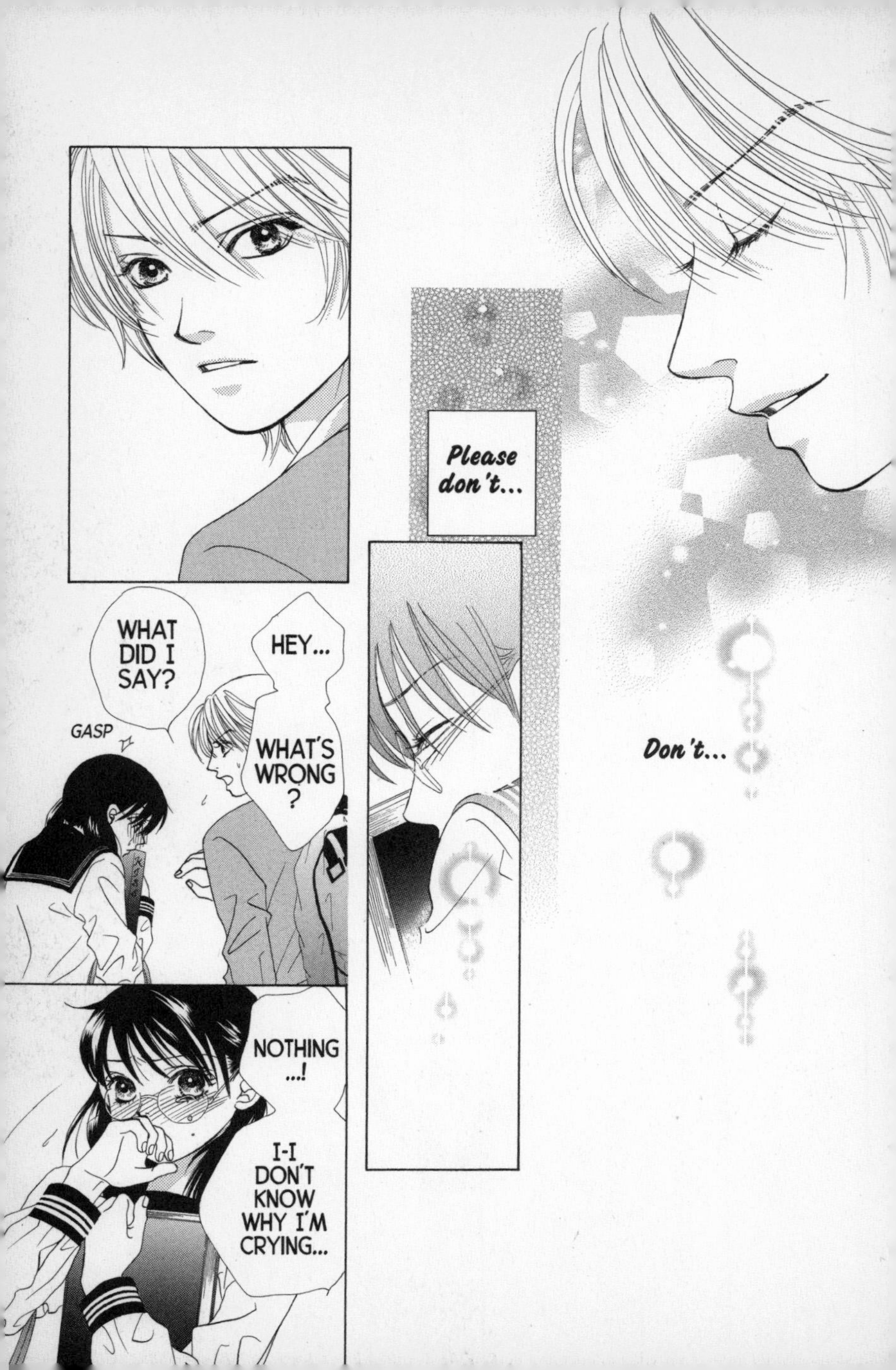
Please don't...
Don't...
HEY...
WHAT'S WRONG?
WHAT DID I SAY?
GASP
NOTHING...!
I-I DON'T KNOW WHY I'M CRYING...

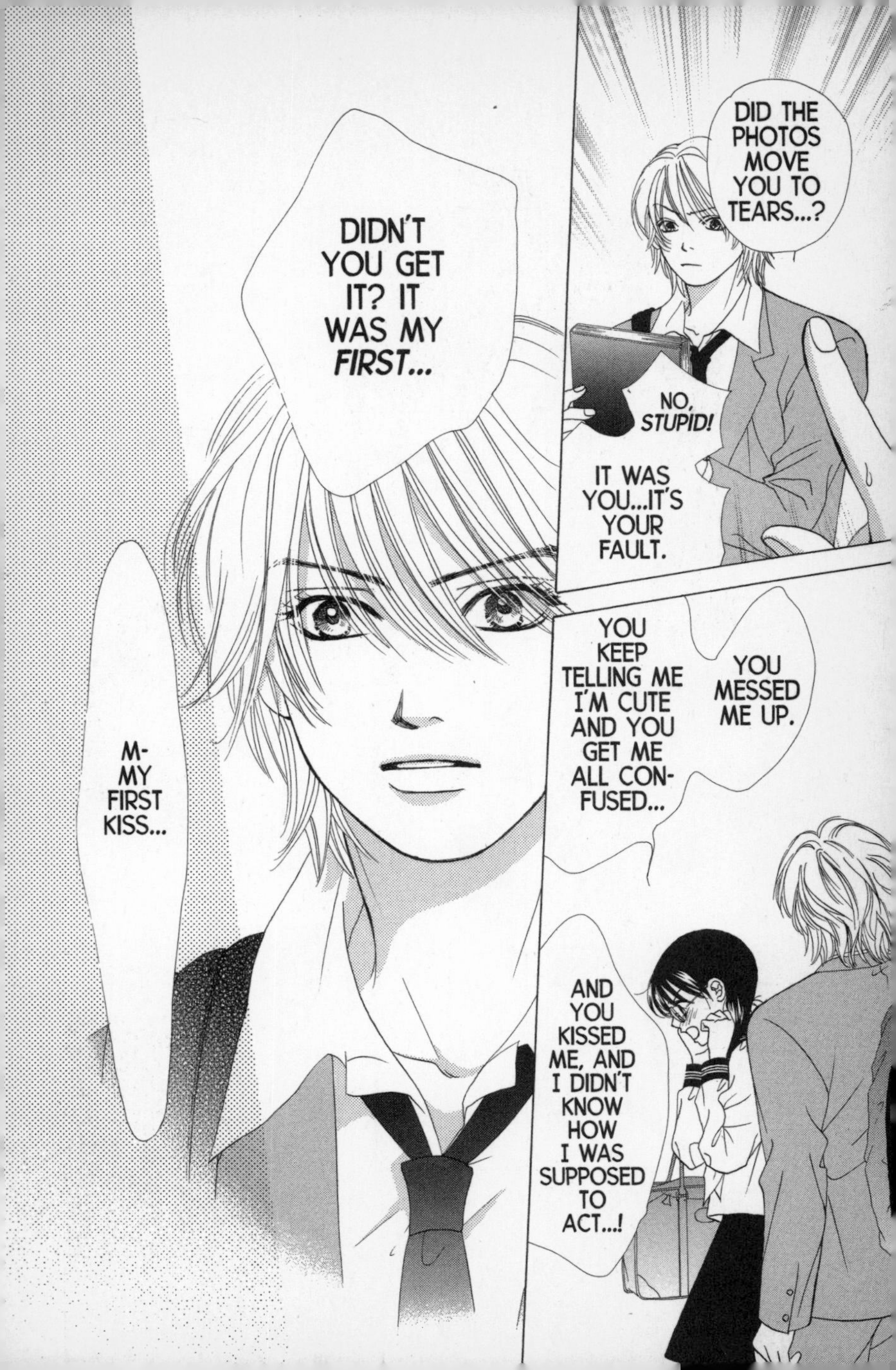
DID THE PHOTOS MOVE YOU TO TEARS...?
NO, *STUPID!*
IT WAS YOU...IT'S YOUR FAULT.
YOU MESSED ME UP.
YOU KEEP TELLING ME I'M CUTE AND YOU GET ME ALL CON-FUSED...
AND YOU KISSED ME, AND I DIDN'T KNOW HOW I WAS SUPPOSED TO ACT...!
DIDN'T YOU GET IT? IT WAS MY *FIRST*...
M-MY FIRST KISS...

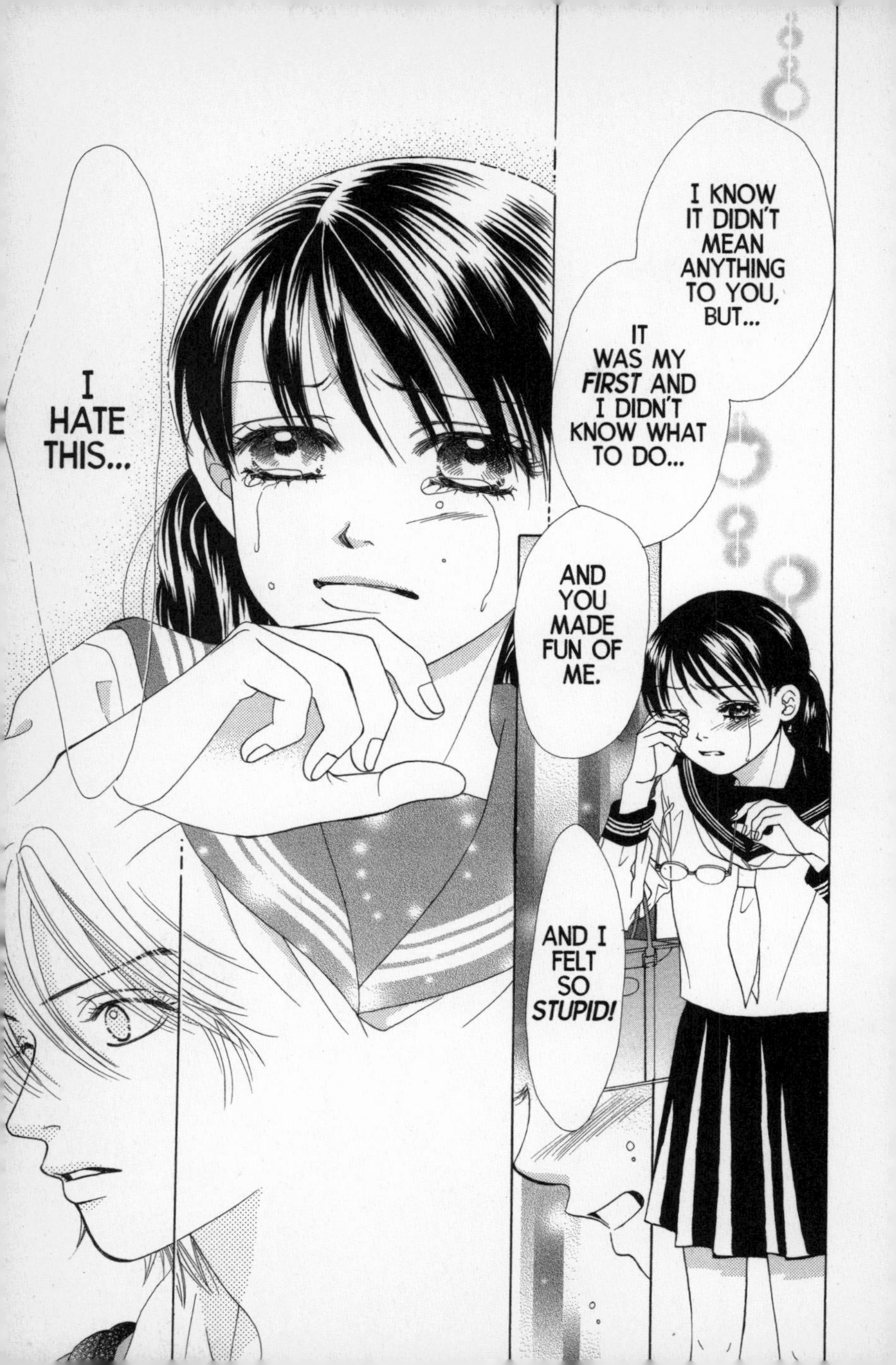
I KNOW IT DIDN'T MEAN ANYTHING TO YOU, BUT...
IT WAS MY *FIRST* AND I DIDN'T KNOW WHAT TO DO...
AND YOU MADE FUN OF ME.
AND I FELT SO *STUPID!*
I HATE THIS...

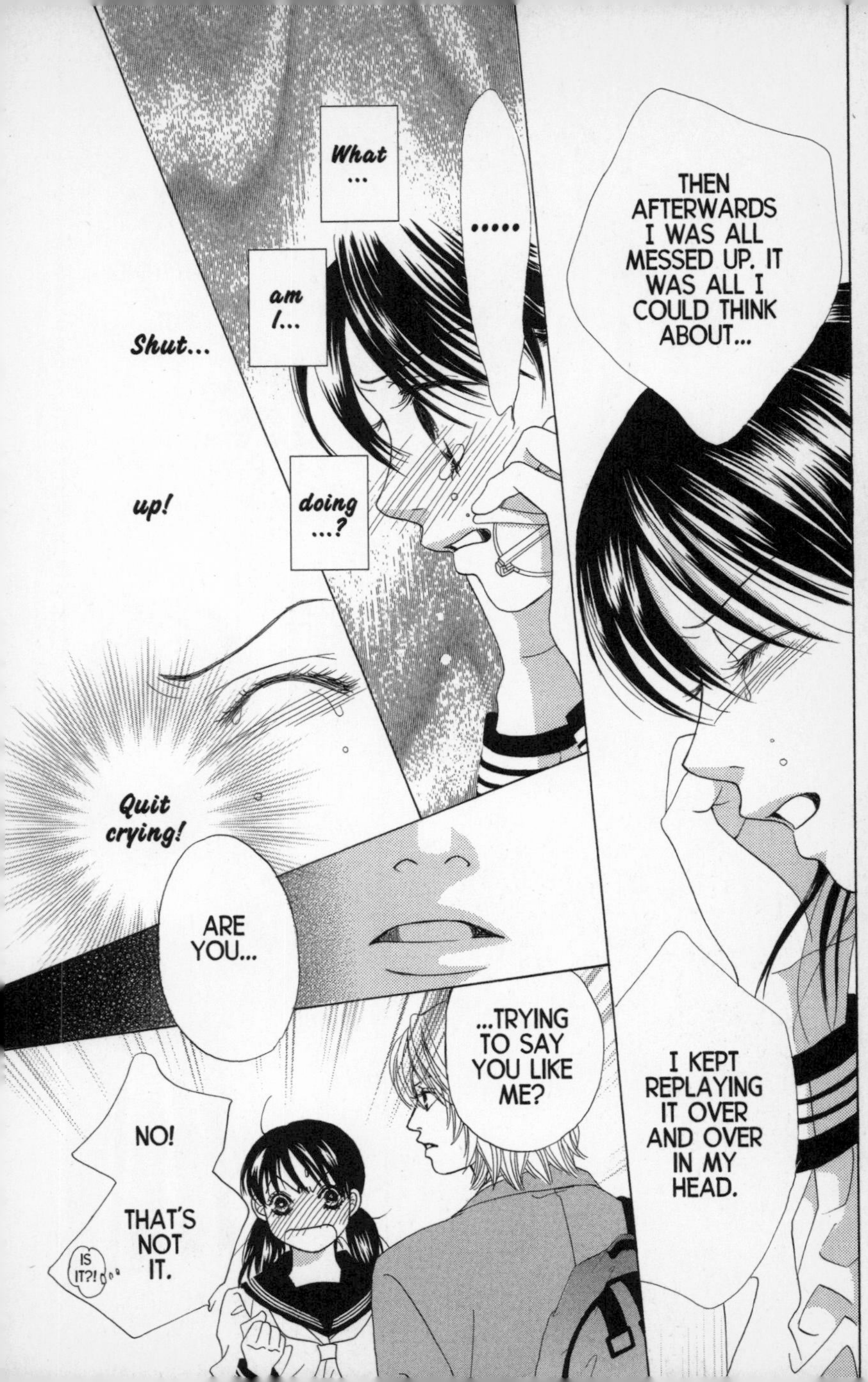
THEN AFTERWARDS I WAS ALL MESSED UP. IT WAS ALL I COULD THINK ABOUT...
I KEPT REPLAYING IT OVER AND OVER IN MY HEAD.
......
What...
am I...
doing...?
Shut...
up!
Quit crying!
ARE YOU...
...TRYING TO SAY YOU LIKE ME?
NO!
THAT'S NOT IT.
IS IT?!

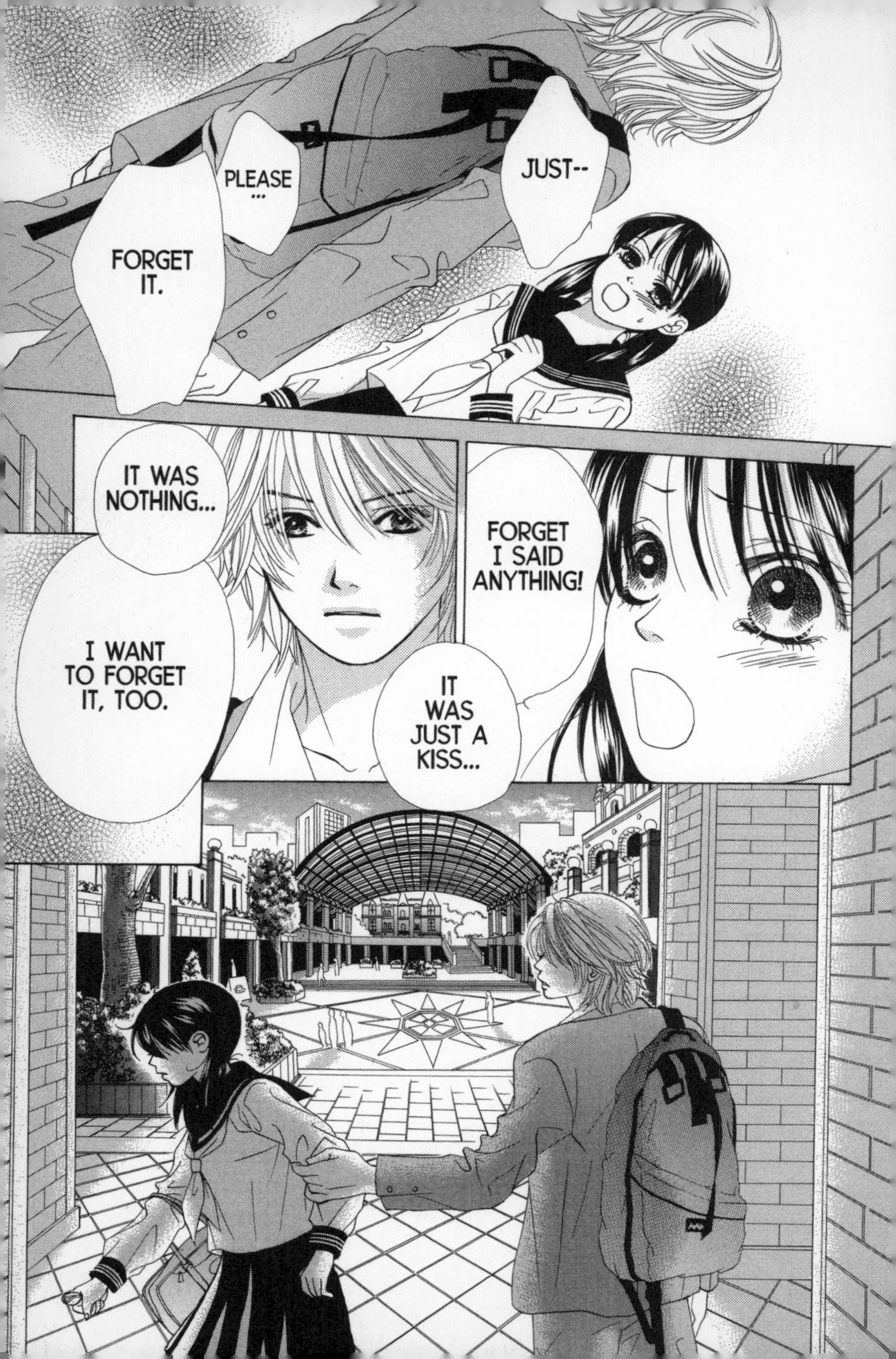
JUST--
PLEASE ...
FORGET IT.
FORGET I SAID ANYTHING!
IT WAS JUST A KISS...
IT WAS NOTHING...
I WANT TO FORGET IT, TOO.

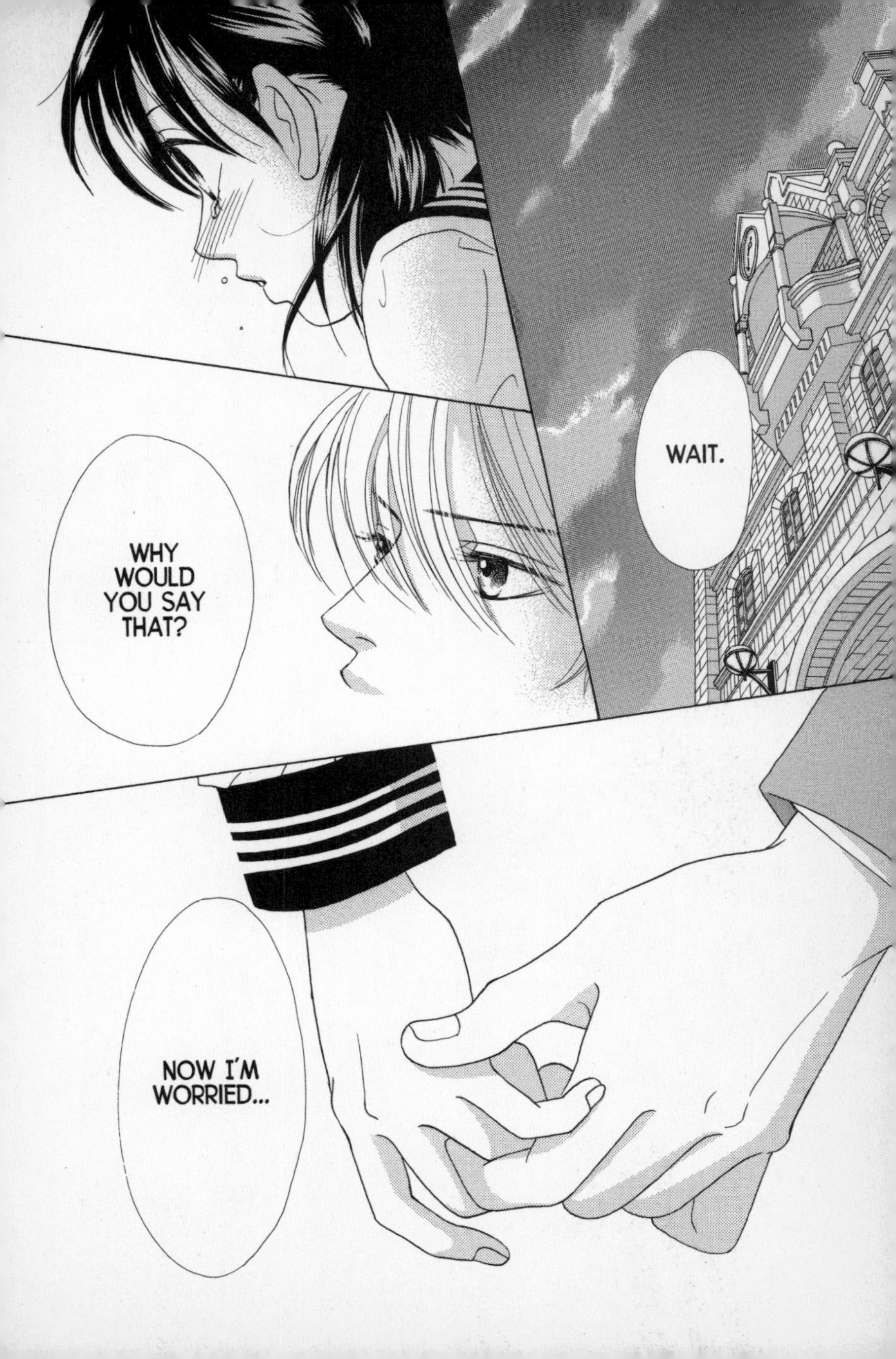
WAIT.
WHY WOULD YOU SAY THAT?
NOW I'M WORRIED...

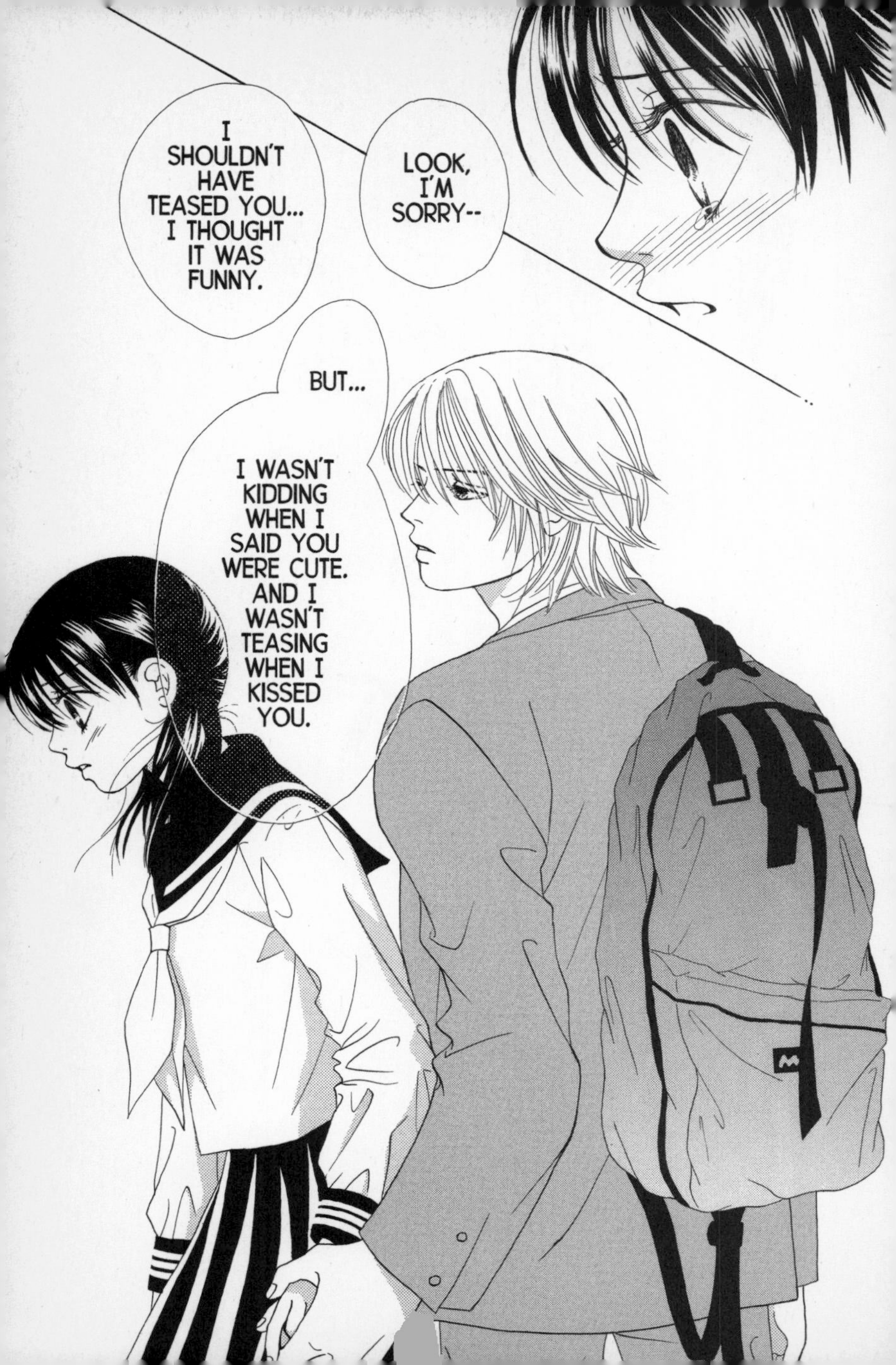
LOOK, I'M SORRY--
I SHOULDN'T HAVE TEASED YOU... I THOUGHT IT WAS FUNNY.
BUT...
I WASN'T KIDDING WHEN I SAID YOU WERE CUTE. AND I WASN'T TEASING WHEN I KISSED YOU.

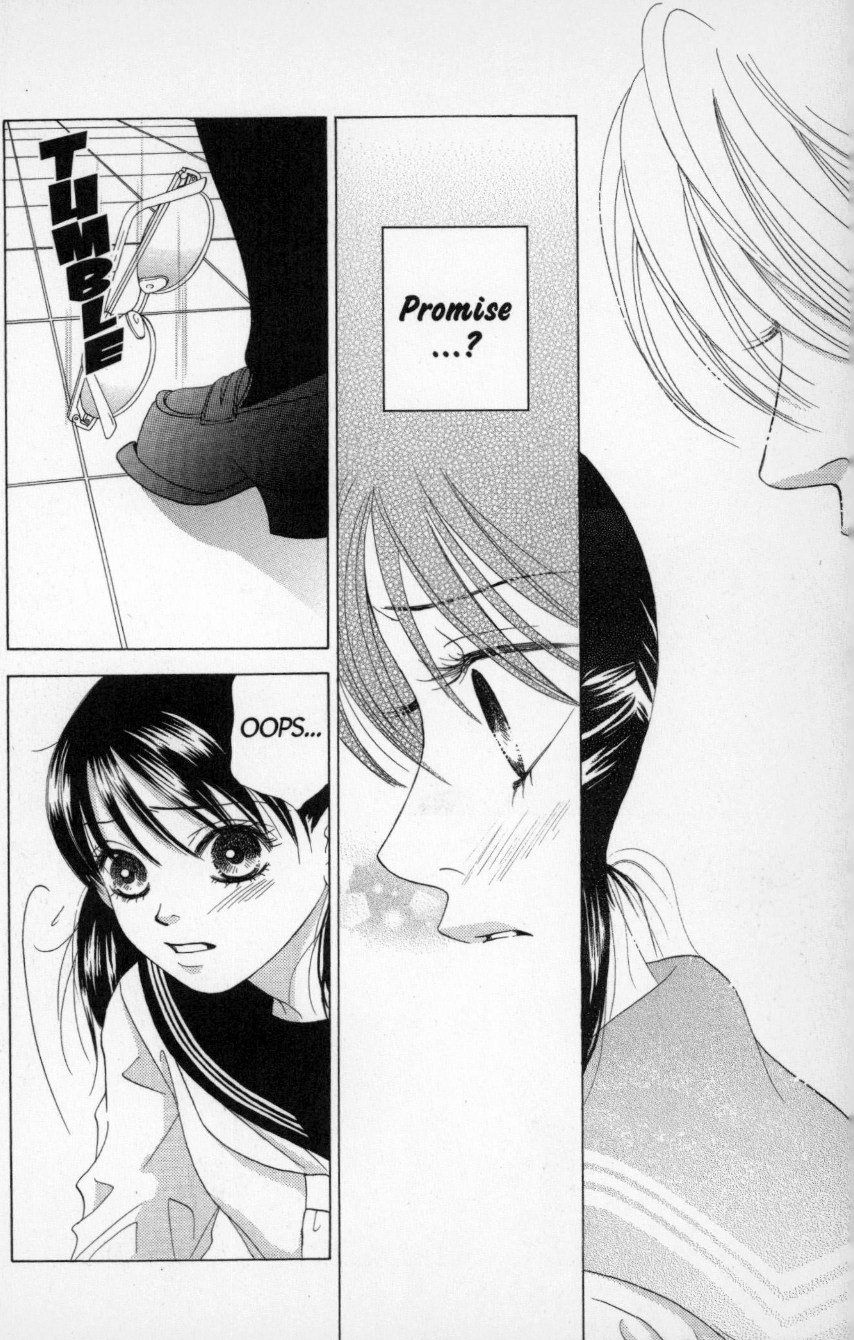
Promise ...?
TUMBLE
OOPS...

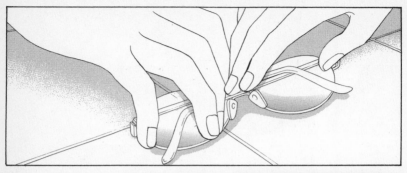

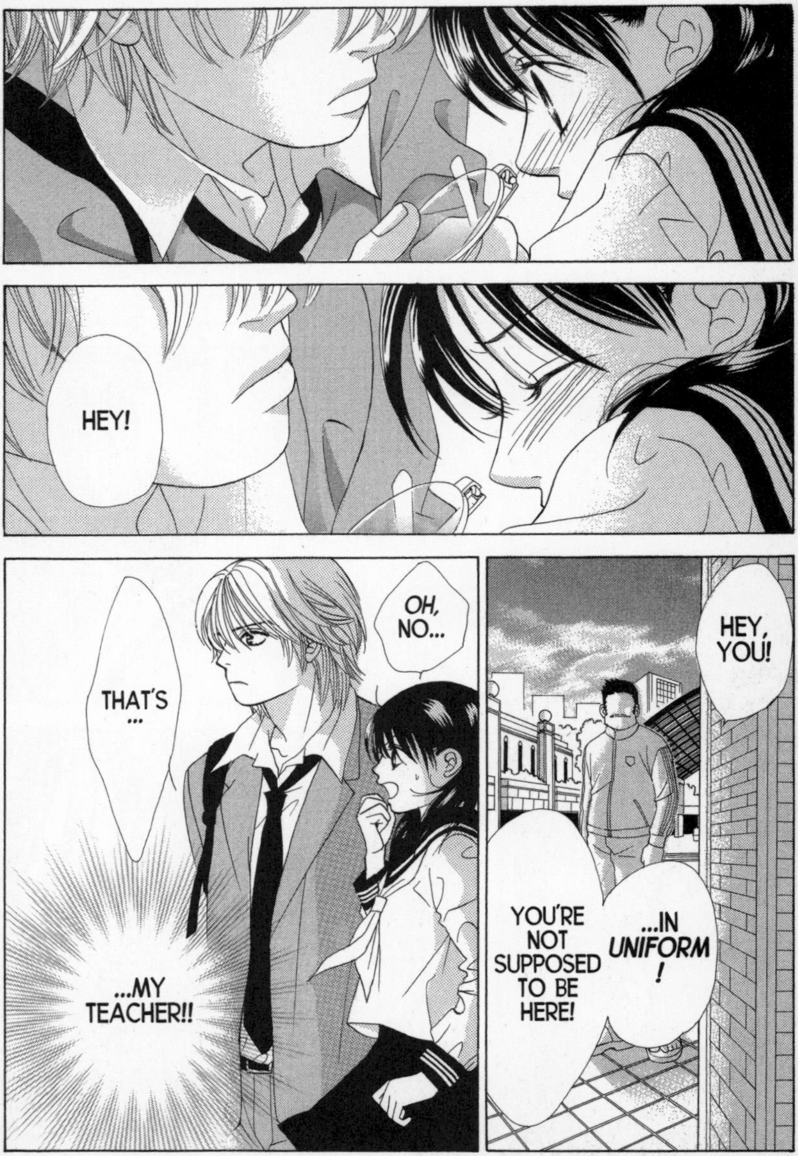
HEY!
HEY, YOU!
...IN *UNIFORM*!
YOU'RE NOT SUPPOSED TO BE HERE!
OH, NO...
THAT'S ...
...MY TEACHER!!

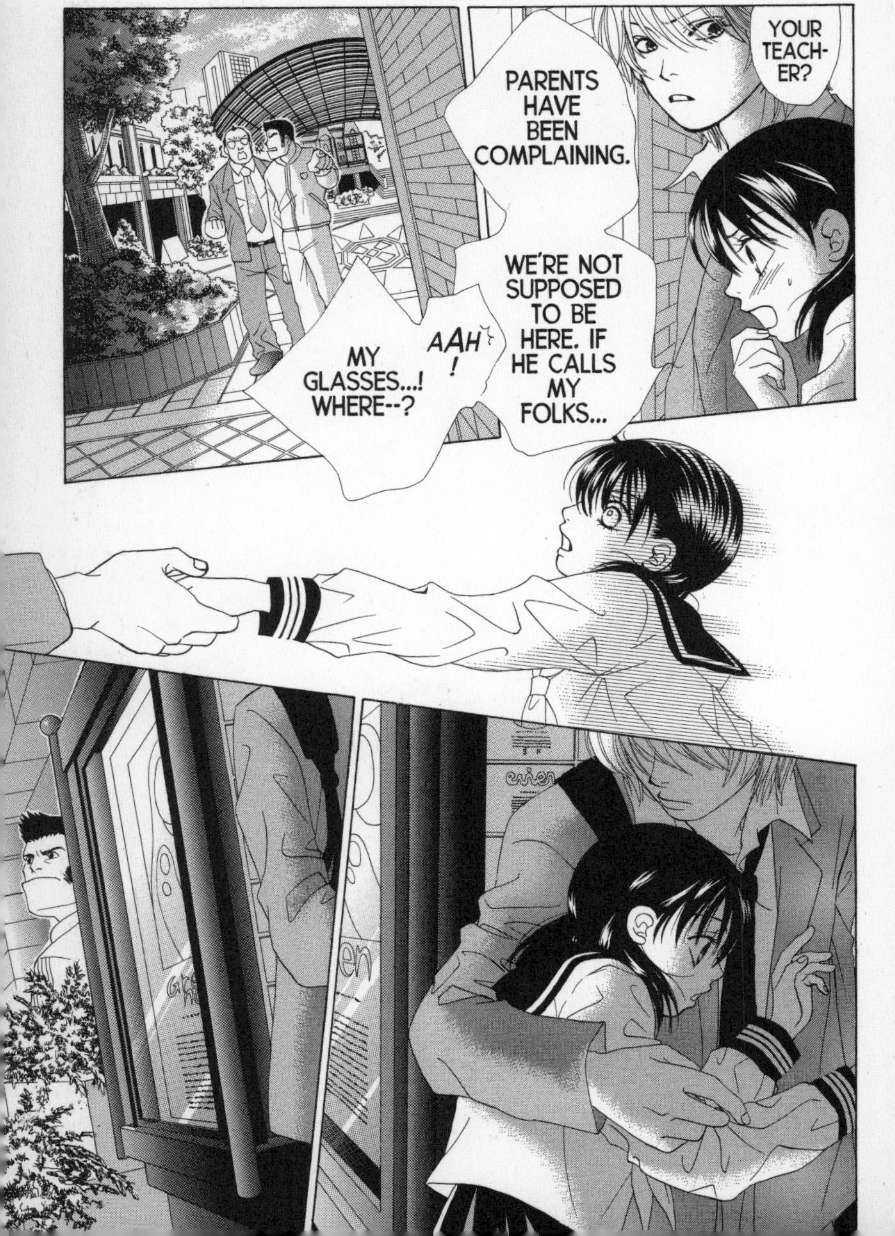
YOUR TEACHER?
PARENTS HAVE BEEN COMPLAINING.
WE'RE NOT SUPPOSED TO BE HERE. IF HE CALLS MY FOLKS...
AAH!
MY GLASSES...! WHERE--?

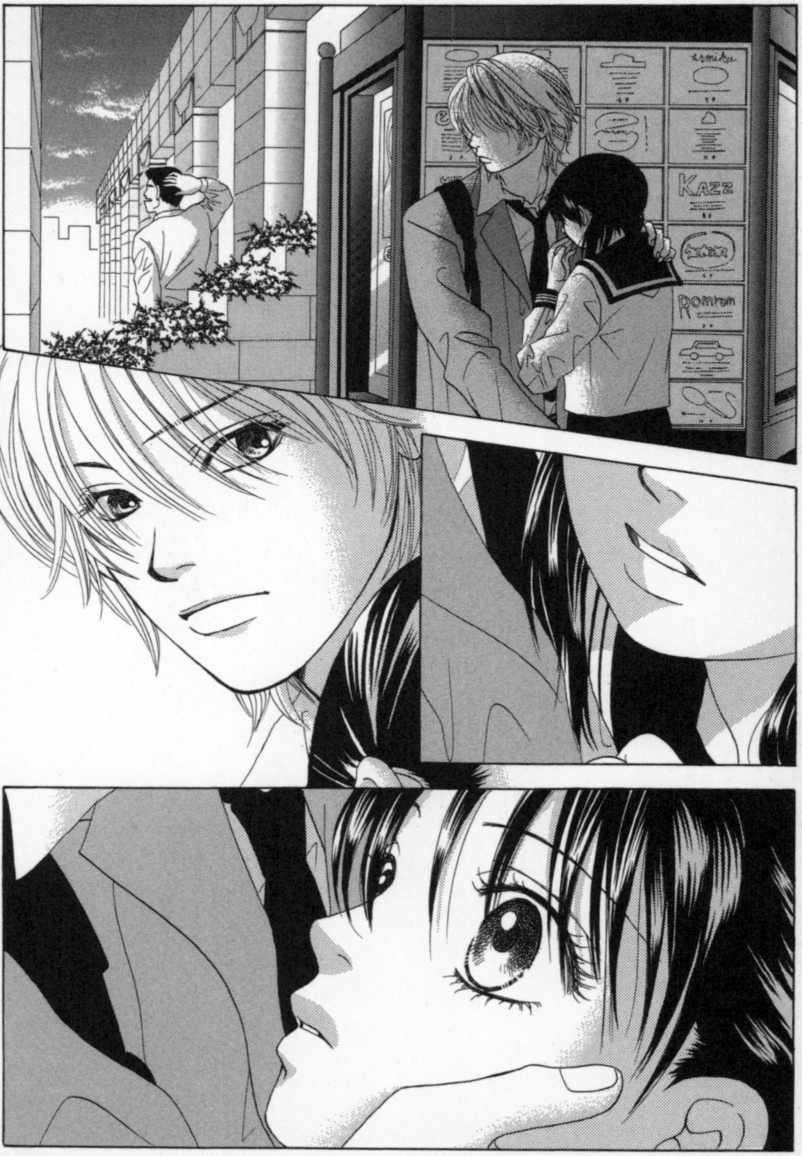
Kazz

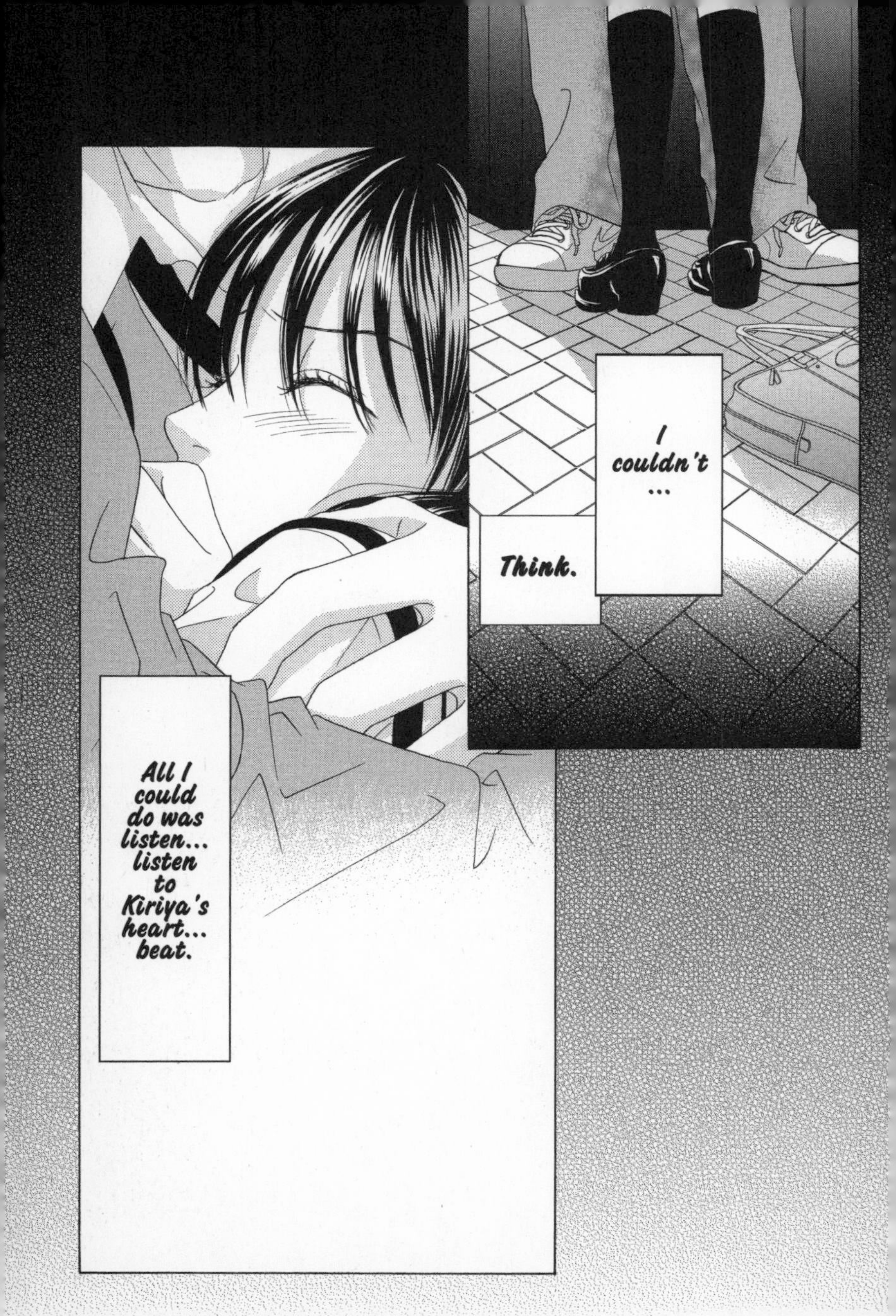
I couldn't ...
Think.
All I could do was listen... listen to Kiriya's heart... beat.

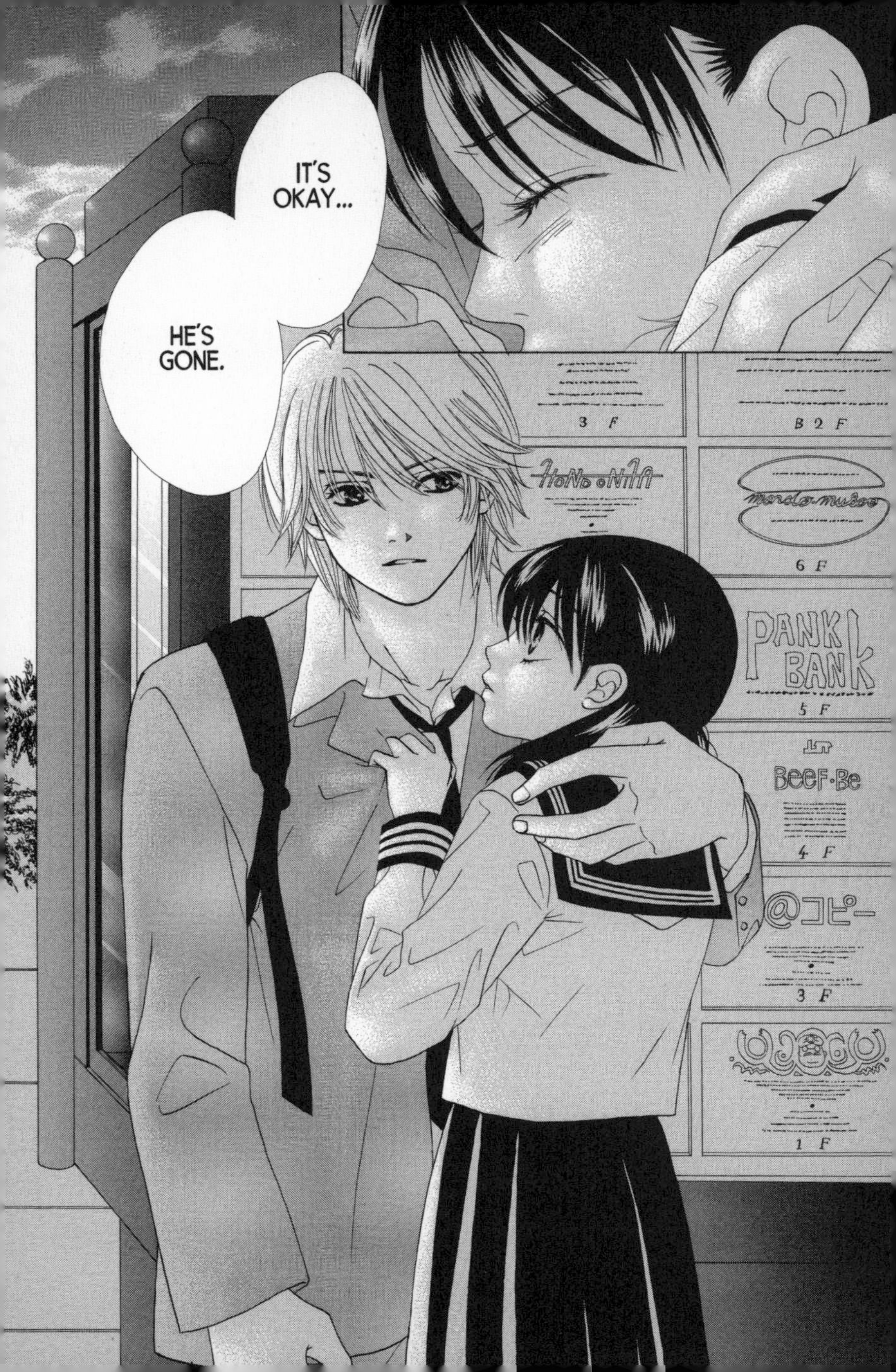
IT'S OKAY...
HE'S GONE.
3 F
B 2 F
6 F
PANK BANK
5 F
Beef・Be
4 F
@コピー
3 F
1 F

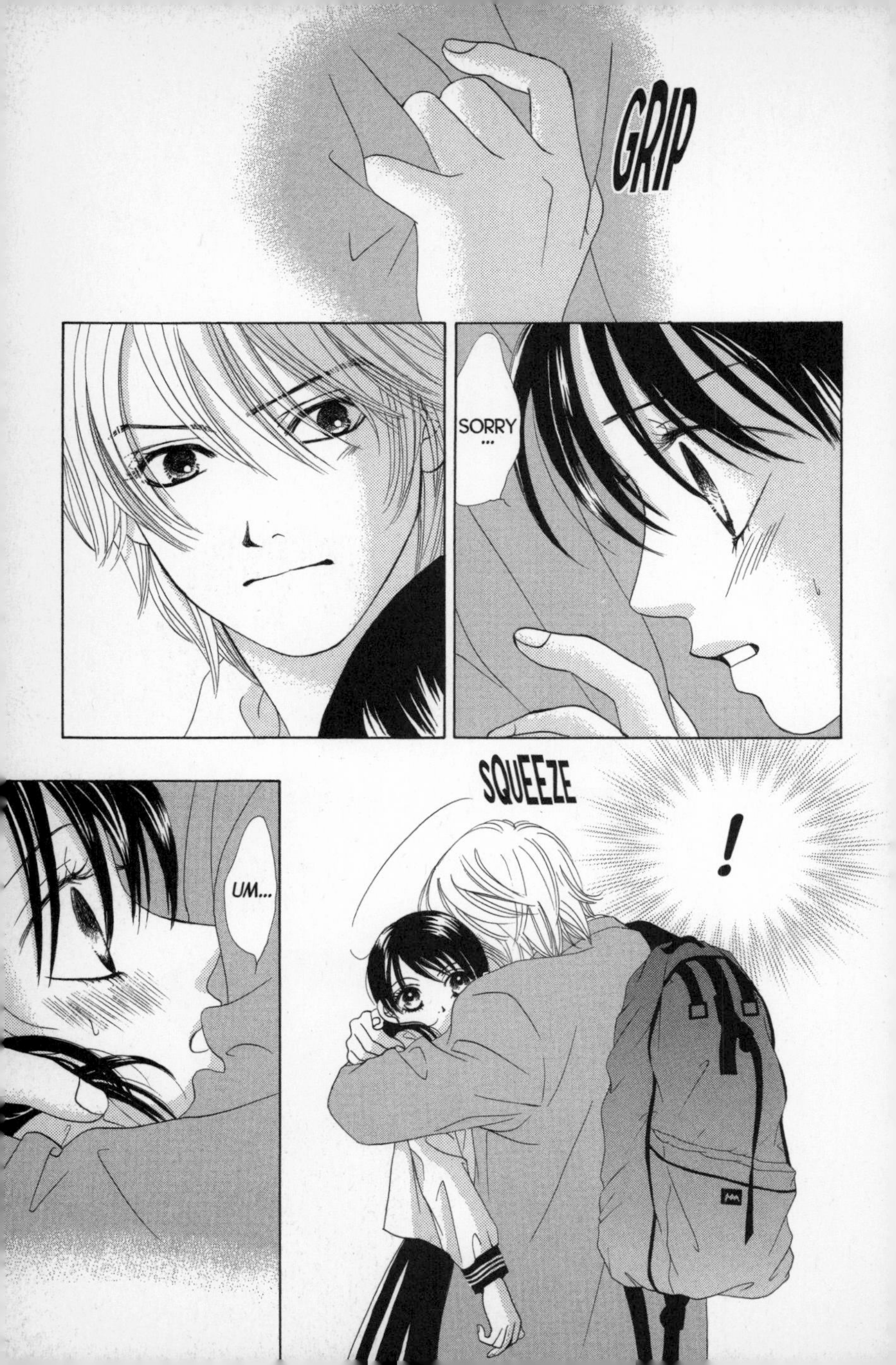
GRIP
SORRY...
SQUEEZE
!
UM...

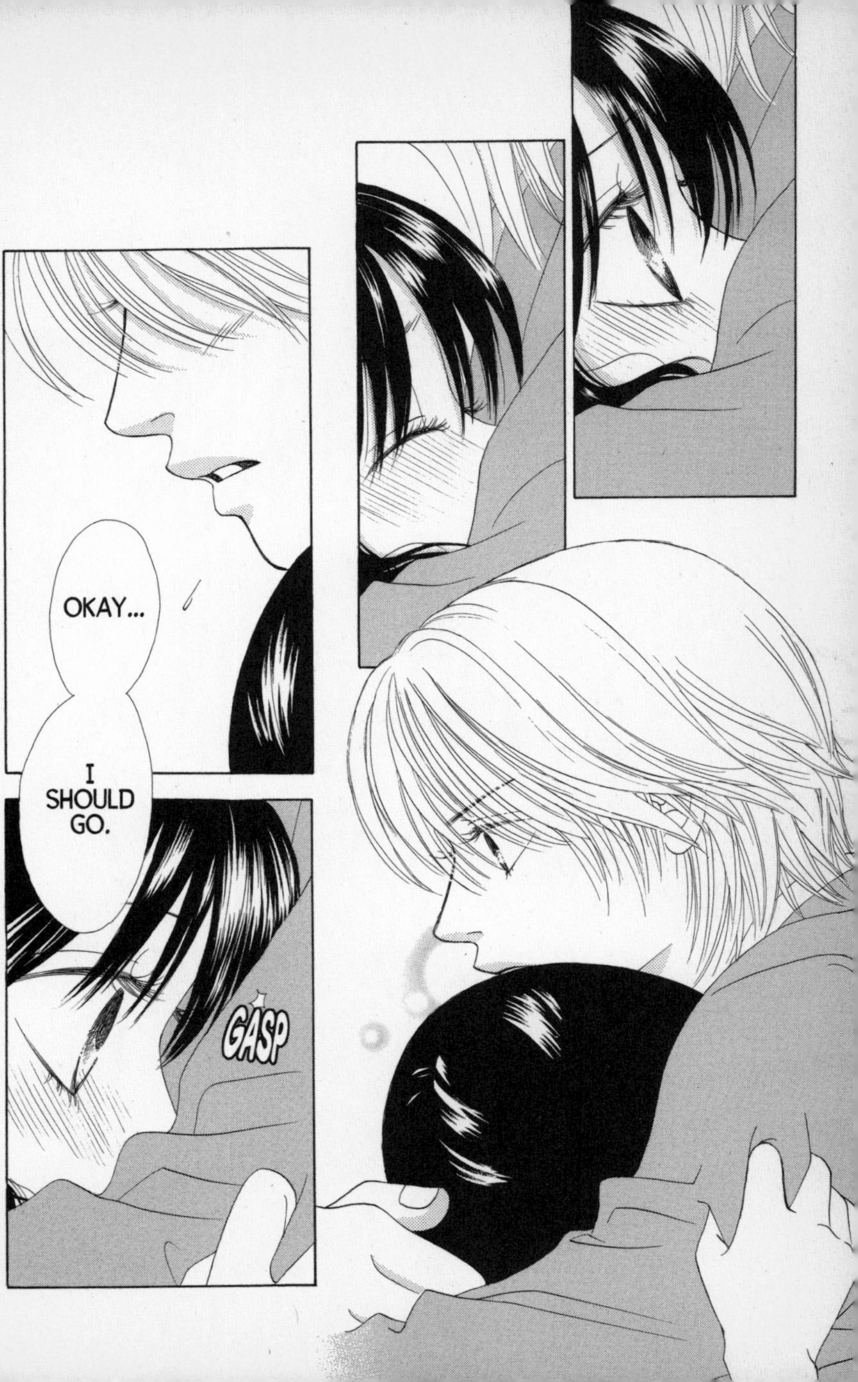
OKAY...
I SHOULD GO.
GASP

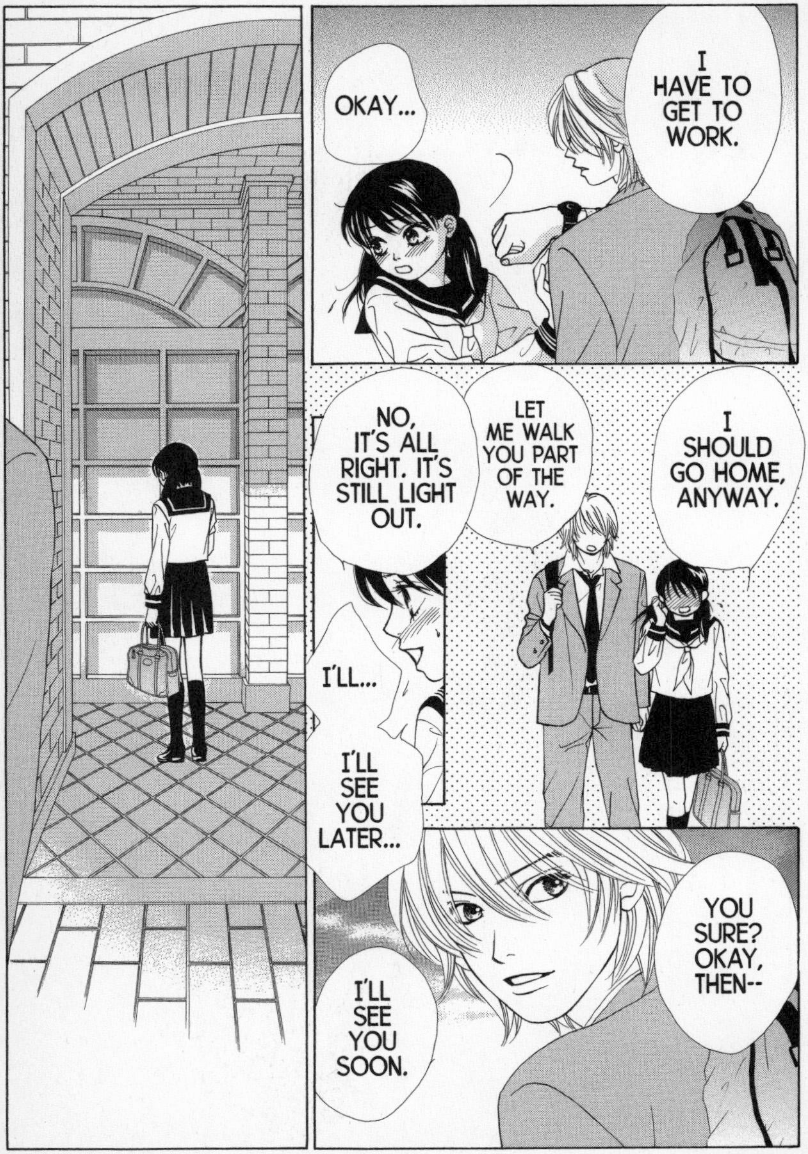
I HAVE TO GET TO WORK.
OKAY...
I SHOULD GO HOME, ANYWAY.
LET ME WALK YOU PART OF THE WAY.
NO, IT'S ALL RIGHT. IT'S STILL LIGHT OUT.
I'LL...
I'LL SEE YOU LATER...
YOU SURE? OKAY, THEN--
I'LL SEE YOU SOON.

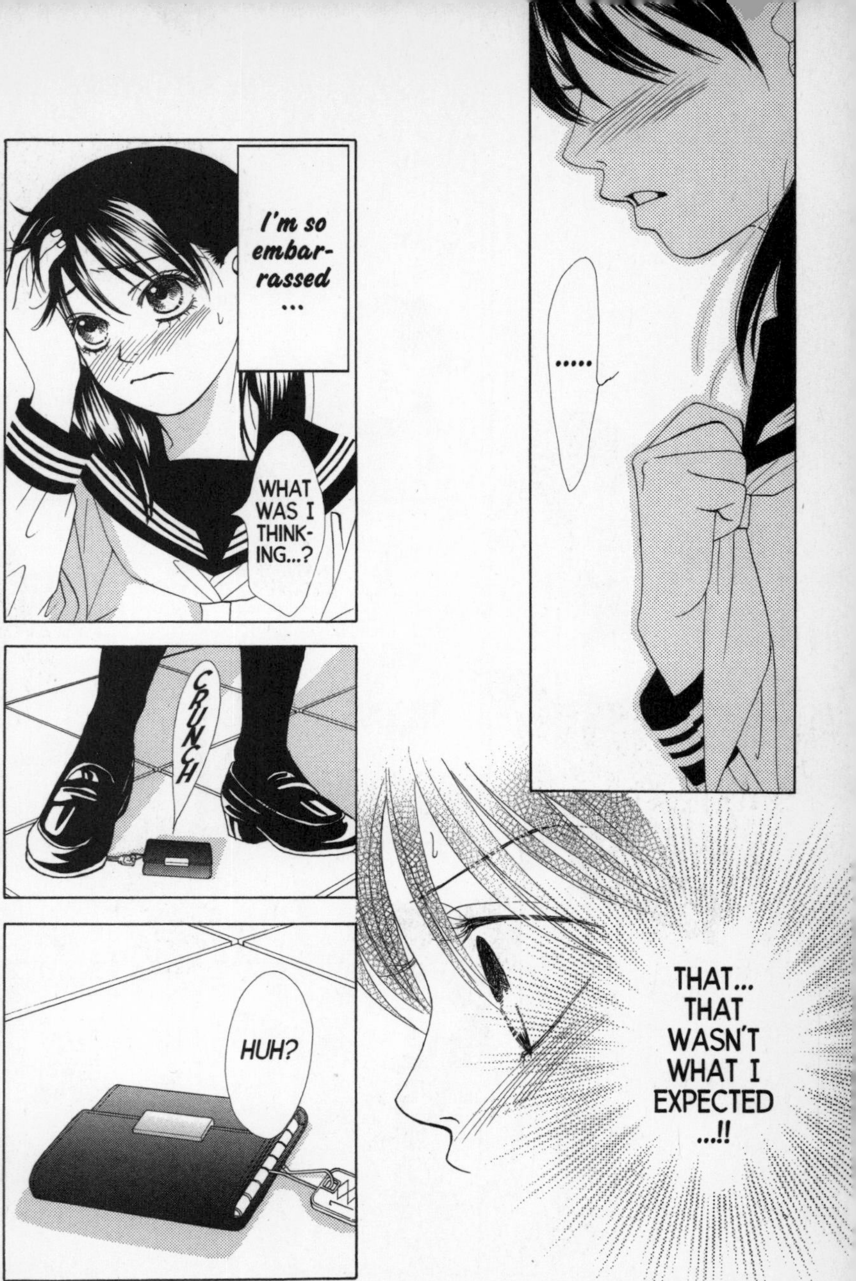
.....
THAT... THAT WASN'T WHAT I EXPECTED ...!!
I'm so embarrassed ...
WHAT WAS I THINKING...?
CRUNCH
HUH?

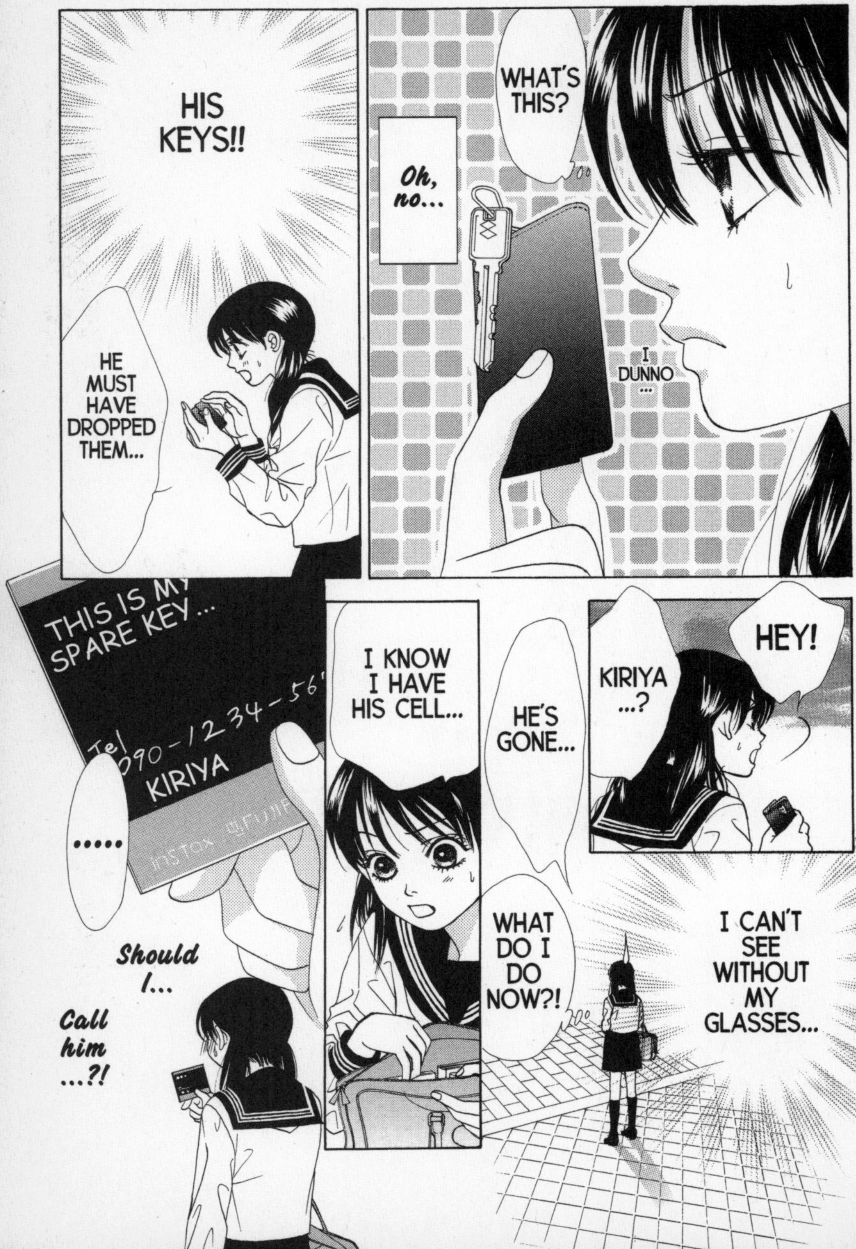
WHAT'S THIS?
I DUNNO ...
Oh, no...
HIS KEYS!!
HE MUST HAVE DROPPED THEM...
HEY!
KIRIYA ...?
HE'S GONE...
I KNOW I HAVE HIS CELL...
WHAT DO I DO NOW?!
I CAN'T SEE WITHOUT MY GLASSES...
THIS IS MY SPARE KEY...
Tel 090-1234-56
KIRIYA
......
Should I...
Call him ...?!

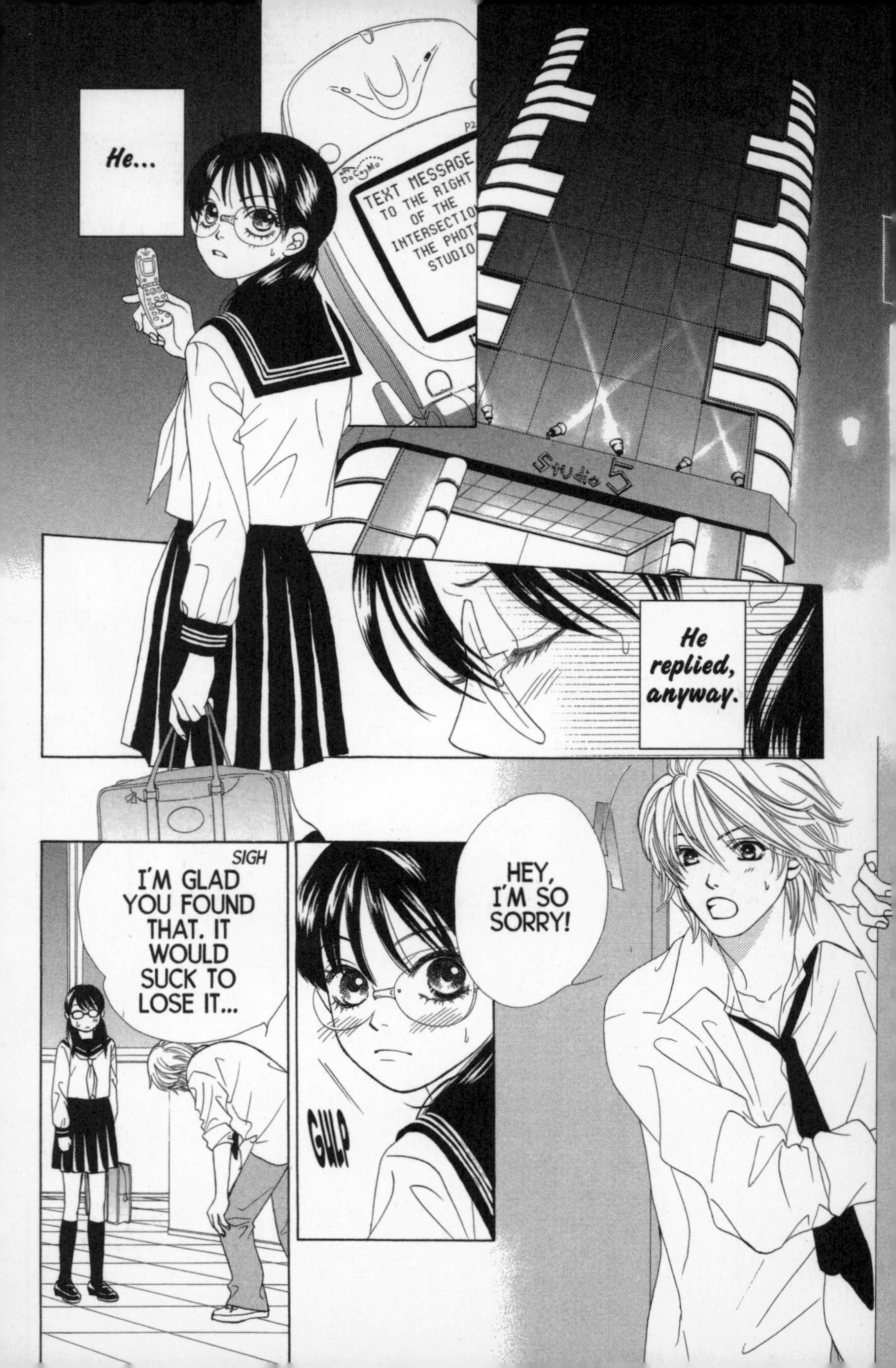
Studio 5
DoCoMo
TEXT MESSAGE TO THE RIGHT OF THE INTERSECTIO THE PHOTO STUDIO
He...
He replied, anyway.
HEY, I'M SO SORRY!
GULP
SIGH
I'M GLAD YOU FOUND THAT. IT WOULD SUCK TO LOSE IT...

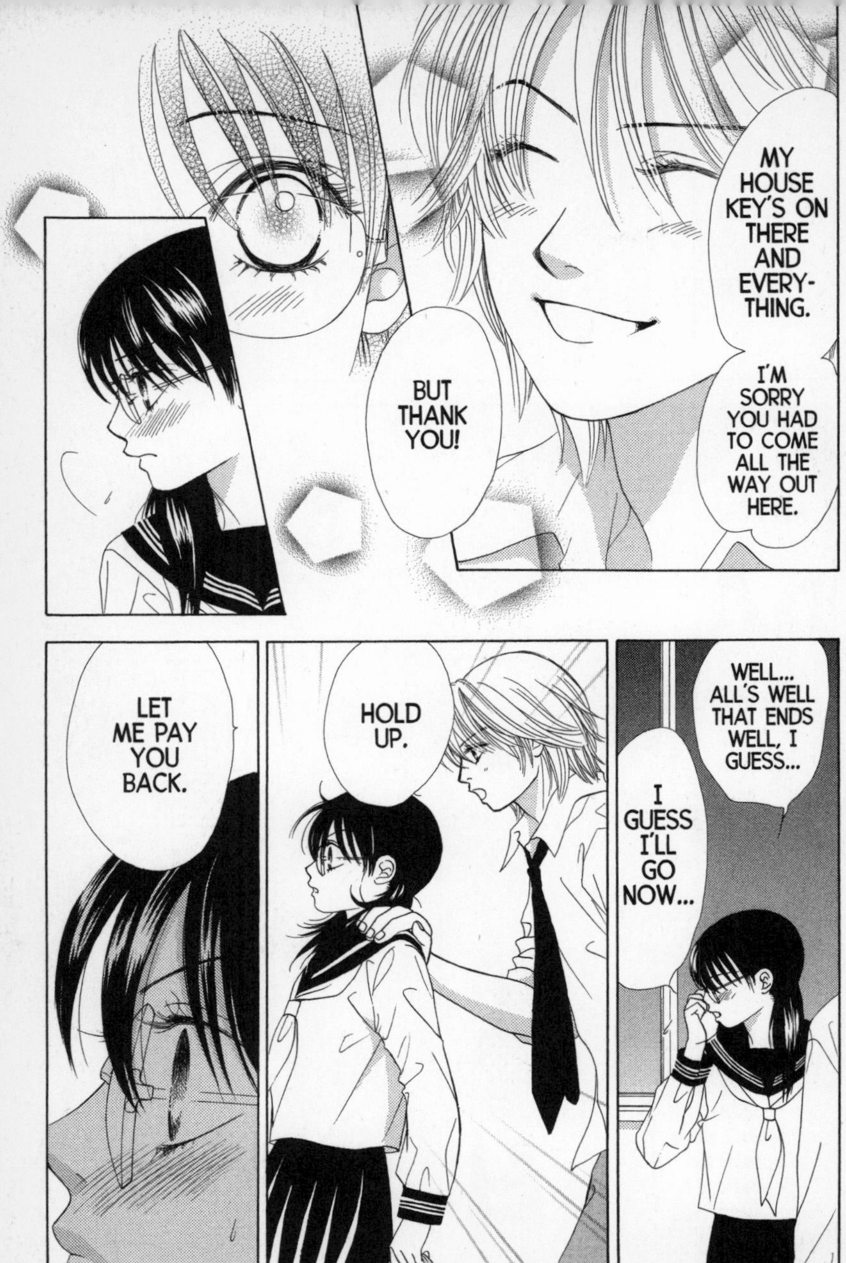
MY HOUSE KEY'S ON THERE AND EVERY-THING.
I'M SORRY YOU HAD TO COME ALL THE WAY OUT HERE.
BUT THANK YOU!
WELL... ALL'S WELL THAT ENDS WELL, I GUESS...
I GUESS I'LL GO NOW...
HOLD UP.
LET ME PAY YOU BACK.

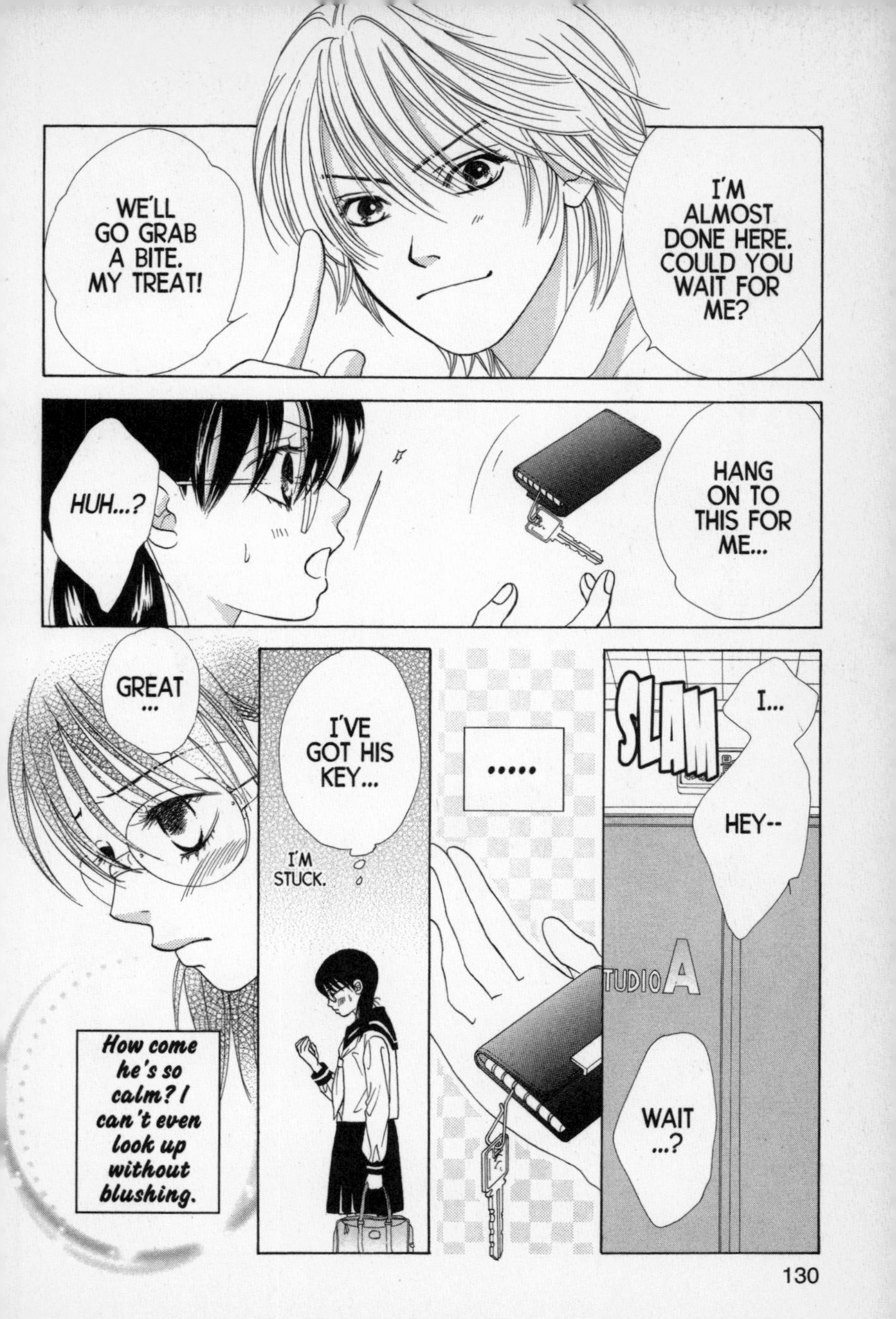
I'M ALMOST DONE HERE. COULD YOU WAIT FOR ME?
WE'LL GO GRAB A BITE. MY TREAT!
HANG ON TO THIS FOR ME...
HUH...?
SLAM
I...
HEY--
WAIT ...?
.....
I'VE GOT HIS KEY...
I'M STUCK.
GREAT ...
How come he's so calm? I can't even look up without blushing.

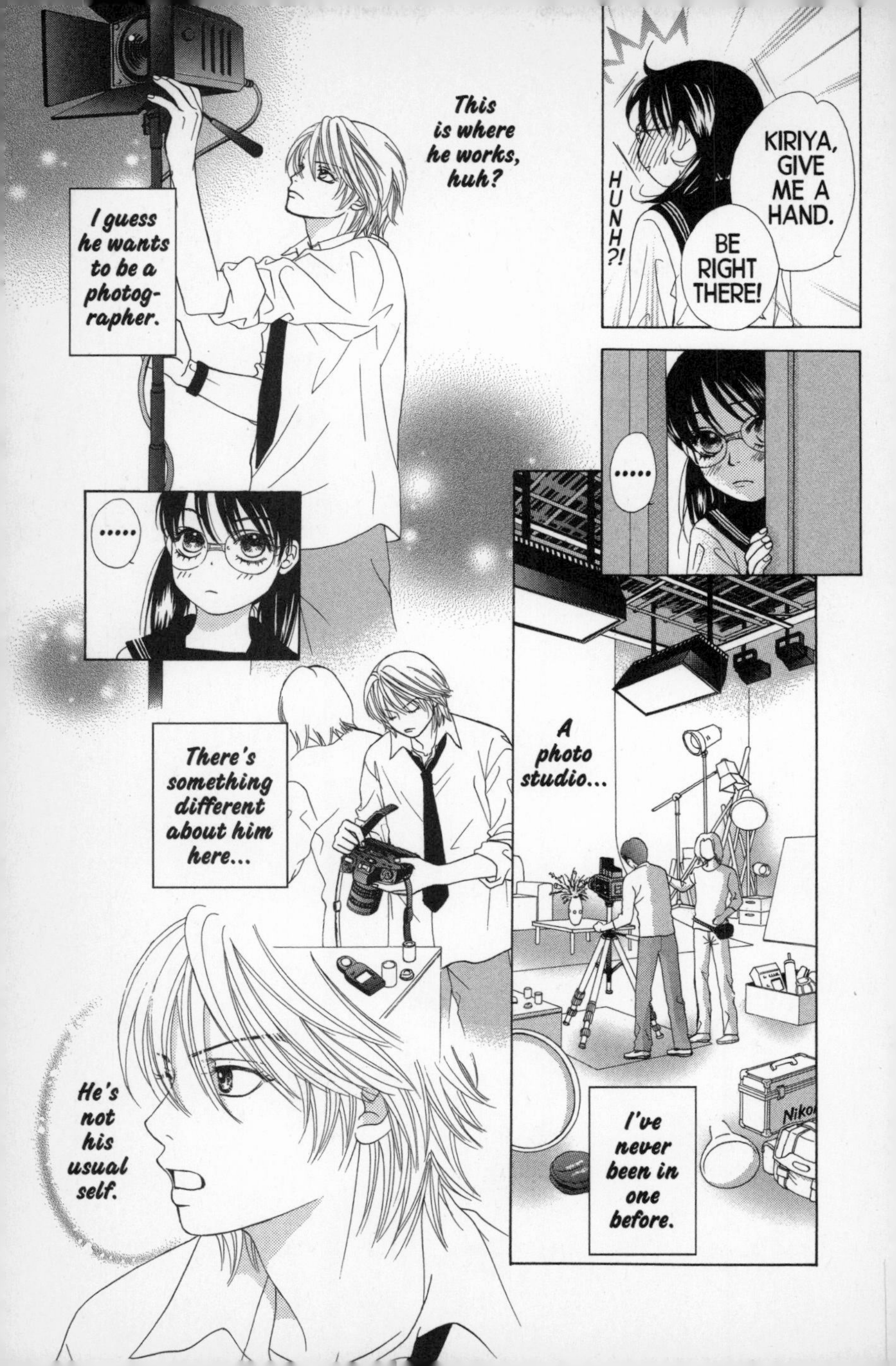
KIRIYA, GIVE ME A HAND.
BE RIGHT THERE!
HUNH?!
.....
A photo studio...
I've never been in one before.
This is where he works, huh?
I guess he wants to be a photographer.
.....
There's something different about him here...
He's not his usual self.

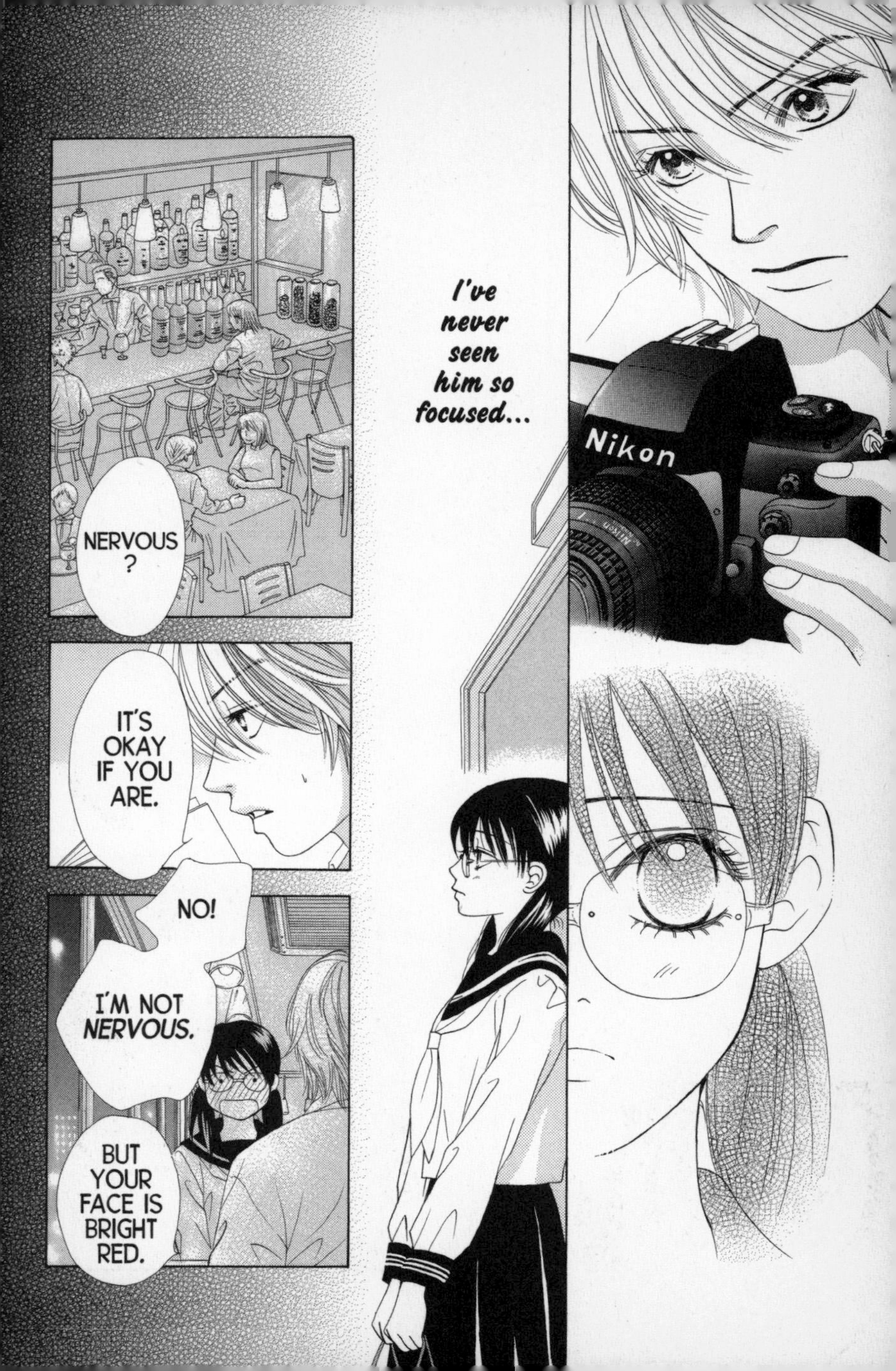
Nikon
I've never seen him so focused...
NERVOUS?
IT'S OKAY IF YOU ARE.
NO!
I'M NOT *NERVOUS.*
BUT YOUR FACE IS BRIGHT RED.

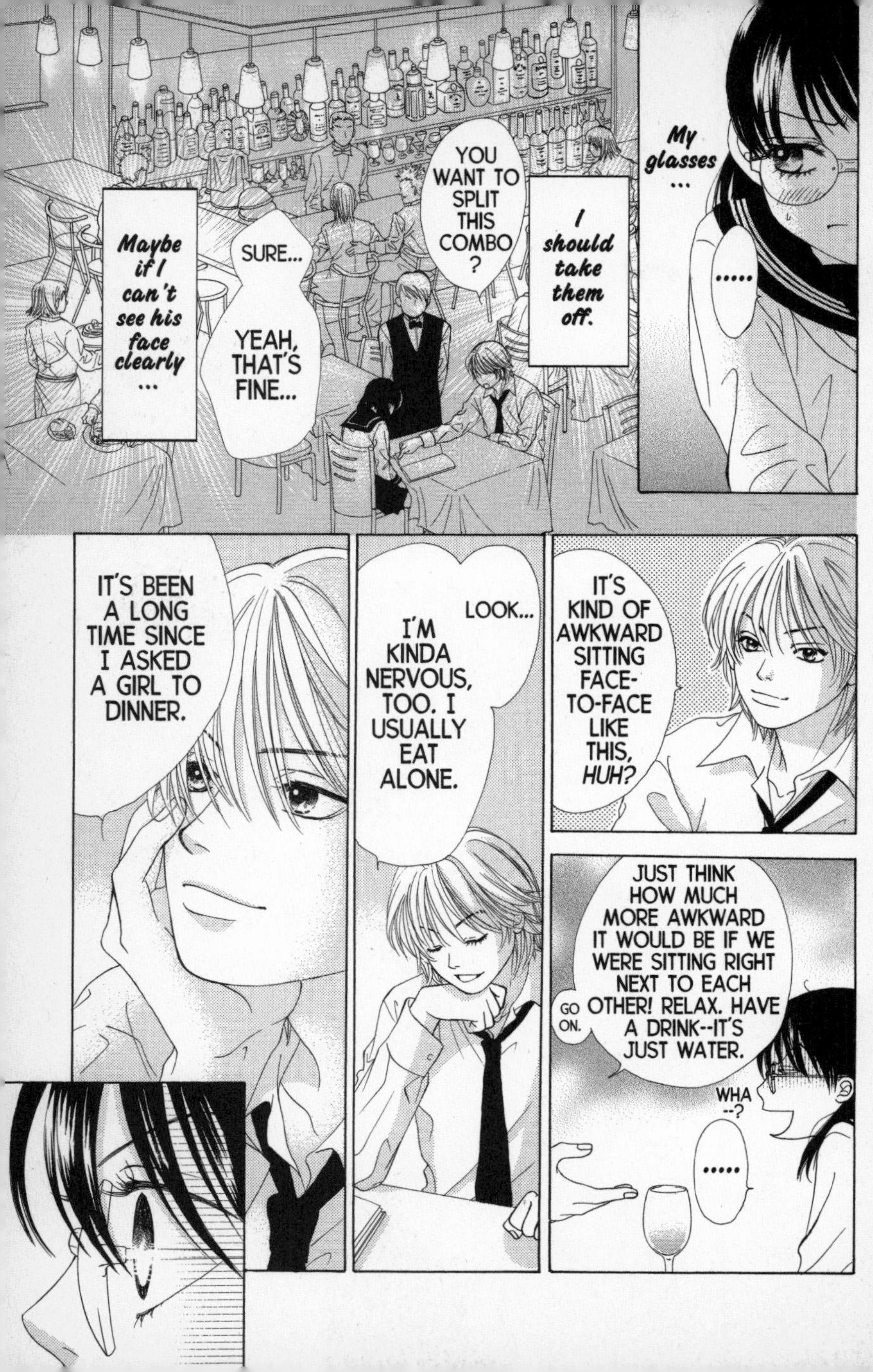

My glasses ...
.....
I should take them off.
YOU WANT TO SPLIT THIS COMBO?
SURE...
YEAH, THAT'S FINE...
Maybe if I can't see his face clearly ...
IT'S KIND OF AWKWARD SITTING FACE-TO-FACE LIKE THIS, *HUH*?
JUST THINK HOW MUCH MORE AWKWARD IT WOULD BE IF WE WERE SITTING RIGHT NEXT TO EACH OTHER! RELAX. HAVE A DRINK--IT'S JUST WATER.
GO ON.
WHA --?
.....
LOOK...
I'M KINDA NERVOUS, TOO. I USUALLY EAT ALONE.
IT'S BEEN A LONG TIME SINCE I ASKED A GIRL TO DINNER.

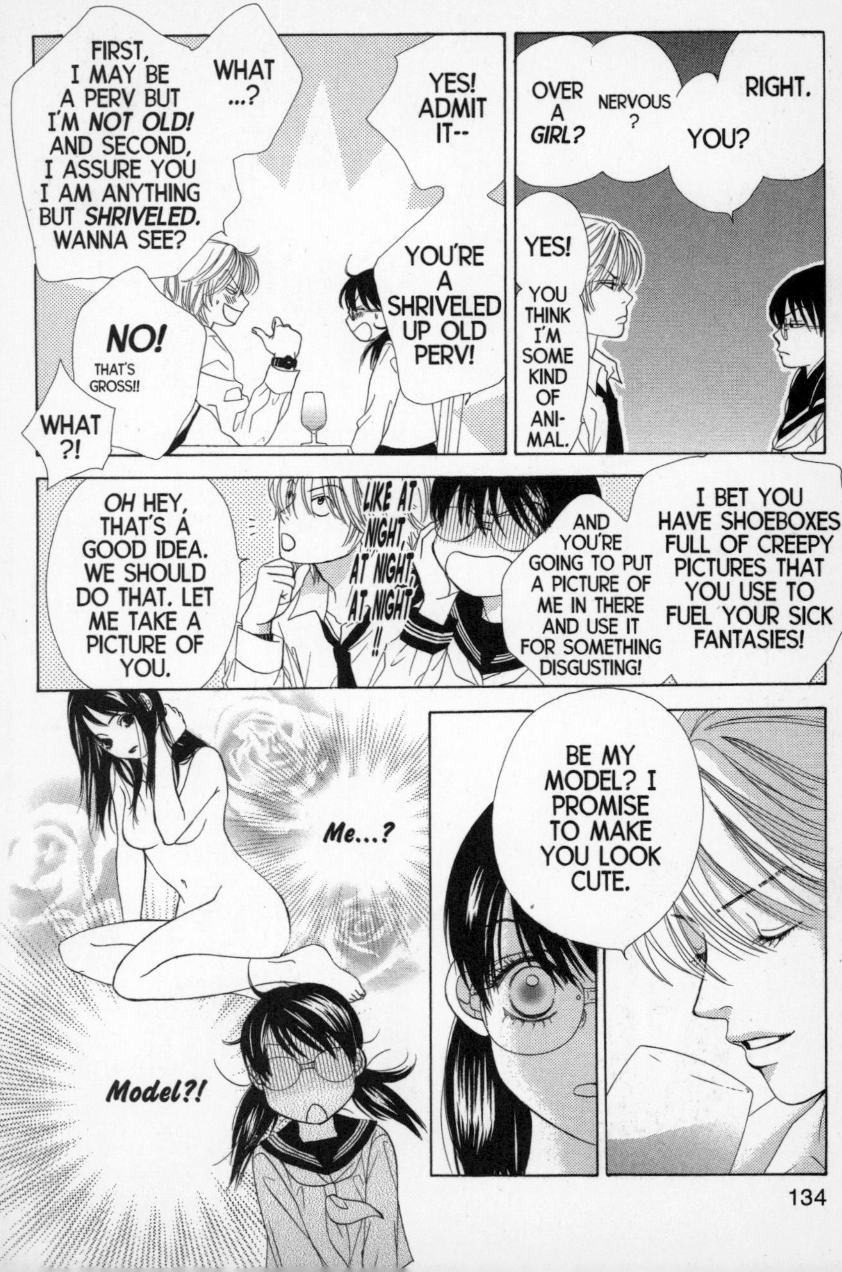
RIGHT.
YOU?
NERVOUS?
OVER A GIRL?
YES!
YOU THINK I'M SOME KIND OF ANI-MAL.
YES! ADMIT IT--
YOU'RE A SHRIVELED UP OLD PERV!
WHAT ...?
FIRST, I MAY BE A PERV BUT I'M *NOT OLD!* AND SECOND, I ASSURE YOU I AM ANYTHING BUT *SHRIVELED.* WANNA SEE?
NO! THAT'S GROSS!!
WHAT ?!
I BET YOU HAVE SHOEBOXES FULL OF CREEPY PICTURES THAT YOU USE TO FUEL YOUR SICK FANTASIES!
AND YOU'RE GOING TO PUT A PICTURE OF ME IN THERE AND USE IT FOR SOMETHING DISGUSTING!
LIKE AT NIGHT, AT NIGHT, AT NIGHT!!
OH HEY, THAT'S A GOOD IDEA. WE SHOULD DO THAT. LET ME TAKE A PICTURE OF YOU.
BE MY MODEL? I PROMISE TO MAKE YOU LOOK CUTE.
Me...?
Model?!

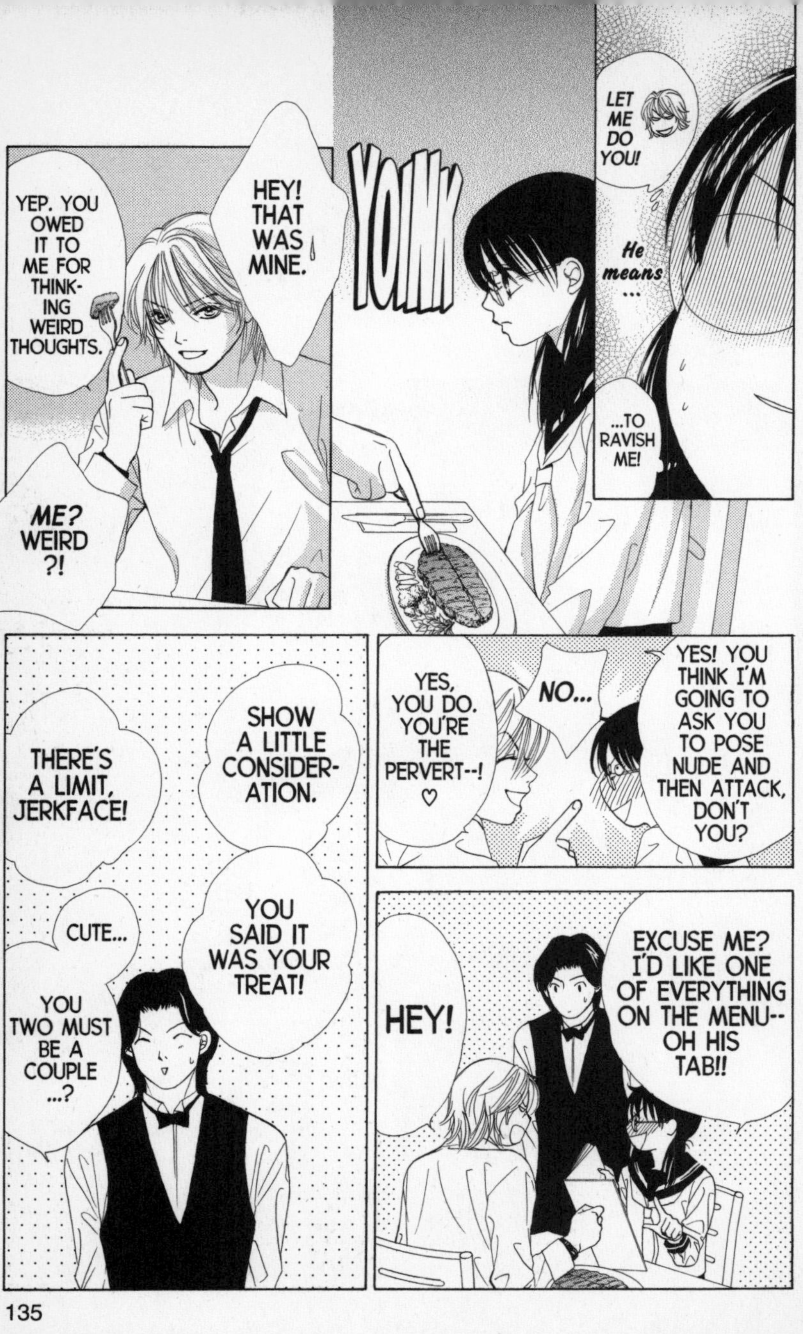
LET ME DO YOU!
He means...
...TO RAVISH ME!
YOINK
HEY! THAT WAS MINE.
YEP. YOU OWED IT TO ME FOR THINKING WEIRD THOUGHTS.
ME? WEIRD?!
YES! YOU THINK I'M GOING TO ASK YOU TO POSE NUDE AND THEN ATTACK, DON'T YOU?
NO...
YES, YOU DO. YOU'RE THE PERVERT--! ♡
EXCUSE ME? I'D LIKE ONE OF EVERYTHING ON THE MENU--OH HIS TAB!!
HEY!
SHOW A LITTLE CONSIDERATION.
THERE'S A LIMIT, JERKFACE!
YOU SAID IT WAS YOUR TREAT!
CUTE...
YOU TWO MUST BE A COUPLE...?

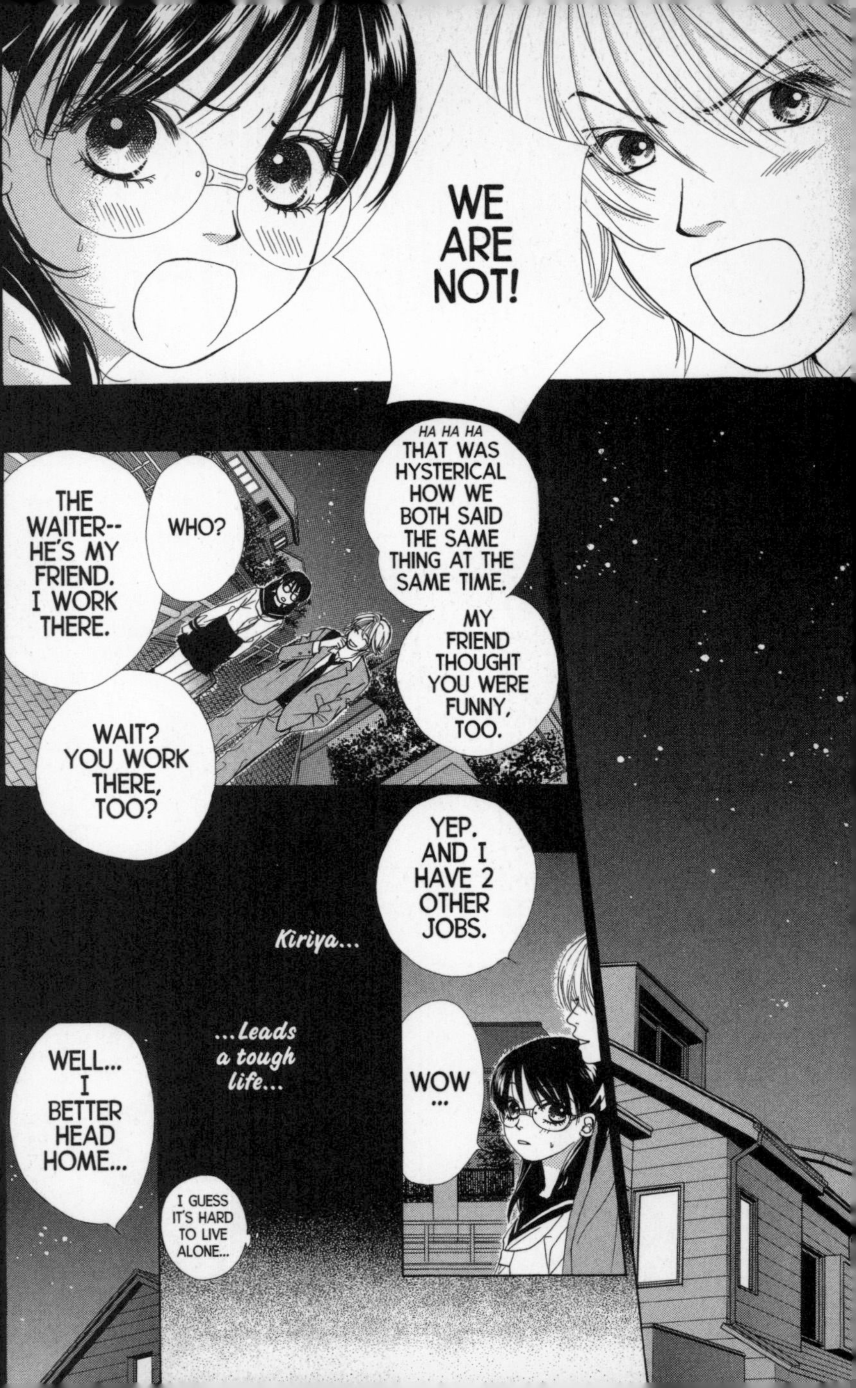
WE ARE NOT!
HA HA HA THAT WAS HYSTERICAL HOW WE BOTH SAID THE SAME THING AT THE SAME TIME.
MY FRIEND THOUGHT YOU WERE FUNNY, TOO.
WHO?
THE WAITER-- HE'S MY FRIEND. I WORK THERE.
WAIT? YOU WORK THERE, TOO?
YEP. AND I HAVE 2 OTHER JOBS.
WOW...
Kiriya...
...Leads a tough life...
WELL... I BETTER HEAD HOME...
I GUESS IT'S HARD TO LIVE ALONE...

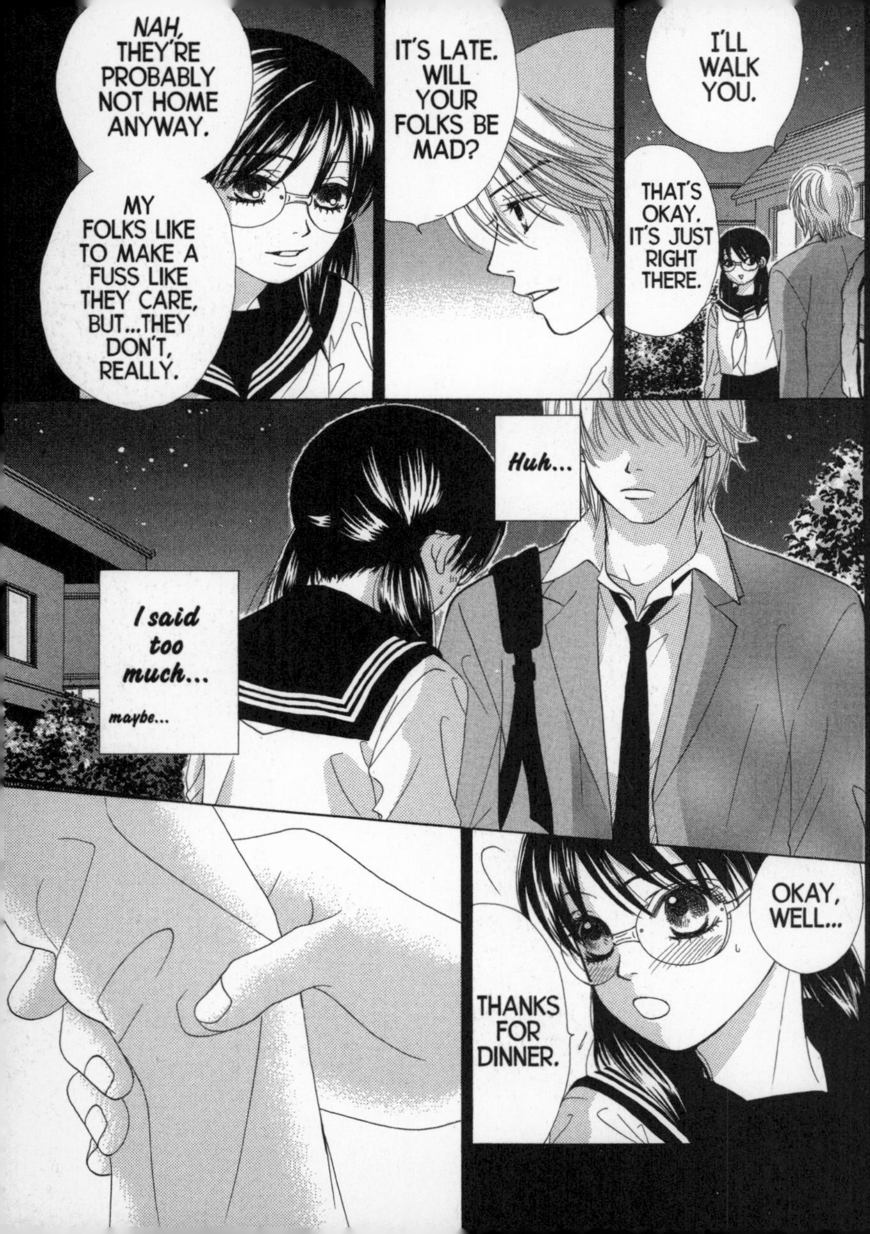
I'LL WALK YOU.
THAT'S OKAY. IT'S JUST RIGHT THERE.
IT'S LATE. WILL YOUR FOLKS BE MAD?
NAH, THEY'RE PROBABLY NOT HOME ANYWAY.
MY FOLKS LIKE TO MAKE A FUSS LIKE THEY CARE, BUT...THEY DON'T, REALLY.
Huh...
I said too much...
maybe...
OKAY, WELL...
THANKS FOR DINNER.

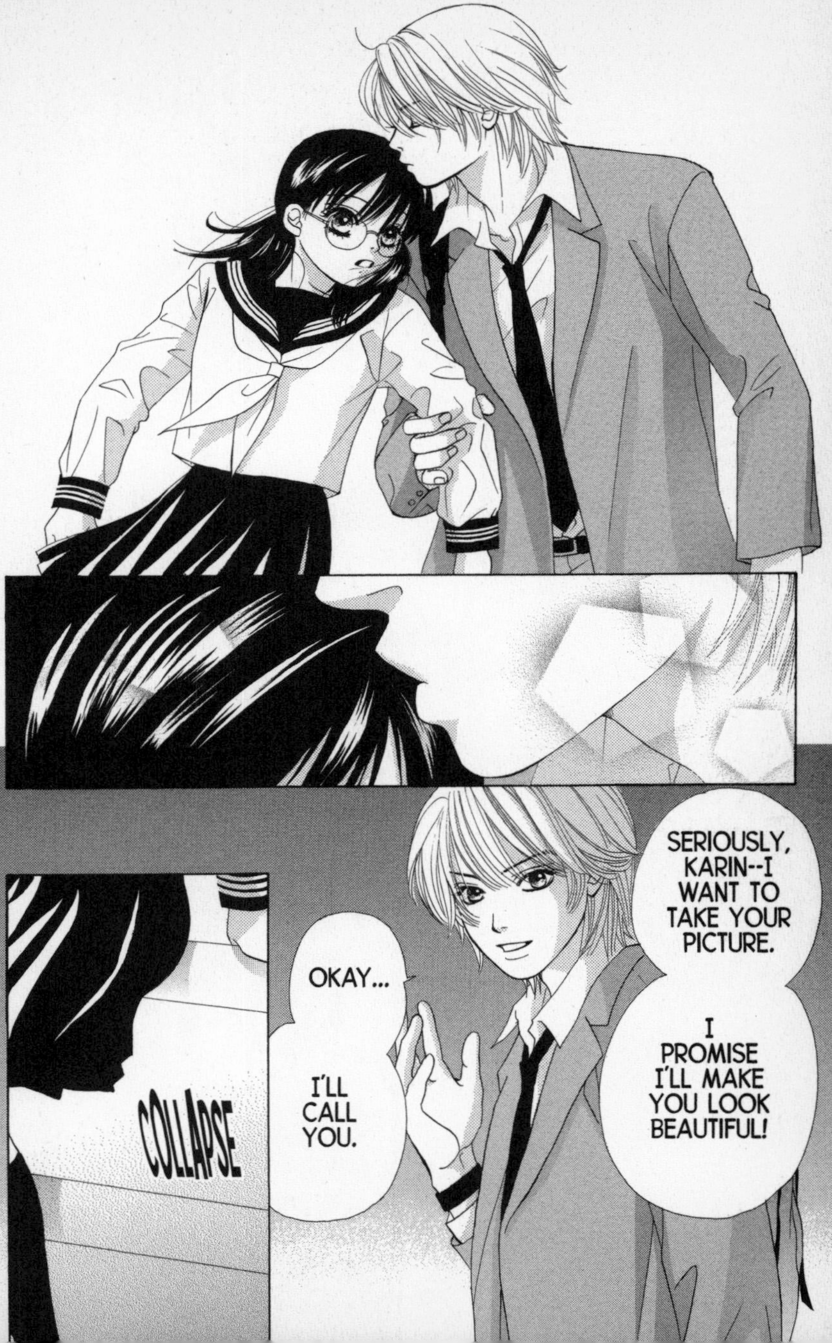
SERIOUSLY, KARIN--I WANT TO TAKE YOUR PICTURE.
I PROMISE I'LL MAKE YOU LOOK BEAUTIFUL!
OKAY...
I'LL CALL YOU.
COLLAPSE

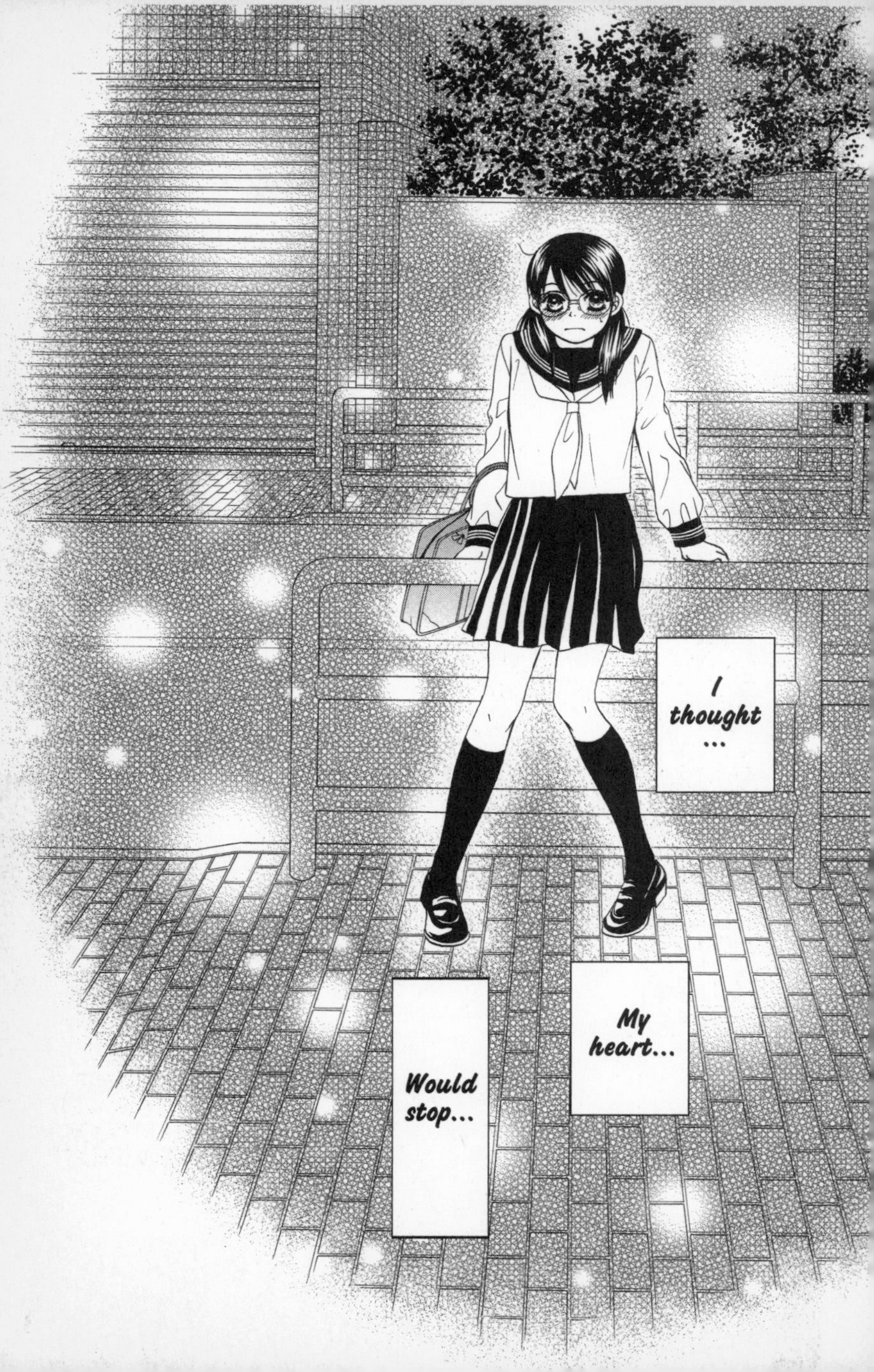
I thought...
My heart...
Would stop...

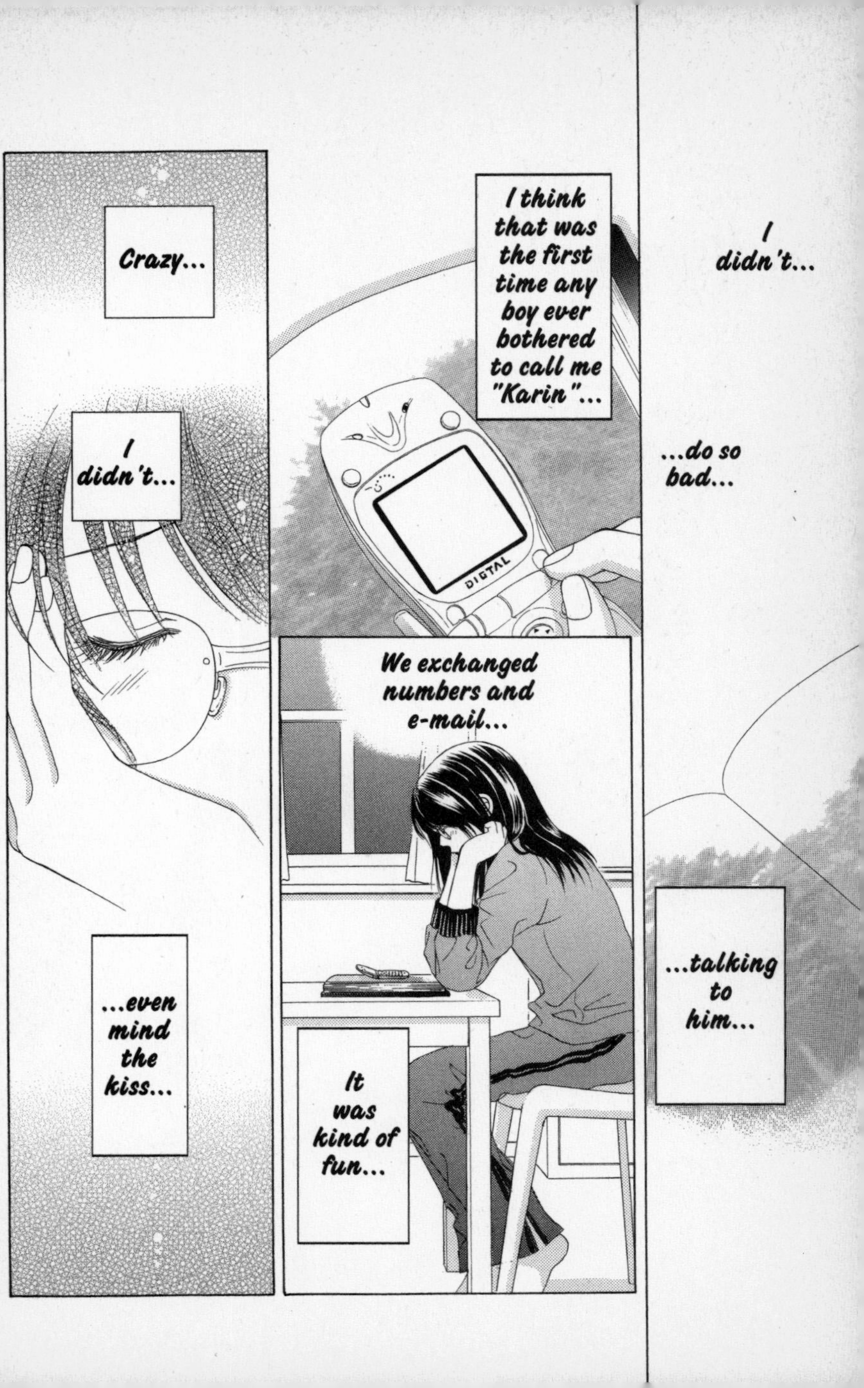
I didn't...
...do so bad...
...talking to him...
I think that was the first time any boy ever bothered to call me "Karin"...
DIGTAL
We exchanged numbers and e-mail...
It was kind of fun...
Crazy...
I didn't...
...even mind the kiss...

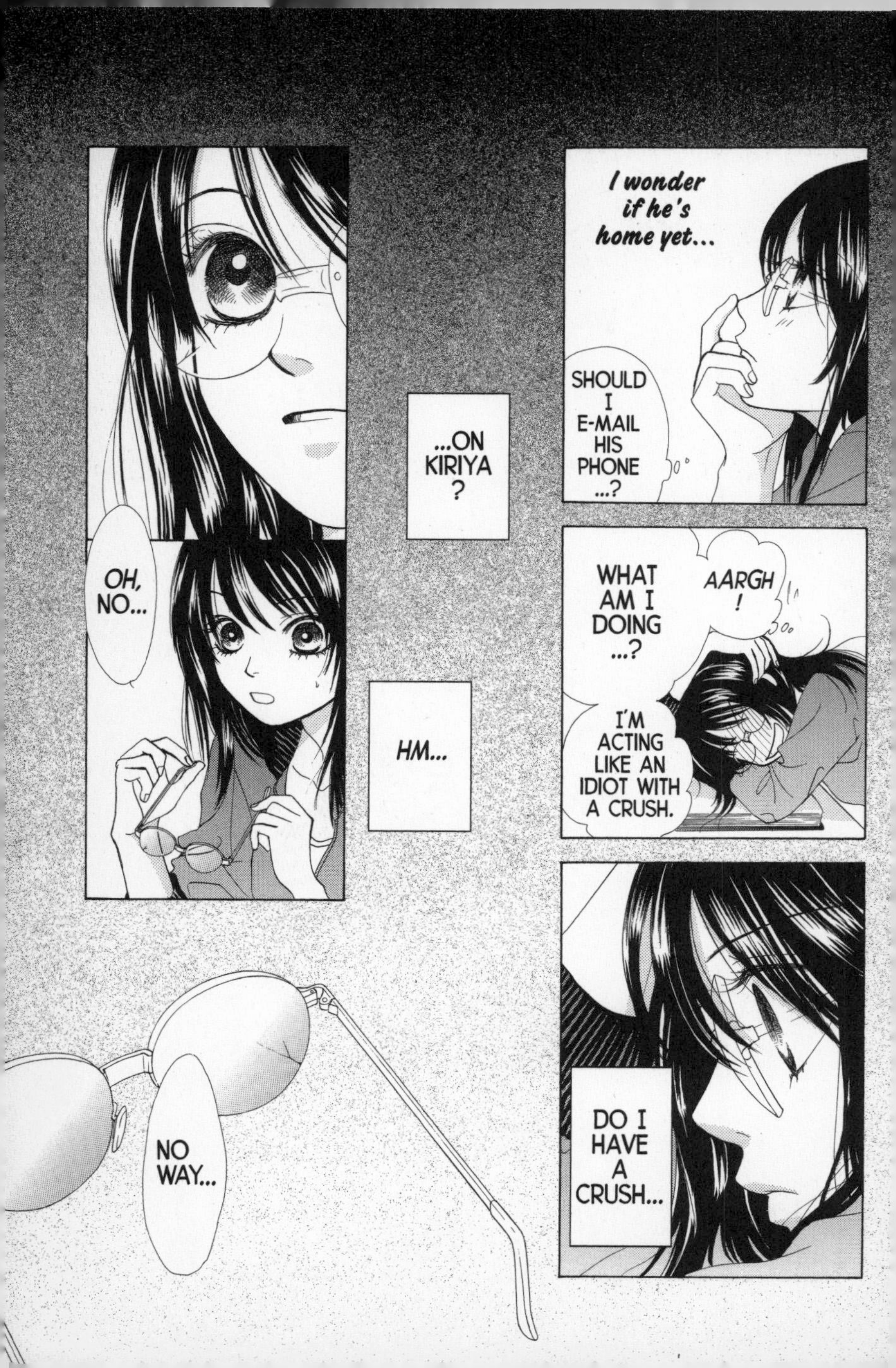
I wonder if he's home yet...
SHOULD I E-MAIL HIS PHONE ...?
AARGH!
WHAT AM I DOING ...?
I'M ACTING LIKE AN IDIOT WITH A CRUSH.
DO I HAVE A CRUSH...
...ON KIRIYA?
OH, NO...
HM...
NO WAY...

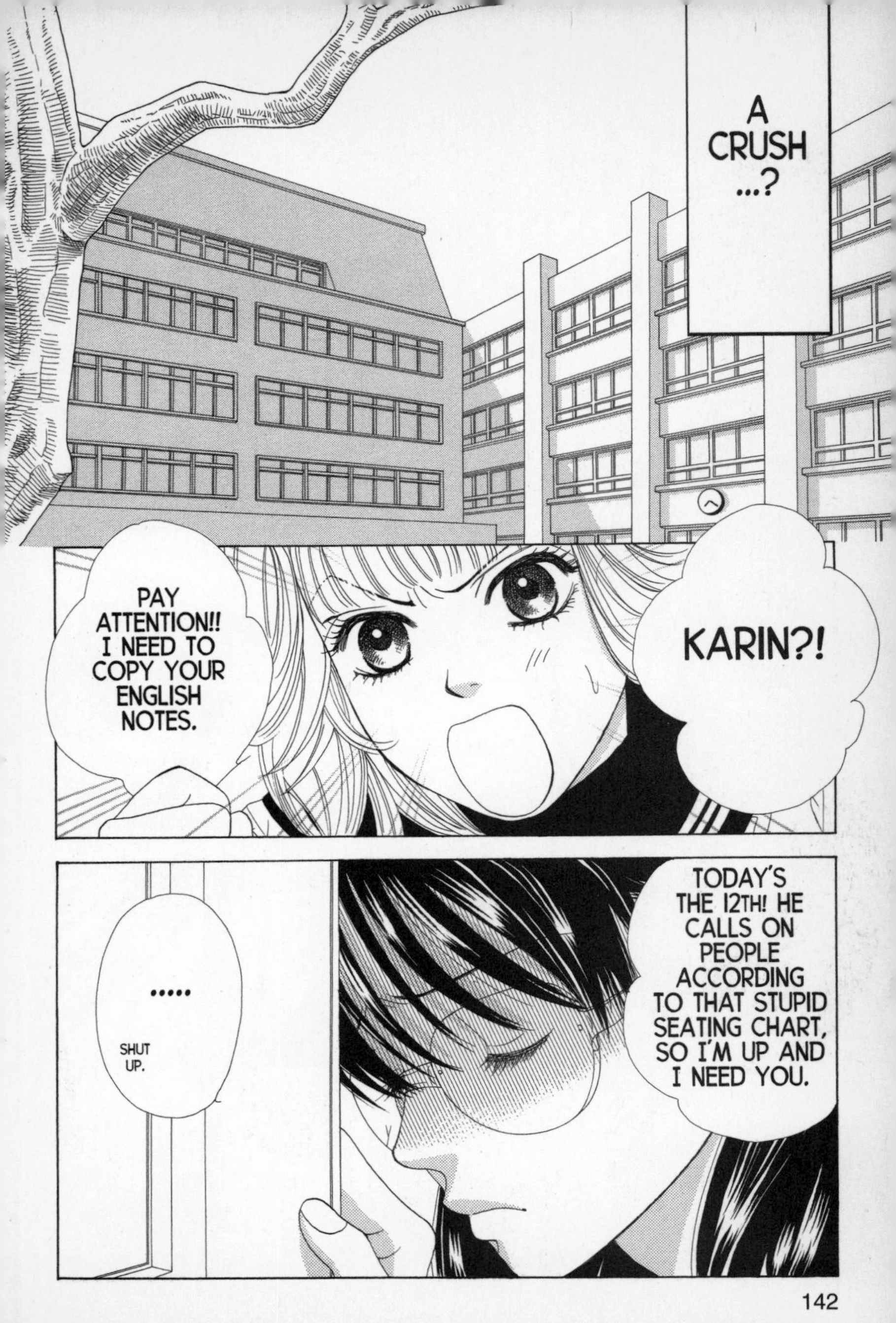
A CRUSH ...?
KARIN?!
PAY ATTENTION!! I NEED TO COPY YOUR ENGLISH NOTES.
TODAY'S THE 12TH! HE CALLS ON PEOPLE ACCORDING TO THAT STUPID SEATING CHART, SO I'M UP AND I NEED YOU.
.....
SHUT UP.

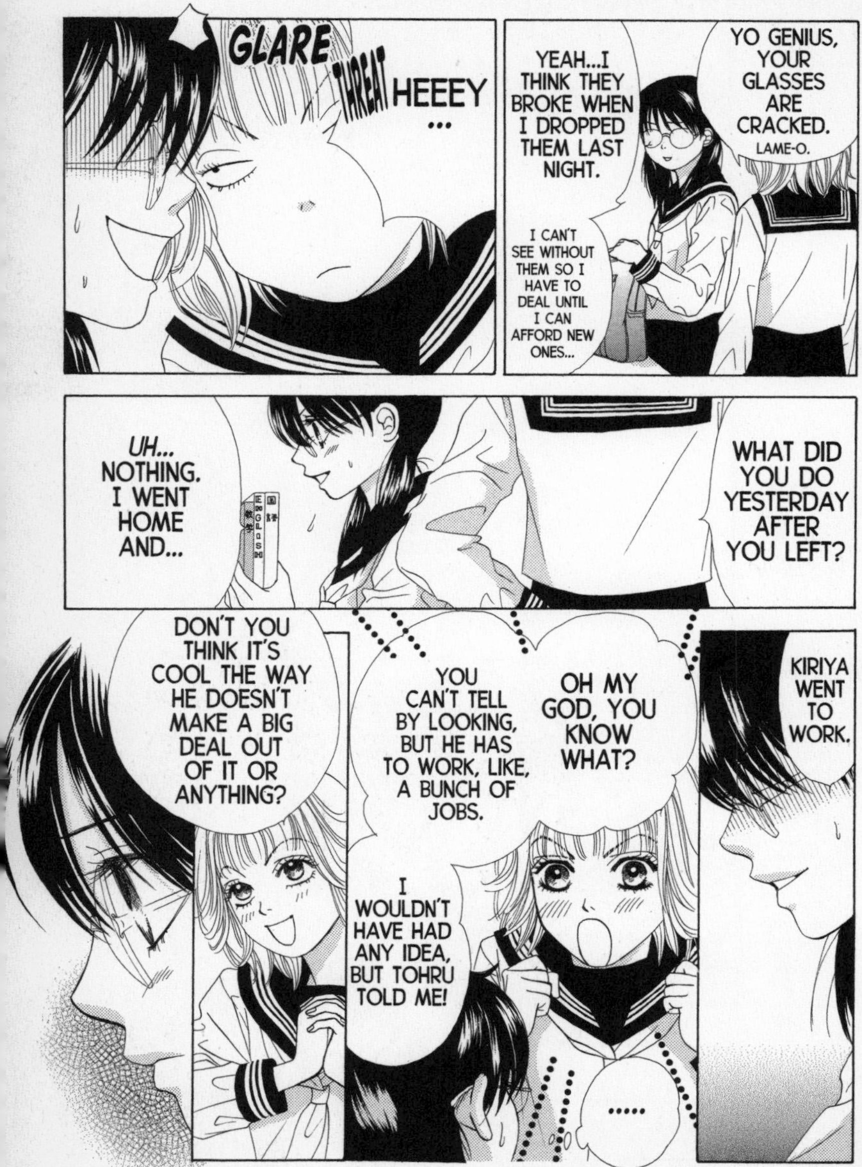
YO GENIUS, YOUR GLASSES ARE CRACKED.
LAME-O.
YEAH...I THINK THEY BROKE WHEN I DROPPED THEM LAST NIGHT.
I CAN'T SEE WITHOUT THEM SO I HAVE TO DEAL UNTIL I CAN AFFORD NEW ONES...
HEEEY ...
THREAT
GLARE
WHAT DID YOU DO YESTERDAY AFTER YOU LEFT?
UH... NOTHING. I WENT HOME AND...
KIRIYA WENT TO WORK.
OH MY GOD, YOU KNOW WHAT?
YOU CAN'T TELL BY LOOKING, BUT HE HAS TO WORK, LIKE, A BUNCH OF JOBS.
I WOULDN'T HAVE HAD ANY IDEA, BUT TOHRU TOLD ME!
.....
DON'T YOU THINK IT'S COOL THE WAY HE DOESN'T MAKE A BIG DEAL OUT OF IT OR ANYTHING?

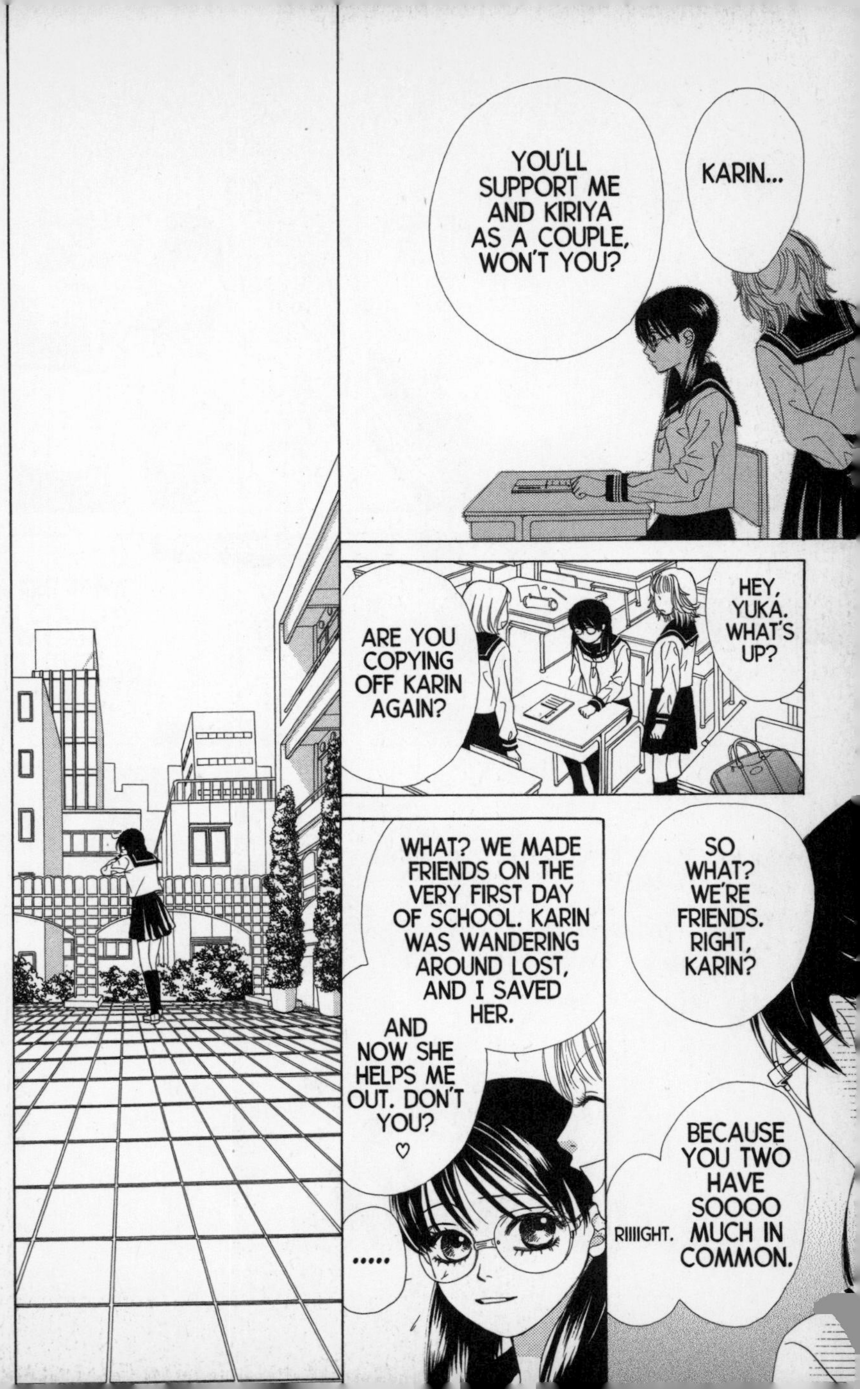
KARIN...
YOU'LL SUPPORT ME AND KIRIYA AS A COUPLE, WON'T YOU?
HEY, YUKA. WHAT'S UP?
ARE YOU COPYING OFF KARIN AGAIN?
SO WHAT? WE'RE FRIENDS. RIGHT, KARIN?
WHAT? WE MADE FRIENDS ON THE VERY FIRST DAY OF SCHOOL. KARIN WAS WANDERING AROUND LOST, AND I SAVED HER.
AND NOW SHE HELPS ME OUT. DON'T YOU? ♡
BECAUSE YOU TWO HAVE SOOOO MUCH IN COMMON.
RIIIGHT.
.....

Yeah...
I guess that makes us "friends"...
Maybe I shouldn't see Kiriya.
Yuka would be pissed if she found out.
She really likes him.
.....
I wonder what she'd do if she knew?
YIKES!
DON'T THINK ABOUT IT.
What about me?
What about my feelings...?
What am I supposed to do...?

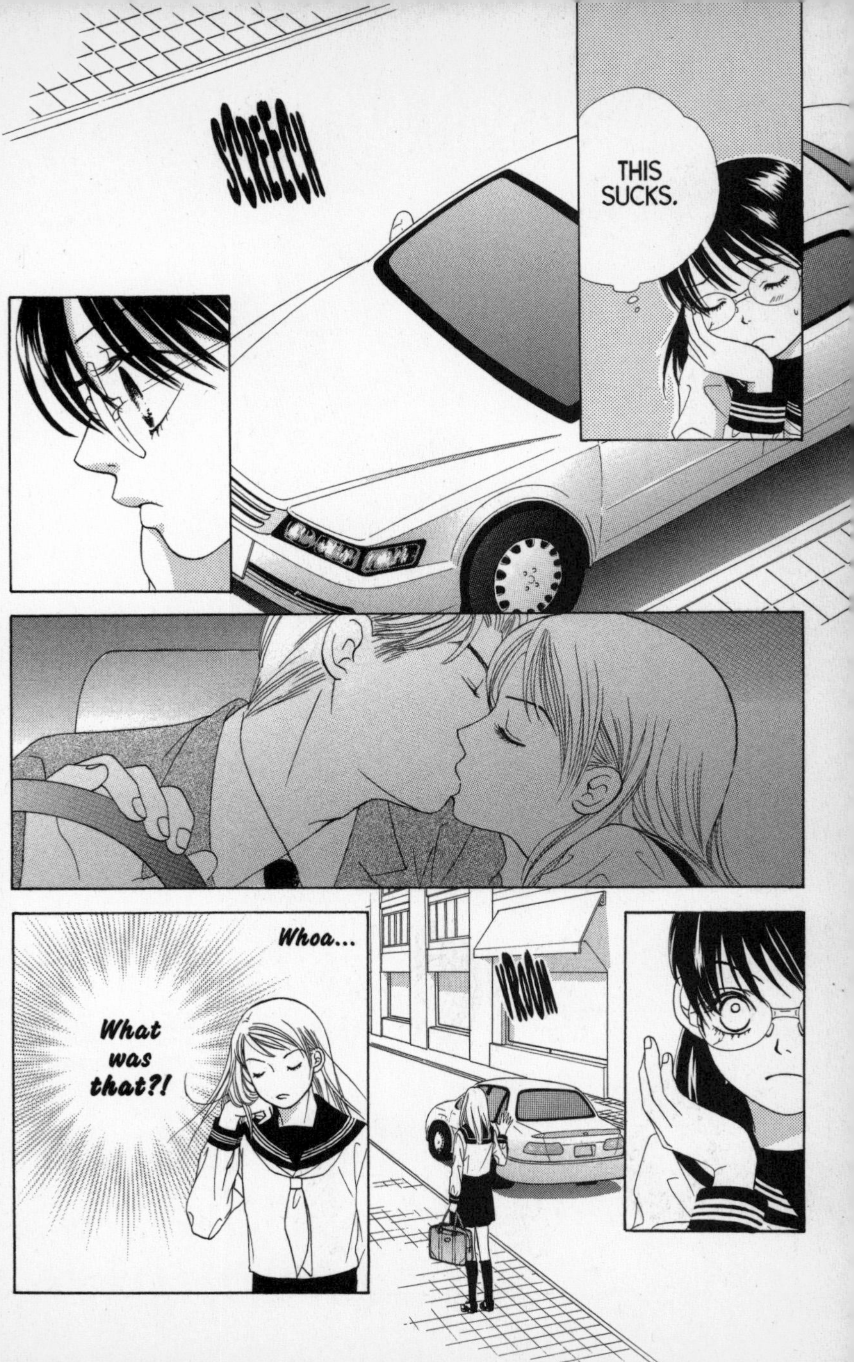
THIS SUCKS.
SCREECH
VROOM
Whoa...
What was that?!

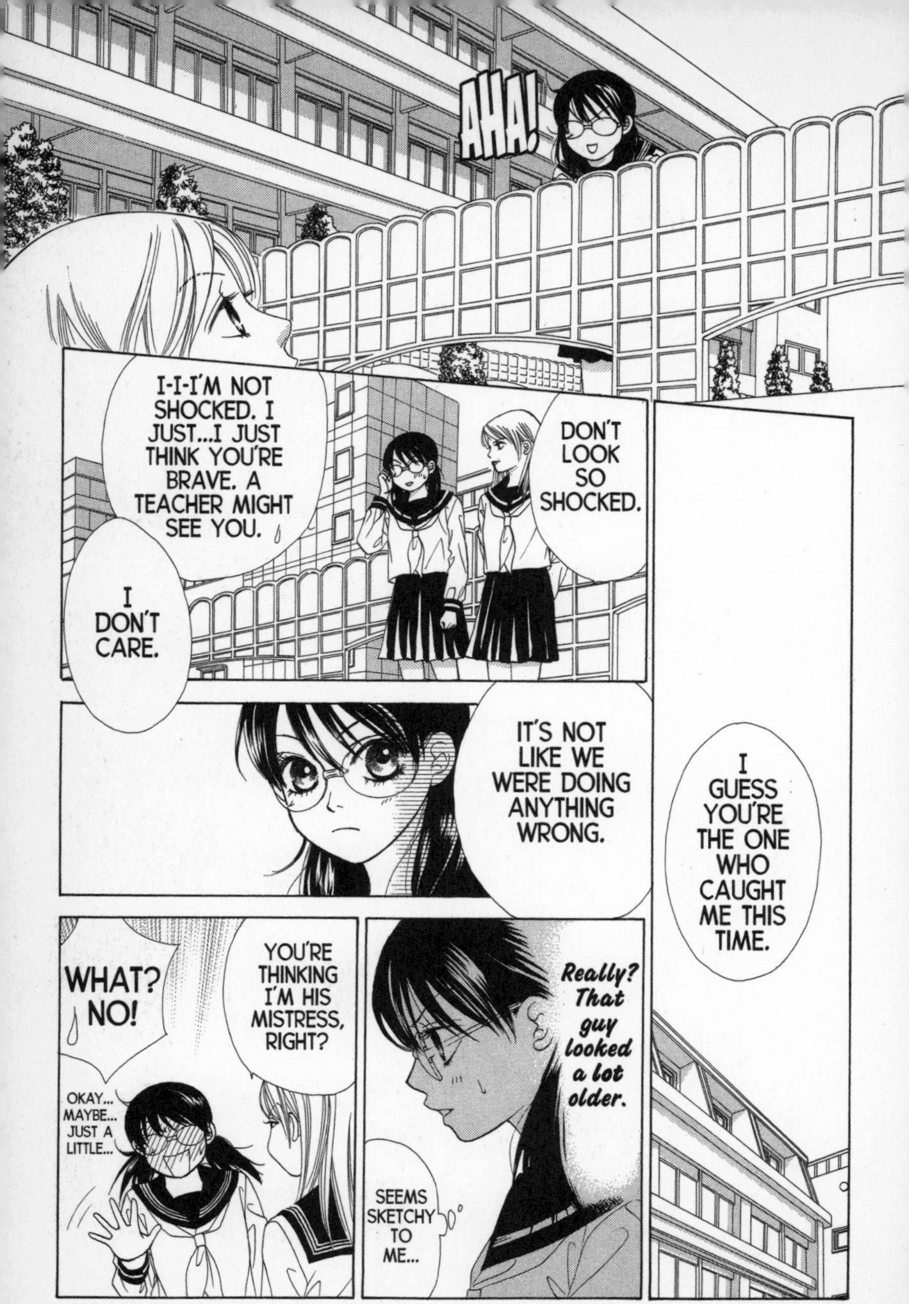
AHA!
I GUESS YOU'RE THE ONE WHO CAUGHT ME THIS TIME.
DON'T LOOK SO SHOCKED.
I-I-I'M NOT SHOCKED. I JUST...I JUST THINK YOU'RE BRAVE. A TEACHER MIGHT SEE YOU.
I DON'T CARE.
IT'S NOT LIKE WE WERE DOING ANYTHING WRONG.
Really? That guy looked a lot older.
SEEMS SKETCHY TO ME...
YOU'RE THINKING I'M HIS MISTRESS, RIGHT?
WHAT? NO!
OKAY... MAYBE... JUST A LITTLE...

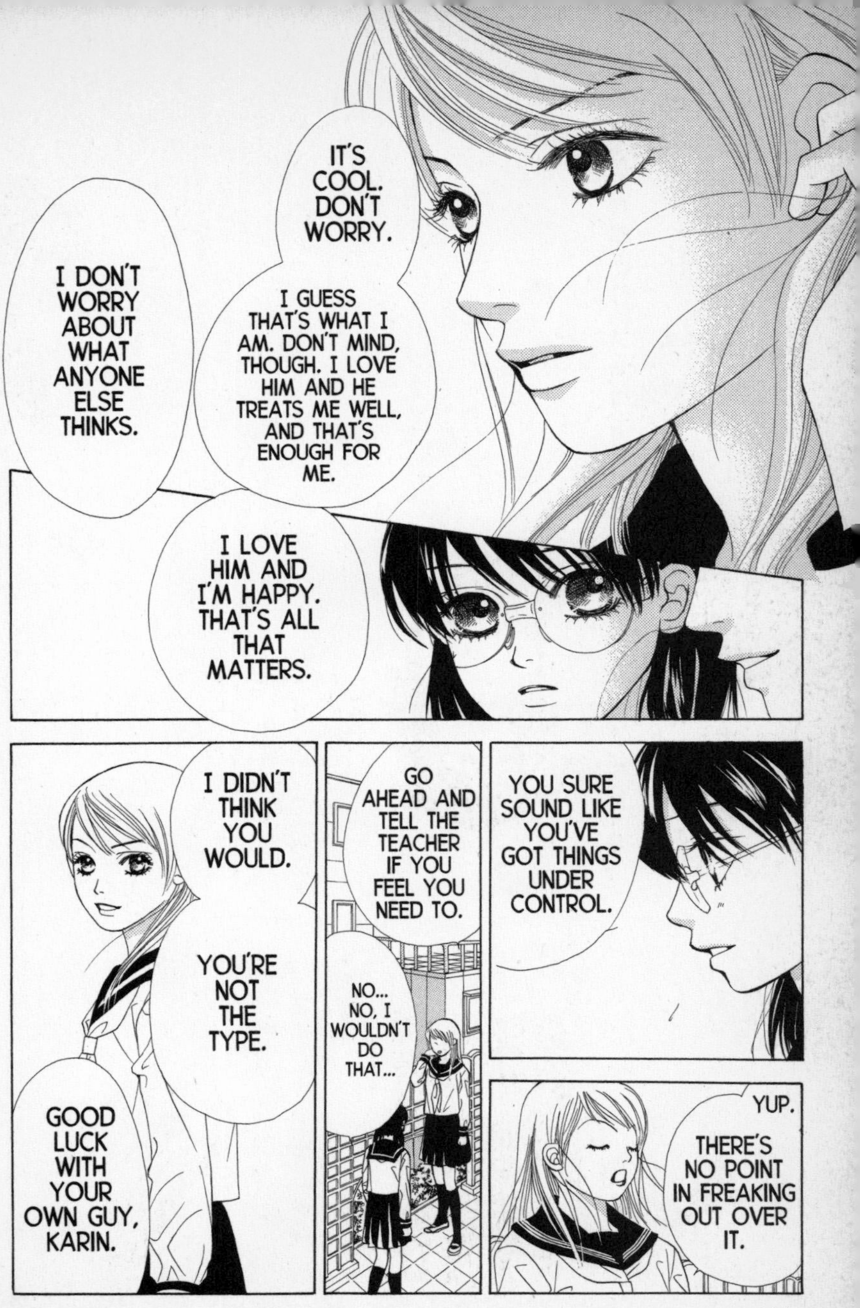
IT'S COOL. DON'T WORRY.
I GUESS THAT'S WHAT I AM. DON'T MIND, THOUGH. I LOVE HIM AND HE TREATS ME WELL, AND THAT'S ENOUGH FOR ME.
I DON'T WORRY ABOUT WHAT ANYONE ELSE THINKS.
I LOVE HIM AND I'M HAPPY. THAT'S ALL THAT MATTERS.
YOU SURE SOUND LIKE YOU'VE GOT THINGS UNDER CONTROL.
YUP.
THERE'S NO POINT IN FREAKING OUT OVER IT.
GO AHEAD AND TELL THE TEACHER IF YOU FEEL YOU NEED TO.
NO... NO, I WOULDN'T DO THAT...
I DIDN'T THINK YOU WOULD.
YOU'RE NOT THE TYPE.
GOOD LUCK WITH YOUR OWN GUY, KARIN.

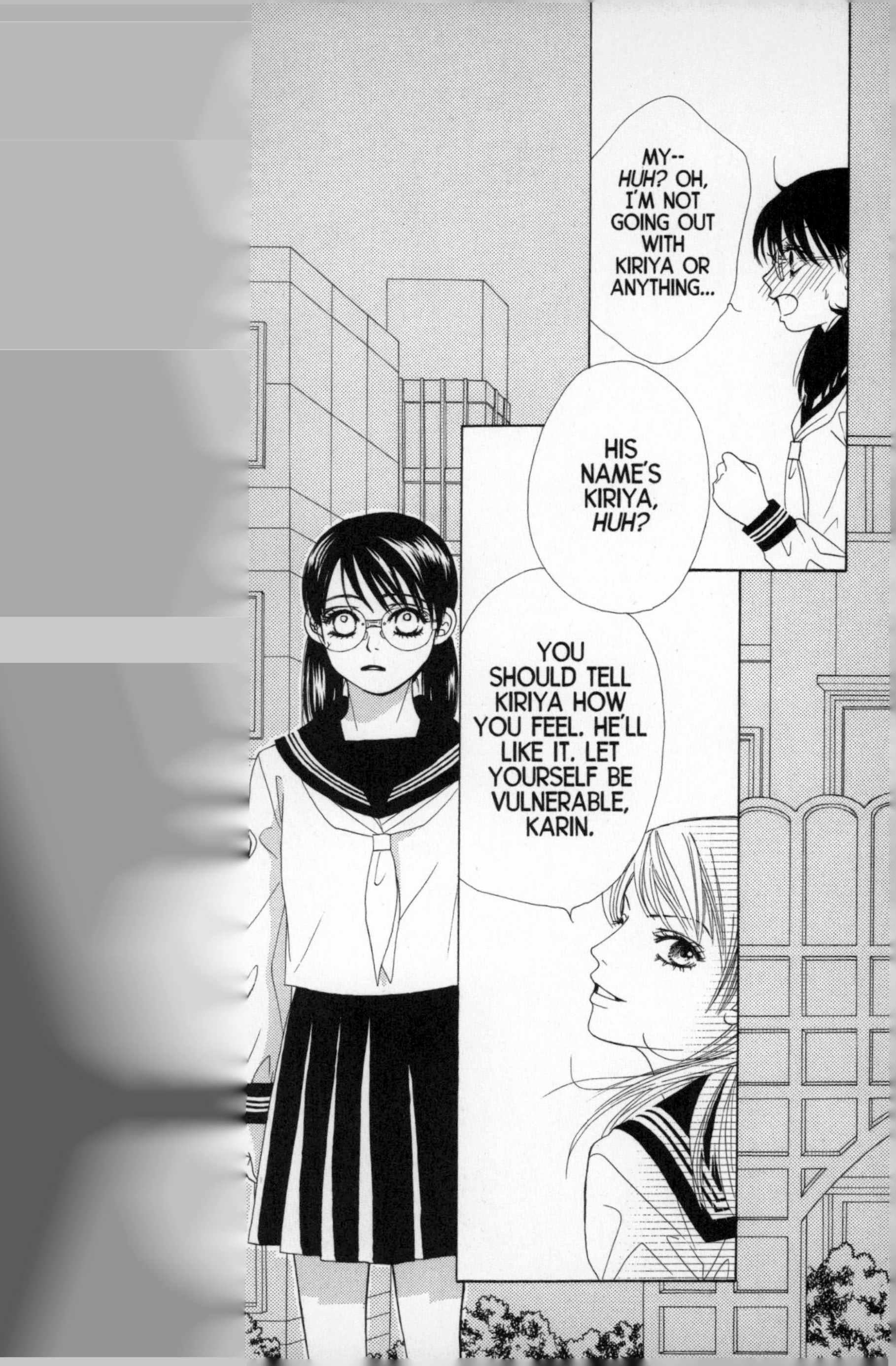
MY-- *HUH?* OH, I'M NOT GOING OUT WITH KIRIYA OR ANYTHING...
HIS NAME'S KIRIYA, *HUH?*
YOU SHOULD TELL KIRIYA HOW YOU FEEL. HE'LL LIKE IT. LET YOURSELF BE VULNERABLE, KARIN.

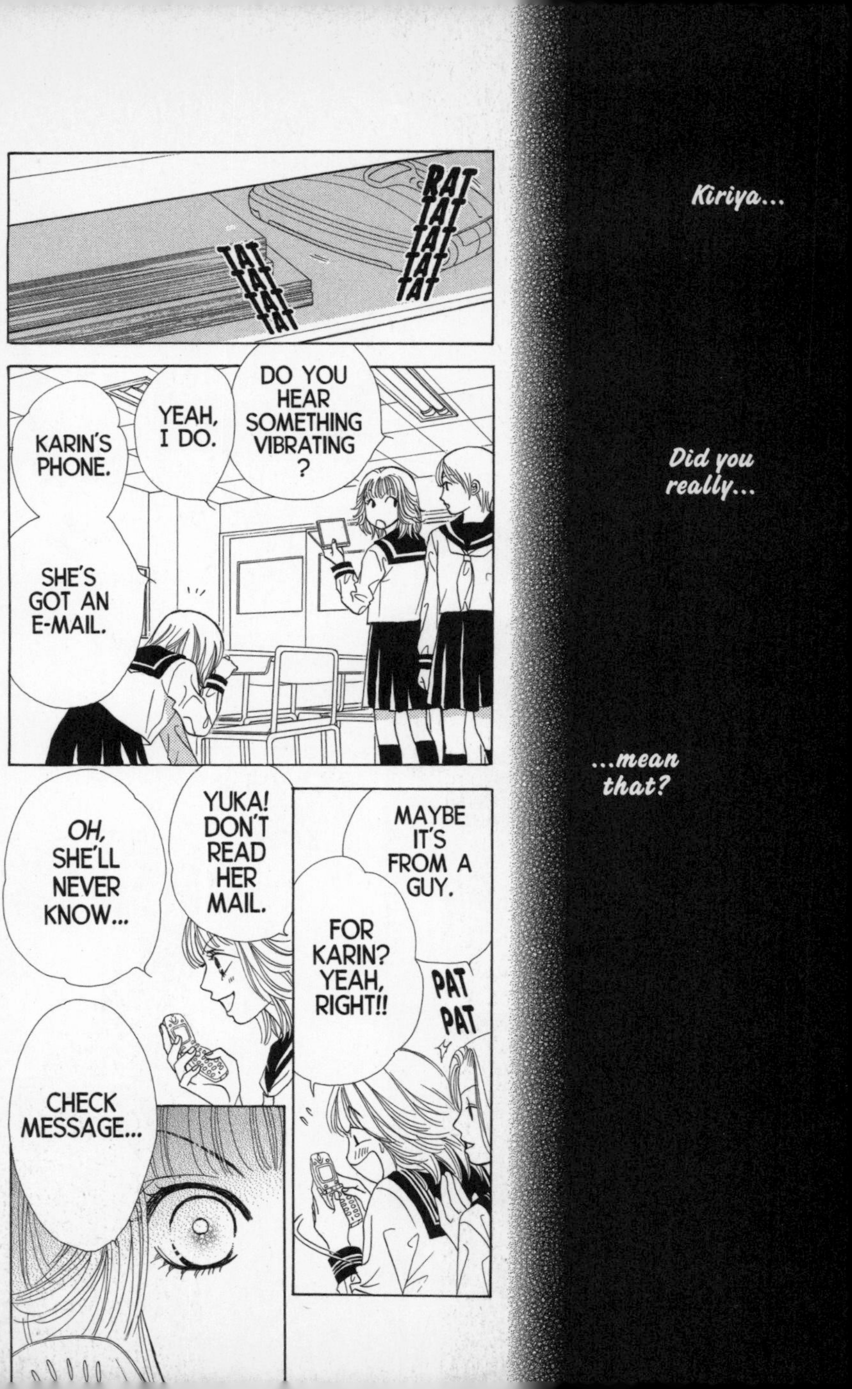
Kiriya...
Did you really...
...mean that?
RAT TAT TAT TAT TAT TAT
TAT TAT TAT TAT
DO YOU HEAR SOMETHING VIBRATING?
YEAH, I DO.
KARIN'S PHONE.
SHE'S GOT AN E-MAIL.
MAYBE IT'S FROM A GUY.
FOR KARIN? YEAH, RIGHT!!
PAT PAT
YUKA! DON'T READ HER MAIL.
OH, SHE'LL NEVER KNOW...
CHECK MESSAGE...

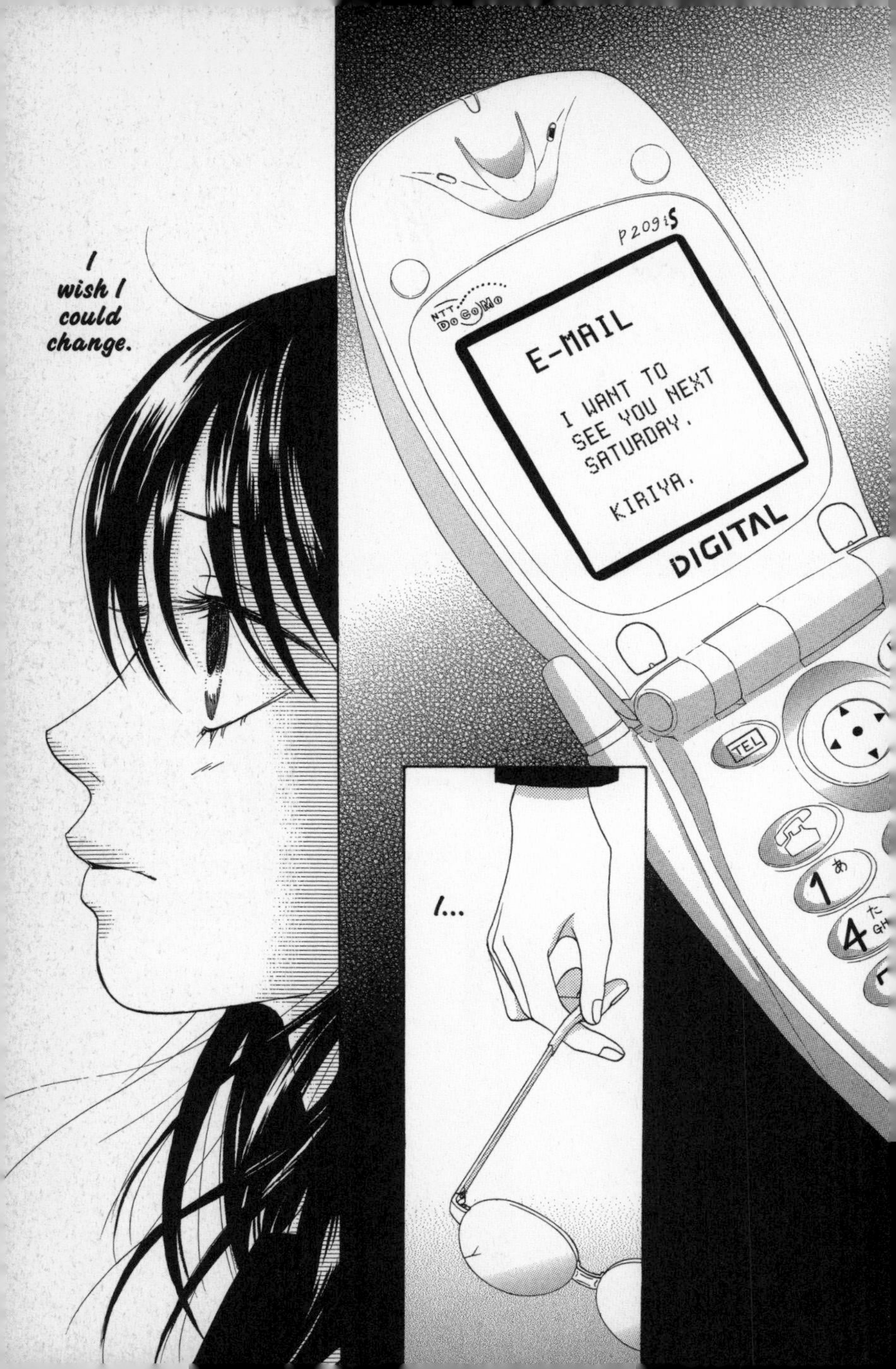
P209iS
NTT DoCoMo
E-MAIL
I WANT TO SEE YOU NEXT SATURDAY.
KIRIYA.
DIGITAL
TEL
I...
I wish I could change.

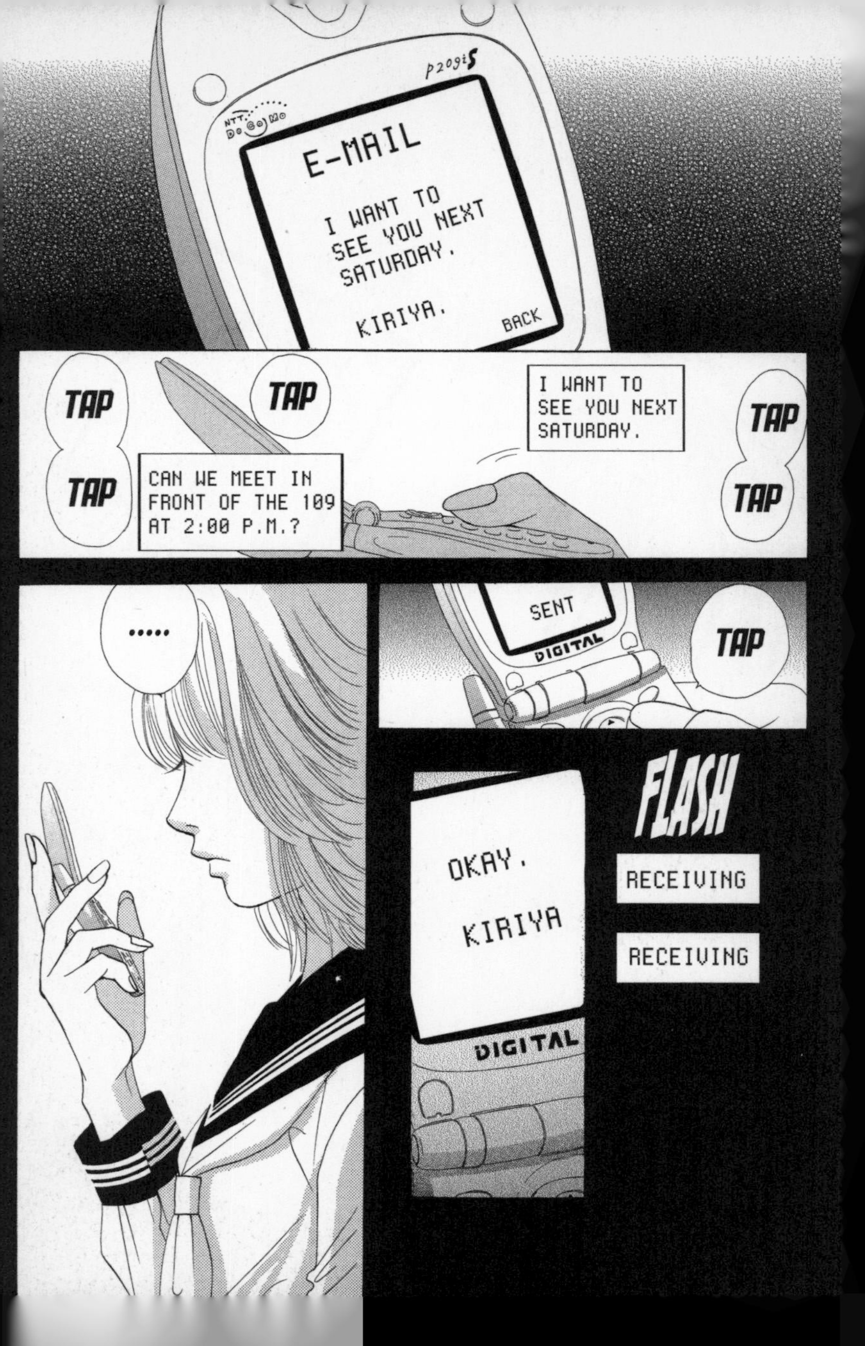

E-MAIL
I WANT TO SEE YOU NEXT SATURDAY.
KIRIYA.
BACK
TAP
TAP
I WANT TO SEE YOU NEXT SATURDAY.
TAP
TAP
CAN WE MEET IN FRONT OF THE 109 AT 2:00 P.M.?
TAP
SENT
DIGITAL
TAP
FLASH
RECEIVING
RECEIVING
OKAY.
KIRIYA
DIGITAL
……

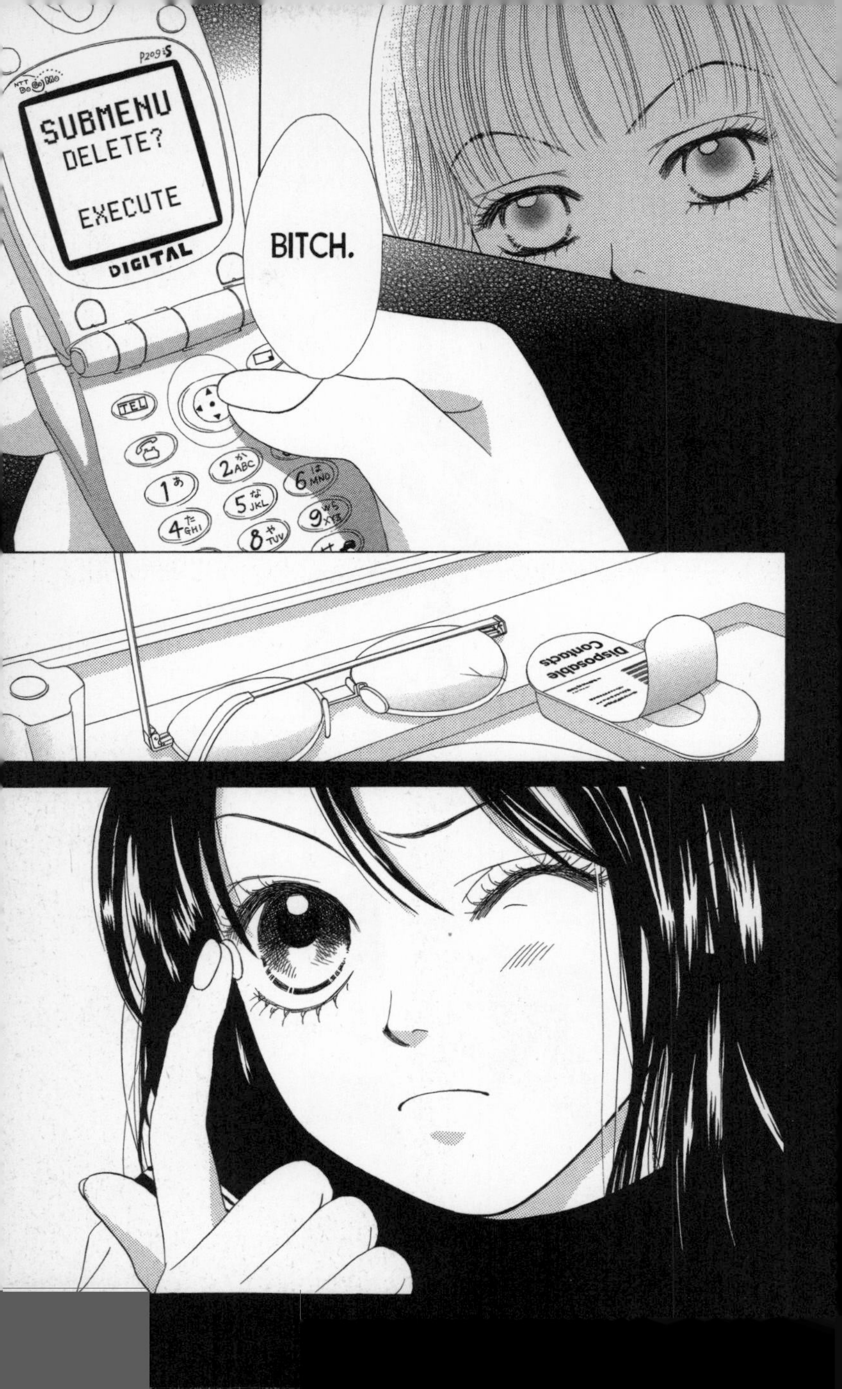
BITCH.
P209iS
SUBMENU
DELETE?
EXECUTE
DIGITAL
Disposable
Contacts

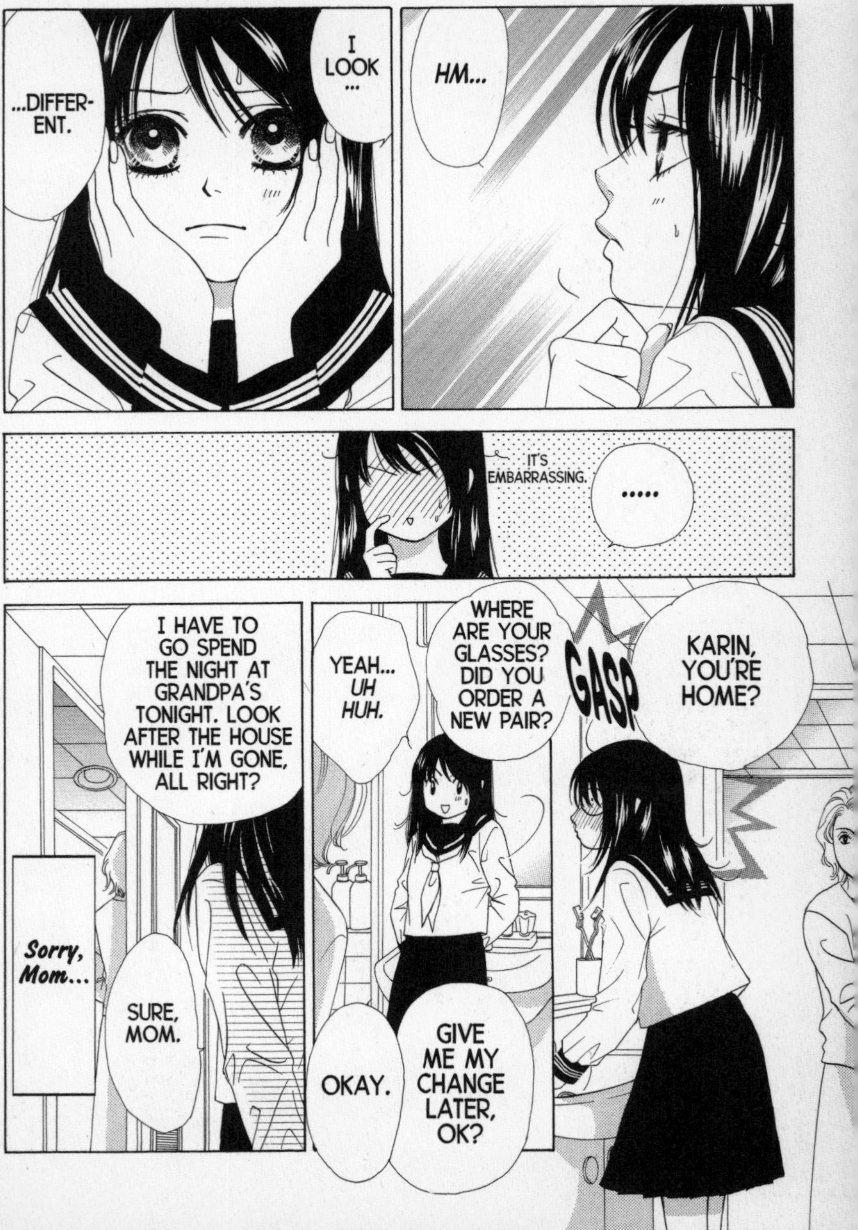
HM...
I LOOK ...
...DIFFER-ENT.
.....
IT'S EMBARRASSING.
KARIN, YOU'RE HOME?
GASP
WHERE ARE YOUR GLASSES? DID YOU ORDER A NEW PAIR?
YEAH... UH HUH.
GIVE ME MY CHANGE LATER, OK?
OKAY.
I HAVE TO GO SPEND THE NIGHT AT GRANDPA'S TONIGHT. LOOK AFTER THE HOUSE WHILE I'M GONE, ALL RIGHT?
SURE, MOM.
Sorry, Mom...

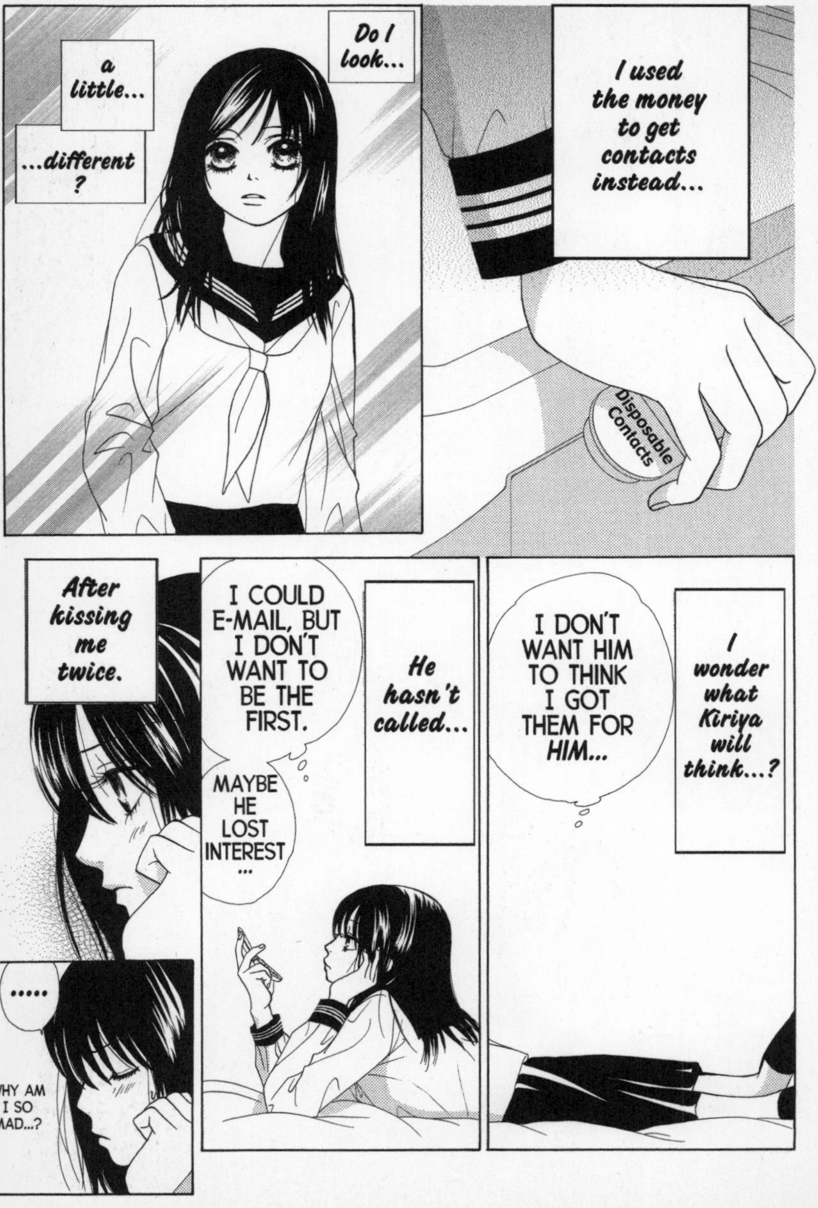
I used the money to get contacts instead...
Disposable Contacts
Do I look...
a little...
...different ?
I wonder what Kiriya will think...?
I DON'T WANT HIM TO THINK I GOT THEM FOR HIM...
He hasn't called...
I COULD E-MAIL, BUT I DON'T WANT TO BE THE FIRST.
MAYBE HE LOST INTEREST ...
After kissing me twice.
......
WHY AM I SO MAD...?

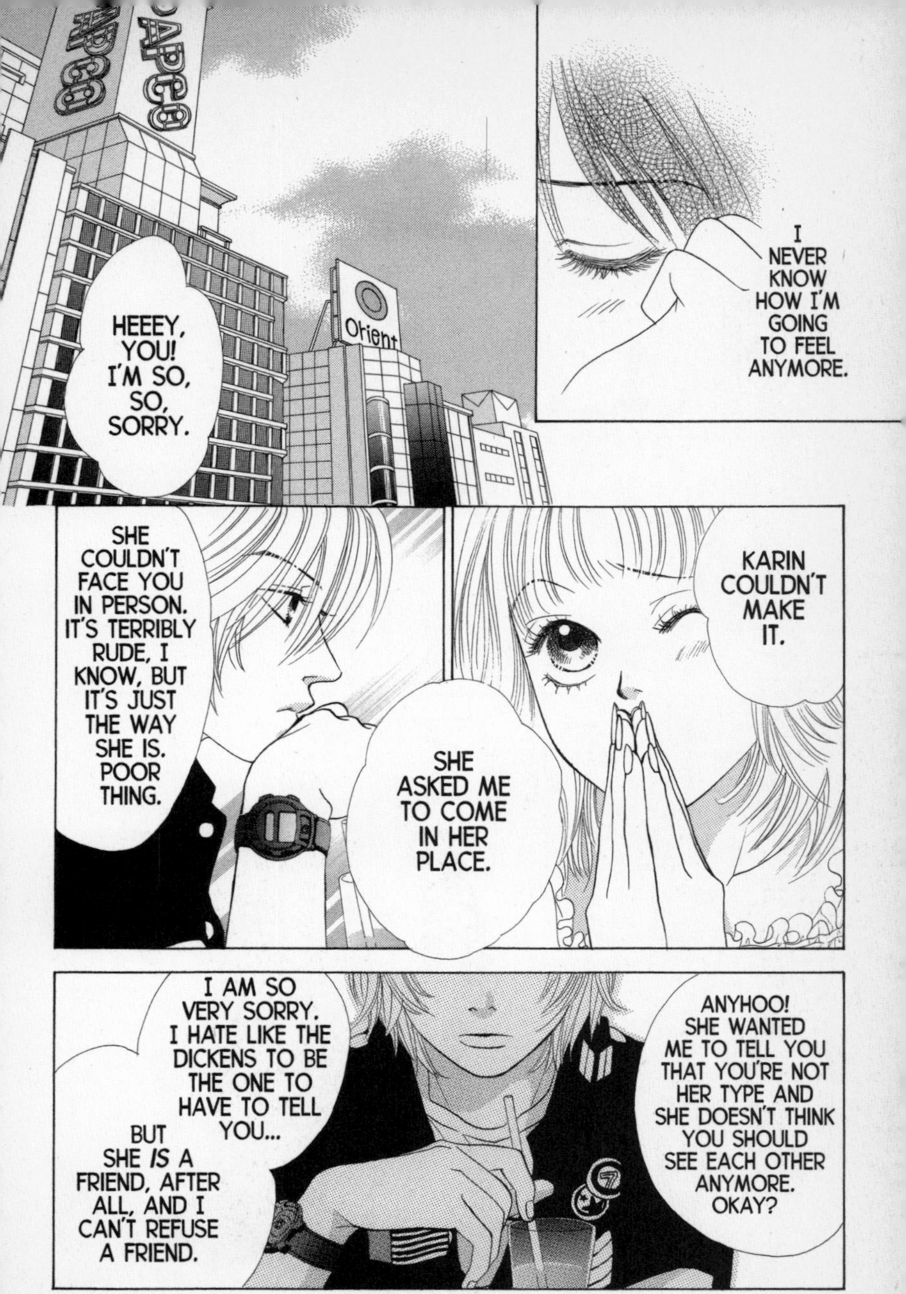
I NEVER KNOW HOW I'M GOING TO FEEL ANYMORE.
Orient
HEEEY, YOU! I'M SO, SO, SORRY.
KARIN COULDN'T MAKE IT.
SHE ASKED ME TO COME IN HER PLACE.
SHE COULDN'T FACE YOU IN PERSON. IT'S TERRIBLY RUDE, I KNOW, BUT IT'S JUST THE WAY SHE IS. POOR THING.
ANYHOO! SHE WANTED ME TO TELL YOU THAT YOU'RE NOT HER TYPE AND SHE DOESN'T THINK YOU SHOULD SEE EACH OTHER ANYMORE. OKAY?
I AM SO VERY SORRY. I HATE LIKE THE DICKENS TO BE THE ONE TO HAVE TO TELL YOU...
BUT SHE *IS* A FRIEND, AFTER ALL, AND I CAN'T REFUSE A FRIEND.

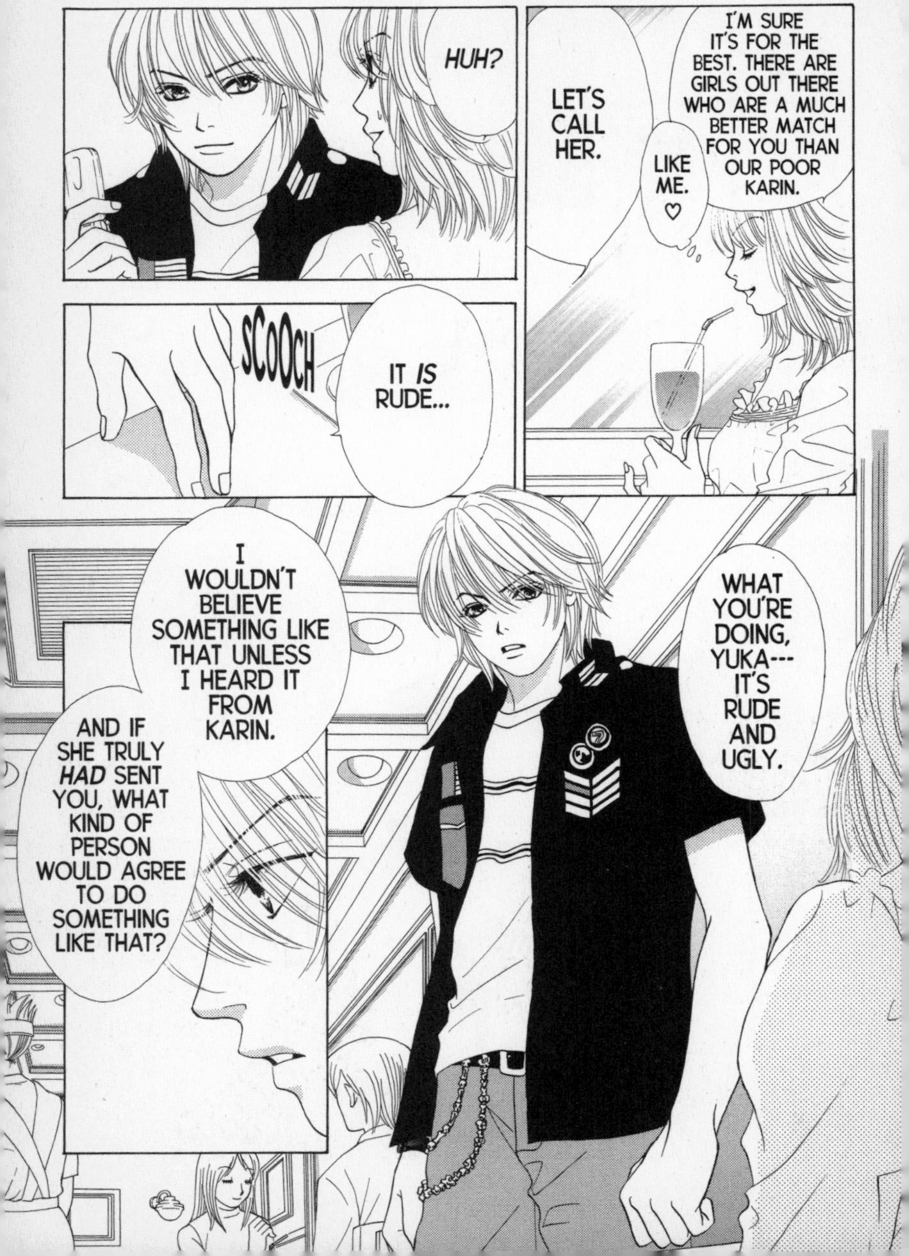
I'M SURE IT'S FOR THE BEST. THERE ARE GIRLS OUT THERE WHO ARE A MUCH BETTER MATCH FOR YOU THAN OUR POOR KARIN.
LIKE ME. ♡
LET'S CALL HER.
HUH?
SCOOCH
IT *IS* RUDE...
WHAT YOU'RE DOING, YUKA--- IT'S RUDE AND UGLY.
I WOULDN'T BELIEVE SOMETHING LIKE THAT UNLESS I HEARD IT FROM KARIN.
AND IF SHE TRULY *HAD* SENT YOU, WHAT KIND OF PERSON WOULD AGREE TO DO SOMETHING LIKE THAT?

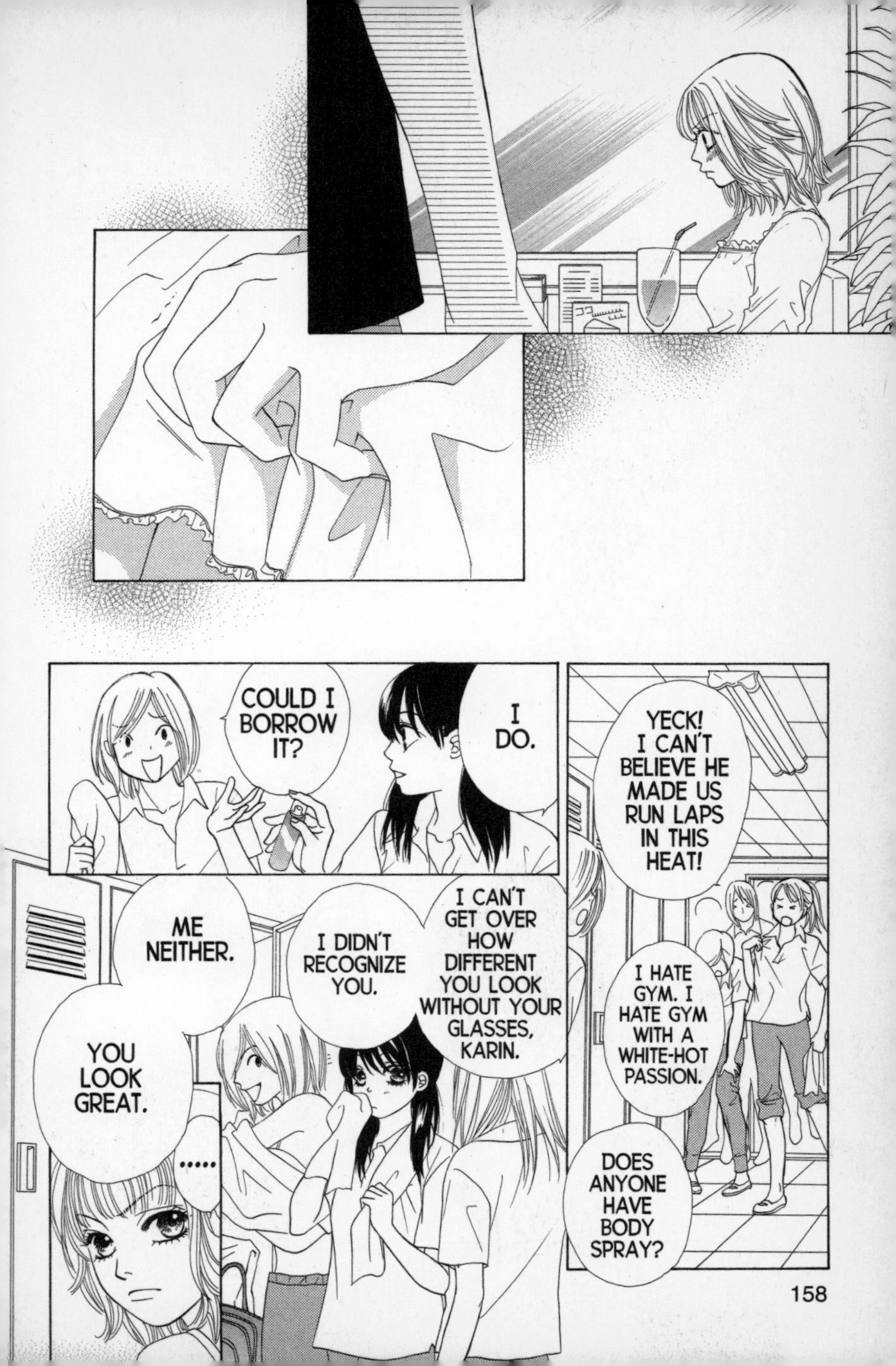
YECK! I CAN'T BELIEVE HE MADE US RUN LAPS IN THIS HEAT!
I HATE GYM. I HATE GYM WITH A WHITE-HOT PASSION.
DOES ANYONE HAVE BODY SPRAY?
I DO.
COULD I BORROW IT?
I CAN'T GET OVER HOW DIFFERENT YOU LOOK WITHOUT YOUR GLASSES, KARIN.
I DIDN'T RECOGNIZE YOU.
ME NEITHER.
YOU LOOK GREAT.
......

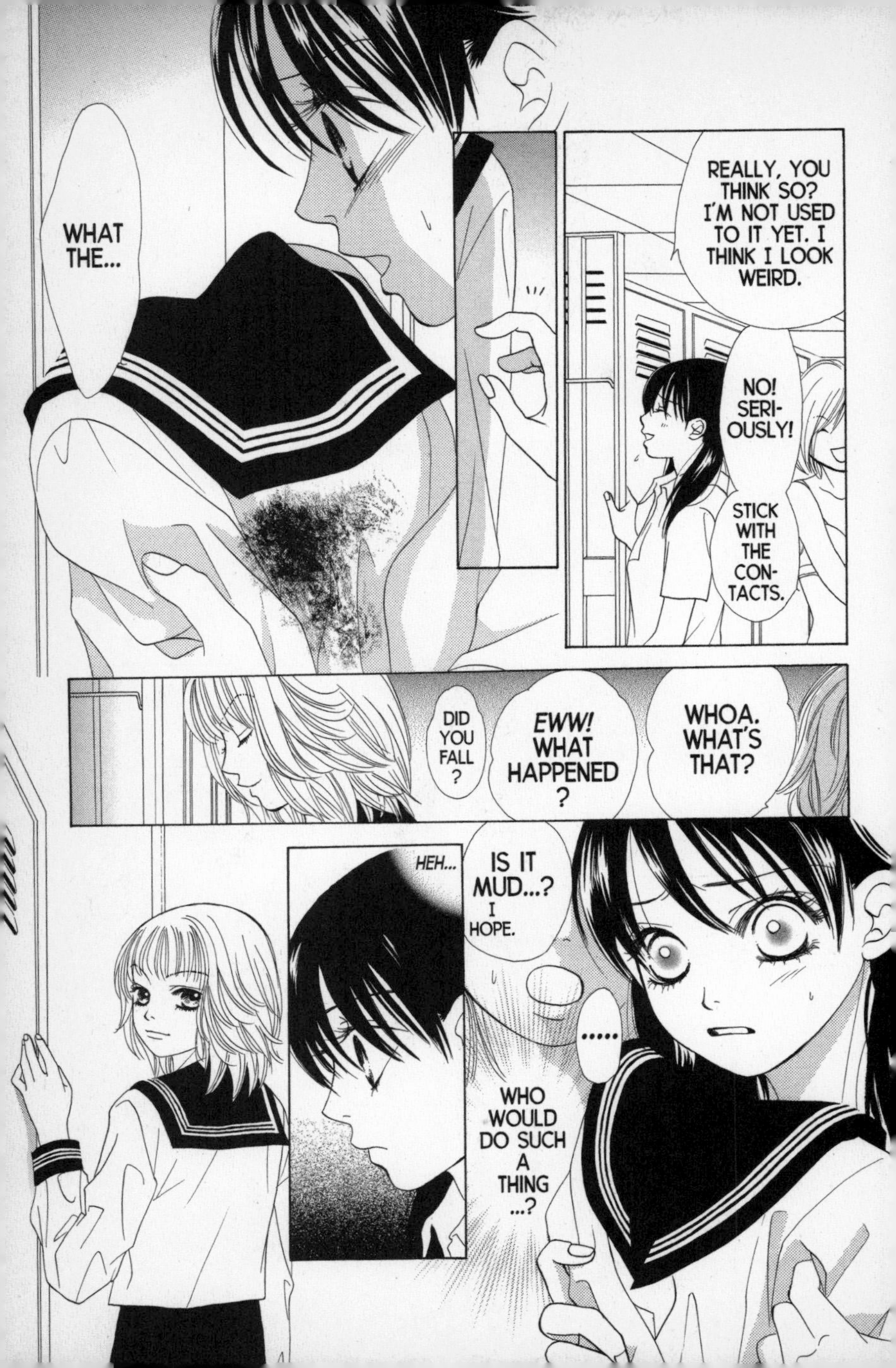
REALLY, YOU THINK SO? I'M NOT USED TO IT YET. I THINK I LOOK WEIRD.
NO! SERI-OUSLY!
STICK WITH THE CON-TACTS.
WHAT THE...
WHOA. WHAT'S THAT?
EWW! WHAT HAPPENED?
DID YOU FALL?
IS IT MUD...?
I HOPE.
......
WHO WOULD DO SUCH A THING ...?
HEH...

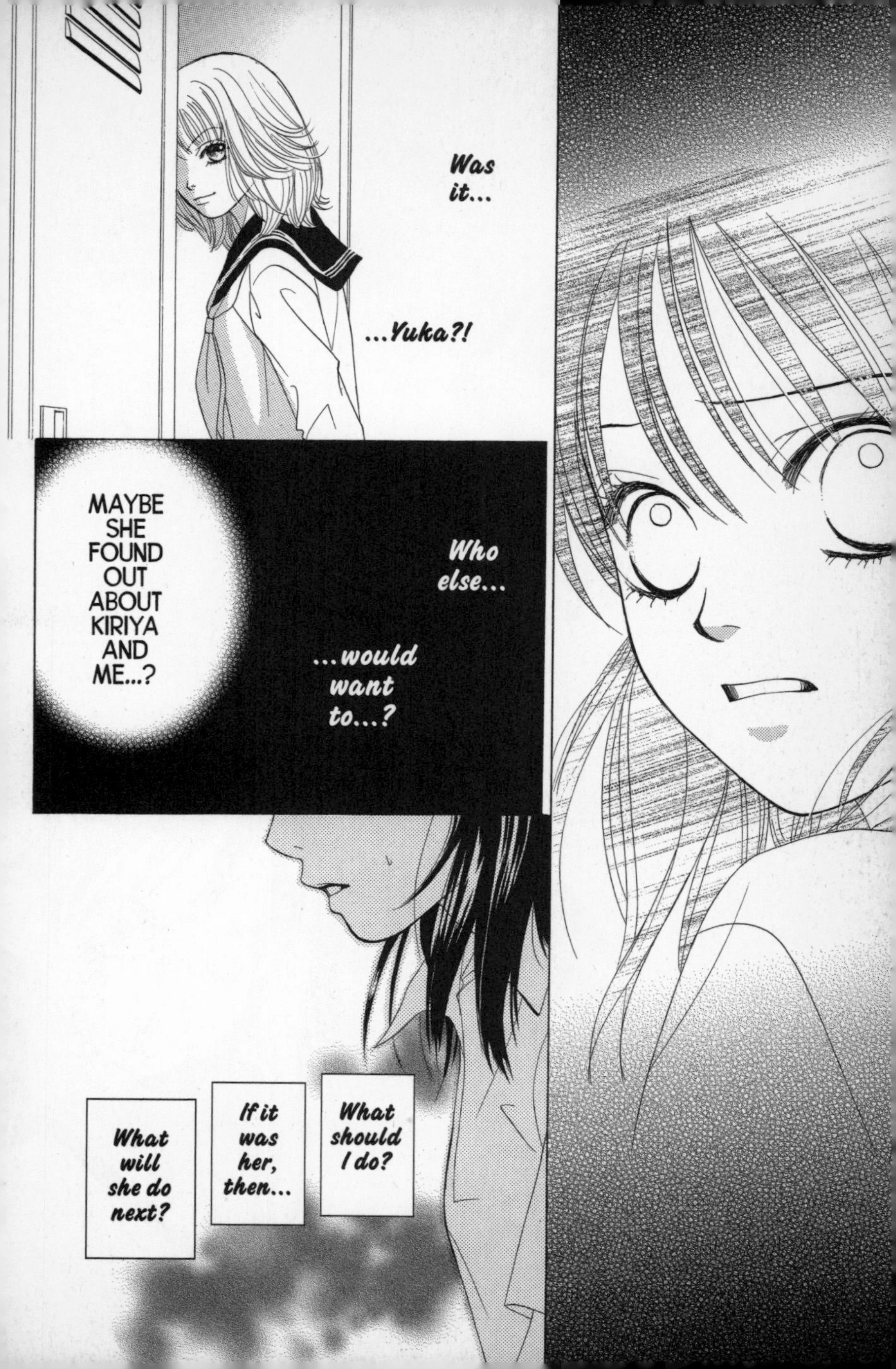
Was it...
...Yuka?!
Who else...
...would want to...?
MAYBE SHE FOUND OUT ABOUT KIRIYA AND ME...?
What should I do?
If it was her, then...
What will she do next?

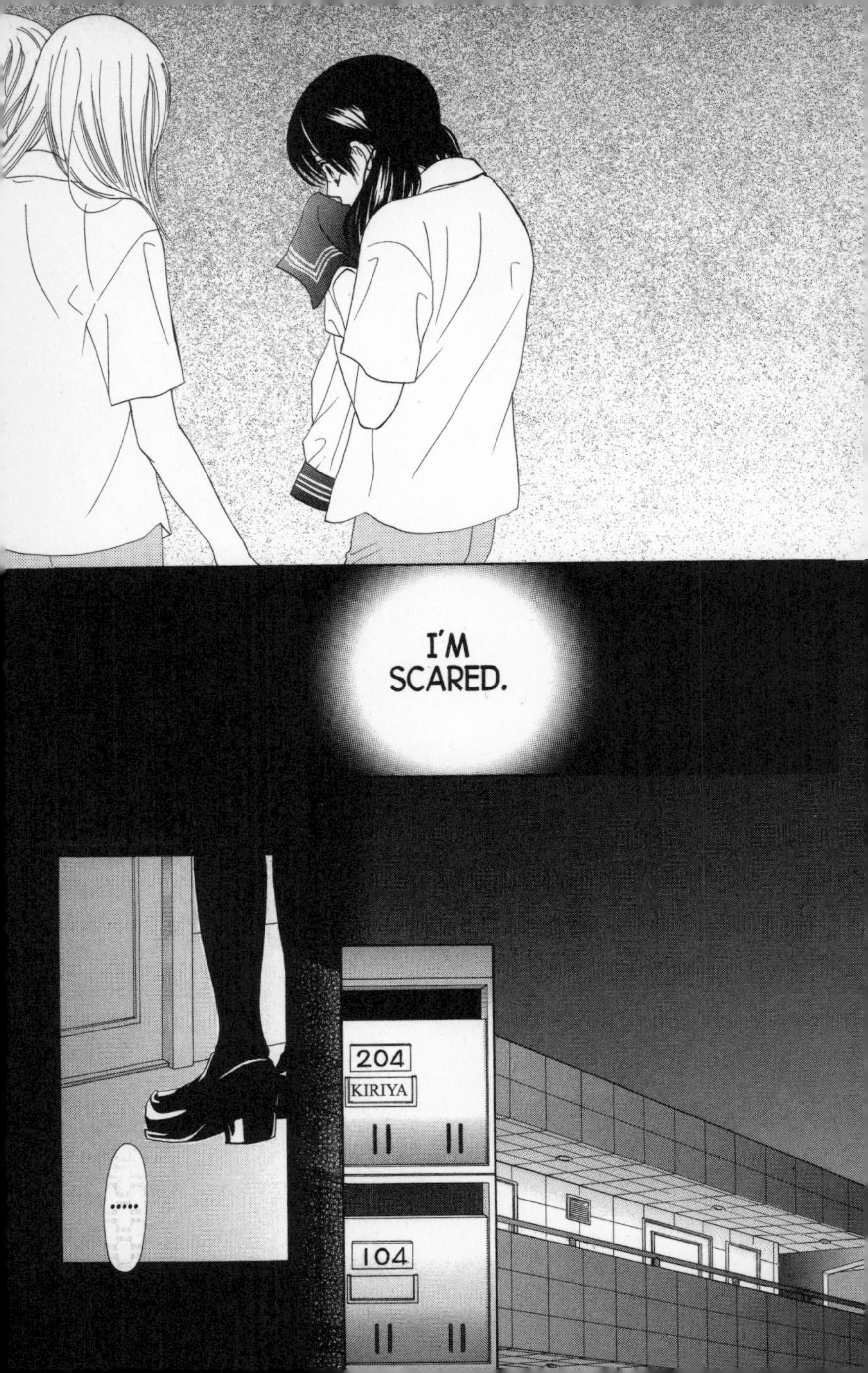
I'M SCARED.
204
KIRIYA
104
......

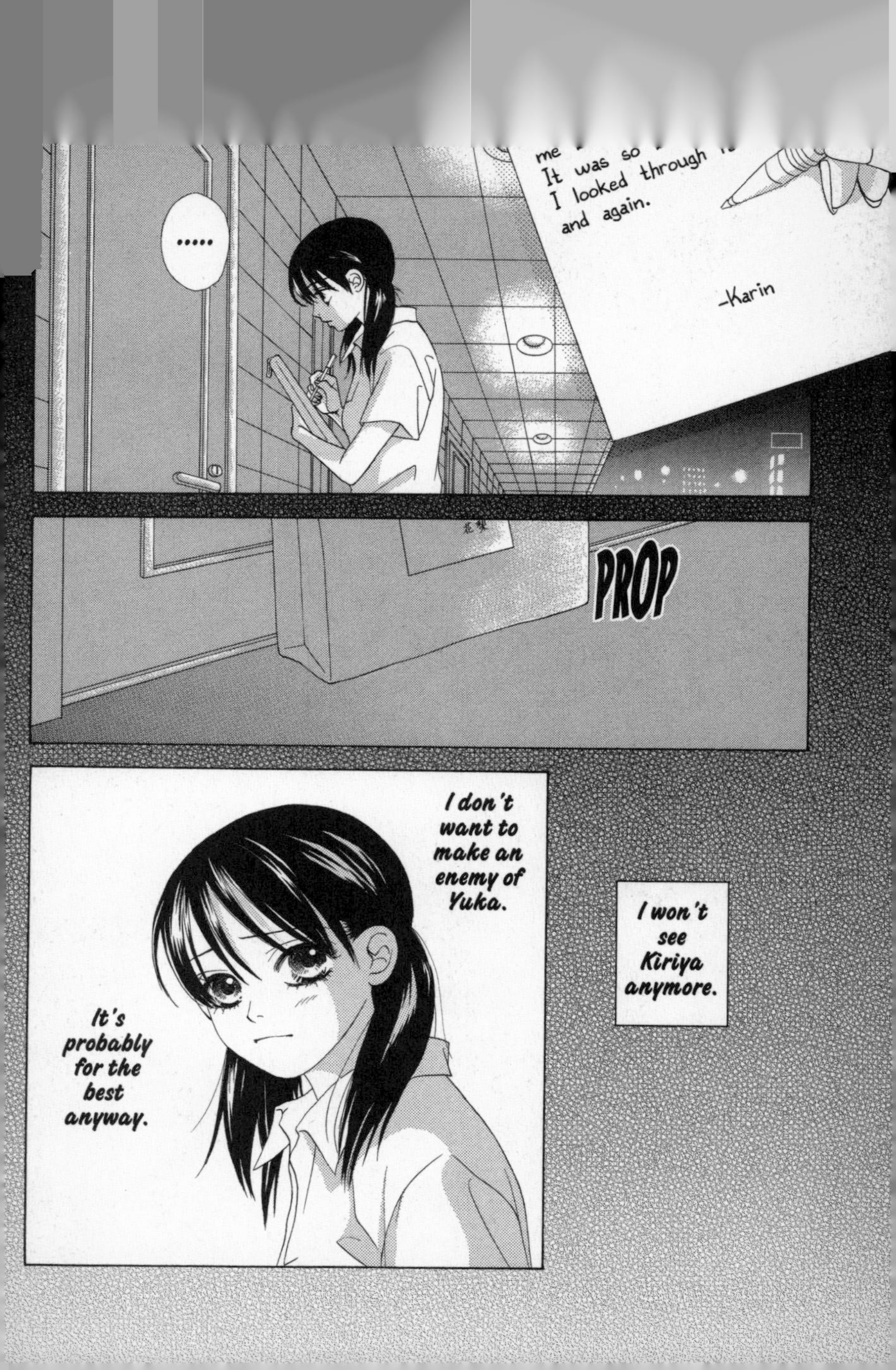
me
It was so
I looked through
and again.
-Karin
......
PROP
I won't see Kiriya anymore.
I don't want to make an enemy of Yuka.
It's probably for the best anyway.

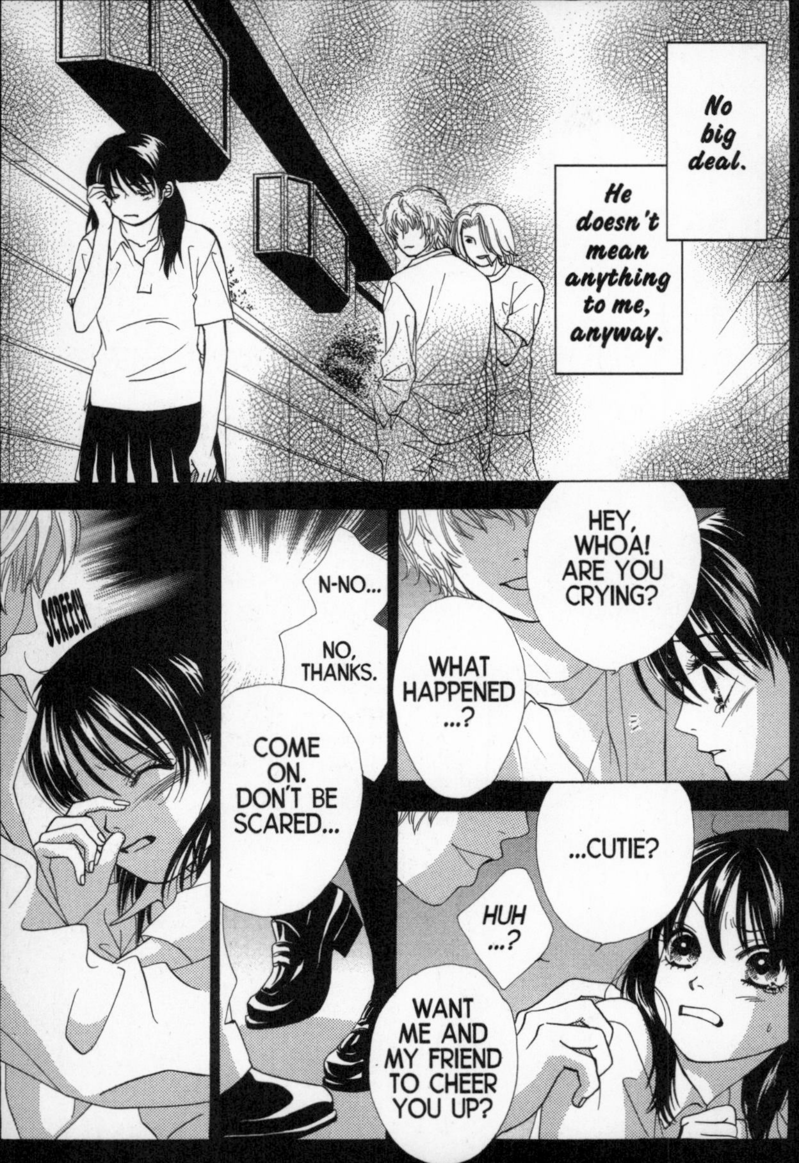
No big deal.
He doesn't mean anything to me, anyway.
HEY, WHOA! ARE YOU CRYING?
WHAT HAPPENED ...?
...CUTIE?
HUH ...?
WANT ME AND MY FRIEND TO CHEER YOU UP?
N-NO...
NO, THANKS.
COME ON. DON'T BE SCARED...
SCREECH

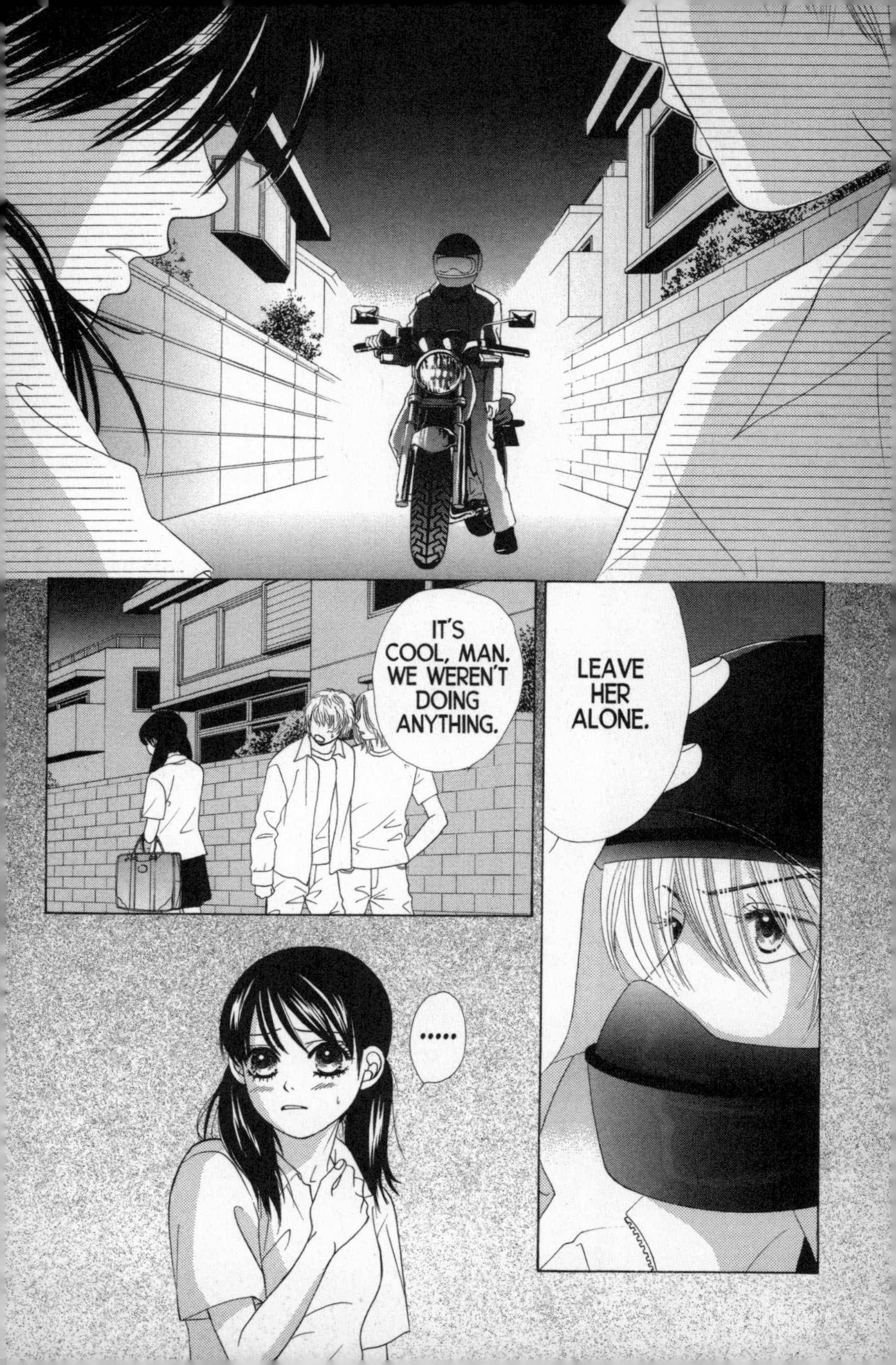
LEAVE HER ALONE.
IT'S COOL, MAN. WE WEREN'T DOING ANYTHING.
......

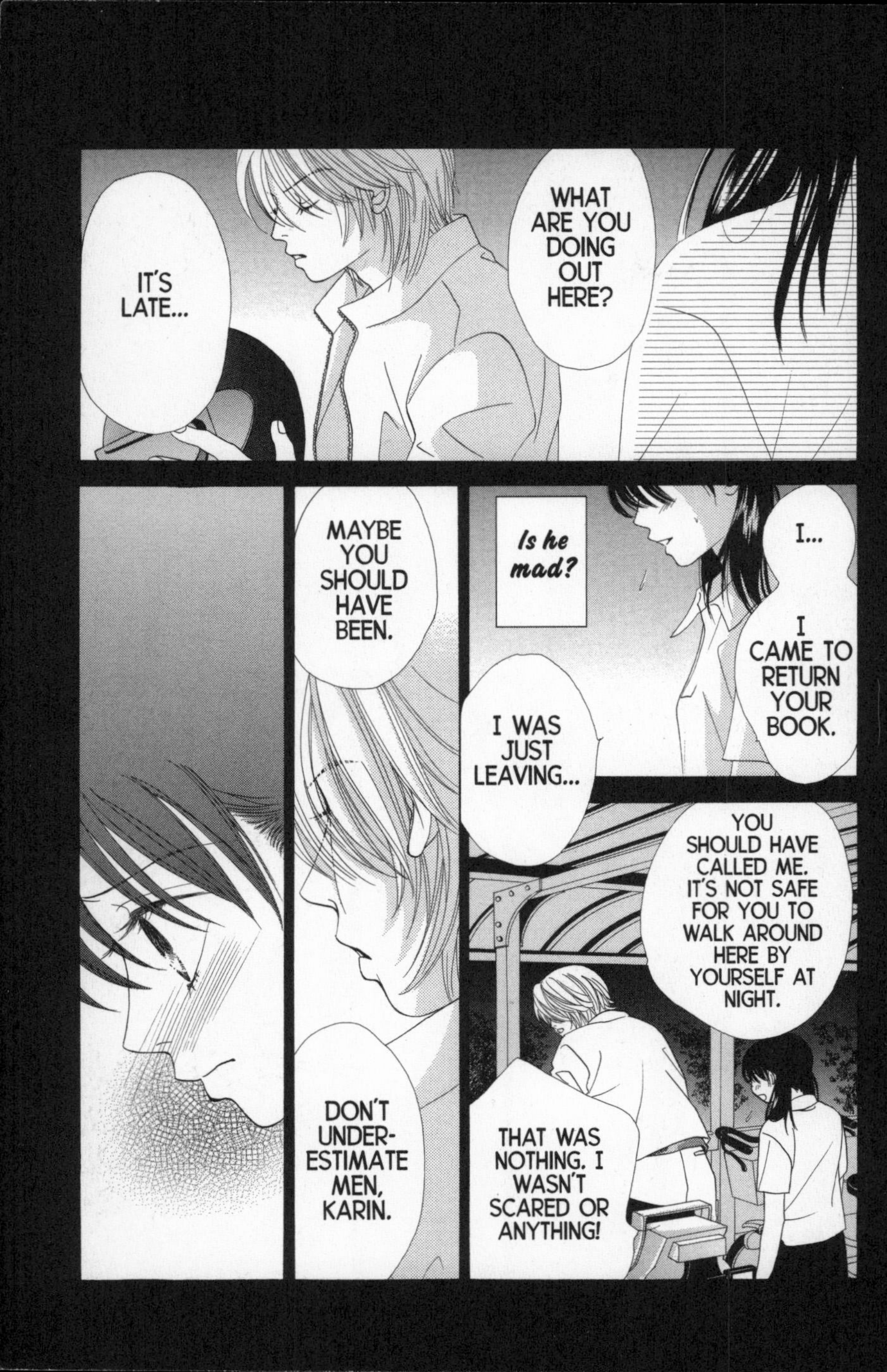
WHAT ARE YOU DOING OUT HERE?
IT'S LATE...
I...
I CAME TO RETURN YOUR BOOK.
Is he mad?
I WAS JUST LEAVING...
YOU SHOULD HAVE CALLED ME. IT'S NOT SAFE FOR YOU TO WALK AROUND HERE BY YOURSELF AT NIGHT.
THAT WAS NOTHING. I WASN'T SCARED OR ANYTHING!
MAYBE YOU SHOULD HAVE BEEN.
DON'T UNDER-ESTIMATE MEN, KARIN.

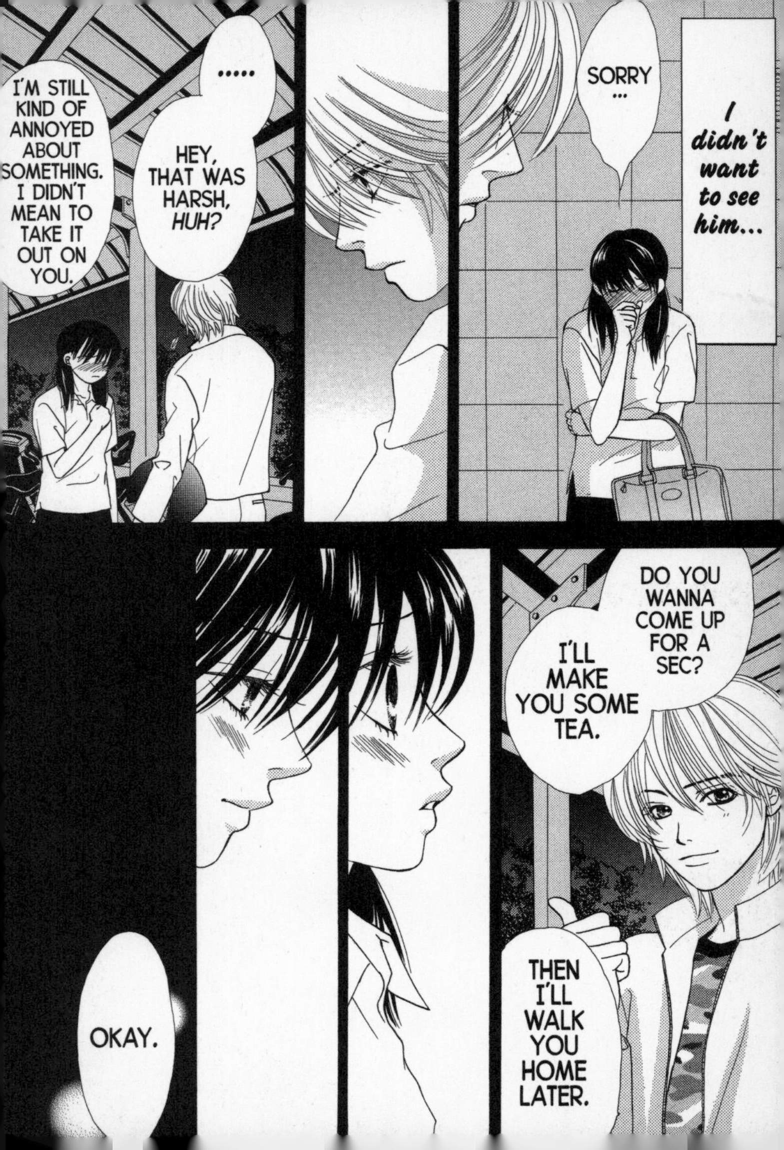
I didn't want to see him...
SORRY...
.....
HEY, THAT WAS HARSH, HUH?
I'M STILL KIND OF ANNOYED ABOUT SOMETHING. I DIDN'T MEAN TO TAKE IT OUT ON YOU.
DO YOU WANNA COME UP FOR A SEC?
I'LL MAKE YOU SOME TEA.
THEN I'LL WALK YOU HOME LATER.
OKAY.

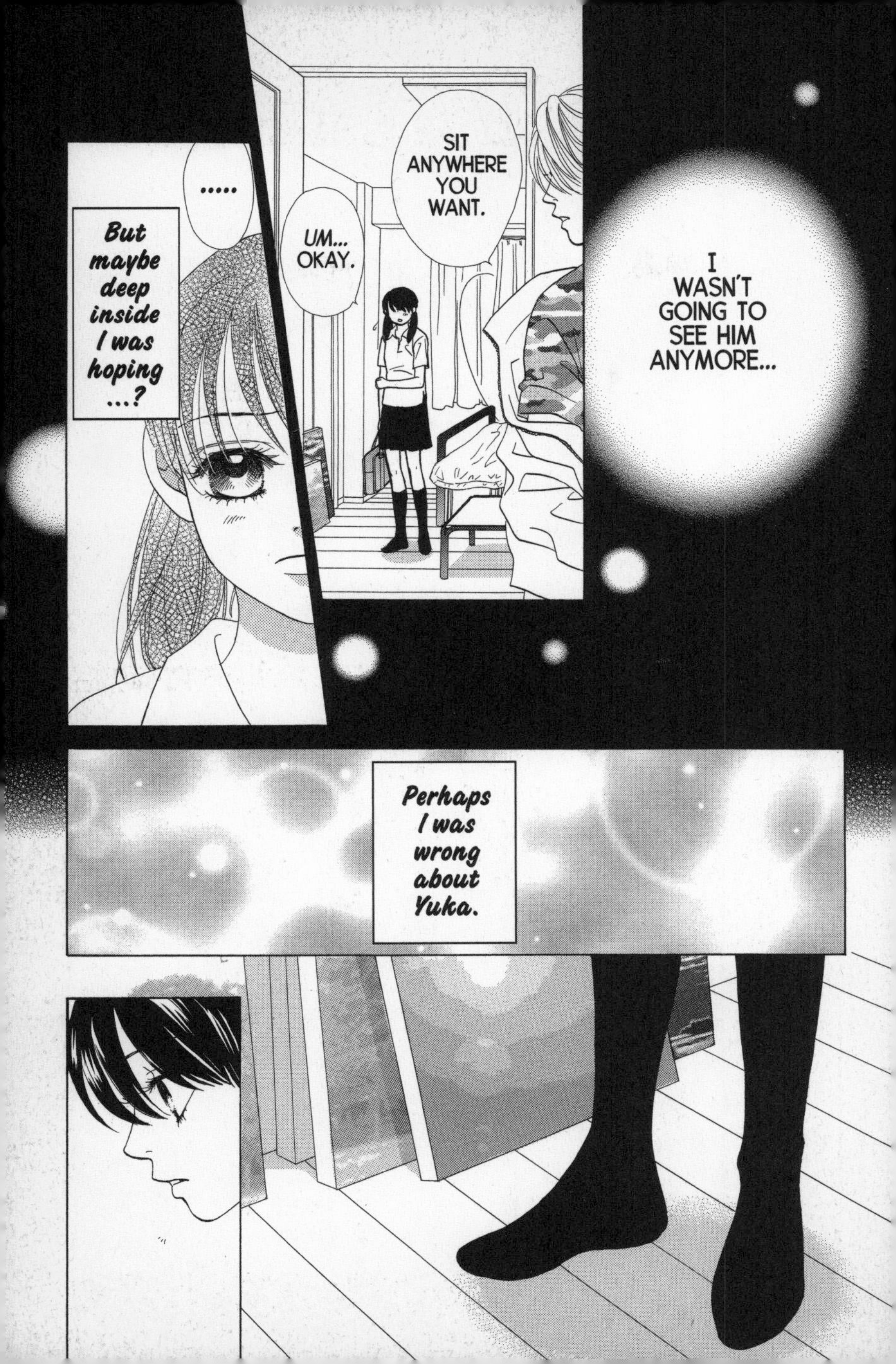
I WASN'T GOING TO SEE HIM ANYMORE...
SIT ANYWHERE YOU WANT.
UM... OKAY.
.....
But maybe deep inside I was hoping...?
Perhaps I was wrong about Yuka.

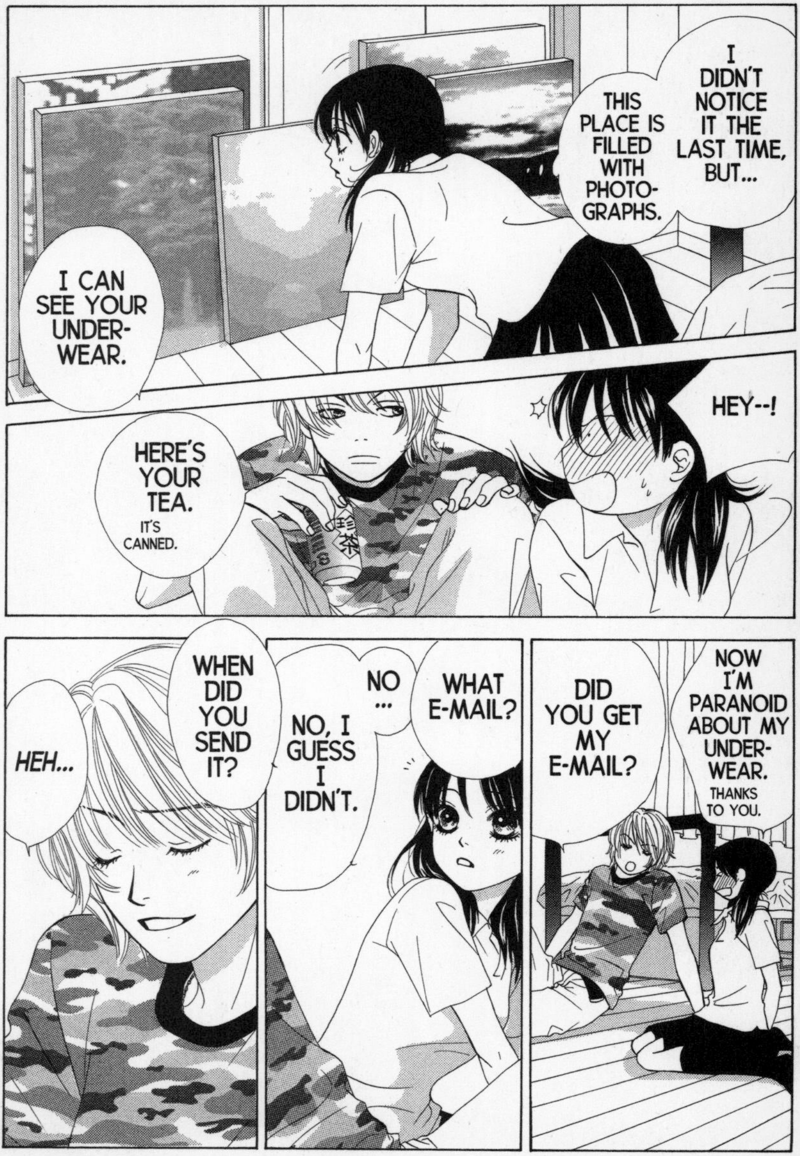
I DIDN'T NOTICE IT THE LAST TIME, BUT...
THIS PLACE IS FILLED WITH PHOTOGRAPHS.
I CAN SEE YOUR UNDERWEAR.
HEY--!
HERE'S YOUR TEA. IT'S CANNED.
NOW I'M PARANOID ABOUT MY UNDERWEAR. THANKS TO YOU.
DID YOU GET MY E-MAIL?
WHAT E-MAIL?
NO ...
NO, I GUESS I DIDN'T.
WHEN DID YOU SEND IT?
HEH...

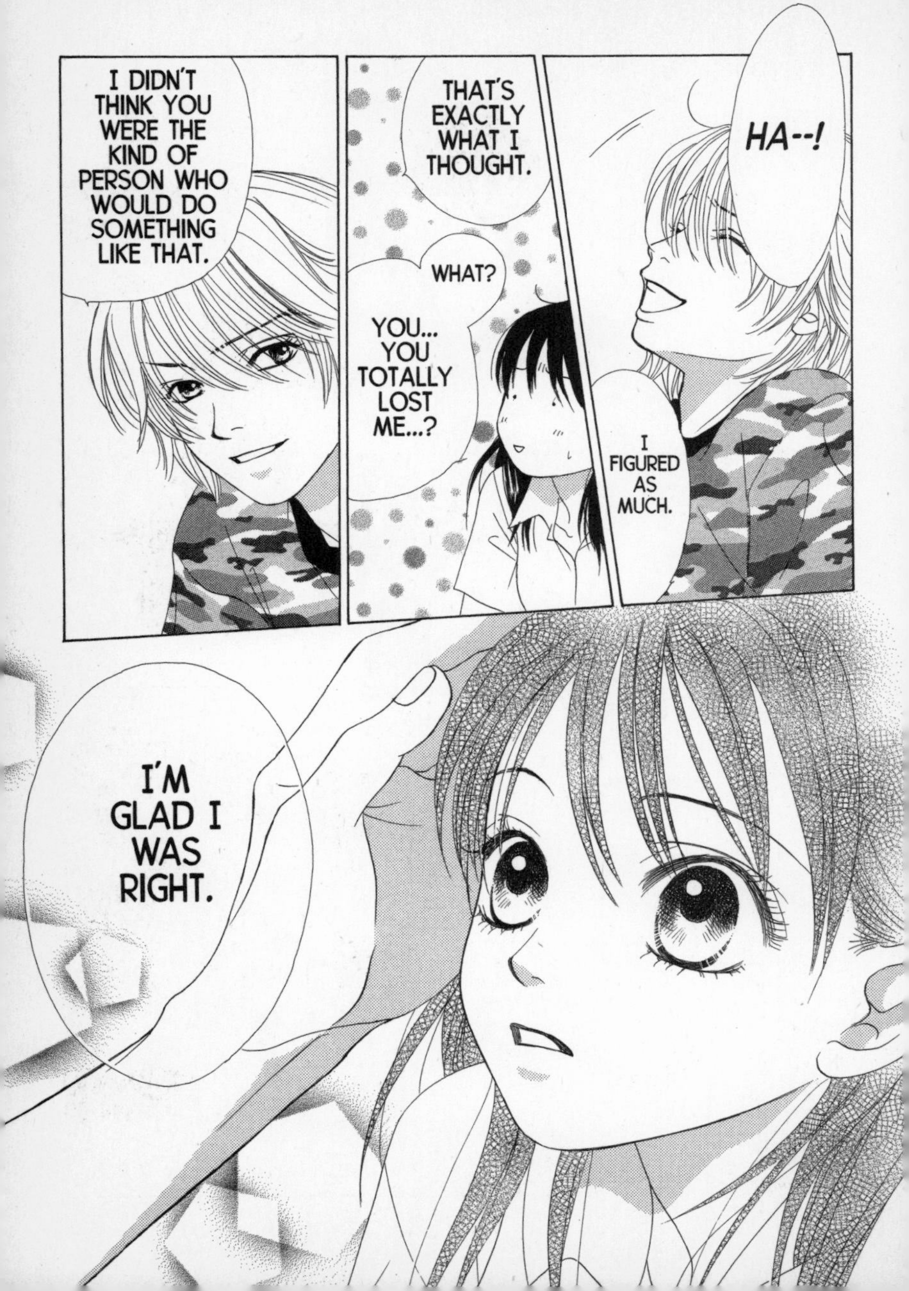
HA--!
I FIGURED AS MUCH.
THAT'S EXACTLY WHAT I THOUGHT.
WHAT?
YOU... YOU TOTALLY LOST ME...?
I DIDN'T THINK YOU WERE THE KIND OF PERSON WHO WOULD DO SOMETHING LIKE THAT.
I'M GLAD I WAS RIGHT.

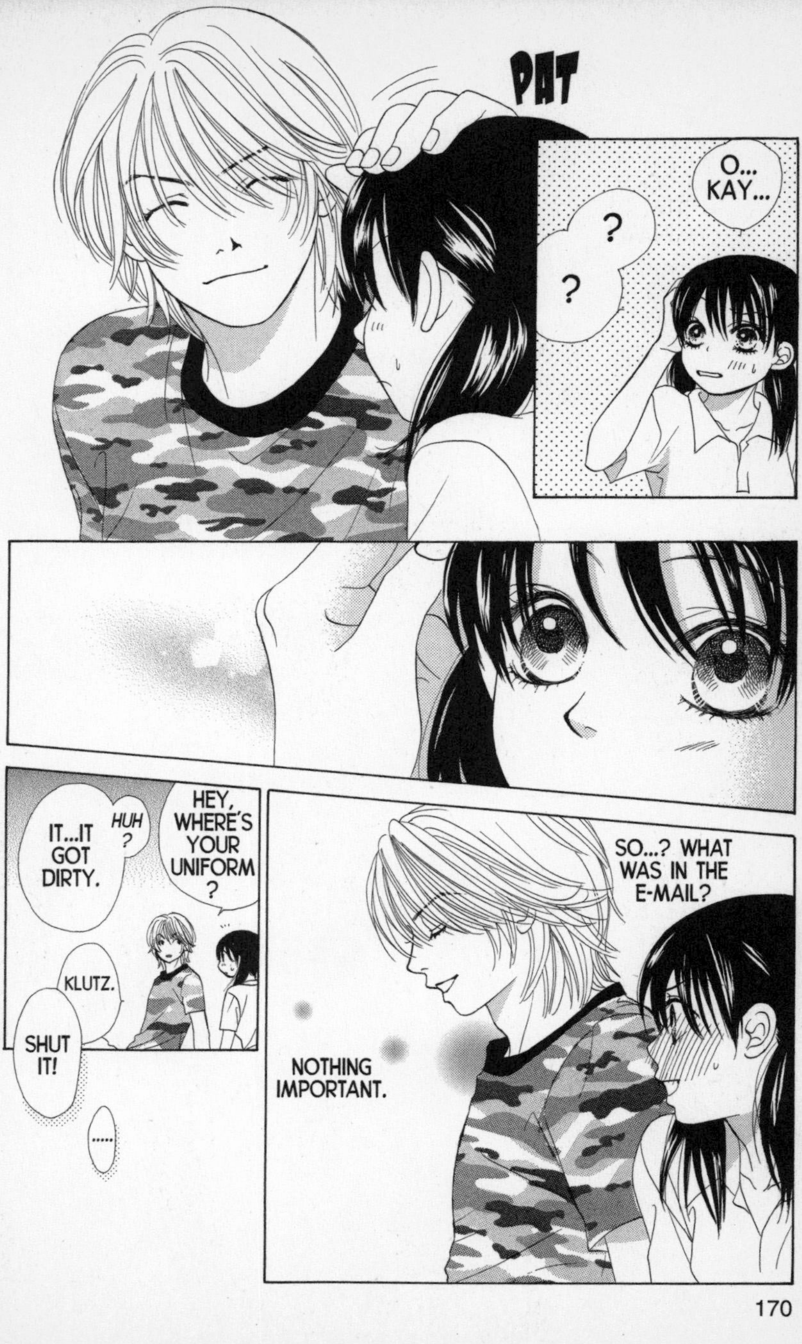
PAT
? ?
O... KAY...
SO...? WHAT WAS IN THE E-MAIL?
NOTHING IMPORTANT.
HEY, WHERE'S YOUR UNIFORM?
HUH?
IT...IT GOT DIRTY.
KLUTZ.
SHUT IT!
.....

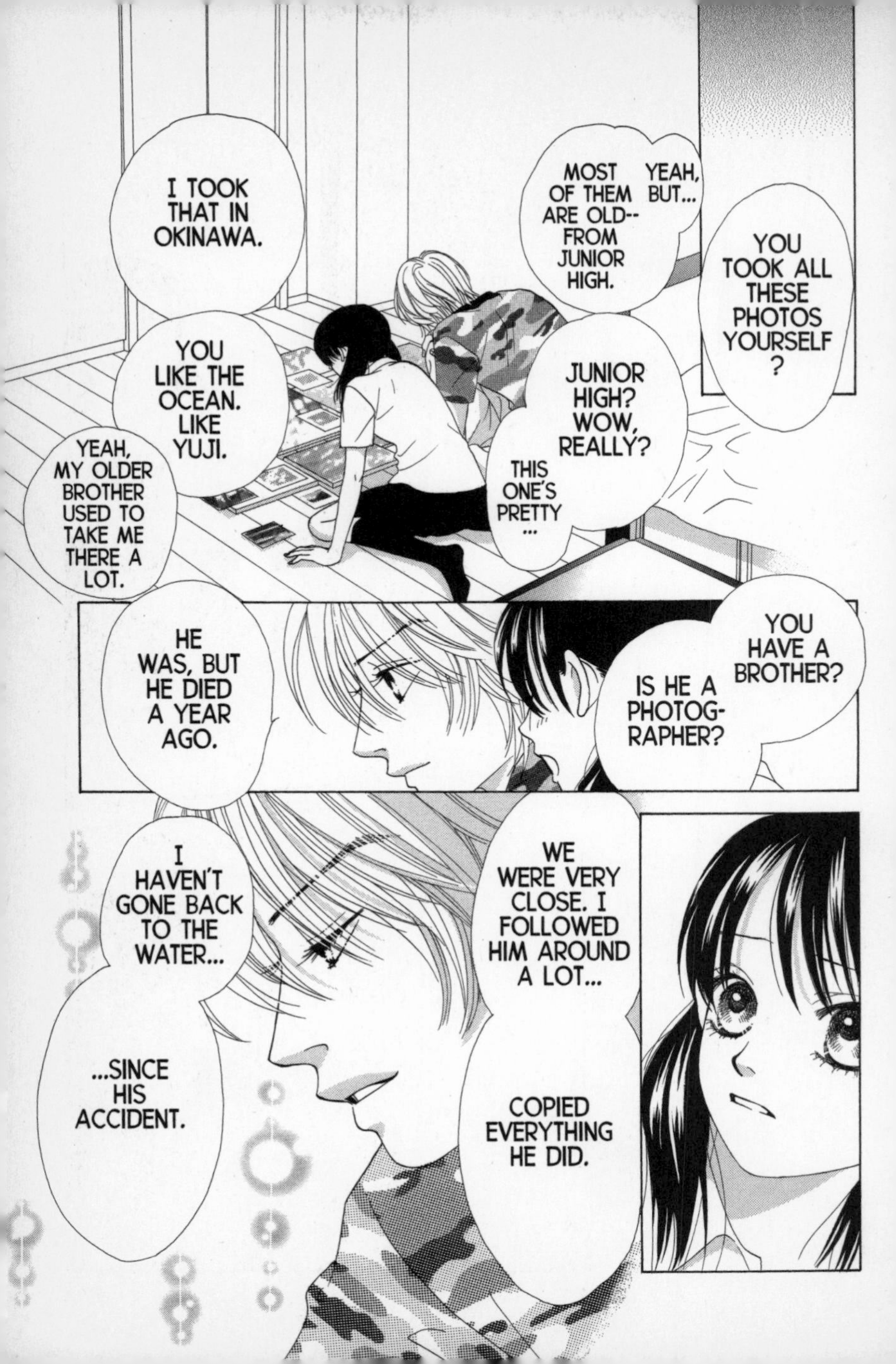
YOU TOOK ALL THESE PHOTOS YOURSELF?
YEAH, BUT... MOST OF THEM ARE OLD-- FROM JUNIOR HIGH.
JUNIOR HIGH? WOW, REALLY?
THIS ONE'S PRETTY...
I TOOK THAT IN OKINAWA.
YOU LIKE THE OCEAN. LIKE YUJI.
YEAH, MY OLDER BROTHER USED TO TAKE ME THERE A LOT.
YOU HAVE A BROTHER?
IS HE A PHOTOGRAPHER?
HE WAS, BUT HE DIED A YEAR AGO.
WE WERE VERY CLOSE. I FOLLOWED HIM AROUND A LOT...
COPIED EVERYTHING HE DID.
I HAVEN'T GONE BACK TO THE WATER...
...SINCE HIS ACCIDENT.

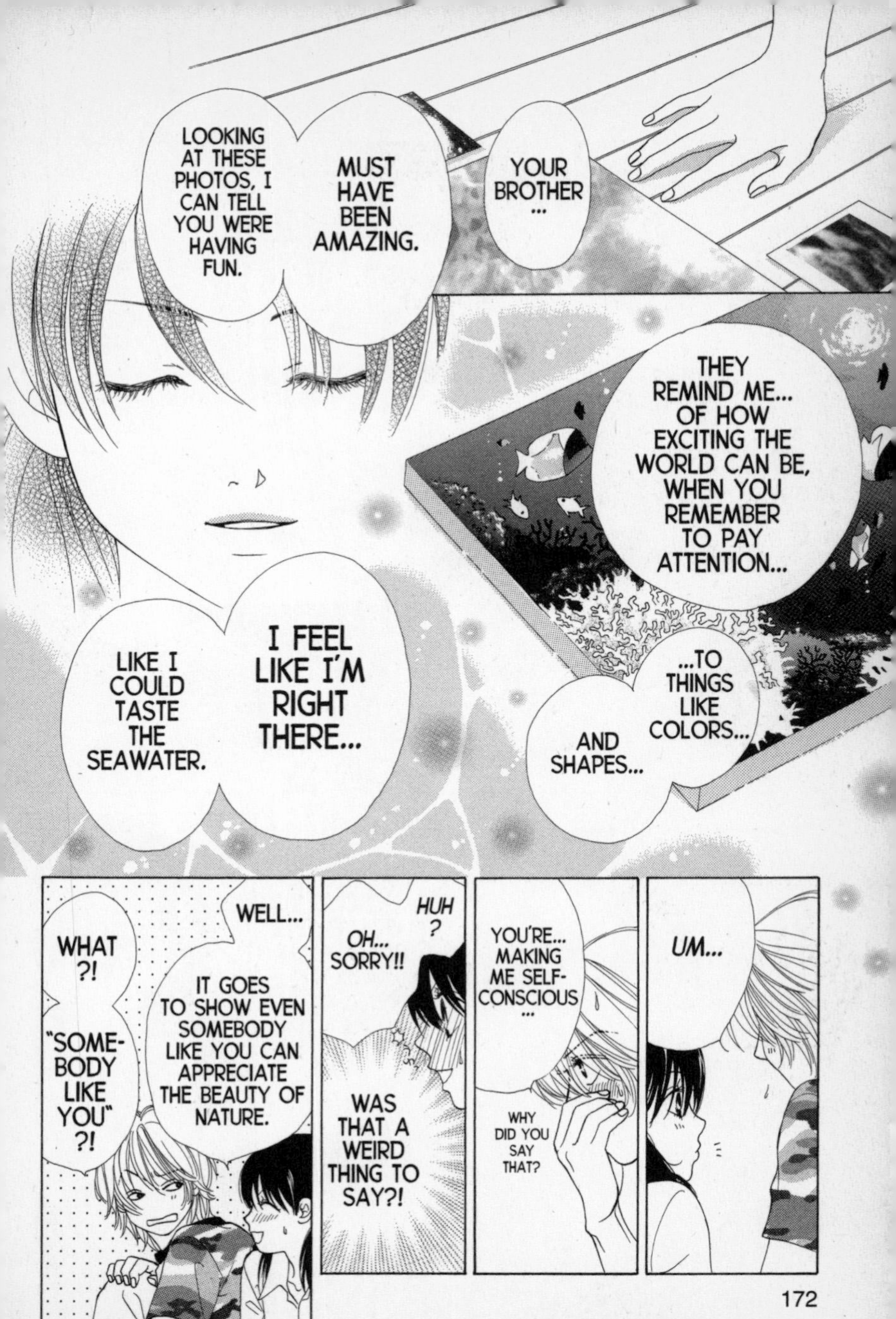
YOUR BROTHER ...
MUST HAVE BEEN AMAZING.
LOOKING AT THESE PHOTOS, I CAN TELL YOU WERE HAVING FUN.
THEY REMIND ME... OF HOW EXCITING THE WORLD CAN BE, WHEN YOU REMEMBER TO PAY ATTENTION...
...TO THINGS LIKE COLORS...
AND SHAPES...
I FEEL LIKE I'M RIGHT THERE...
LIKE I COULD TASTE THE SEAWATER.
UM...
YOU'RE... MAKING ME SELF-CONSCIOUS ...
WHY DID YOU SAY THAT?
HUH ?
OH... SORRY!!
WAS THAT A WEIRD THING TO SAY?!
WELL...
IT GOES TO SHOW EVEN SOMEBODY LIKE YOU CAN APPRECIATE THE BEAUTY OF NATURE.
WHAT ?!
"SOME-BODY LIKE YOU" ?!

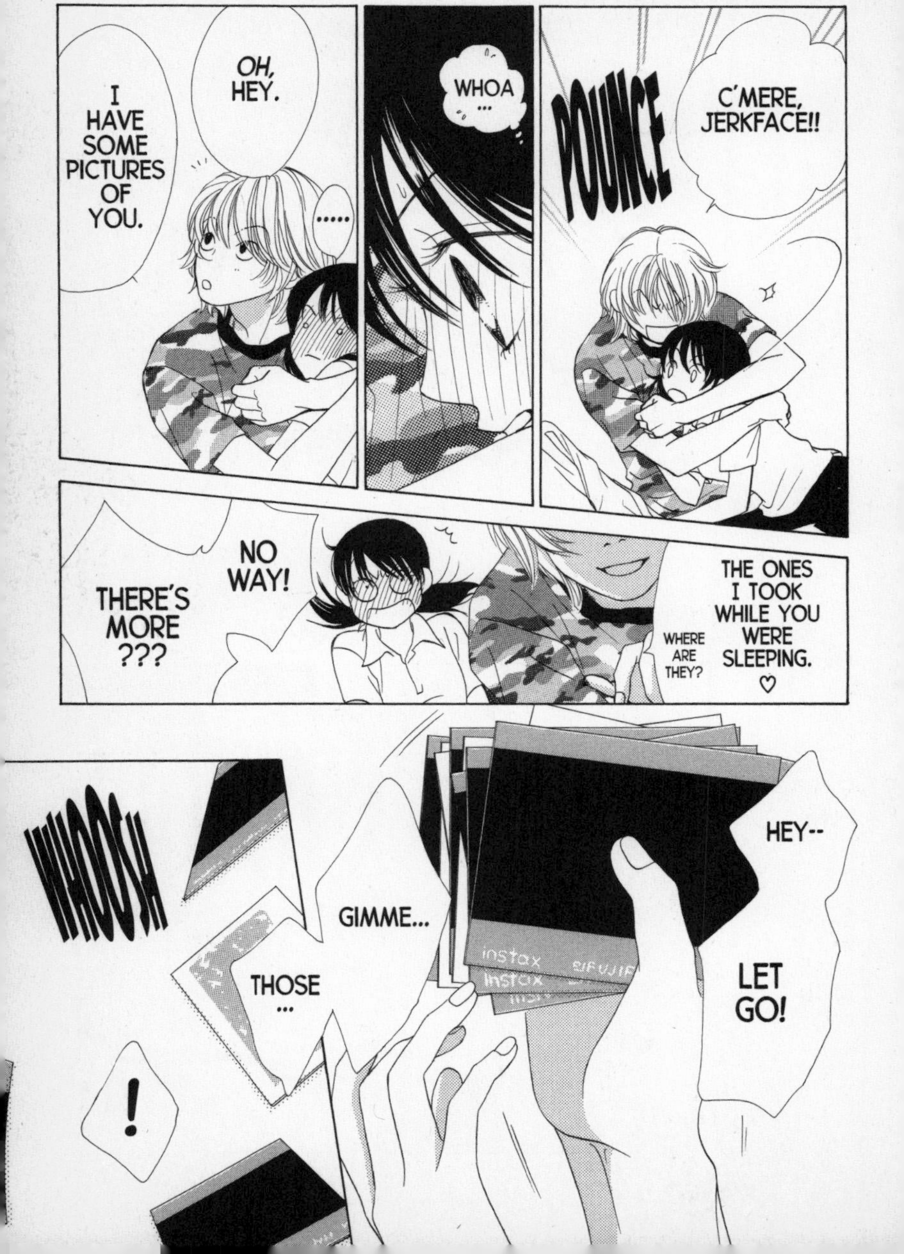
POUNCE
C'MERE, JERKFACE!!
WHOA ...
OH, HEY.
.....
I HAVE SOME PICTURES OF YOU.
THE ONES I TOOK WHILE YOU WERE SLEEPING. ♡
WHERE ARE THEY?
NO WAY!
THERE'S MORE ???
HEY--
LET GO!
GIMME...
THOSE ...
WHOOSH
!

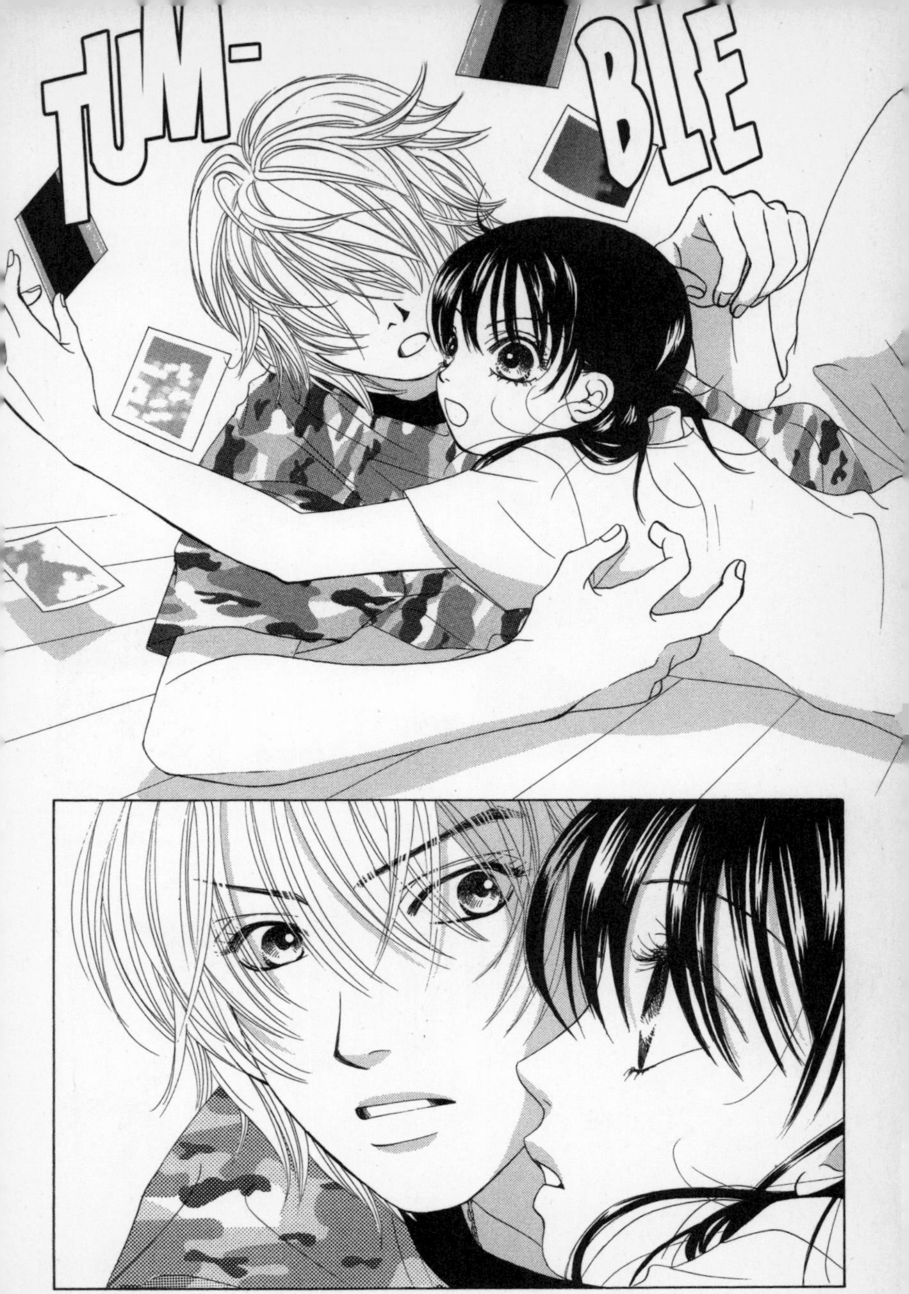
TUM-BLE

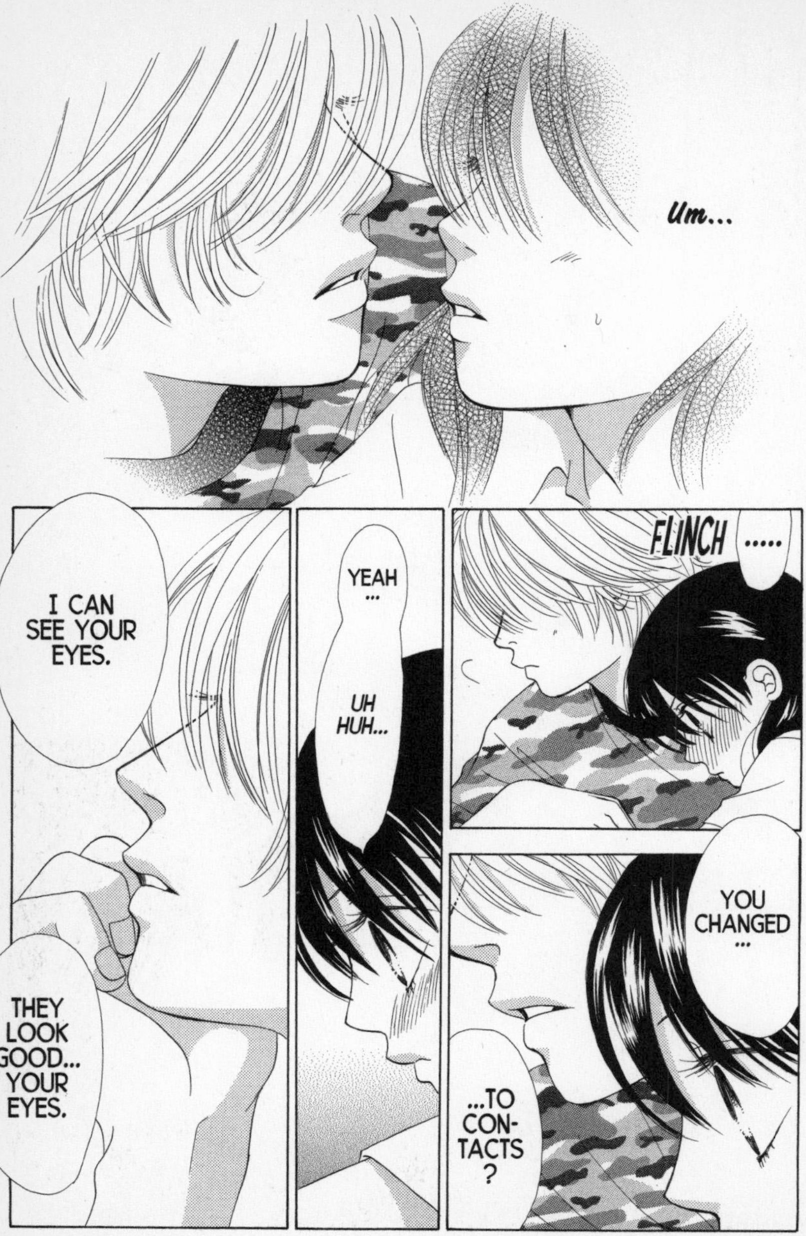
Um...
FLINCH
.....
YOU CHANGED ...
...TO CONTACTS?
YEAH ...
UH HUH...
I CAN SEE YOUR EYES.
THEY LOOK GOOD... YOUR EYES.

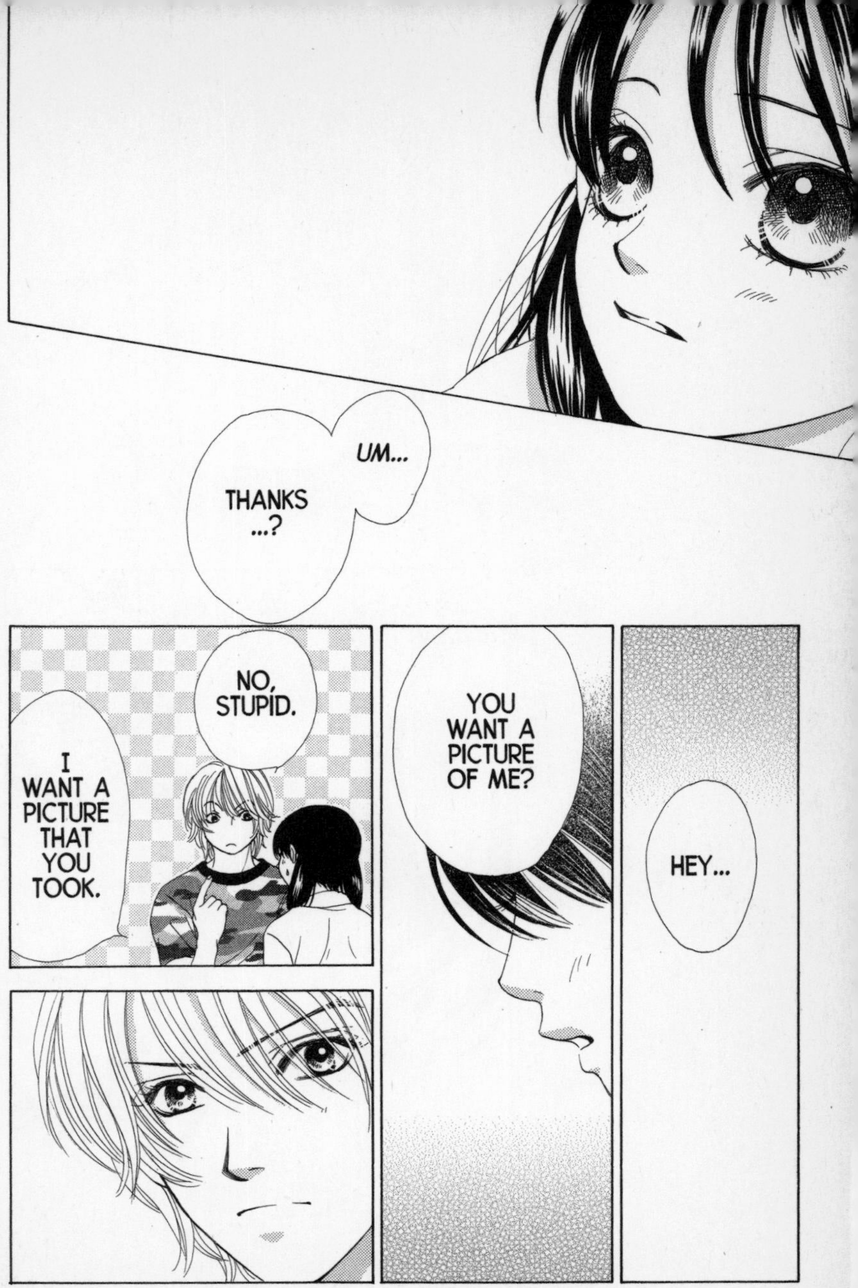
UM... THANKS ...?
HEY...
YOU WANT A PICTURE OF ME?
NO, STUPID.
I WANT A PICTURE THAT YOU TOOK.

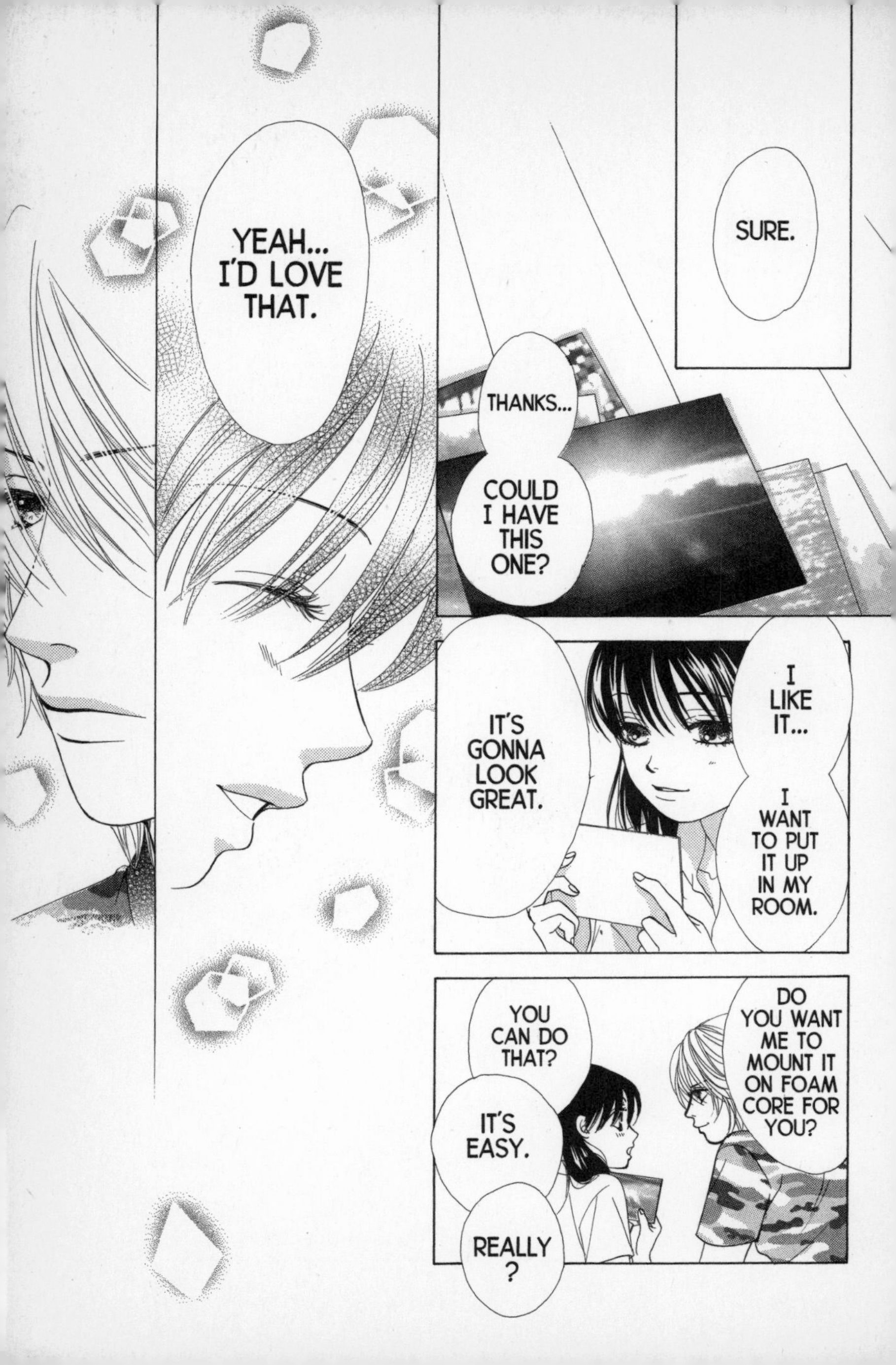
SURE.
THANKS...
COULD I HAVE THIS ONE?
I LIKE IT...
I WANT TO PUT IT UP IN MY ROOM.
IT'S GONNA LOOK GREAT.
DO YOU WANT ME TO MOUNT IT ON FOAM CORE FOR YOU?
YOU CAN DO THAT?
IT'S EASY.
REALLY?
YEAH... I'D LOVE THAT.

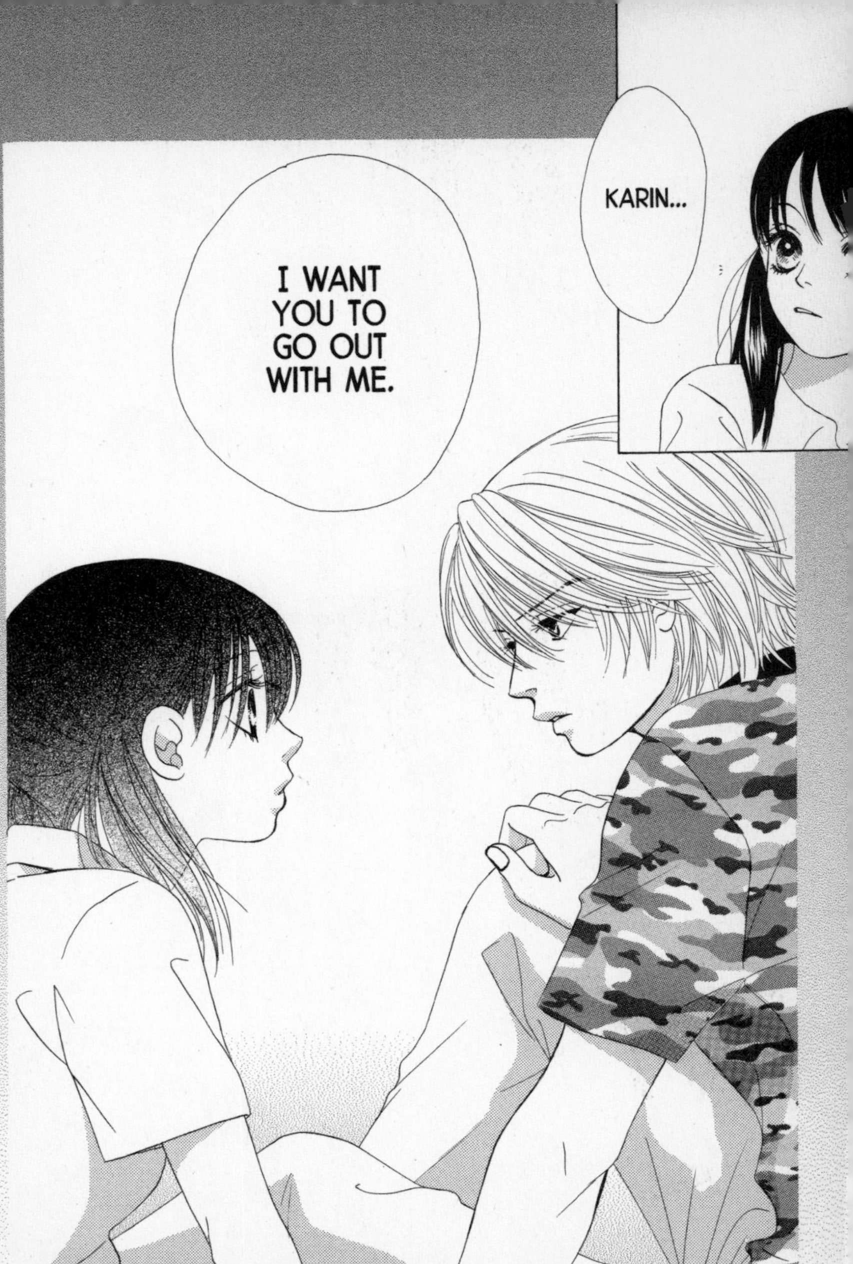
KARIN...
I WANT YOU TO GO OUT WITH ME.

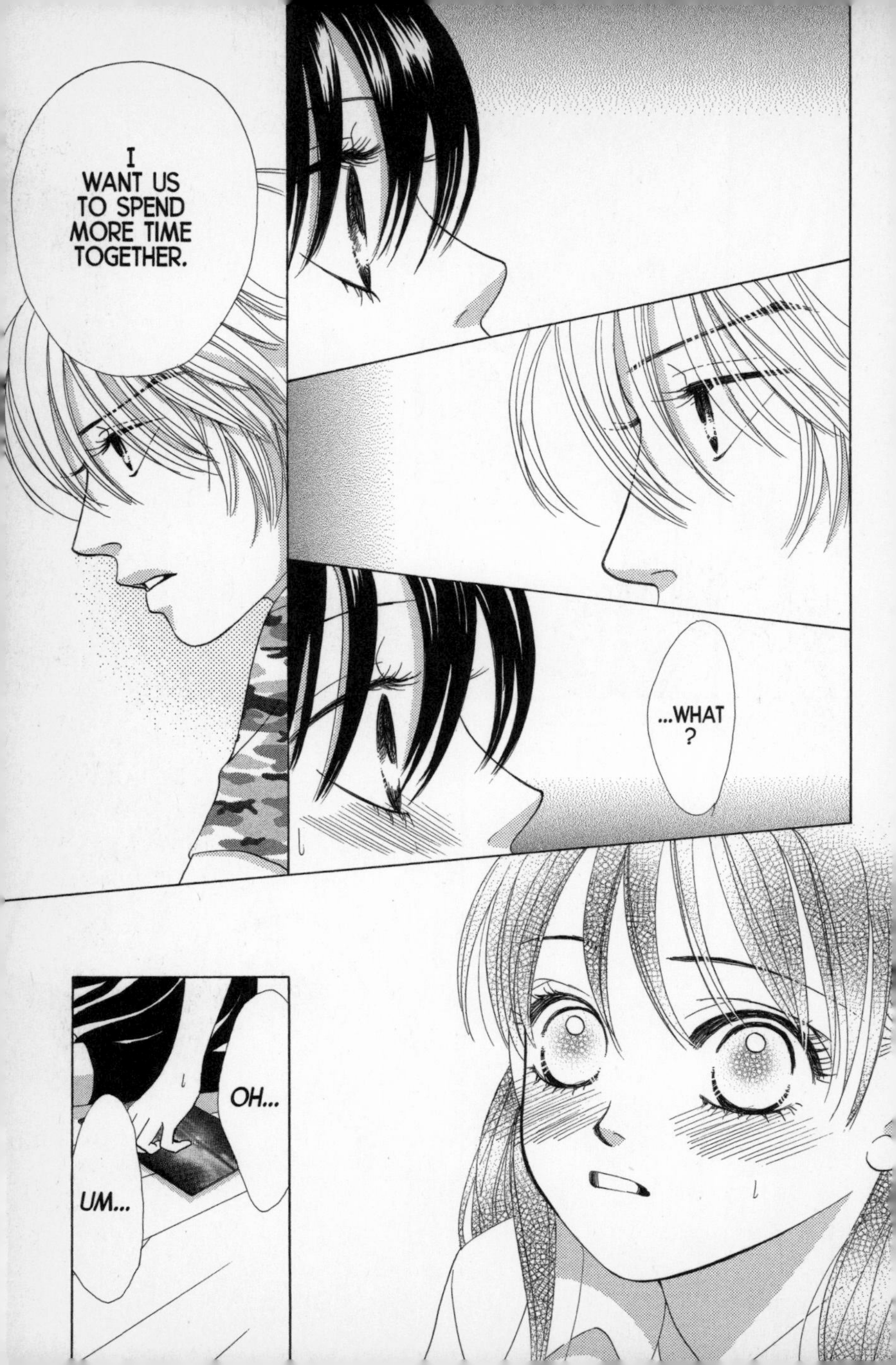
...WHAT?
I WANT US TO SPEND MORE TIME TOGETHER.
OH...
UM...

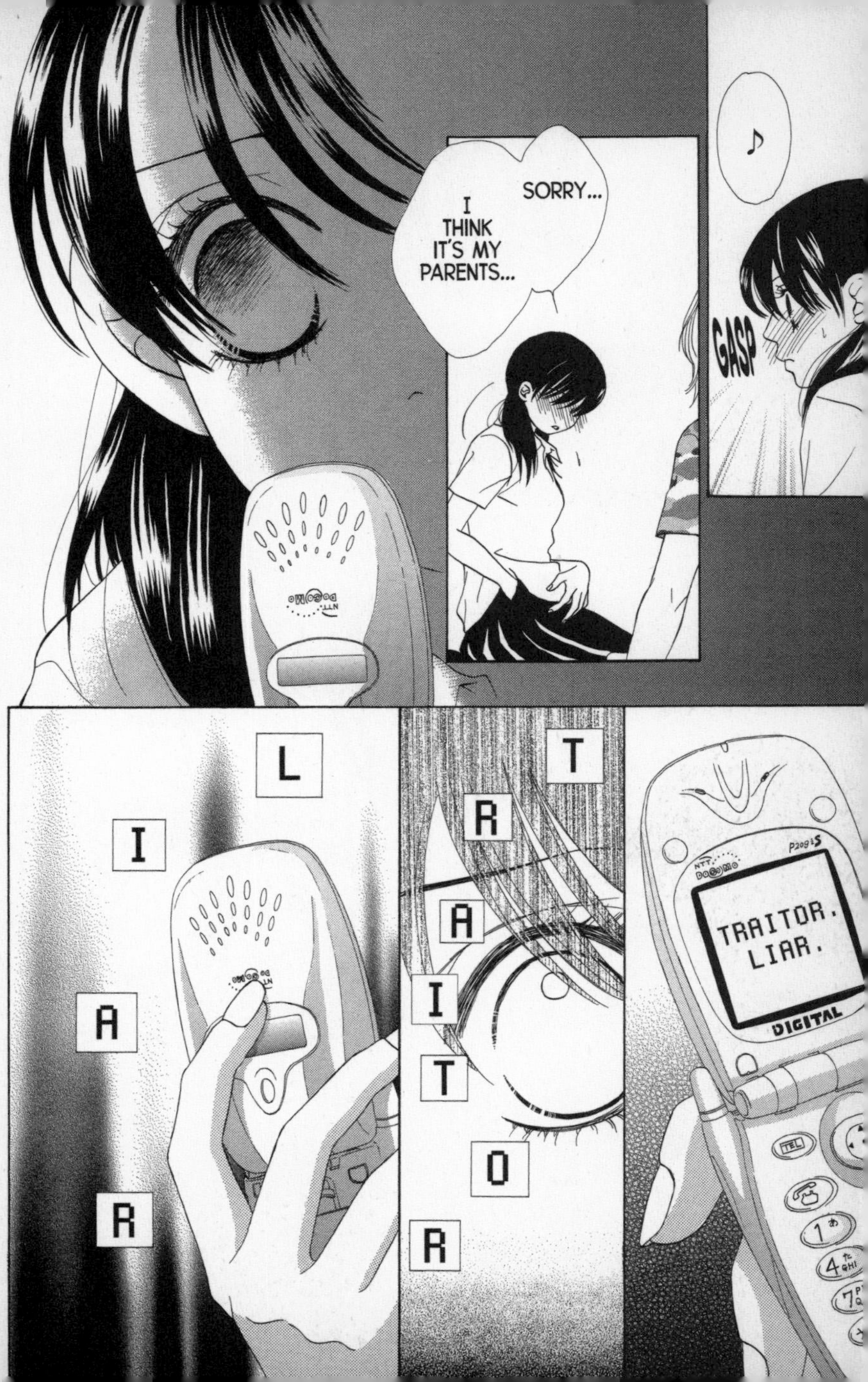
♪
GASP
SORRY...
I THINK IT'S MY PARENTS...
TRAITOR.
LIAR.
DIGITAL
T
R
A
I
T
O
R
L
I
A
R

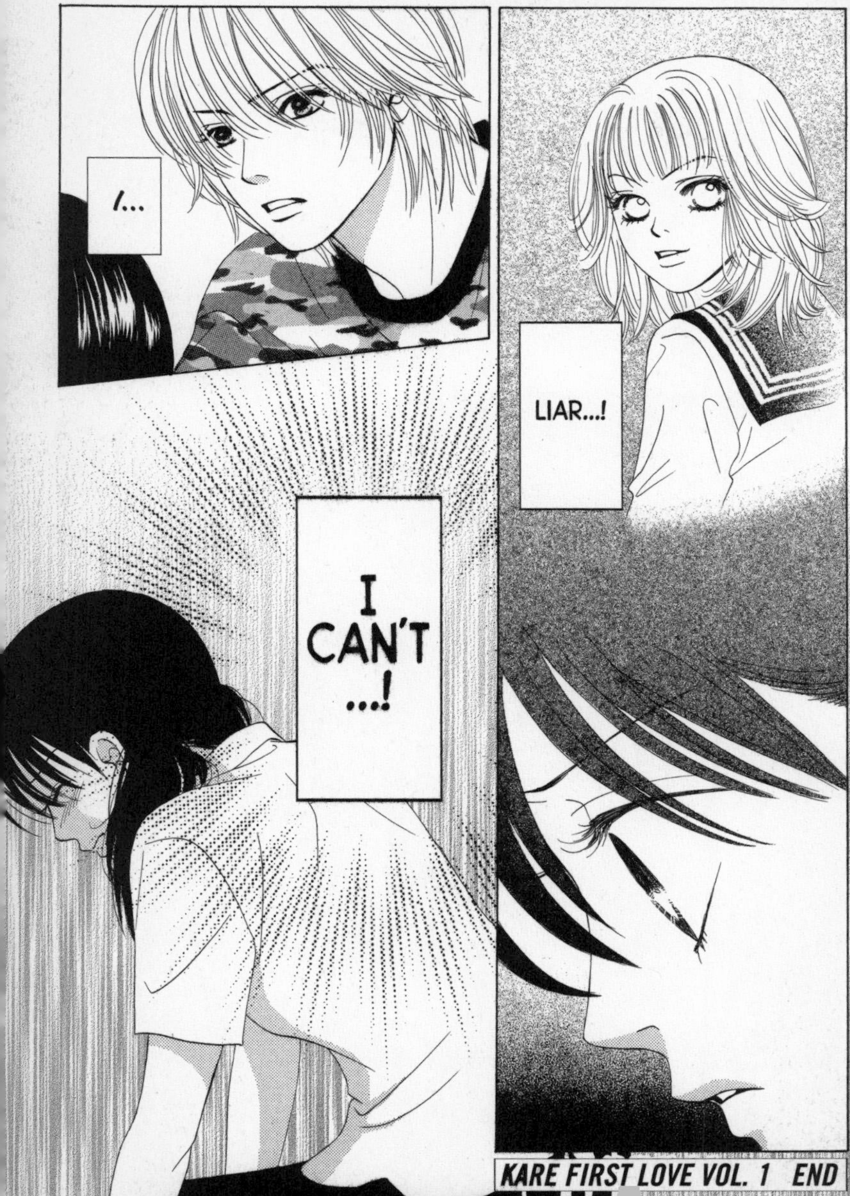
LIAR...!
I...
I CAN'T ...!

KARE FIRST LOVE VOL. 1 END

Kaho Miyasaka
official site

Love✳Factory

http://www.k-miyasaka.com/

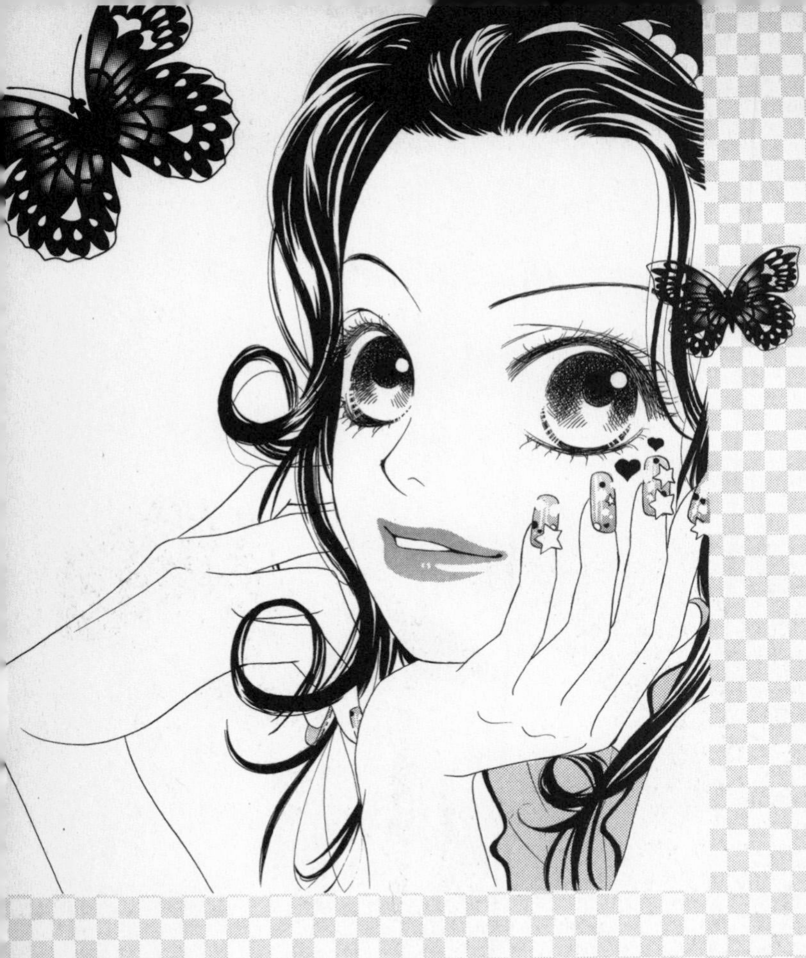

Illustration gallery

Illustration gallery

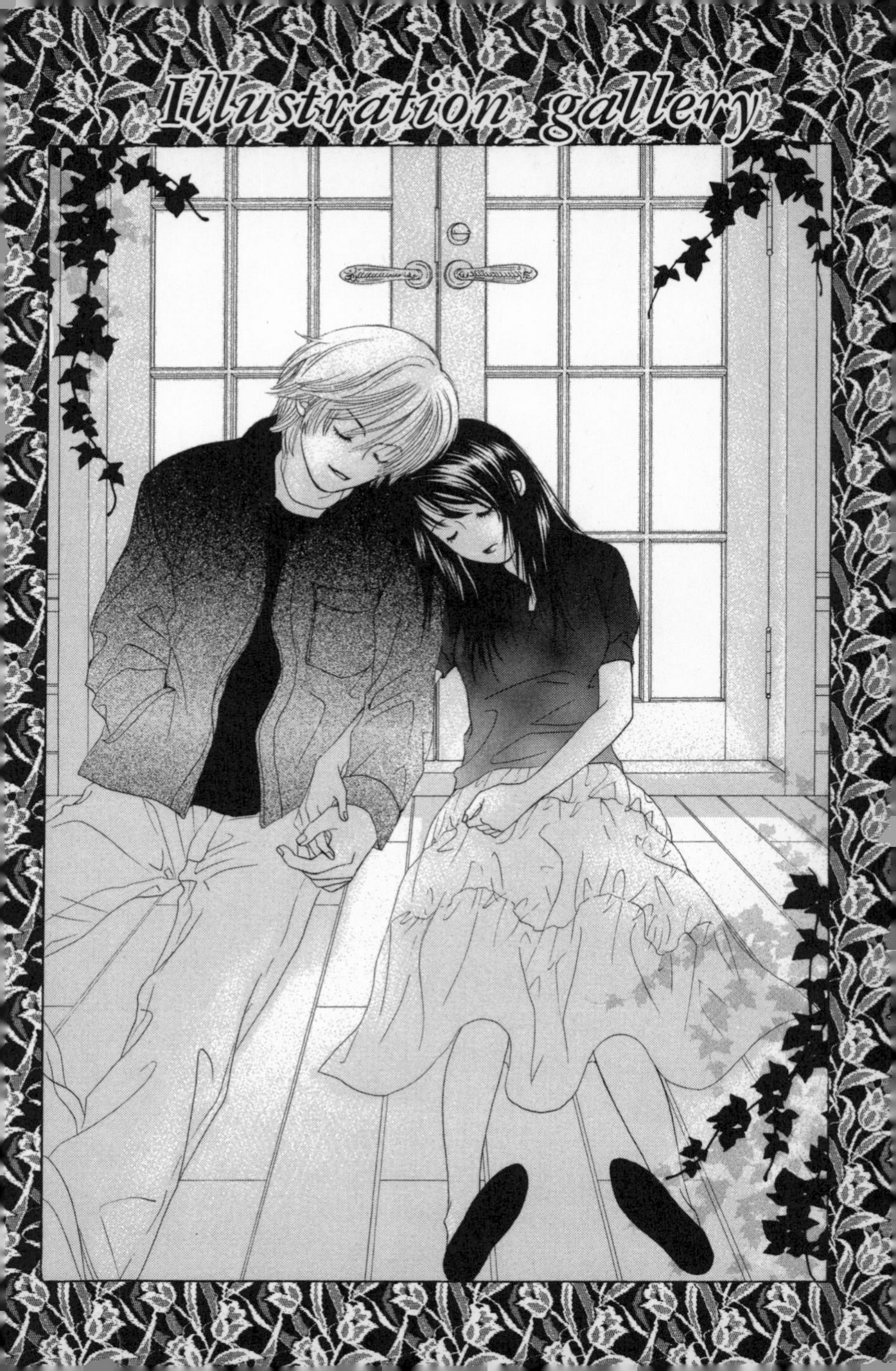

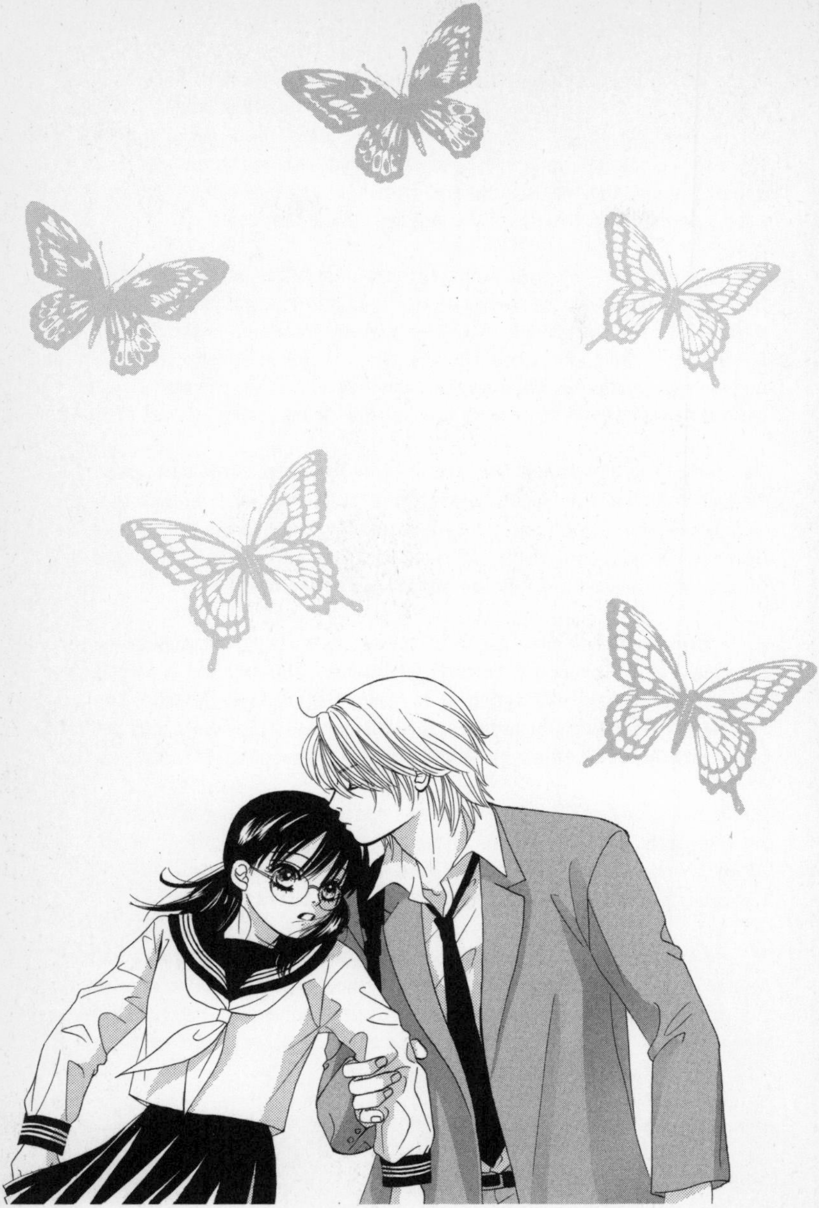

If there's one thing that could make or break a child's view of the world at a young age, it's *trust*. Nothing can be more devastating than having it broken very early in life. As children, we trust that our parents—or guardians—will be there to feed us, give us a home and, hopefully, embrace us enough times to diminish the chance of us turning into the next batch of celebrated serial killers portrayed on Forensic Files. At least, that's the ideal.

We learn early on that those two adults sleeping in the next room will come running when we wake up sweating after a bad dream, screaming like our butts are on fire. We go to bed trusting that we'll wake up in the same bed we fell asleep in the night before. We trust that the box of sweet, colorful cereals on the kitchen counter will have the same heavenly flavor the next time we slurp it down with our favorite chocolate milk. Some things are just a given.

Fast-forward to high school life, and children find themselves navigating through halls and classrooms filled with potential friends, sweethearts and vicious enemies! It's an endless task of weeding through the folks we encounter and labeling them as "friend" or "foe." And some of those who touch—or taint—our lives become our friends or enemies for life.

Kaho Miyasaka's *KARE FIRST LOVE,* a hit manga series in Japan, depicts the drama of being a plain-Jane teenage girl muddling through life in a zoo known to many as "high school." Serialized in comic magazines in Thailand, Korea and Taiwan, Miyasaka's beautifully crafted story and art offers a microscopic look at the core of a young girl groping for the sweet spot of trust.

Main character Karin Karino tackles the dilemma of trusting her own judgment of people and the actions of the people in question—if popular boy Kiriya is sincerely attracted to her; if her classmate Yuka truly is a friend; if her cocky acquaintance Nanri really is her silent but faithful ally.

We are privy to Karin's thought process and inner struggle to strike the right balance socially, academically, and even in this hugely unfamiliar concept to her called "love." Through Miyasaka's deft use of soliloquies, we become fully aware of what Karin is going through and appreciate her efforts to make 1+1=2 in her daily life.

And speaking of soliloquies, I better end this one.

Michelle Pangilinan
Editor of *KARE FIRST LOVE*

If you liked Kare First Love, you might want to try these!

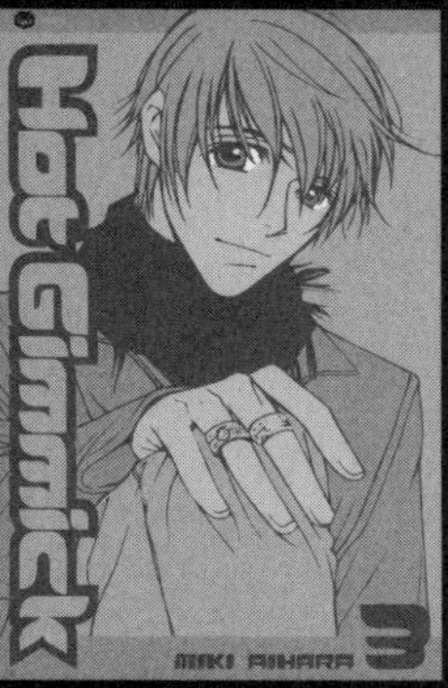
Hot Gimmick
MIKI AIHARA
3

HOT GIMMICK

The apartment complex in which high-school girl Hatsumi Narita lives is run by the rumor-mongering, self-righteous Mrs. Tachibana. Tenants, beware! Get on Tachibana's bad side, and you'd wish you lived in a hell worse than you've ever known. When Hatsumi purchases a pregnancy test for her popular sister Akane, Mrs. Tachibana's son, Ryoki, who used to bully Hatsumi as a kid, promises not to tell the world about Hatsumi's secret—if she becomes his slave.

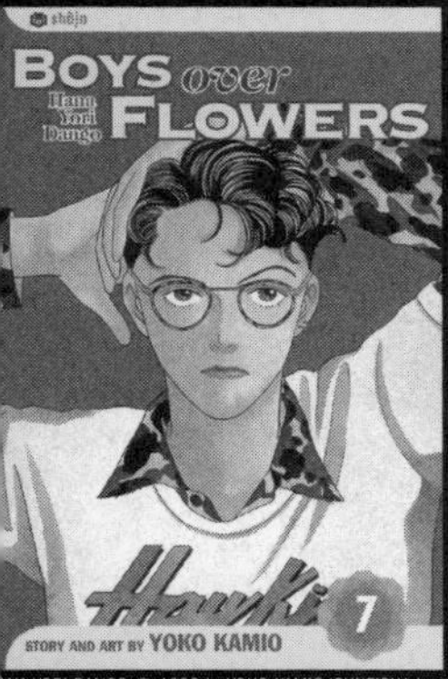
shôjo
BOYS over FLOWERS
Hana Yori Dango
7
STORY AND ART BY YOKO KAMIO

BOYS OVER FLOWERS

From a middle-class background—and poor compared to her classmates—Tsukushi Makino has been accepted into the prestigious Eitoku academy. A diploma from Eitoku would give her the freedom to pursue her dreams. But life takes a dramatic turn for Tsukushi when her only friend, Makiko, falls on Tsukasa Domyoji, the explosive leader of "F4," a group of the four most handsome and affluent young men at the school.

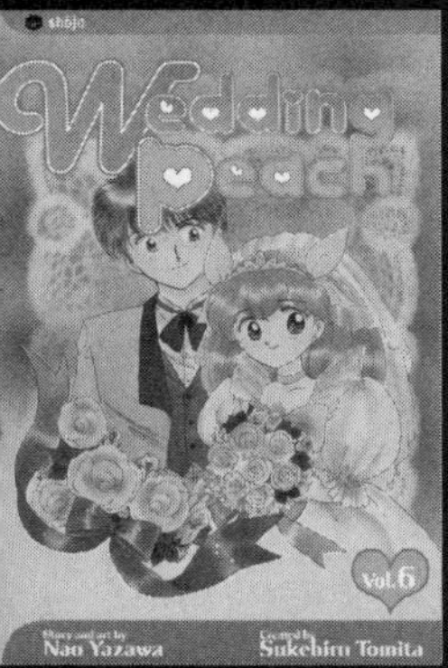
shôjo
Wedding Peach
vol.6
Story and art by Nao Yazawa
Created by Sukehiro Tomita

WEDDING PEACH

In an eccentric universe in which the wedding chapel has become the proverbial battleground between good and evil, three young girls morph into feisty warriors of love. WEDDING PEACH features first-year middle-school student Momoko Hanasaki and her two friends Yuri and Hinagiku—all of whom transform into demon-slaying superpower angels when they aren't busy ogling the captain of their school soccer team!

Every Secret Has a Price

Hatsumi will do anything to keep a family secret — even enslave herself to her childhood bully, Ryoki. Forced to do what he wants when he wants, Hatsumi soon finds herself in some pretty compromising positions! Will Azusa, her childhood friend and current crush, be able to help? Or does he have an agenda of his own?

From the top of the Japanese manga charts, HOT GIMMICK is now available for the first time in English.

Start your graphic novel collection today!

Only $9.95!

 www.viz.com
store.viz.com

© 2001 Miki Aihara/Shogakukan, Inc.

To Get Everything You Want, You've Got To Give Everything You've Got!

Airi wants fame and fortune, and for teens in Okinawa the answer is an *American Idol*-like TV show called *Boom Boom*. But first, she must enroll in a big city actor's school where competition can be ruthless.

Can Airi pass her classes, find a boyfriend, secure her father's approval, *and* make her dreams come true?

B.B. Explosion ™

shôjo

Only $9.95!

Start your graphic novel collection today!

VIZ

www.viz.com
store.viz.com

©1997 Yasue Imai/ Shogakukan, Inc.

shôjo

AT THE HEART OF THE MATTER

- *Alice 19th*
- *Angel Sanctuary*
- *Banana Fish*
- *Basara*
- *B.B. Explosion*
- *Boys Over Flowers ***
- *Ceres, Celestial Legend ***
- *Descendants of Darkness*
- *Fushigi Yûgi*
- *Hana-Kimi*
- *Hot Gimmick*
- *Imadoki*
- *Kare First Love*
- *Please Save My Earth ***
- *Red River*
- *Revolutionary Girl Utena*
- *Sensual Phrase*
- *Wedding Peach*
- *X/1999*

Start Your Shôjo Graphic Novel Collection Today!

FRESH FROM JAPAN
日本最新 **VIZ**

© 2002 KAHO MIYASAKA/SHOGAKUKAN, INC.

www.viz.com

STARTING @ $9.95!

**Also available on DVD from VIZ*

COMPLETE OUR SURVEY AND LET
US KNOW WHAT YOU THINK!

☐ Please do NOT send me information about VIZ products, news and events, special offers, or other information.

☐ Please do NOT send me information from VIZ's trusted business partners.

Name: _____

Address: _____

City: _____ **State:** _____ **Zip:** _____

E-mail: _____

☐ **Male** ☐ **Female** **Date of Birth** (mm/dd/yyyy): __ / __ / ____ (Under 13? Parental consent required)

What race/ethnicity do you consider yourself? (please check one)

☐ Asian/Pacific Islander   ☐ Black/African American   ☐ Hispanic/Latino

☐ Native American/Alaskan Native   ☐ White/Caucasian   ☐ Other: _____

What VIZ product did you purchase? (check all that apply and indicate title purchased)

☐ DVD/VHS _____

☐ Graphic Novel _____

☐ Magazines _____

☐ Merchandise _____

Reason for purchase: (check all that apply)

☐ Special offer   ☐ Favorite title   ☐ Gift

☐ Recommendation   ☐ Other _____

Where did you make your purchase? (please check one)

☐ Comic store   ☐ Bookstore   ☐ Mass/Grocery Store

☐ Newsstand   ☐ Video/Video Game Store   ☐ Other: _____

☐ Online (site: _____)

What other VIZ properties have you purchased/own? _____

_____

How many anime and/or manga titles have you purchased in the last year? How many were VIZ titles? (please check one from each column)

ANIME
- [ ] None
- [ ] 1-4
- [ ] 5-10
- [ ] 11+

MANGA
- [ ] None
- [ ] 1-4
- [ ] 5-10
- [ ] 11+

VIZ
- [ ] None
- [ ] 1-4
- [ ] 5-10
- [ ] 11+

I find the pricing of VIZ products to be: (please check one)
- [ ] Cheap
- [ ] Reasonable
- [ ] Expensive

What genre of manga and anime would you like to see from VIZ? (please check two)
- [ ] Adventure
- [ ] Comic Strip
- [ ] Science Fiction
- [ ] Fighting
- [ ] Horror
- [ ] Romance
- [ ] Fantasy
- [ ] Sports

What do you think of VIZ's new look?
- [ ] Love It
- [ ] It's OK
- [ ] Hate It
- [ ] Didn't Notice
- [ ] No Opinion

Which do you prefer? (please check one)
- [ ] Reading right-to-left
- [ ] Reading left-to-right

Which do you prefer? (please check one)
- [ ] Sound effects in English
- [ ] Sound effects in Japanese with English captions
- [ ] Sound effects in Japanese only with a glossary at the back

THANK YOU! Please send the completed form to:

VIZ Survey
42 Catharine St.
Poughkeepsie, NY 12601

All information provided will be used for internal purposes only. We promise not to sell or otherwise divulge your information.

NO PURCHASE NECESSARY. Requests not in compliance with all terms of this form will not be acknowledged or returned. All submissions are subject to verification and become the property of VIZ, LLC. Fraudulent submission, including use of multiple addresses or P.O. boxes to obtain additional VIZ information or offers may result in prosecution. VIZ reserves the right to withdraw or modify any terms of this form. Void where prohibited, taxed, or restricted by law. VIZ will not be liable for lost, misdirected, mutilated, illegible, incomplete or postage-due mail. © 2003 VIZ, LLC. All Rights Reserved. VIZ, LLC, property titles, characters, names and plots therein under license to VIZ, LLC. All Rights Reserved.